An Extra-Ordinary Beginning

The Adventures of Eric and Ursula

A.D. Winch

First published in 2012

ISBN: 9781301880331
ISBN-1301880337

Printed and bound in the European Union.

DEDICATION

For Christophe.

ACKNOWLEDGMENTS

I would like to thank Deborah for her support. She was an excellent editor and was always, and is, my muse. A big thank you to my brother, K.J. Winch, for his creativity in designing the front cover and images on www.winchad.com.

My parents for their encouragement. My brothers for being inspirational.

I would like to thank Fiona and Veronika for helping with the title, Mark for the concrete mixer and Helen for not being offended.

I would also like to thank the friends who gave me valuable feedback.

Finally, thanks to my other editors Helen, the greatest lover of books I have ever met, and Robert who went through my manuscript with a fine tooth Dutch comb
.

PROLOGUE

OVER TEN YEARS AGO

The explosion ripped through the European Space Station with the speed of a bullet. In less than a second, one hundred metres of metal, plastic, complicated circuitry and solar panels were silently reduced to a billion new satellites orbiting the earth. Hidden amongst the debris were two platinum pods. They had been shot away from the space station, moments before the explosion, into the Earth's atmosphere and onto their programmed locations.

Moments earlier Professor Larsen had blinked back a tear and watched, through sky blue eyes, as her lifetime's work left her forever and escaped the coming disaster. She had expected this to happen, had accepted the fact and was only thankful that it had taken them this long to find her. She hoped she had done enough.

Down on the planet in the Main Control Room at the European Space Operations Centre in Germany everybody was in shock. The sudden disappearance of the biggest European space project in history was met with disbelieving gasps and then frantic action as the control room came to life. Technicians, scientists and computer experts searched hurriedly for the cause of the problem. No one believed that a space station could suddenly vanish. Computers were rebooted, millions of lines of software code were scanned for bugs, the position of radars were checked and the tracking stations of the ESTRACK network were contacted. The two stations in Australia were unable to locate the space station and the same was true of those in Kenya, French Guinea, Sweden and Spain.

In desperation NASA was contacted. They did not answer the call.

It soon became clear that there was no glitch in the system and a powerful digital telescope in Belgium was trained on the coordinates, where the space station should have been. As these images appeared on the seven large plasma screens dominating the room, the busy movements and conversations began to peter out. The hive of worker bees were turned into wax work dummies with mouths open.

A hush fell over the room, broken only by the voice of a skinny scientist who wouldn't give up on the woman who had always been there for him. Speaking calmly, patiently and expectantly he repeated the same words over and over again. "Professor Larsen, this is ESOC, please come in. Professor Larsen, this is ESOC, please come in. Professor Larsen..."

Tears streamed down his cheeks.

1

ON THE ROOFTOPS OF PARIS

Ursula stood on the flat roof of the Palais Omnisports indoor stadium. Four floors below her was the busy Boulevard de Bercy but up on the roof all was calm. Her black pony tail reached the warm tiles on which she sat and she could feel the heat through the holes in her jeans. A thin layer of moisture stuck her white vest to her back and, as she wiped her dirty hands across its front, railway tracks of grey appeared where her ribs protruded. From her stomach came a deep rumbling. She tried to ignore it as she had more important things to think about. Gingerly she placed her dark hand into the front pocket of her grubby jeans, to check that its contents were still there. As her bony fingers felt the edge of the small cardboard box she let out a sigh of relief and lay back to look at the sky.

It was a beautiful day in Paris. The sky was bright blue and fluffy clouds drifted aimlessly, creating shapes for anyone who had a mind to see them. Ursula loved watching the clouds. She fixed her chocolate brown eyes upon them and before long could make out a vicious fire-breathing dragon, a long-eared rabbit and the outline of Italy. These gradually became a horse on a cold day, a round teddy bear and a lady's pointed boot, before merging together and blowing into the distance.

Her grandmother and neighbours had been moaning about the heat since it had risen to tropical temperatures three weeks previously. It was the subject of conversation every time they met on the graffiti covered passageways outside their flats. Anyone nearby would happily join in with their opinions on the, 'stifling temperatures.' At first Ursula had been honest and told the adults how much she loved the heat and felt energized by the sun. However, after the tuts, disapproving looks and comments such as, 'you're only eleven, you wait until you're our age,' she decided it was probably best to just agree and enjoy the sun in private.

For Ursula nowhere was more private than the rooftops of Paris. High above the busy streets, tooting cars, grumpy commuters, lost tourists and stressed shoppers she was alone. Hidden behind billboards, advertising products people did not need, she was free from disapproving glances, nasty comments and away from prying eyes. She relaxed, took the little Sudoku book and pencil from her back pocket, flicked to the only one she had not yet completed and rolled onto her front to do it. As the sun beat down on her back her brain came to life and she set about solving the puzzle in front of her. It was rated 'very difficult'. Within two minutes it was almost complete. She wrote the last number, nine, in a small square on the page and allowed a thin smile of satisfaction to creep across her slim face. Just a bit longer then I'll go home, she thought to herself, appreciating her solitude. However Ursula was not completely alone, she was being watched. On a tall floodlight overlooking the indoor stadium and advertising boards was a CCTV camera and it was trained firmly on the Palais roof.

"Geez, this kid is something else," exclaimed Agent Hoover in the near darkness, relaxing his bloated body into the swivel chair that was his home every day. "I mean she's a worthless thieving little punk, who deserves a brief stretch in the joint, but you've got to admire her style."

He sat forward again, placed his podgy elbows on the glass desk in front of him and rested his head in his swollen hands.

Ursula returned the pencil and book to her back pocket and sat up, unaware of the attention she was receiving. She was on a small screen marked 'Boulevard de Bercy, Paris, France.' Surrounding it, on a wall the size of a tennis court, were thousands upon thousands of similar tiny screens all marked with the names of streets, towns and countries in Europe. The flickering pictures provided the only light in the air-conditioned room and reflected off Agent Hoover's blotchy red face. Behind him, lurking in the shadows, a short sinewy figure remained silent.

Agent Hoover continued talking to himself, "I tell you something for nothing, next time I see her I'm going to bring her down, she may be a skinny little runt but that's about twelve drug stores she's held up now."

Suddenly, he felt as if someone had just stabbed his brain with a pin and then he heard his own voice in his head. "We are not looking for French juvenile petty criminals."

He pulled his eyes away from the screen showing Ursula, slumped back in his chair and took in all the screens in front of him. He did not know how he could watch and process so many at once but he thanked the stars and stripes that he had been born into this TV nation.

Ursula stood up and walked across the tiles on the gym roof. Without making a sound she knelt down beside a large skylight and peered into the indoor stadium below. The Palais Omnisports was holding a gymnastics event. Parallel bars, high bars, hoops, beams, a large blue floor mat, and a host of other gymnastic equipment filled the arena. Around the edges, underneath flags and billboards, the stands were full of people showing their appreciation. In the centre two boys, in their countrys' tracksuits, stood on a podium with a bronze and silver medal around their necks. They belonged to a world that Ursula dreamed of but knew she would never be part of. She hated being part of *les exclus*: the people whom no one wanted.

Upset by her thoughts Ursula crept back from the skylight, jumped up purposefully, twisted before she landed and ran towards the blue metal supports that criss-crossed around the edge of the arena's roof. The moment she reached the edge she sprang up like a cat and launched herself into the air. From the Palais below she heard a man's nasal voice announce that the gold medal winner in the under thirteen category was Eric Meyer.

Eric walked confidently towards the other two medal winners with his head held high. He brushed his blond hair away from his high forehead and used the movement as an excuse to briefly look at the audience. He could not see his parents but it was a big crowd and he decided to look again once he was on the podium. Eric jumped up on to the step reserved for the gold medalist. He raised his toned arm in the air and, acknowledging the clapping and cheering, slowly turned on the spot. His dark brown eyes searched the audience as he turned but his parents were nowhere to be seen. On the outside his body remained tall and powerful but inside Eric slumped and his strong shoulders drooped forward.

A grey haired man in an ill-fitting grey suit, who was introduced to the audience as 'today's main sponsor', approached Eric. The tender skin on Eric's palms stung as the man limply shook his hand. Together they posed for the cameras which flashed around them. Eric then bowed towards the sponsor and his prize was placed delicately over this head. The ribbon slid over his ears and the gold medal hung, swinging from his neck. As he stood up to his full height he saw his nanny, who doubled as his maid and driver, standing beside the exit. Her skin was so pale that she stood out in a crowd, especially in the summer time when everyone else was sporting a tan. She wasn't his parents but at least someone Eric knew had been there to see him win. In fact Miss Duna, or Andrea as she liked to be called, was always there. Whether it was picking Eric up from school or gymnastic competitions or sports matches or guitar performances it didn't matter, she was there.

The national anthem began and flags, half the size of the mobile phone adverts that ringed the area, began their slow journey towards the ceiling. Eric lowered his head respectfully and stared at his feet, which he felt were too small for his body. It was always better to look down than try to sing along. He knew the words but also knew that he couldn't sing and hated the idea of making a fool of himself in front of a large crowd, or anyone for that matter. To the spectators he looked like a model gymnast, tall and slim with muscles starting to develop on his young body. He also looked deep in thought. Most people watching felt he was enjoying this winning moment but he wasn't.

Eric's thoughts were hijacked by the list of broken promises that his parents had made. They had promised with hands on hearts that they would be here today, and the time before and the time before that. His mind wandered. Despite all his achievements maybe they just weren't proud of him. He had always tried to be the best but maybe he had to try even harder to be even better. Maybe only then would they notice him and reward him with some recognition.

The anthem finished and Eric hopped down from the podium, stumbling with tiredness as he hit the floor. He hoped that no one had seen and was relieved to see the spectators streaming towards the exits oblivious to his near fall. Wearily he picked up his heavy gym bag, slung it over his shoulders and walked towards his leather clad nanny. It never ceased to amaze him that whatever the weather Andrea would be wearing the same leather trousers and same leather jacket. The only item that seemed to change was the long-sleeved T-shirt she wore underneath it.

Today she was wearing a Nirvana one from her never-ending supply.

"I would like to leave now, please Andrea," requested Eric, saying every word clearly and properly.

"Okay," answered Andrea in an accent that had been formed behind the Communist Iron Curtain and added, almost as an afterthought, "you did well today Eric."

"I'm glad someone thinks so," replied Eric, a little more sharply than he would have liked.

"They all thought so," said Andrea waving one of her slight arms at the leaving crowd.

"You know who I mean;" and Eric handed Andrea his heavy gym bag. She barely noticed the weight and turned to lead Eric out of the stadium. For a moment Eric forgot the crowds around him and gazed solely at Andrea. She was a petite woman, barely one metre fifty, with an elfin frame. Eric often thought that she had once been a tall woman who had shrunk in the rain. In spite of her size she was not puny and, from head to toe, she was as solid as a rock. One of Eric's earliest memories was of the difference between being held by his soft and warm mother and being held by Andrea.

"It is time to go," she said over her shoulder and, without barging or pushing, his nanny walked calmly into the throng of people who parted before her like Moses and the Red Sea. Eric loped behind her, appreciating the path she created through the crowd.

Once outside in the sun Eric's tiredness seemed to drift away and his plan to become even better began to take shape. The more he thought about it the more it made sense. His father was, according to newspapers, the best poker player on the planet and his mother was a former Miss World. They were therefore used to being THE BEST and for them only THE BEST would do.

Eric continued to follow Andrea along the busy Boulevard de Bercy but his thoughts were elsewhere. His idea needed some direction and, as he reviewed his achievements, he set himself new goals. In gymnastics, as of today, he was the European champion so his next step had to be World Champion. That would put him on par with his parents. In school he was quite certain that he was top of the class, even though his teacher never told him, but he would now get top marks in every test to prove it. When competing in tennis and swimming for the school he would beat all opponents and in football he would be the star player of the team. He would stand out from all the other children in school and be admired because of it. During the guitar and kick boxing lessons that his parents arranged for him in his free-time, he would excel. Admittedly he was already at Grade 7 for guitar and a black belt in kick boxing but this did not mean he could not improve further.

Eric was too caught up in his thoughts to notice the world around him. One step behind him was a man in red baseball cap worn low over his eyes. In front of Eric was Andrea, whose brisk pace came to an abrupt end when she suddenly stopped. Eric clattered into the back of her. A rock being hit by a toy action man would have moved more.

"Sorry, Andrea."

"No problem, Eric."

The man behind side stepped the pair, tutted, and walked off into the distance.

Andrea had stopped in front of the Meyer's new top of the line Range Rover. It was silver with dark tinted windows and grey door handles. She opened the rear door and seemed to strain not to wrench it from its hinges. The new car smell, mixed with the leather aroma of the seats, wafted out of the vehicle as Eric climbed in.

Once his nanny had sat down on the cream driver's seat she turned like a clockwork toy to face Eric. "I will repeat what I said earlier, you did well today. You are only eleven years old and you are now the under thirteen European champion. That is quite an achievement."

A hint of a smile briefly appeared on her face and she raised her non-existent eye brows. There was not one hair on her pale face and Eric was certain that her short blonde bob was a wig. In spite of how she looked Eric felt safe and secure around her. If Andrea said she would do something she did it, if Andrea was asked to do something she did it and on the very rare occasions that she could not do something she would say so beforehand. If only his parents could be the same.

"Thank you," said Eric quietly, "I'm glad you were there."

"Always a pleasure, Eric," and Andrea started the car. The V8 Supercharged engine roared into life and she pulled cautiously away into the afternoon traffic.

In front of Eric on the back of Andrea's headrest and fixed into a Mahogany casing was a LCD screen. It was showing a map of their journey home and as she took lefts and rights Eric followed the Galileo satellite navigation system. They were just coming onto Place Felix Eboue when 'Incoming Call' flashed three times on the screen before disappearing. The screen flickered with colour and then a woman's beautiful face smiled at Eric.

His mother's jet black hair cascaded down her well-tanned face and she flicked it over her shoulder before she spoke.

"Erika, bambino," she purred.

"Mother," replied Eric through clenched teeth. He hated being called Erika and bambino more than he hated losing.

"Did you win?" she asked with the Latin accent that Eric knew turned grown men to gibbering wrecks.

"Yes."

"I knew you would, that's why I knew you it would not be a problem if I was not there."

"You said you would!" Eric replied angrily.

"I know what I said bambino but I managed to get a last minute appointment with Pierre La Vache before he flew off for the Milano show. He is such an exciting young fashion designer with so many wonderful ideas on how to use fabrics for women that I just had to meet him. If I hadn't met him today it could have been up to two weeks before I got another appointment."

"Oh, lucky you," Eric didn't know what else to say.

"I knew you would be happy for me Erika. I have to go as I'm half way through being measured. Ciao bambino, see you at home."

No sooner had the screen turned blank than it filled with colour again. This time a man appeared. He had a long angular face and blond hair in a side parting, similar to Eric's.

"Hi son," Eric's father never called him by his name, "Andrea's been telling me you vere great today."

"I won," was all Eric could think of to reply.

"You von," Eric's father could not say 'w'. "Of course you did. I expect nothing but the best from my boy."

"It would have been nice if you had been there father." Eric almost swallowed the words as he said them.

On the screen Eric's father appeared to squirm. "Sorry son, you know I vood have loved to but these rich Parisians have, how do you say in English, so much money and so little hours."

"Time. So little time," corrected Eric. "What happened?"

"I von," Eric's dad leaned forward and looked around him to make sure no one was listening and whispered, "six point seven million."

"Well done," said Eric but there was no conviction in his praise.

"Thanks, son. It vill make sure your mother has clothes for a few more day, no?" Eric's father laughed falsely and then raised his voice. "Can you hear me, Andrea?"

"Yes, Sir."

"Good job on the competition in the newspaper, vell

done," congratulated Mr Meyer. "I saw it was in Le Monde, El Pais, Das Bild and The Times in the hotel *tabac* vhere I vas playing poker."

"Thank you Sir, it was in every national newspaper in Europe."

"Including, San Marino?"

"Of course."

"What competition was this father?" asked Eric, suddenly concerned that there was something he did not know about.

Once again Eric's father began to squirm and Eric knew he wasn't going to like it when his father replied, "At home I vill tell you."

After his father signed off Eric asked Andrea semi-seriously if it was possible to divorce his parents.

2

PARENTS PET PROJECT

A black crow circled over Ursula's head before landing on a broken CCTV camera only a few metres from where she stood. It stared at her through its beady dark eyes and gave a loud squawk. Even the birds have attitude in *les banlieues*, thought Ursula and tried to scare it off. The crow refused to move and continued to stare, challenging her right to be there on the roof, eight floors above the ground.

"I'll only be a minute," Ursula told the crow who, apparently satisfied with this statement, flew away over her head. Ursula followed him with her eyes, as he flew across her neighbourhood and towards the Stade de France.

Despite being only half a kilometre from Ursula's home it was another world away. The stadium was covered in advertising boards and was made of the latest materials all welded and concreted stylishly together. It was an arena which people flocked to and marveled at. When people saw Ursula's neighbourhood, les banlieues at Saint-Denis, they were just relieved that they did not live there and beat a quick retreat.

Ursula lived in an eighth floor apartment on a square of four high-rise blocks. It was a concrete cuboid embedded with small windows, balconies that rarely saw any sunlight and passageways where lights, if they were working, were permanently on. None of the CCTV cameras which watched these areas worked and like the blocks themselves they had been painted grey. The occasional flashes of colour, on these crumbling urban tombstones, were impressive pieces of graffiti that belonged to unknown nocturnal artists or flags of the residents' home countries. From numerous windows proudly hung the flags of Algeria, Burkina Faso, Cameroon, Chad, Congo, Djibouti, Guinea, Cote d'Ivoire, Morocco, Togo, Tunisia, Zaire and more. To residents they were colourful symbols, which scattered across the four high-rises brought welcome relief from the oppressive and over bearing grey. To middle class Parisians who walked past, on their way to the stadium, they were viewed as warning signs telling them to stay away. Ursula liked the flags, could name them all, and was proud of the fact that so many different nationalities were present in her neighbourhood of only four apartment blocks.

Enclosed by these high rises was an outside communal area made up of a basketball net woven from metal chains, three trees which continued to live in spite of the amount of engravings on their trunks, several broken benches and, below them all, more concrete. Ursula knew that there were better places to live but she liked the area anyway and it even had its own soundtrack. As she stood on the roof she could hear Arabic Rai, Euro Pop and French Rap echoing between the blocks.

On the corner of her building she had painted a little white cross, next to the edge and overlooking the communal area. She approached like a panther and, bending down, placed her hands firmly between the cross and the edge, kicking her legs in the air as she did so. The world turned upside down and she gazed momentarily at the building above the sky before swinging her legs down and gripping the edge tightly. Her body turned through one hundred and eighty degrees, she let go and landed almost silently on a balcony below that was completely covered in lush green plants.

The plants emerged from numerous yoghurt pots on the balcony's ledge, from old plastic buckets on the floor and from burst footballs hanging from the ceiling.

Amongst them all, in a large flowery nylon dress and with a watering can in her hand, was Ursula's Grandmother Benjamin or Mémé, as she liked to be called. She was a short woman shaped like a pear with the largest bottom in the block. Her black hair was wrapped around dusty pink and baby blue curlers and she looked decidedly unimpressed.

"*Salut*, Mémé," greeted Ursula and smiled meekly.

"I've told you not to jump down onto the balcony. You will get yourself killed," she scolded in her thick French African accent, "where have you been anyway? You have been a long time!"

"*Pardon* Mémé, I was enjoying the weather."

"At least someone is. I'm hotter than a burning coconut. It wasn't even this hot when I lived near the equator."

"I know, you keep telling me."

"You have been enjoying it for a whole afternoon, the pharmacy is only over the road," and she pointed into the distance.

"It was closed," lied Ursula, and hated herself for saying this the instant the words left her lips. "I had to go to another one." This bit at least was true.

Mémé clasped her rough hands around the battered watering can and looked at Ursula with eyes that had seen it all. She knew Ursula was not being completely truthful, but the girl had been brought up to know the difference between right and wrong and did what she was told without complaint.

"Well, at least tell me you've got Granddad Benjamin's medicine."

"Yes, it's here," and Ursula pointed to her pocket.

Mémé's face softened and, still clasping the metal can, she waved Ursula towards the balcony door with her fleshy arms. Ursula squeezed between the plants and her grandmother. As she passed she gave Mémé a quick sneaky hug before being shooed away by the smiling old lady.

The balcony door led directly into the living room and Ursula stepped inside onto the orange paisley carpet. Instantly Mémé appeared in the door way.

"Take off your trainers, *ma cherie.* I've just cleaned."

Ursula did as she was told and placed them on the mat besides the feeble looking door. The room was sparsely furnished, containing only a brown and beige sofa which Ursula found too itchy to sit on, a huge old television with a small screen placed dangerously on a rickety metal stand, a fold up white formica table with matching chairs and, in pride of place near the window, a glass cabinet full of random trinkets. These included five blown glass animals, a wind up clock standing on a CD which they never played, Kinder egg toys and china ornaments. These ornaments, and the furniture, were all much older than Ursula but the room was spotlessly clean and everything had been carefully looked after.

Ursula walked through, past the kitchen and to the short hallway that led to the other three rooms in the flat: the bathroom, her room and her destination, her grandparents' bedroom.

It was dim in the room but she could still see her Granddad, laying fast-asleep on top of the yellow nylon sheets. He was wearing a string vest and baggy faded black trousers held up by green braces. A thin beam of sun light, from a crack in the purple curtains, bounced off his bald ebony head and lit up the glass on the circular bedside table. Inside it, covered in water, were his dentures. One day, when she had money, Ursula wanted to replace these with a pair of wind-up teeth. The thought of them in his mouth chattering away uncontrollably often made her giggle and she knew he would chuckle at it too. Granddad Benjamin had the best and loudest laugh in the world, a roaring infectious laugh which everyone who heard it would join in with. Unfortunately, he also had the worst and loudest snore in the world, a trumpet blasting snore which could have been put to better use warning ships in fog. Ursula decided to save her ears, sat softly on the end of the bed, away from the noise, and took hold of Granddad Benjamin's naked left foot. Gently, she shook it until the old man woke up.

"Hello Granddad," she said, "I've bought your medicine."

Ever since Ursula was a baby Granddad Benjamin had only spoken English to her, while Mémé spoke French, and he expected only English to be spoken back. He had told on her numerous occasions that he had had to learn English, French plus his own language and if he could learn three then he was sure she could learn two.

He raised his head to look at Ursula, smiled a gummy grin and replied, "Fang oo, dear."

"Put your teeth in Granddad."

"Solly," he sat up and in one movement took his teeth out of the water, threw them in the air and caught them skillfully in this mouth. Once again he smiled but this time his teeth were at right angles to where they should have been. Ursula laughed and he waved his hand in front of his mouth until he revealed a beaming white crescent moon of a smile. Granddad Benjamin was full of little tricks and, even though Ursula had seen them many times, she still couldn't see how he did them.

"Hand it over then little miss," he said with a smile as he put out a calloused palm.

Ursula retrieved the box from her pocket and asked, "Will I get your illness, Granddad?"

"Oh no, I suffer from a problem only men and normally only old men get. With better medicine I would be much better, but these are the best for now," and he shook the box. "But you are trying to distract me. Where is my change?" he asked gently.

Ursula sighed, removed the twenty Euro cents from her pocket and handed it over.

"Is that all?"

"I bought some *bonbons*," she lied.

"After running around for your Granddad I'm sure you deserve them. But don't tell your Grandmother."

Ursula smiled with relief and promised she wouldn't. She hated lying but she felt she really had no choice. Granddad Benjamin needed the medicine and it was her job to get it for him.

Since Granddad Benjamin had developed his mysterious illness, and Mémé refused to leave the flat without him, Ursula had inherited all the outside chores. This meant, primarily, shopping and going to the pharmacy for medicine. At first it was difficult for their weekly allowance to stretch to both but Ursula learnt to shop around, soon found the cheapest shops for different items and used her keen mental mathematics ability to make it work. However, when prices rose during the financial crisis this quickly became impossible. Ursula's grandparents, who were not economically minded, could not understand it and, even if they did, they did not have enough money to change it. As a result Ursula was forced into an impossible situation: get Granddad his medicine and have no food, or buy food and deny Granddad his medicine. Neither was a good option so Ursula, even though she knew it was wrong, chose a third one. She was thinking about this when Granddad Benjamin playfully hit her with a newspaper.

"Hey daydreamer, take a look at that," and he thrust a tightly folded paper into her hand.

Ursula took it, opened it out in front of her and scanned the front page. It was the previous day's Le Monde, which a neighbour always kept for her Granddad. The headline announced, 'Hailstones Destroy Vineyards' and Ursula was not interested enough to read on.

"What's the big deal?" asked Ursula scratching her head.

"Not that," said her Granddad, shuffling up the bed to sit beside her, "but this."

He opened the paper to page 3 and tapped a full page advert repeatedly with his finger until Ursula started to read it.

WIN 10,000 EURO!
10,000 Euro prize money will be given tax-free to anyone in Europe who can solve this puzzle!

She glanced briefly over the puzzle and then read below:

All entries should include name, age and address and are to be received within seven days of publication at the following address:
WIN 10,000 EURO PUZZLE, BP 1357911, FRANCE
In case of a draw please include a similar puzzle you have written with its solution.

"So what do you think?" Granddad Benjamin asked, barely able to contain the excitement in his voice.

"What do I think about what?" Ursula was confused.

"For a smart girl you are slow sometimes." he mocked. "The puzzle! Do you think you could do it?"

Ursula stared intently at the puzzle. It took up most of the page and was made up of an irregular hexagon with letters, numbers and symbols she had never seen before, dotted around its outside edges. Some of them appeared inside smaller hexagons within the larger one but they were scattered around in what appeared to be a totally random pattern. There were no instructions, no rules and no guidelines given.

Granddad Benjamin took her arm with a sweaty hand and looked at her expectantly. "Well, can you?"

"Granddad this puzzle is in Le Monde, a newspaper for adults. How am I supposed to do it? I'm only eleven."

In spite of what she had said Granddad Benjamin still looked excited. His hand left her arm, patted her on the back and he said, "I know but if anyone can do it you can."

"Okay Granddad, for you I'll try," Ursula declared, gripped the paper tightly and strode purposefully out of the room.

Granddad Benjamin lay back on his bed and thought about what he would do with the money. It was a simple dream, but one that would not go away and one that he had had since Ursula first started talking many years earlier. He would place it all in a savings account and, when Ursula was old enough, he would send her away to get a good education, to university, and out of the les banlieues forever.

Ursula's room was only big enough for a small bed, wardrobe and desk. The neatly made bed rested against one wall and on top of the pink blanket slept Ursula's teddy bear, Fred. On the opposite wall, separated by a thin strip of carpet underlay, was a wardrobe and the desk. The wardrobe was so old that the wood had warped and the doors no longer shut. Mémé would not permit anything to be stuck on the walls of the room, as she thought it looked unsightly, but allowed the wardrobe to be used instead. Because of this Ursula had completely covered the wardrobe in cut outs from Granddad Benjamin's newspapers. Zinedine Zidane fought for space with cyclists in the Tour de France who overlapped with French astronauts who partially covered Lady Diana who nudged against Nelson Mandela and so on. Next to the wardrobe Ursula sat at her worn little desk. It had been used so much that the letters, words and sentences were etched into the wood. Until Granddad Benjamin placed a piece of glass on the surface it had been difficult to use but now it was perfect and, if Ursula became bored while working, she could read what was written underneath it. At the moment she was not bored. School work bored her as it was all too easy, crosswords and puzzles from Mémé's magazines bored her but this puzzle was something else and it definitely was not boring.

There was a quiet knock at the door and Granddad Benjamin entered sheepishly. Ursula was so deep in concentration that she didn't notice. On the desk in front of her the puzzle lay untouched, next to an old chess set, but she frantically turned a short stubby pencil in her left hand as she pondered it. Granddad Benjamin watched and leaned against the wardrobe door which creaked and broke Ursula's concentration.

"Granddad, what are you doing out of bed?" she asked caringly, for he rarely left his bed other than to visit the toilet, which he did often.

He gave her a big warm smile and placed one of his wife's homemade sunflower seed biscuits delicately on the desk so as not to disturb the puzzle. Placing a finger to his bald head he silently mouthed, "brain food," and shuffled out in small, careful steps.

The moment he closed the door behind him the smell of the biscuit reached Ursula's nose and it smelt delicious. It was still warm as she picked it up and it felt comforting in her skinny fingers. She ate in small bites, savouring every mouthful, and catching any crumbs that fell in her palm. Mémé's biscuits were the best in the world, better than any Ursula had eaten from a shop, and the sunflower ones were her favourite. She finished off the remaining crumbs from her hand and, feeling suitably energized, she continued to work on the puzzle.

Within sixty minutes she had completed it and within another thirty she had written her own similar puzzle, with solution, and was sitting on her grandparents' bed explaining how she had done it. Outside, the sun had set but Ursula was basking in the warmth of her Granddad's delighted smile.

"I knew you could do it," he said, more excited than he had been for years.

"And I knew I would find you with your Granddad," interrupted Mémé, appearing in the bedroom doorway. "It's bedtime for you young lady," she ordered.

Her hands were placed forcefully on her hips and Ursula knew that this pose meant Granddad Benjamin was in trouble.

"But Marie-Thérèse," he pleaded, in French, as his wife spoke limited English. "Ursula has just solved the prize puzzle in Le Monde,"

"I don't care if she's just solved the planet's energy crisis. It's bedtime! And that applies to you too, Jerome. I'm not happy with you at all, NOT AT ALL, I say."

Granddad is in for it now, thought Ursula and looked for a place to hide, in case Mémé started throwing things at him. Even though Mémé had not done this for years Ursula did not want to get caught in the cross-fire in case it happened again.

"The whole of Europe will be entering that competition, millions and millions of people who are probably a lot cleverer than Ursula." She looked at Ursula, apologized for the last comment, and continued, "Which means absolutely no chance of winning. Getting Ursula excited for no reason is one thing but getting yourself so excited at your age, and with your health, and with a lack of proper medication is just, just," she hunted for the right word, "Dangerous." She pointed at Ursula, "Come on you, au lit!"

Ursula was glad to leave before Mémé gave her Granddad a proper roasting. She had only done the puzzle to make him happy, she hadn't meant to get him excited or get him into trouble. Leaving the newspaper and her puzzle on the bed she stood up miserably and walked towards the door.

"*Bonne nuit*, Mémé," she said and gave her Grandmother a kiss on the cheek.

"Bonne nuit, ma cherie," replied Mémé, moving away from the door.

Behind his wife's back Granddad Benjamin pulled a rude face which made Ursula giggle as she tiptoed past her Grandmother.

The moment she had left the room Mémé picked up Le Monde and Ursula's puzzle and waved them in her husband's direction. "I mean it Jerome, Ursula will be devastated if she lost you and so would I."

Granddad Benjamin dropped his head solemnly and mumbled an apology but his wife hadn't quite finished yet. She kept shaking the newspaper and puzzle, which were now screwed up together, and continued.

"And none of this puzzle nonsense!" she warned before storming out of the bedroom, turning out the light as she went.

In the darkness Granddad Benjamin whispered, "She's a softy, really. She'll send it." A victorious smile appeared across his face and he promptly fell fast asleep.

The next morning at dawn, before anyone was up, Mémé took the screwed up newspaper and unfolded it as if it was made of gold. She cut out the puzzle, as neatly as she could, and put it with the puzzle Ursula had written. Taking extra care she ironed each one and then placed them in an envelope she had addressed the previous evening. As quiet as a mouse she slipped out of the flat, took the lift down to the post box on the ground floor of the block and secretly sent off Ursula's entry.

Eric gripped Le Monde tightly in his right hand and a fountain pen in his left. He was worried but he did not let it show as he stood in the centre of his parent's luxurious Parisian living room. They had four other properties around the world but this was undoubtedly his least favourite and, at nearly two hundred and fifty years old, the oldest. In his opinion it belonged in the years before the French Revolution with its grandiose furnishings, marble flooring and fireplace the size of a shed. The decadent crystal chandelier alone had just been valued at over one hundred thousand Euros and his parents adored it. He could understand why the French peasants had wanted to chop off aristocratic heads when they entered these buildings. Simple bad taste in furnishings alone was reason enough in Eric's mind. However, the worst thing about the room, which he loathed more than everything else put together, was the smug family portrait. It hung above the crafted mantelpiece in a gold gilded frame and dominated the room. There were two reasons he hated it so much. Firstly, he had not posed for it. Secondly, it had been painted in a romantic style with pinkish rose hues that made him want to retch. To keep his food down he looked from the painting to his parents. They were sat in front of him on a rich burgundy sofa with finely carved teak legs.

Mr and Mrs Meyer were sat very close together with knees touching and hands resting in each other's. Eric had watched his father play poker and had seen that where money and gambling were concerned, he was supremely focused. Eric had watched his mother on the catwalk and had seen that she oozed confidence from every beautiful pore. However, where Eric was concerned they were neither focused nor confident. Most of the time they just avoided Eric and when they did spend time with him, they didn't really know what to do, unless it involved giving presents.

"So, let me get this absolutely clear," said Eric throwing the pen above his head. It spun around in the air so close to the expensive chandelier that his mother winced. "The only thing you wanted to tell me this evening is that you are running a rather childish competition in the international press of Europe and the person who solves this silly little puzzle will win ten thousand Euros?"

"It's not that silly, bambino," said his mother looking hurt and pouting.

"It took me slightly longer than an hour to complete it and I'm ONLY eleven! Of course it's silly."

"But it vas designed by a man I hired vith an IQ plus 200, son," his father said.

"Next time why don't you save yourself some money

and ask me to do it." Eric was on edge, he knew that his parents were avoiding telling him something else. Their stalling was unnerving his Saxon reason and awakening his Latin temper. "I'll ask again, the only thing you wanted to tell me this evening was about this competition?"

Mr Meyer's eyes moved away from Eric and made contact with his wife's. Without speaking but with an unsubtle nodding of his head he prompted his wife to tell Eric the news. She looked guiltily flustered, began to pout again and shot glances at her son. Even though he looked calm and stood almost like a statue, inside Eric was turning to jelly. All he wanted was a normal family life, but his parents seemed opposed to such boring matters as bringing up a child. What else could he expect from a beauty queen and poker king who met in Vegas, dated in Monaco and were married by a pastor dressed as Elvis on the Great Barrier Reef?

The pouting stopped and Mrs Meyer began, "Erika, bambino."

Eric's back tensed. His mother would never let him forget that he was not the daughter she had so desperately desired.

"We are worried that you are lonely. That you are talented and... gifted and... special."

Eric did nothing but waited for the punch line. He was being complimented which, he had learnt from experience, meant the news he was about to receive was really bad. His mother continued.

"Therefore, we wanted to find someone who was a match or an equal to you."

"In other vords, son," his father interrupted, "ve have decided to use the 'Meyer Foundation for the Deprived, Needy and Challenged' to find you a friend."

"I don't need your foundation for the poor, dirty and stupid to find me a friend. I don't need friends," Eric stated forcefully and then blurted out, "I just need you."

If his parents had been tortoises they would have

chosen that moment to retreat sharply into their shells and not re-emerge until Spring.

"If a suitable person enters a vinning puzzle into the competition, son, ve vill use the foundation to avard them a scholarship to your school in Prague."

Just as Eric was about to say, "Great! I'm going to bed," Mr. Meyer nudged his wife. This new development was frightening, it meant they had not finished yet. Eric's mouth froze before he could utter the words.

"As well as the scholarship, bambino, we will also support the winner financially in Prague."

There was more to come, Eric could feel it, and his blood started to boil.

"And Erika," she paused, fearful to go on, "they can live in our house too."

That was it, the big news that they were scared to tell him was out in the open, the bombshell had been detonated. Phew, it's over, thought Eric. Despite being mightily annoyed at the future intrusion on his privacy he let his shoulders drop and he relaxed. He congratulated his parents on such noble charity work; applauded his 'Parents' Pet Project' as he instantly named it. He hoped that the PPP would be happy in the cellar with the rats, bid his parents a good night and spun round to leave. Behind him his father let out an extremely false cough that he normally reserved for waiters in fancy restaurants. Eric stopped in a heartbeat and without hurrying, for fear of showing his concern, turned around on the spot.

"You have not fully understood, son," said Mr Meyer stumbling over his words as he said them. "They von't be staying vith the rats, they'll be staying vith us, sort of, in a manner of talking, if you see vhat I mean."

Eric's mind went into overdrive. Shared dinners, wet towels in his bathroom, fights over the television channel, locks on his room, no chocolate biscuits... but all he could think of saying was, "Fine, I don't have to communicate with your PPP, I'll just ignore it and speak to you instead."

Mrs Meyer removed a frilly handkerchief from a satin sleeve and dabbed her forehead delicately. "Erika, bambino, you may have to if we are not there."

"I'll wait until you get home," he answered assuredly and crossed his arms securely to show that he meant what he said.

"That might be hard, son, because your mother and me, ve have been speaking and next month is our anniversary of fourteen years."

"Congratulations," said Eric flatly but his father ignored him.

"So ve decided to go on a second honeymoon."

"Good for you," said Eric without any trace of enthusiasm. "Take a week or two weeks, I'm sure I can handle the PPP for that long."

Suddenly Mrs Meyer blurted out, "We'll be gone from September until April."

Eric's jaw hit the floor. "What? Eight months!"

"Yes, we've decided to make good use of the yacht and sail around the world," declared his mother as if she was just going down the shops. "But don't worry, Andrea will be here to look after you both."

In a fraction of a second Eric's blood reached boiling point and his brain spun out of control. He had no idea who was now talking to him. It could not be his parents. Parents would never leave their child for eight months! On the sofa, with reassuring smiles plastered all over their faces, sat his mother and father. They looked as if they did not have a care in the world. With a jolt that made him wince Eric's mind went blank. The thoughts that had been exploding in his mind like fireworks stopped and a new one emerged. It flashed in his head like breaking news on the television, 'PARENTS AWAY FOR EIGHT MONTHS TO BE REPLACED BY INSIGNIFICANT PPP FLAT-MATE. ERIC MEYER WHEN ASKED TO COMMENT STATED...' In truth Eric did not know what to say; his dream of a normal family life had been put on hold for yet another eight months and he felt, he felt, he felt...

His thoughts were broken by a rather uninformed and ill-timed comment from his mother. "Cuddle, bambino?"

It was the straw that broke the camel's back and Eric felt his rage about to spin out of control. His parents took this point to stand up, walk quickly behind the sofa and out of the living room into the hallway. They didn't even say good night. Eric saw in quick succession yellow, orange and then RED. Without thinking he charged, like an Olympic long jumper, towards where they had been sitting and sprang into the air. Eric hit the well sprung sofa with the speed of a train, his feet sunk into the cushions and he sprang backwards up towards the high ceiling. He twisted effortlessly in the air, dropped Le Monde, put out his hands and caught hold of the chandelier. The force of his movement swung the chandelier upwards and just before it made contact with the ceiling Eric let go. He somersaulted towards the door, landed calmly on his feet and walked quietly out of the room as if nothing had happened. Behind him there was a thunderous crash as the chandelier hit the ceiling and smashed into countless crystal hailstones which rained down upon the room.

When at last the glass and dust settled Eric's parents appeared from the hallway door.

"I thought that vent vell," said Mr Meyer gleefully.

"I agree," purred his wife. "Let's go out for dinner."

3

THE COMPETITION

Within three days of the competition being published the first entry arrived. It had been sent from Portugal and arrived in a manila envelope with looping handwriting on the front. Attached to the entry was a letter praising the puzzle and offering, it claimed, an even more challenging version. The solution was wrong. Andrea filed it carefully in the paper recycling bin and opened the second envelope.

Andrea was working in a windowless office in the Meyer's Parisian apartment. It was hot and stuffy in the room, due to the large number of sacks full of entries. They were piled up high and blocked the vent leading to the central air-ventilation shaft, which ran through the building from the basement to the roof. Amongst the sacks, and almost hidden, was a laptop with a special scanner attached. Andrea was sitting in front of it.

The process was simple. First she would open the envelope, with a well-manicured fingernail, and place the solution under the scanner. She would wait zero point five seven seconds for the laptop to declare if the solution was correct and then file the entry. Winners were placed in a wire mesh tray, losers in the recycling bin. It was a laborious and mechanical task but she didn't mind. She had been asked to do it and she would. For four days she worked tirelessly, going through the entries one-by-one. By the morning of the fifth day she had handled, and the computer had scanned, 837,496 entries. Some were only slightly wrong and contained only one or two errors. Others were not even close. A huge number of people had blatantly filled in the puzzle randomly and hoped they would win. Over a thousand people sent begging letters and seventeen more sent threats. Only twenty-eight entries were correct and, of these, only four contained alternate puzzles that worked.

Andrea took the winning entries from the tray and looked them over in detail. The first winner was from Finland. Her name was Aamu Kuusi and she was twenty-six years of age. She would receive the prize money but was not a suitable 'friend' for Eric. Jose Moreno from Spain was in his eighties. Eliisabet Raudsepp from Estonia was fifteen and 'Fraser' from Scotland did not give his age but claimed he was, "no spring chicken." Andrea's head dropped, none of the winners fitted the criteria she had been given. Mr and Mrs Meyer would not be happy. She picked up a headset attached to the laptop and used it to call Serge.

Serge had managed the Post Office where the Meyer's PO Box was based, for seventeen years. Not only did he work in the Post Office but he also lived there. Serge was scared of the randomness of the outside world, the dangers it possessed and the people it housed. He was sitting in his office when the phone rang, admiring stamps and reflecting on the predictability of letters. They were written, sent, arrived and read, altogether a very straightforward routine.

He answered in a gruff voice and spoke as if he wanted to be off the phone before he had even picked up, "Bonjour."

"Serge, it's Andrea Duna."

At the sound of Andrea's voice Serge instantly relaxed and his voice mellowed. He did not like people but he had warmed to Andrea because, like letters she was predictable and followed routines. "Andrea, what can I do for you?"

She explained that the competition was over and the

PO Box could be closed. Serge looked around himself; he was drowning in sacks of entries.

"What shall I do with the remaining ones?"

"Recycle them," answered Andrea.

"I would be delighted," Serge already knew the postal employees who were to have the pleasure of this task.

"Shall I bring in the empty sacks for you?" Andrea asked.

"You can keep them. There is no need," Serge knew the post office would not miss one or two empty post sacks.

"There are over two hundred, Serge."

For a moment Serge reflected on the cost of all these sacks and then answered. "In that case you had better return them, the post office closes at five."

Andrea promised she would be there and then ended the call. She would now have to face the Meyers and break the bad news.

The Meyer's living room had been hoovered, swept and brushed since Eric had destroyed the chandelier. In its place now hung what looked like a giant ice-cube with a spinning fan below it. It was a light completely out of character with the room and as such Eric could not decide if that made it better or worse.

Since he had been told about the competition he had kept tabs on Andrea and monitored her every movement. From the arrival of the first post bag four days ago to the phone call earlier that morning Eric knew exactly what was happening. During the call he had been hiding in the ventilation shaft, perched on a narrow ledge five floors above the basement and listening to every word. When Andrea put the phone down he tiptoed around the ledge and snuck through the loose air vent back into his room. He crept silently through the hallway, into the living room and hid on the floor behind the chaise longue. His parents were sat upon it reading. Eric heard Andrea enter and followed her footsteps with his ears as she approached the expensive sofa. She greeted his parents, sat down on an Edwardian armchair next to the mantelpiece and told Eric's parents what had happened.

Mrs Meyer brushed the news away as if it was really of no importance at all. This was a reaction she had perfected at beauty contests, and she used it whenever events did not go the way she had hoped. Her husband showed no reaction, his face and body language were impossible to read. An altogether unsurprising reaction from an experienced poker player. They sat in silence wondering what to do next until Andrea asked if she should re-advertise the puzzle in children's magazines. Her suggestion was declined on the basis that Eric never read them so a suitable 'friend' would not be found there either.

"Maybe we should do what we have talked about for a long time and send him to boarding school," said Mrs Meyer banging her fist smartly on the sofa arm to make her point.

Hidden behind the chaise longue Eric shook his head and mouthed, "No!"

He would much rather be left alone than go to boarding school and lose all his freedom. The idea of having to share a dorm room with other boys his age, and having all his time scheduled by teachers, he found terrifying.

"You are correct my darling," agreed Mr Meyer. "Miss Duna, please contact the best boarding schools in England and Svitzerland, make a decision and enroll Eric in one you feel vill best suit him. Thank you."

Andrea replied that she would start the task once she had returned the sacks to the post office, and that Eric would be enrolled in the best boarding school by the end of the following day. She left purposefully through the same door she had entered from. Eric slithered out of the room on his belly, like an army commando. He was biting his tongue so hard that he could taste blood.

Granddad Benjamin was lying on his bed not feeling well. During the night, while asleep, he had knocked all his medicines from the bedside table onto the floor. This would not have been a problem but before sunrise Mémé had decided to clean. Not wanting to disturb her husband, who was deaf while asleep but woke at the slightest change in light, she had vacuumed in the dark. Her ancient beast of a hoover had greedily sucked up his multi-coloured tablets. He had therefore missed his morning medication and his lunchtime tablets too. Ursula had left for the pharmacy after breakfast but it was now almost four and she had still not returned. A frown began to sketch across Granddad Benjamin's face, he was in pain. His pills were not the best but they did help. The frown stretched further as he thought about the puzzle competition. They should have heard by now that Ursula had won. Maybe his wife had been right when she said that the chances of winning were hopeless. However, if she had really felt this then she wouldn't have posted the entry. After forty-nine years of marriage he knew that she also had dreams and most, like his, were for Ursula. If she could do anything to achieve these for her granddaughter she would. He was convinced Ursula had won and decided he just had to wait patiently to be told. Pushing his head back into the pillow he tried to relax and focus his thoughts on something else.

The high ceilinged post office was not busy. A few elderly women queued up in front of glass counters, moaning about the hot weather while they waited. The automatic doors opened and Andrea entered clutching twelve blue and yellow postal bags. Each of these bags was stuffed full of more bags. She strode to the front of the queue, apologized for pushing in and asked to see the manager. The post office clerk phoned Serge and then directed Andrea towards the office door. The gossiping quickly stopped and all eyes turned to Andrea. Nobody ever saw the manager. Nobody had ever seen the manager since his arrival many years before. Nobody could even remember what he looked like. The chattering began again as Andrea moved away from the queue towards a plain grey door. This time the subject of conversation was her. The ladies shuffled their positions so they could watch but made sure they would not lose their place in the queue.

There was creak as the door moved slightly on its hinges followed by shh-ing from the women in the queue. The door squeaked more as it opened and gingerly Serge stepped into the doorway. A stunned silence fell over the room. His head bent down and he looked over the grey tiled floor to make sure there was no obvious danger. Reassured by the lack of water, or other slippery liquid, he stepped cautiously out of his office. He was an average size man with prematurely thinning hair which failed to cover his bald patch. Conscious of this fact he tried to brush the hair with his fingers so it rested more evenly over this head. Feeling more confident in his appearance he moved towards Andrea and greeted her with a hesitant kiss on both cheeks. Andrea thanked Serge for all his help and placed the sacks she was carrying by the door against the wall. Kissing him on both cheeks she apologized for the short visit and left the post office to gasps from the watching women.

Serge watched her leave, his head sunk and he turned to the pile of sacks that Andrea had delivered. Keeping his back straight, to avoid pulling anything he shouldn't, he bent down, picked up a blue sack and promptly dropped it again. It was far heavier than he had expected and he did not want to risk an injury. The sack swayed before falling onto its side and spilling out all its contents onto the clean floor. The old ladies laughed and Serge silenced them with a glare. Blue and yellow sacks now littered the area outside his office and he knelt down to pick them up. As he picked up the first bag he noticed a glimmer of white amongst the yellow and blue. He moved forward and picked up a small crumpled envelope with a Parisian post mark. It had been used more than once but written above crossed out writing was the competition address. Serge stood up and carefully walked across the foyer to the post office's doors. He would have run but he was bound to slip on the polished tiles and had no desire to go to hospital. However, he wanted to catch Andrea before she drove away and he knew this would mean leaving the safety of the post office. In front of him the automatic glass doors opened and closed in time with Serge's quickening breath. He clenched his fists and went outside.

Outside it was noisy, busy and muggy after the calm and the cool of the post office. Cars rushed down rue Paul Baudry, zooming in front of Serge's eyes, but none contained Andrea. Rotating his head steadily he surveyed the road, but he could not see her. Disappointed, he turned to go inside when he saw a silver Land Rover indicate and pull out from the other side of a parked butcher's van. Serge was relieved to see that Andrea was driving and she was heading in his direction. As wary as a deer he stepped into the road, between two parked scooters, and waved to the Land Rover as it approached. He did not want to step out too far in case he was hit by a car and had to be taken to hospital. The Land Rover slowed down and came to a stop beside him. The passenger window hummed as it opened and Andrea leant across towards it.

"Serge, are you okay?" Andrea asked, concerned that he had left the safety of the post office.

"I'm, er, fine," replied Serge and moving towards the window he produced the letter. "I found this," and he dropped it through the window.

"Thanks," said Andrea taking the envelope and opening it in one movement.

She scanned the puzzle solution written in neat childish writing, glanced at the written puzzle, looked at the age of the entry and smiled. The entry would need checking back at the apartment but she knew it was correct.

Serge withdrew his hand from the window. Andrea closed it, waved goodbye and drove away. Delighted with his achievement Serge turned around carefully, admired his post office, stepped forward and disappeared down an open drain. Three old ladies rescued him and the ambulance arrived to take him to hospital, twenty minutes later.

Agent Hoover stopped laughing at the man who fell down the gutter when he saw Ursula skip past the ambulance. With energy that he normally reserved for tracking bank robbers he took note of the street name, rue Paul Baudry, and scanned his computer database for drug stores on that street. The computer gave him two matches. From watching Ursula for several weeks he knew that she had already been to the Pharmacie Europa but she had yet to visit the newly opened Pharmacie Baudry nearby. With more speed than his hot dog fingers seemed capable of he typed the name into his computer, found the pharmacy's telephone number and used the computer to call.

A Frenchman with a bass drum voice answered, "*Bonjour.*"

"Hello," he drawled, "you gotta a kid coming into your drug store in a minute and she's gonna swipe some of your drugs. I'm just warning ya."

The pharmacist was confused, "*excusez-moi, mais je ne comprend pas.* I... er... not... understand."

Agent Hoover leant forward into his chair, moved his hands in the air to make his point and tried to make the pharmacist understand. "YOU GOTTA A KID COMING INTO YOUR CHEMIST AND SHE'S GONNA SWIPE SOME OF YOUR MEDICINE! YOU UNDERSTAND NOW?"

Demonstrating a remarkable amount of patience the pharmacist replied, "*Non*, no."

"Geez, buddy it's about time you got with the program

and learnt some English. Let me spell it out for you. Black girl, thin, thief, medicines, okay?"

"Okay," replied the pharmacist.

"Understand?"

"Er...yes...thief...take medicaments."

"Whatever you say bud," and Agent Hoover ended the call.

For once he was alone in the large dark room and had decided to have a well- earned break by catching this thieving punk instead of his usual search. His fingers sprang to life over the keyboard again and, within a few seconds, live feed from the Pharmacie Baudry security camera appeared on one of the countless screens in front of him. The black and white grainy footage showed a well-built man in square glasses and a white coat standing behind a counter covered in medicine. Behind him were white shelves and drawers full of more tablets, creams and sachets. In front of him the pharmacy's door opened and Ursula entered.

On her first step into the pharmacy, Ursula had located the medicine her Granddad needed behind the counter. By the second step she had spotted the most difficult to reach tablets and sized up the agility of the pharmacist. On the third step she had to fight back the urge to flee and convince herself that what she was doing was for the best, even though she knew it was wrong. Before she reached the counter she had to perfect her most innocent and helpless look. She managed all of these and stood facing the full figure of the pharmacist. Pointing high above his left shoulder she asked if she could have the Anusol cream in the blue and white box in the corner of the top shelf.

The pharmacist moved away from the counter but his movements were slow and looked too deliberate. Ursula instantly felt that something was wrong. As the pharmacist reached up Ursula's hand darted forwards. Silently she grabbed the medicine she needed and moved them under her white vest and into her jean's pocket. She followed this by announcing loudly that she had left something in the shop next door and she would be back in a minute. As she twisted around towards the exit she saw the white and blue police car pulling up in front of the pharmacy. It stopped her dead and then she sprang for the door. She sped out at the same time as two policeman left the car. The taller of the two, who was closest to Ursula, put out an arm to stop her but she ducked underneath and broke into a sprint. Her heart was racing.

Three weeks out of the National Police Institute at Clermont Ferrand, Officer le Blanc was young and fit. During this training he had shaved three seconds off the Police Force four hundred metres record. He felt confident that he could afford to give the girl a fifty metres head start.

"Follow in the car," he told his fellow officer and began the chase on foot. The girl was slightly further than fifty metres ahead by this time but he was sure that she wouldn't pose a problem. There were only a few pedestrians on the pavement and he knew they would move as he began his pursuit.

As she wove around a woman with a pram Ursula shot a glance over her shoulder. The police car was pulling away and a tall, shaven-headed officer was chasing after her. High above the hot sun beat down, but Ursula's perspiration was not due to the heat. She saw a side road about three hundred metres ahead, dug her heels in and accelerated up rue Paul Baudry. As she sprinted the police car pulled up beside her and shadowed her while the Officer followed.

It had taken her five hours to find a suitable pharmacy that she had not stolen from before. According to the speed she walked Ursula thought that she was probably about fifteen kilometres from home. "Fifteen kilometres!" she exclaimed to herself between breaths, she couldn't run for fifteen kilometres!

Slaloming through shopping families she reached the side road and turned down it. The police car followed but was forced to stop as Ursula sprinted across the road in front of it and down the opposite pavement. A Renault 6 behind the police car, the driver distracted by a loose chicken in his car, shunted into the rear. Ursula breathed a short sigh of relief. The police car had been lost. Unfortunately the policeman was just crossing the road, having narrowly avoided becoming part of the smash.

Cutting down a grubby alleyway behind some shops Ursula slipped on some mushy old fruit. She just managed to retain her footing and skidded away. The alley was long and littered with old food, cardboard boxes, plastic bags and packaging. In the distance she could see the end of the alley and glimpses of the Avenue de Champs Elysées. If she could get there she knew she would be safe. She sprinted over the rubbish, striding over the small bits and expertly hurdling the larger pieces. About halfway along a black cat strolled out in front of her looking for affection. Ursula jumped. Her right foot missed the cat by a whisker and sent it scampering away towards the policeman. At the end of the alleyway she reached the busy Champs Elysées. Skidding out from the dirty alley she bumped into a well-padded German tourist with a handlebar moustache, bounced off him and shot into the crowds.

Officer le Blanc smacked into the already flustered German and scanned the crowds. He was stunned. A girl of about ten years of age had just outrun him and then disappeared. Admittedly the alley had not been wide and the car crash, plus the cat, had slowed him down. However, he should have still caught her. There was no real excuse and he would be a laughing stock back at the station when the other officers found out.

Thirty minutes later the police car, which now had two smashed rear lights, pulled up beside him and he jumped in. Before he could say what had happened his colleague spoke. "We have been given some information.

Unsurprisingly it looks as if she is heading for les banlieues, near the Stade de France at Saint-Denis. We will drive over there and see if she shows up."

Le Blanc nodded his approval and they drove off.

Dark black clouds had formed in the sky by the time Ursula saw the square of apartment blocks which she called home. Her heart slowed down and she began to relax as large drops of rain started to fall. She ran down the road towards the path that led to her apartment block. On the street opposite, parked between a silver Land Rover and a faded bronze Peugeot 205, was the police car. It was parked underneath a very old cigarette advert, heavily tagged with graffiti, and the two policeman were still inside. They waited until Ursula was a safe distance away and then left their vehicle to follow her. Ursula was so happy to be home that she didn't even notice they were there.

The path that she took to her apartment block was one she normally avoided. Dog poo, broken bottles and syringes covered the cracked path. Despite appearances Ursula felt safe. The door to her block was always open, after somebody had accidently broken it, so she entered easily and skipped up the eight floors to her grandparents' flat. After four knocks on the door it was opened by Mémé who scolded her for being late, reminded her to remove her shoes and then let her in. Ursula made straight for her bedroom, lay down on her bed and closed her eyes. The moment she did this she heard urgent knocking on the front door, followed by the sound of Mémé opening it.

"Bonjour Madame, I am Officer Massot and this is Officer le Blanc. We are looking for a thin girl aged approximately ten. Would you be able to help us?"

Clutching hold of Fred, fear gripped Ursula like a vice and a deafening clap of thunder did not help her mood. Mémé had always told her that lying was wrong, she would tell the policemen the truth, get Ursula from her room and hand her over. Before Ursula did anything she waited to hear what her Grandmother said.

"I'm very sorry but I think you have the wrong apartment. It's only me and my husband who live here and he is very sick. You will have to excuse me as I was just looking after him when you knocked. Au revoir."

She shut the door shakily. Ursula breathed a sigh of relief, she was out of the frying pan but into the fire. She heard her Granddad get up and shuffle into the hall.

"Who was that Marie-Thérèse?" he asked.

"Nothing for you to worry about, Jerome. Go back to bed and relax it was nothing important."

Granddad Benjamin did what he was told, but he was not convinced by his wife's words.

Footsteps approached Ursula's room and she watched as her door handle turned. Before the door was pushed fully open there was another knock at the front door and Ursula's door was slammed shut.

On opening the front door Mémé was greeted by a slight woman wearing leather trousers, a leather jacket and a T-shirt upon which was written 'The Pixies.'

"Bonjour," greeted Andrea and continued in perfect French, "I'm looking for Ursula Benjamin."

Looking Andrea squarely in the eye and without batting an eyelid, Mémé said, "I'm sorry, *madame*, but there is no one of that name who lives here. You must be mistaken. Au revoir."

Calmly and politely she shut the door. Andrea knocked once more. At first Mémé ignored it but the persistent tapping forced her to open the door yet again. "I'm sorry but I think you have the wrong apartment," she said holding back her temper.

Before Mémé could close the door Andrea placed her foot in the open door way, speaking calmly as she did so. "Madame Benjamin, I am not the police or a detective, I promise, though there is a police car parked in the road and I passed two police men on the stairs coming up."

The words seemed to reassure Mémé who paused from

slamming the door shut. Andrea continued, slightly slower now that she felt she was not going to be shut out again.

"My name is Andrea Duna and I represent the Meyer foundation. I am here about the competition."

From the bedroom there was a loud thump as Granddad Benjamin fell out of bed, followed by a groaning shout of, "For God's sake Marie-Thérèse, let her in!"

The three Benjamins sat attentively on the itchy brown and beige sofa. . In the centre, and slightly elevated due to the weight of her grandparents on either side of her, was Ursula. She sat motionless, more worried about the trouble she was in, and whether she would go to prison, than the puzzle competition she had won. Her Grandmother had not invited Ursula to the living room, she had summoned her. Likewise she had been told to sit down rather than asked. As they sat there Ursula felt that the usual warmth she received from Mémé had been replaced by a very cold shoulder. Granddad Benjamin knew something had happened but as he was fast asleep when the police called he had no idea what. Experience had taught him not to ask questions in these situations, if he didn't want to get caught in the middle. Also, after hearing the words 'Meyer' he had stopped caring about what may have happened anyway.

On one of the white formica seats opposite them sat Andrea. She had finished explaining that Ursula had won the competition, would receive ten thousand Euros and was about to share the other news.

"I have been asked to inform you of another competition that you have also won which was not advertised in the newspapers along with the puzzle."

Granddad Benjamin's ears pricked up and he leaned forward while trying to contain his excitement, "Another competition?"

Surprised that she needed to confirm this Andrea simply nodded her head. She proceeded to explain that the

Meyer Foundation wished to offer a scholarship for an exclusive school in Prague - a scholarship which would cover Ursula's education until she was eighteen. During the explanation Andrea mentioned that this was the same school that the Meyer's own son also attended. She did not say that it was hoped that Ursula would be a companion, and hopefully, a friend for Eric while his parents toured around the world on their yacht.

The Benjamins had heard of the word scholarship but as it had never applied to them they did not fully understand what it meant. They asked for an explanation.

"To put it simply," explained Andrea, "we would fly Ursula to Prague, house her, clothe her, feed and water her, supply her with pocket money and pay for her to attend the Prague Anglo International School."

"That sounds great," announced Granddad Benjamin genuinely, "what a super opportunity! It is what we have always dreamed of for Ursula," and he looked at his wife.

Mémé had started to fidget and Ursula sensed that the cold shoulder was thawing quickly.

Trying to keep her voice steady Mémé added, "Jerome is right. We always wanted Ursula to have opportunities that we never had, but I never imagined they would be in another country. She will be able to come home every weekend, won't she? Prague is not that far away, is it?"

Her hand moved to Ursula's knee and held on as if she was about to fall. Ursula relaxed slightly and felt that it was only the police she had to worry about now. She looked at Andrea and waited for her answer.

"I do not think that would be possible," Andrea replied sympathetically. On seeing the Benjamin's faces drop she added, "But she would be back during the holidays. This is not a question of money. It is about doing the best for Ursula. Traveling between Prague and Paris every weekend would exhaust her."

Faking a look of comprehension Mémé nodded unconvincingly. She and her husband had arrived in

France on a boat and taken a steam train to Paris. They had never been in an aeroplane and in fact had not visited an airport either. The closest they had come to a plane was watching them in the sky above their apartment. In other words she did not understand. Over Ursula's head Mémé looked desperately at her husband. After so many years together he knew the look and took over the conversation.

"It would not be easy for us to lose Ursula," he said.

Andrea shook her head slowly and smiled sweetly. "I understand but you would not be losing her. We will insist she stays in contact with you and we will set up a video phone, and pay for all calls, so you can see her when you speak to her. There is no obligation for you to say yes and no obligation for Ursula to go. Think about it this way, we are just providing Ursula with a better school to go to and because it is far away we will take care of her as well."

During the adult's discussion Ursula had sat silently. She did not know what to say. She did not want to leave her grandparents but she did want to escape the police. She did want to explore new places but she was scared of not knowing somewhere. She wanted to learn more but she found school boring. Her silence was due to her confusion. Over the years her grandmother had taught her that if she didn't know what to say it was best to say nothing at all. Unfortunately Ursula was unable to stay silent because Andrea then asked her what she wanted to do. Another one of Mémé lessons had been that it was rude to ignore questions. Therefore Ursula was forced to answer. Not knowing what to say, she avoided speaking and shrugged her shoulders.

Pushing her seat back towards the table Andrea stood up. The Benjamins obviously had to talk about this and she believed it was best if she left them to do so.

"You do not need to make a decision today but may I ask for one by tomorrow evening?" Andrea requested.

The three Benjamins politely stood up and nodded like

a small Mexican wave. Together they followed Andrea to the hallway. At the front door Andrea handed over her telephone number on a small playing card to Mémé. Granddad Benjamin opened the front door in a gentlemanly fashion and Andrea, followed by his wife, stepped outside into the passageway. Indoors Granddad Benjamin placed his arms around Ursula and held her close to him like a precious stone. Outside Mémé pointed at the two of them.

"You can see it is not easy," she sighed.

A tear formed in her eye at the thought of losing Ursula. Delicately she wiped it away and as she did so she saw the two policeman, poking their heads around the stairwell, at the end of the passageway. The moment they saw Mémé they hid. Disappearing quickly behind the peeling walls and badly spelled graffiti like rabbits down a hole. It was their not-so-secret spying that prompted Mémé to invite Andrea back into the house.

Once they had returned to the living room and were sitting relatively comfortably again Mémé cleared her throat.

"I can see it would a great opportunity for Ursula, as my husband said, but as I said it would not be easy to let her go. I don't know a lot but I do know that Ursula does not stand a good chance of a good life if she stays here." She paused, choosing her next words carefully. "But I need to know that she will stand a better chance of a good life somewhere else, even if we are not there."

A feeling of loss started to eat away at Ursula. They had talked as a family about their dreams but the reality was very different.

Andrea looked concerned, "Mrs Benjamin, I would like to stress that we are not taking your Granddaughter away from you. And she will always come back as well as staying in contact with you."

Placing his arm tenderly around Ursula's shoulder Granddad Benjamin began to speak but his words had difficulty leaving his throat. "I think really," he coughed, "it is Ursula's decision."

Up to this point Ursula had been content with the adults talking about her, as she still did not know what she wanted to do. Suddenly this changed and all eyes were upon her. After an initial shrug of her shoulders she whispered, "I think it would be good..." There was a long pause and then she spoke from the heart, "...if I didn't love my grandparents so much I would go."

Granddad Benjamin took her right hand, looked her in the eyes and said gently, "That's no reason to say no. Love can travel over long distance and survive over periods of time."

Taking her left hand Mémé continued, "And Miss Andrea said you could write to us and do that phideo vone thing."

Ursula felt her heart rise and fall at the same time. Tears were welling up in her eyes but she tried to ignore them.

"When you are older you won't regret the things you did," said Granddad Benjamin, "only those you didn't."

The tears had filled her eyes and were slowly meandering down Ursula's cheeks.

Andrea broke the silence, "If you do want to do this, then we will leave Paris in two days." Her tone was warm but functional. "Ursula will need a suitcase of clothes and anything else she wants to bring. And, of course, she will also need her passport."

Ursula's grandparents looked at each other. On their faces more wrinkles had appeared at Andrea's last request. Andrea looked at Granddad Benjamin who began to talk, "Ursula does not have a passport. None of us do. We..."

"...had a fire," Mémé interrupted. "We lost them all in a fire. We lost everything including the passports and we never felt we needed new ones."

"That is fine," Andrea was not concerned, "we can get a new one. All I need is a birth certificate."

Looking down at his feet Granddad Benjamin uttered quietly, "We don't have it, as my wife said we lost everything."

Andrea tried to reassure them, "That makes it a bit harder but I know someone who can help. When I give him Ursula's name he will be able to provide us with a new birth certificate from the existing records."

Granddad Benjamin was still looking at his feet. "I don't think he will be able to help either as we..." he paused, pressing his fingers into his forehead as he did so, "...never registered her."

"Not that it was our job to do it," Mémé was keen to explain. She spoke very quickly and babbled, "Obviously it was Ursula's parent's job but they went away shortly after the birth, rock climbing, and when they didn't come back it was hard and then Ursula was with us, and we thought they had done it but they hadn't and we had other things to do and then, shortly after, we had the fire and we lost everything, well nearly everything, all the important things anyway and it was a very difficult time and..."

Gently, Andrea interrupted, "I am sure it was. Do not worry, no problem is unsolvable. Ursula had already proved that by winning the competition. I'm sure we can solve it."

After checking her watch Andrea excused herself and stood up. Before she left she made the Benjamins promise they would phone if they had any problems or second thoughts. At the front door she told them that she would see them in two days, if they did not change their minds, and walked off towards the staircase. As she turned onto the stairwell she stood on Officer Le Blanc's hand, who has been lying on the floor spying. While he rolled around in agony his partner asked her if there was a young girl in the apartment that Andrea had just left.

"None at all," she replied confidently and continued walking down the stairs.

4

AU REVOIR

In the centre of the Meyers' mahogany dining table stood two silver candlesticks. The flames slowly danced in the hot summer breeze and the net curtains moved in time with them. Outside, the deep orange sun had set, turning a bright day into a dark night. The only light in the large dining room came from the flames at the end of the wax candles. They were slowly melting and wax dripped onto the mahogany.

There were fourteen high-backed chairs around the oval table. However, Eric and his parents only sat around one end. Mr Meyer was tucking into a meal of truffles, fine sausage and exclusive Foie Gras paté. His wife was nibbling on a lettuce leaf from her Waldorf salad and picking around the other ingredients. Eric was eating a beef burger made from maize fed Argentinian cows. It was squashed between a freshly made wholemeal bun covered in sesame seeds. According to the chef, who also worked in a four star hotel famed for its food, it was a designer burger. This meant, as far as Eric could see, that the pickles and garnishes were artistically arranged but it still tasted the same as every other burger.

The Meyers ate in silence, the only sounds in the room coming from the cutlery as it scraped against the plates. Outside the dining room window a cat's quiet miaow could be heard coming closer. It became louder until a grey Persian cat suddenly appeared at the window, jumped silently onto the table and then once more on to the floor.

Dark wooden panels covered the wall opposite the window. They stretched from the floor to the ceiling and hid the only entrance to the room. Slowly a wooden panel moved and the hidden door opened. A thick ray of light cast itself across the table. Andrea entered and stood in its glow as the cat bolted past her. She faced the Meyers and spoke matter-of-factly and without emotion.

"I am sorry to interrupt but I have good news. I have found someone who has won the competition and who also fills your requirements for the scholarship. She is the same age as Eric and, I assume from her puzzle entry, equally as intelligent. She lives with her grandparents here, in Paris, and they have agreed to let her study in Prague. I shall be collecting her the day after tomorrow, early in the morning before the flight. I will take Eric with me and then the three of us will journey to Prague."

"Bravo!" cried Mrs Meyer.

"Well done!" congratulated her husband.

"Pile of poo!" muttered Eric under his breath.

Andrea turned and left as swiftly as she had arrived. The door closed without a sound and the thick beam of light retreated from the room. Spitting out a piece of burger that he had been unable to swallow Eric stood up. He leant forward until his lips could feel the warmth of the candles and blew. The flames struggled and fought but Eric blew harder until they gave up and went out. A black sheet draped itself over the three diners and Eric returned unseen to his seat.

"Just pretend I'm not here," he uttered while straining to hold back his tears, "that shouldn't be too hard for you."

Mr Meyer asked his wife if she would like a dessert. She declined.

From behind a large board advertising petrol, on top of one of the four apartment blocks, a red sun rose. White clouds, barely visible before the sun came up, turned to pink candy floss. The resulting light bathed les banlieues of Saint-Denis in a warming glow. Ursula looked down on her neighbourhood. She knew that she was going to miss it, in spite of its appearance.

Sitting on the roof, above the eighth floor of her block, she could look down and see it all. She was wearing her favourite clothes; her threadbare black jeans, a plain yellow vest top and her greying white trainers. Her feet dangled over the side and moved in small circles above her grandparents' balcony. They were being watched by her Granddad and Mémé.

Both were standing still in their dark living room. The rose light reflected off their faces and spot lit their hands as they held each other tightly. Over the last two days they appeared to have aged. Their backs had started to curve, their steps dragged, Granddad Benjamin's jokes had dried up, and they both looked to have shrunk. Ursula had promised them all the money she had won but no money could replace their granddaughter. They felt selfish and knew deep down that this was a wonderful opportunity for Ursula but this thought did not help them to feel any better.

Thirty minutes earlier Andrea had called on them. She had brought, among other gifts, enough medicine for the next two years for Granddad Benjamin. She gave them the video phone, set it up and showed them how to use it, plus she a laptop for email and handed over the prize money. After reassuring the elderly couple that their granddaughter would phone every night, she picked up Ursula's luggage. It was a beaten, brown suitcase scratched by time. Originally it had been Granddad Benjamin's and was so old that it was made of stiff card. The plastic handle was, by modern standards, like a razor blade but Andrea did not notice.

Inside the suitcase were Ursula's clothes and a few sentimental possessions - Fred, a silver outfit she had worn as a baby and a photo of her grandparents. Only one item of Ursula's was not in the suitcase. It was too precious to be kept amongst her clothes and losing it was too big a risk. The object looked worthless but to Ursula it was priceless. Granddad Benjamin and Mémé had given it to her on her sixth birthday and it was a small piece of rock from her parents' last climb. Her grandparents had told her that it was the only item they had left from Ursula's parents. All the other mementos and photos they had owned had been destroyed in the fire when Ursula was still a toddler. The little coin-sized rock was her only link to them. It hung around her neck, turned into a necklace by Mémé as a leaving present, and Ursula promised it would always stay there.

The necklace swung in front of Ursula's chest as she leaned forward to see what was happening eight floors below. She watched as Andrea left the block with the suitcase. Ursula did not know yet if she liked Andrea or not. Andrea seemed fine but Ursula had thought that about some of the teachers at school who soon became monsters. From far below, Andrea looked up. Swinging her arm in the air she beckoned Ursula down and walked away.

This was the moment which Ursula had been dreading, the time to leave. Before coming up to the roof, to avoid an emotional scene in front of a near stranger, she had said a long tearful goodbye to her grandparents. She had then come up on the roof to say goodbye to the neighbourhood - her neighbourhood. On the road next to her block, she could see that Andrea had reached a silver Land Rover and had put her suitcase down on the tarmac.

Pulling her legs back up to the roof, Ursula stood. She pirouetted until there was no roof below her and only her toes clung to the ledge. Slowly she took a deep breath in. With her eyes closed she tilted her head up towards the sky and as she opened them again she hopped backwards. She dropped like a stone past her grandparents' window and caught the balcony before she fell any further. She had fallen two and a half metres. At the same time as her hands clenched hold of the railing she heard Mémé shout, "Wait!"

Seven floors above the ground Ursula hung onto the railing. The sound of the creaking balcony door opening reached her ears, followed by the shuffling of feet, as her grandparents came outside. On looking up Ursula was greeted by her Granddad's smiling face.

"I'm looking forward to using this new video phone thing," he said and grinned broadly. "Take care, my love."

A hand appeared and pulled him out of the way. Mémé appeared in view. "I'll miss you, ma cherie," she said.

"I'll miss you too, Mémé."

A tear fell from Mémé's left eye onto Ursula's forehead. It felt as heavy as an ocean. Unable to support the weight, Ursula opened her bony fingers, let go and dropped down to the next balcony, grabbing hold of the railing as she had done previously before falling further.

"You're going to be filthy before you even reach the ground and you know I worry to death when you do this," scolded Mémé.

"Last time," shouted back Ursula, smiled and let go. She fell to the sixth, then fifth, fourth, third...

From his comfortable office chair Agent Hoover watched via satellites. Before Ursula reached the ground he lost her. There were no working security cameras near the ground in Saint-Denis and too many places to vanish. He sunk back into his chair, adjusted the air conditioning and turned his head to scan the other small screens. That was when he saw it.

A silver glint caught his eye. It was on a screen marked strada Stadionului/Stadium Street, Sfantu Gheorge, Romania. As he watched, he saw a rusting bulldozer remove it from the ground. It was covered in mud but it was unmistakably a silver bulb shape, approximately the size of small car. It was the object he had been instructed to find. With sweaty palms he lifted up the black phone on his desk and started to dial the number he knew by heart though he had never read, seen, heard nor been told it. Behind him, lurking in the shadows, a sinewy figure wheezed expectantly.

5

FINDING THE TREASURE

The referee put the whistle to his lips, blew forcefully and FC Sfantu Gheorghe kicked off against their rivals. The football pitch had baked hard over the summer and the ball bobbled on the bumpy surface. On hitting a divot it was miskicked, bounced around all the players and rolled off the pitch for a throw in. The small crowd, who were watching from a grass bank, booed. Amongst them was a man of average height with well-kept, black hair down to his shoulders. He was dressed in a purple addiddash shell suit and wore a new FC Sfantu Gheorghe scarf around his shoulders. He was known as Mihai Ionescu and his forehead was dripping with sweat. Despite his scarf Mihai was not a soccer fan and watched the match half-heartedly. From where he stood he could see almost all of Stadium street, the potholed road where the stadium was situated. In between breaks in play, so as not to draw attention to himself, he tried to take the location in.

Mihai saw the hilly road he had driven up to get to the stadium, and could see only one other road wide enough to get away. His car was a black GMC Yukon, a Sport Utility Vehicle or SUV. It was big, fast and powerful; he could drive it almost anywhere and he could bully other drivers with it. Dotted between these two roads, or 'exit points' as Mihai called them, were seven apartment blocks known as *panelaks*. The balconies and windows had been painted recently but the plaster on the walls was cracked and crumbling.

Almost hidden beneath two panelaks was a brightly coloured school. Around its grounds were tall dense trees which stopped the sun reaching the car park and hid cars from the sky. Further along, and opposite the stadium, a rundown hospital spat smoking patients out onto the road. They mooched outside the main entrance in their pyjamas, holding cigarettes and listening to the sound of the football game. When they heard the referee whistle for the end of first half they lost interest. Back in the stadium the players, pouring with sweat, trotted off the pitch towards the changing room.

The man known as Mihai Ionescu watched them leave and turned around. Behind the stadium was a newer, unnamed road. It ran away from Stadium street, towards a dead end, and what looked like a building site. Green, sloping fields on the edge of the town, had been divided up like a patch work quilt and were now being dug up. On every available plot houses of all shapes and sizes were being built, all the way to the edge of a forest.

At the top of the sloping fields, overlooking the haphazard building site, Mihai could see a Roman style villa. It was the house he had been told to locate first, the marker. To the right of it was a plot of land where nothing had yet been built. Large piles of bricks and breeze blocks were scattered around its border like badly constructed pyramids. Near the centre, a clogged up concrete mixer stood idle against sacks of sand and a dirty tarpaulin covered an unseen object. The intelligence had all been good, everything fitted, and under the black tarpaulin he was sure he would find the object they had code named 'the treasure'.

Four deeply tanned workmen, with skin like leather, chatted amicably in the sun. Dusty mud covered them from head to foot and in their hands they held well used shovels. Nearby, a rusty old bulldozer carved out a hole in the ground and dumped the soil in a pile beside them.

Mihai Ionescu touched a small device resting in his left

ear with his index finger. "This is Agent Ion. I have found the X that marks the spot," he said in English, and pretended to scratch his head.

Agent Hoover considered what he should say. In front of him a thin microphone stood upright on his glass desk. Before he had a chance to reply a strong hand gripped his shoulder and pushed him away from the microphone. Agent Angel stepped forward and spoke. His deep voice, scarred by years of smoking, boomed the response and filled the room. "Find the treasure, gentlemen," he bellowed, "find the treasure!" He stepped back and let Agent Hoover reclaim his desk.

The screens which dominated the front of the room were no longer showing images from cameras around the world. A very small number were showing footage from every security camera in Sfantu Gheorghe. The rest of the displays had become an IMAX size screen and were showing footage from a satellite positioned directly above the stadium.

As the players came out of the changing rooms for the second half the man known as Mihai Ionescu left the stadium. He was followed by a man and a woman. He walked past the changing rooms, stepped into the street, and made his way to the plot of land. It was time to retrieve the treasure.

A temporary fence made of different sized planks of wood enclosed the plot. To its left was the villa and to its right a half-built home-ade of breeze blocks. Both had mean looking dogs in the gardens patrolling their territory. On seeing Mihai approach they growled and began to bark menacingly. He was not bothered by the barking as it was usual in the town. However, he did not want to go any further until the workers had left. He stopped next to a shed by the dusty path. The shed's low window had been removed and underneath it, lined up like soldiers, were

American cigarettes and fizzy drinks on a roughly made shelf. Crouching down he ordered a cola, in Romanian, put his money on the shelf and waited. An old lady took a glass cola bottle from a small fridge and handed it shakily to Mihai.

"If you are going to take it away you will have to pay for the bottle as well," she replied, sounding as if she was telling off a small child.

"I'll drink it here, don't worry," replied Mihai with a kindly smile.

The woman had given him a good excuse to stay exactly where he was and watch what was happening on the plot of the land.

A man in a sweat stained vest, which barely covered his hairy beer belly, got out of the bulldozer. Tapping his watch he signaled to the four men that it was time to go. The workmen, obviously tired from their day's work, threw their spades to the floor. They were happy to be going home and moved towards the gate with a spring in their step. As they did so an old truck with a brown cab chugged past Mihai. Thick smoke billowed from its exhaust, causing him to cough until his lungs were clear. Even though it was not going fast, the brakes screamed as it slowed down near the plot's gate. It stopped in front of the workmen, blocking their way. The engine ticked over with a horrible grinding sound and more smoke coughed from the exhaust pipe. A bald driver put his head out of the cab, waved a small black wallet and spoke with the workers. What he was saying was obviously not welcomed by the tired men. A man in a red baseball cap leant out of the other window and pointed at the tarpaulin. From the looks on the workmen's faces, and their tense body language, Mihai could see that they were far from happy.

The driver retreated into his cab and re-emerged with a stack of bank notes. The workers' shoulders relaxed but they did not look any more co-operative. One bank note after another was counted out to each man until they stopped frowning. Stuffing the money into their pockets they walked in the direction of the dirty black tarpaulin. Gears crunched, smoke spewed from the exhaust pipe and the truck followed them.

Everything that was happening was unexpected and Mihai was confused. Bribed men and an empty truck were not part of the brief he had been given. Rocking back on his feet and leaning against the shed he felt the comforting shape of his gun pressing into his back. Carefully he raised his finger to his earpiece and spoke, "there are pirates on board. Stand by."

The man and the woman, who had followed Mihai, suddenly appeared from hiding places around the plot of land. They nodded and then disappeared again.

The earpiece fizzed into life and Agent Hoover's Texan drawl could be heard clearly. "Do not engage the pirates, gather intelligence, stay put."

Mihai did exactly what he was told. During the next twenty minutes all he did was buy himself a second drink and watch.

With a loud screech the truck came to a stop next to the concrete mixer. From the passenger door the man in the red cap slowly got out. He looked around the plot as if expecting someone else to be there. Once satisfied that the surroundings were clear, he jumped down from the cab. His red cap was worn low over his forehead and he was wearing large, mirrored sunglasses. Below them his face was covered in black stubble that had been stylishly trimmed. His only distinguishing feature was a long pink scar which ran across his right cheek from the corner of his mouth to the top of his ear. He was wearing a tight red T-shirt which emphasized his lean figure and large arm muscles. Despite his build he seemed to be deliberately slouching, keeping his chin close to his body and never looking up.

He walked towards the tarpaulin like a child approaching a Christmas tree. Crouching down he lifted up a corner so that only he could see what was beneath. His face lit up. He placed his arm under the sheet and began to stroke whatever lay below it until the bulldozer pulled up beside him.

The man in the red cap stood up and motioned that the object should be lifted, and then he pointed towards the truck. The man in the string vest skillfully manoeuvred the bulldozer and the four workmen held the object in place under the tarpaulin as the command was carried out. When the object was in position and the bulldozer had reversed away the four workmen climbed up onto the truck and secured it in place. At one point the tarpaulin brushed against a workmen's leg and folded back to reveal a silver curve that glinted in the sun like a mirror. It was instantly covered again. Once the job was done the man in the red cap handed out more money and sprang back into the cab. As the truck drove out of the gate the workmen followed, cheerlessly waving goodbye.

Before the truck reached him Mihai covered his mouth and nose and held his breath. The truck chugged down the road covering everything in its wake, including Mihai, in polluting exhaust. When it reached the junction it turned right onto Stadium street and disappeared from his view.

As Mihai put down his cola the ear piece, once again, fizzed into life.

"We are tracking the pirates using satellites, confirm the treasure is gone," requested Agent Hoover.

Mihai walked calmly towards the plot. He waited until the workmen were out of sight and then vaulted over the fence. After searching the area he found what he had expected.

"Confirmed. The treasure has gone," said Mihai touching his ear.

Agent Hoover watched as the truck slowly approached the school and the large trees that surrounded it. He leaned back in his chair, whistled through his teeth and exclaimed, "Well I'll be damned!"

"You will be if you lose that truck Agent Hoover," barked Agent Angel taking a drag on his cigarette.

Agent Angel was a bear of a man, with arms and legs the size of logs and a torso like a barrel. He had no neck and his shoulders sloped directly up to his hairy chin. Agent Angel was covered in grey hair. It was difficult to spot where his neat beard stopped and his closely cropped hair started. He was in his eighties but was as strong as an ox, and as sharp as any of the younger agents. Some agents joked that whereas the army, navy, airforce, CIA and FBI answered to the President, the President answered to Agent Angel. Nobody, however, would say this to his face. Agent Angel had been working at the OSS longer than anyone remembered and he was feared like no other man.

Slowly, almost lovingly, he stroked his finger and thumb around Agent Hoover's ear lobe. Just as Agent Hoover was about to ask what was going on he felt Agent Angel's nails pinch into his ear.

"Geez, that hurts," cried Agent Hoover trying to shake his ear away from Agent Angel's grasp.

Agent Angel dug his nails deeper into the lobe and started to twist them. The pain got worse and Agent Hoover shook his head wildly, trying to escape.

"You think this is something? Do you? This will be nothing if you lose that truck," threatened Agent Angel and he released Agent Hoover's ear.

Swiveling on his chair Agent Hoover, who was not used to being bullied, looked the Section Head directly in the face. Agent Angel did not flinch. Pain and anger shone from Agent Hoover's eyes. Agent Angel's smiled sinisterly and held out his left hand. He opened his palm to reveal four truncheon fingers and a banana sized thumb. With the cigarette in his other hand he pointed back towards the screens. Agent Hoover did not move.

One by one the thumb and fingers were folded down and Agent Angel mouthed slowly, "Five, four, three, two, one."

He savoured each word as he did so, looking forward to what was to come. On 'one' he broke eye contact and turned away to look into the shadows.

Suddenly Agent Hoover felt a sharp prick in his head. All the things in the world that he didn't know about, and had never thought about, began to enter his mind. His brain started to fill but the thoughts did not stop. Just as he felt his brain was going to explode he spun away from Agent Angel and back towards the screens. Instantly the thoughts stopped and his own voice in his head told him to follow the truck. It seemed like a good idea.

Agent Angel patted Agent Hoover on the back like an owner petting their dog. Agent Hoover thanked him for all his support. He had no memory of what had just happened, it had simply disappeared. Unfortunately so had the truck, it was nowhere to be seen on any of the screens. From the satellite images Stadium street was empty and apart from some wisps of smoke near the school the truck had been lost.

It remained missing for six hours.

Just before night fall in Romania, Agent Hoover relocated the truck on the screens in front of him. It was on the other side of Sfantu Gheorghe crossing a damaged bridge above a snaking river. Spewing out grey smoke the truck approached a junction overlooked by a massive statue of a soldier and turned right onto the road which led out of town. It passed disused factories and headed for the E60 motorway.

Above the mountains in the distance the sun had started to set and the light was beginning to fade. The truck continued on, the tarpaulin was still secure and the secret cargo lay hidden below it. By the time the truck reached the motorway the sun was down and night had begun.

The motorway was quiet and dark. It ran parallel to a railway line and as a train roared past light streamed out from the carriage windows bathing it in yellow. Then it was gone and night engulfed the motorway once more. There were no street lights lining the side of it only fields and a few scattered trees. So, when three black Yukons, with their headlights off, drove down a dirt track and pulled onto the motorway they were unseen.

Behind one of the steering wheels was the man known as Mihai Ionescu. It was a cool night but his windows were closed and the air conditioning was blasting. He checked in his rear-view mirror to make sure that the other two black SUVs were following. Reassured that they were there, he concentrated on driving and tried to ignore the noise. The road had been badly laid and every few metres the tyres thudded as they drove over gaps in the tarmac. It was like the countdown on a time bomb, and it put Mihai on edge

Approximately two kilometres ahead of them, and chugging along at around one hundred kilometres an hour, was the truck. Mihai put his foot to the floor and his Yukon accelerated to speeds far greater than the truck could ever achieve. The gap between the Yukons and the truck narrowed quickly and when they were only a few hundred metres from it Mihai took his foot off the accelerator. As he slowed down to the truck's speed he checked his rear-view mirror again; the other two Yukons were still there. Due to the darkness, and the absence of other traffic on the motorway, Mihai was convinced they had remained unseen. The truck had not changed its speed and the driver had not noticed the three SUVs lurking behind. Ahead of the truck was a disused bridge. This was the point Mihai had just been briefed on. This was the point to act.

Pushing his foot hard on the accelerator pedal Mihai overtook the truck and pulled in front of it. He kept a short, safe distance from the truck and made sure his speed was the same. Looking in the wing mirror he could see the second Yukon pull level with the truck on the outside lane. He moved his eyes to the rear view mirror and could just see the third Yukon bringing up the tail.

The repetitious thud, thud, thud of the tyres on the tarmac was interrupted by a hiss in Mihai's ear.

"Time to make the pirates walk the plank, we are coming in," said a distorted female voice which Mihai had not heard before.

On cue Mihai and the other two SUVs turned their headlights and fog lights on. Mihai lifted his foot from the accelerator and slowed down. The other two Yukons dropped their speed as well. Boxed in, and with nowhere to go, the truck had no choice but to do the same.

"Where are you?" Mihai asked the night. "Where are you?"

He looked feverishly out of the front windscreen, his side window and then the passenger window. Nothing. Nothing but darkness. Suddenly he heard it. The sound of blades chopping air. Checking his rear-view mirror he saw the outline of a Black Hawk helicopter as it rose up from behind the last Yukon. Caught in the head lights it looked like an enormous dragonfly hovering above the ground.

The Black Hawk flew forward and the pilot positioned it directly above the moving truck. From fifty metres above the road six ropes, attached to winches, were thrown from the helicopter. They silently fell through the sky and landed in coils on the truck's cargo area. Six people, clothed from head to foot in black cat suits, abseiled down and stood steadily upon the back of the moving vehicle. Each of them knelt down and unfastened the object from its bindings. A lightweight material cradle was rapidly lowered down and the six abseilers positioned it safely under the object. They raised their hands, and gave thumbs up signs to the sky. The six of them were hurriedly winched back up into the belly of the helicopter.

Carefully the Black Hawk rose. The object lifted off the truck and swung like a pendulum in the sky while the tarpaulin flickered in the breeze. When it was higher than the truck's cab the helicopter banked sharply to the left and disappeared into the night. The retrieval of the 'treasure' had taken less than a minute.

In the truck's cab the man in the red cap could do nothing but watch through a small rear window and punch his chair repeatedly.

The other two Yukons overtook the truck and Mihai. They sped off along the motorway and were soon nowhere to be seen. Mihai checked his rear view mirror and saw the man in the red cap lean out of the cab window and throw something at his Yukon. It made a small clunk as it hit the rear door and caused Mihai to laugh at the man's anger.

"You're not playing with rookies," he muttered to himself and smirked as the man attempted to throw something else at his car.

Ignoring the man's tantrum Mihai accelerated away and touched his ear piece, "The treasure is now in our possession."

6

PARIS TO PRAGUE

As they began their descent, Ursula reflected on the journey. Flying as a passenger was not as exciting as she had hoped. Admittedly the events from earlier had somewhat soured, and sweetened, the experience. However, even without these, Ursula had come to the conclusion that flying was not all it was cracked up to be.

The man at check-in had been polite but he had looked closely at Ursula, after Andrea gave him Ursula's temporary passport, and rubbed his hairless chin repeatedly. The photo was unclear and he did not fully trust the leather clad woman in the 'The Sisters of Mercy' T-shirt.

When he finally made up his mind that he would allow them to travel, he checked them all into row two and dismissed them with a gruff, "Have a good flight."

The business lounge had been very fancy but, apart from free packaged food and drink, it was still only a dressed-up waiting room and Ursula found it quite boring. Men and women in dark suits sat around reading documents, writing reports or instructing someone else on their mobile phones. When they weren't doing anything they looked down their noses at Ursula, in her grey streaked, vest top.

Paris' Charles de Gaulle Airport was large but was jam-packed with people bustling to-and-fro trying to get from one place to another. They were all being herded like mooing cattle, with worried expressions on their faces and passports in their hands.

Until Ursula boarded the plane and found her place, she had seen nothing but the backs of the people in front of her and the newspapers they were carrying. When she finally sat down she was able to have a look around. The plane's interior was light cream with blue seats which looked like leather but were not. Gradually these seats filled until there were no more spaces left on the plane. In fact the only place where Ursula had seen similar amounts of people bunched together was on the Champs-Elysées. With the thought of the Champs-Elysées came memories of being chased by the police and Ursula's heart quickened. She took deep breaths to calm herself and tried to focus on the fact that she was escaping them.

Being a passenger on an aeroplane was, Ursula decided, dull and monotonous. She was stuck in a long metal tube without any freedom, which she found very hard to deal with. Normally she loved being above the ground. She could jump, spring, do somersaults and look down on the world when she had finished. But in the aeroplane she was strapped down in her seat unable to move anywhere and surrounded by chattering people who looked down on her. At least they were all quiet now, she thought to herself.

The plane was silent. If it hadn't been for the engines one could have heard a pin drop. Nobody spoke, nobody whispered and nobody even moved. Every single person was trying to make themselves look invisible while the three hostesses patrolled the aisle like prison guards. Ursula felt it was probably her fault. She hadn't meant to cause such a fuss but... enough was enough and, she had been forced to act. She wished her grandparents were with her but consoled herself with the thought that at least she had made one friend in the commotion. In an attempt to distract herself further she looked out of the plate-sized window.

They were circling above Prague, waiting. As they had

arrived late they had missed their landing window and were waiting for 'the tower', as the Captain called it, to allow their descent. At least it gave Ursula a chance to continue gazing, through the scratched perspex, at Prague below.

From high up in the sky Prague looked picturesque, like an old model village. A dark river cut the city in two and flowed under ancient, old and new bridges. Green copper roofs were dotted amongst terracotta ones, and there were spires and towers everywhere. The biggest of them didn't seem to belong - it looked more like a space rocket than a tower. Ursula thought she would climb it at some point. Surrounding the old centre, like a gigantic grey wall, were ugly apartment blocks. They reminded her of home and she sighed sadly as she thought of her grandparents. Turning towards Andrea, who was sat rigidly beside her, she asked, "Are those les banlieues of Prague?"

"No," replied Andrea flatly in a business-like tone, "they are called panelaks but they are also apartment blocks similar to those in les banlieues."

Andrea could never forget this flight from Paris, and ran through the events again in case she received any unwanted calls from the press. The two children, Eric and Ursula, as well as the adults on the plane, had surprised her so much that she would have to review all her studies on psychology.

From the moment Ursula and Eric had met in the Range Rover there had been problems. There had been no welcome from Eric; the only introduction had come from Ursula who really made an effort.

Eric had been unhappy that Ursula had been sitting in his seat. Andrea had been unaware that Eric 'had a seat' but Ursula moved. He had then been upset that his seat belt was dirty. He took great pains to clean it with tissues, then wiped away imaginary stains from his well-cut beige jeans and invisible smears from his light summer jacket.

During the journey he had ignored Ursula and spoken only to Andrea. He had not uttered a word to Ursula but had referred to her on three separate occasions.

On the busy motorway, on the way to the airport, they drove past an open sewage works. The putrid smells from the open vats had seeped into the car before Andrea could close the windows. Eric learnt forward as far as his seat belt would allow him and pretended to whisper but his voice was loud. "Andrea, that smell really is intolerable, please could you instruct the PPP as to how a bath works and inform her that we expect a higher state of cleanliness in future."

Ursula heard every word but stayed silent.

When they pulled off the motorway a small hill-sized rubbish tip could be seen high above a row of bushes. At its entrance was a long forgotten caravan. The plastic door hung from its hinges, windows had been bashed in and the roof had peeled away from the walls like a tin of beans. Eric pointed towards it, "Andrea, please ask the PPP if this is where she comes on holiday?"

Ursula looked the other way.

As Andrea parked the Range Rover into a private car park space reserved for the Meyer's, Eric tapped her on the shoulder. "You had better explain to the PPP that flight is statistically the safest way to travel. I wouldn't bother explaining the physics of it to her if I were you as I am sure she'll be lost after the word 'thrust'".

These comments continued at check-in, in the business lounge and into the aeroplane. Andrea was surprised at how unrelenting Eric had been with his remarks. However, she had been even more surprised at Ursula's lack of response. That was until they were above Germany.

The other passengers on the plane were chirpy. Tourists were chatting happily to their neighbours, lovers were kissing, business people were working on their laptops and the stewardesses had just begun to serve food.

Andrea was sat between the children with Eric by the aisle and Ursula in the window seat.

A tall, blonde stewardess placed a pre-packaged lunch on Eric and Andrea's trays but, as she leant across them to give Ursula her lunch, Eric nudged her. It wasn't a big nudge but enough for the stewardess to drop the package. The food landed upside down on the tray and spilt out of the pack like a splat of vomit. Carrots, sliced potato, stringy meat and a pepper sauce covered the tray in a sloppy mess. Eric apologized innocently to the hostess and Ursula did not move. Accepting Eric's apology the stewardess took a green cloth from the trolley. She leant across Eric and Andrea again, to clear up the mess, but Eric took her arm.

"Don't worry, it is still a better meal than mummy and daddy..." He stopped and for a moment looked genuinely apologetic for what he had said. "I meant to say. It is still a better meal than her grandparents have ever served her."

To her right Andrea felt Ursula flinch. To her left she watched Eric relax, let go of the hostess and continue eating. Andrea knew instantly that Eric had hacked into her computer again as there were no other records on Ursula's family. Before she could decide what to do, events moved so quickly that Andrea barely had time to log them.

While the last scraps of slop were being cleared away from Ursula's tray she undid her seat belt. The stewardess moved away and Ursula pounced up onto the top of her chair like a cat.

"I say," blurted out the man behind, spraying food all over himself.

Ursula bounced away from him to the chair behind Eric. She landed with a foot on each of the arm rests and her bottom in the face of a prim and proper lady who froze.

"*Mon dieu!*" cried another man and he was joined by chorus of fellow passengers who were vocal in their astonishment.

Ursula grabbed Eric's hair, pulled his head back with one hand and swiped the stewardess' dirty cloth with the other. Before the stewardess realized the cloth had gone it had been smeared all over Eric's face. Carrot dangled from his eye lashes, potato mashed against his teeth, the meat was rammed up his nose and his skin took on a peppery glow.

Hopping down from the chair Ursula apologized to the woman, who was still frozen, and looked down the plane towards the tail. A sea of shocked faces stared back at her. They did not look welcoming so she spun around, slipped past the trolley, ducked under the hostess' legs and walked towards the front of the plane. A secure looking door opened and another hostess came out. Assuming it was a toilet, Ursula dived in and shut the door behind her. It wasn't a toilet. It was the cockpit.

Just after the door closed the plane hit an air pocket, and then another, and then another. It rose and fell like a rickety old roller coaster.

Somebody near the front of the plane shouted, "Terrorist!"

Somebody else screamed, "We're being hijacked," and then there was uproar. Nobody seemed to notice that the plane was now flying normally again.

Andrea looked around herself; she found this whole situation baffling. Meanwhile Eric cleared food from his face ignoring the commotion around him. After all, this whole situation was hardly his fault, he thought to himself.

On the flight deck a kind eyed Captain, with smiling wrinkles and a bushy salt and pepper moustache, turned to face his unexpected guest. Ursula stood transfixed, like a rabbit caught in car headlights.

"Hello," he greeted in a deep kindly voice, "I am Captain Hudson. May I ask if you have ever been on a flight deck before?"

"No," she replied, "I thought it was the toilet."

Captain Hudson and his first officer laughed.

"Do you need the toilet?" he asked warmly.

"No."

Captain Hudson grinned like Ursula's Granddad and said slowly with a glint in his eye, "Then this is a very curious situation we find ourselves in."

Unable to stop herself Ursula told the Captain everything that had happened to her during the day, from leaving her grandparents to arriving on the flight deck. Captain Hudson listened sympathetically, his ears pricking up when he heard the name 'Meyer'.

"Curious," he said, lost in thought, "after all these years."

Ursula did not understand his reaction but was prevented from asking about it by the first officer, an orange haired lady to the Captain's right who spoke urgently. "Captain we have a problem."

She held out a slender finger and pointed at a monitor showing the inside of the plane and the panicking passengers. Ursula glimpsed at it before returning to gaze at the Captain.

"Oh dear," said Captain Hudson calmly and without rushing picked up the microphone. "This is your Captain speaking," he said slowly in French, and looked at the monitor.

People were still screaming and jumping up and down in their chairs like monkeys in a zoo. No one heard his announcement even when he increased the volume.

"Oh dear," he repeated.

Unbuckling his seat belt, he stood up. Ursula remained transfixed and admired his uniform. It was a deep blue, with brass buttons and yellow stripes on the shoulders. Underneath the jacket he wore a crisp, white shirt and an Air France tie.

One day, she hoped, I will be able to wear something like this.

Reaching out, the Captain took his peaked hat from

behind the door and, instead of putting it on his own head, placed it gently on Ursula's.

"You're the Captain now," he told Ursula, shuffled her towards his Captain's seat and sat her down.

In front of her was an instrument panel covered in soft switches like those on an iPod, six different digital displays showing various patterns and shapes, flashing lights, levers, a throttle and two sticks which Ursula thought looked like ones used to play computer games.

Above the panel three windows joined together to give a one hundred and eighty degree view of the outside world. Ursula thought it was probably the best view she had ever seen. Kilometres and kilometres of vast empty blue were laid out in front of her. Little, fluffy, white clouds were dotted upon it and, in the distance, was a line that another aeroplane had drawn across the sky. Ursula sat and marveled. She now knew what she wanted to do when she was older.

"You had better instruct our new Captain what some of these buttons do," he told the First Officer and winked. He placed a lumpy finger on a yellow button and whispered in Ursula's ear, "Whatever you do don't touch this one."

"Is it the ejector seat?" asked Ursula innocently.

"No, it's the loop-the-loop button. Very messy, you'll have food and drink everywhere. First Officer Auteil, please inform Prague we will be slightly late," he instructed and left the flight deck.

The scene in the main body of the plane was one that he had not witnessed in thirty two years of flying. Apart from the petite lady in leather and the boy with an obvious chip on his shoulder, it was hysterical.

Somebody spotted him and shouted, "It's the Captain, the terrorist is in charge of the plane!"

Oh dear, thought Captain Hudson, if they are going to act like children then I had better treat them as such. He picked up the cabin telephone, switched it to the speakers, put an index finger to his lips and shh-ed. On his third attempt he had silence. Slowly and calmly he explained what had happened, told everyone off for acting stupidly and knelt down beside Eric.

For a few seconds he just stared at Eric as if he knew him. His eyes glazed over and he was lost in private thoughts. Eric coughed, falsely like his father, and a returning memory brought Captain Hudson back to the present.

Placing a strong hand on Eric's shoulder he introduced himself. He explained that he had just become Ursula's guardian angel and that Eric should think very carefully about what he says and does to her in future. While he was doing this he winked knowingly at Andrea, who secretly nodded. Eric did not know what to say; he was not used to being told off and was left doing an impression of a goldfish. Captain Hudson returned to the cockpit and, interrupting the flying lesson, gave Ursula his phone number, in case of emergencies, and asked her nicely to return to her seat.

Eric said nothing as Ursula stepped over him to her chair. He was deep in thought, concentrating and reflecting on the day's events. As the plane began its descent he was still reflecting. Walking through passport control and customs he was still reflecting. And when they got into a silver Range Rover, identical to the one in Paris, he was still reflecting.

It had been one of the worst days ever but also one of the most intriguing. Before leaving the Parisian apartment he had been forced to say goodbye to his parents. As they could not be bothered to spend eight months with him he didn't see why he had to be bothered to spend eight seconds saying goodbye to them.

Eight months! Eight months! The thought kept circling around his head like a needle on a record. It was almost the same length of time as a woman is pregnant or the football season or a school year. In spite of the anger he felt, he almost cried as he walked out of the apartment and got into the Range Rover. He tried not to look at them, as Andrea drove away, but he found himself craning his neck to stare back until they were completely out of sight. His last view was of them standing beside each other on the marble entrance in front of the concierge. His mother dabbing her eyes with a handkerchief, his father pulling her close and them both waving, almost desperately, at him. He tried to fix this picture on his brain. For eight months he would not see them and it seemed like forever.

From the Meyer's apartment they went directly to meet with the PPP. When they arrived in Saint-Denis Eric decided it was best to wait near the Range Rover in case of car-jacking. He also had no desire to enter the building to meet the street urchin. A police car was parked nearby and he decided to hang around it for protection. While he waited he talked in French with the two officers. During a break in the conversation he looked up and saw something fascinating. He tried to show the policemen but they were too interested in their newspapers and breakfast croissant to pay any attention. The PPP had fallen from the seventh or eighth floor, he did not know which, to the one below that and the one below that and so on until she reached the ground. He knew of only one gymnast in the world who could do something similar and he was in the Chinese Olympic team.

From the moment he met her Eric was deliberately mean to the PPP but despite all his best sarcastic comments he had failed to make her react. That was until he had mentioned her parents on the plane. This was a useful weapon which he would not forget in a hurry. At school he could wind up most children with a few chosen words but the PPP was obviously made of sterner stuff. However, he had found a chink in her armour which he would use again when needed. It had even been worth the food make-up and the lecture from the Captain to discover it.

There was something else about her that fascinated him. The PPP's speed and agility when she covered his face in food was remarkable. She had been as fast as him on a gym mat, as balanced as him on the beam and as strong as him on the hoops. He could think of only two or three gymnasts who came close to his talent but the PPP looked annoyingly like an equal. Maybe she did solve the puzzle as well and maybe she was as skillful mentally as she was physically. These were all things to think about.

Slowly, and worryingly, an unwelcome feeling of admiration grew inside his head. He did not want it there but it would not go away. Just because I admire what she did, he thought, doesn't mean I have to like her. She had replaced his parents. If Andrea had not found her maybe his parents would not have left him so eagerly. Bitter thoughts towards the PPP pushed the admiring ones to the back of his brain. If it wasn't for the PPP his parents would be there, they would not have gone. So, if he could get rid of her then they would have to come back. Eric had found his mission and he made it his goal to achieve it.

7

IN THE CELLAR

The Range Rover skirted in and out of parked cars on the busy cobbled streets. They were on their way to the Meyer's Prague residence. Ornate old buildings, with impressive statues which guarded the entrances, rose up from the pavements. They cast long shadows over the cars parked on the kerb. The shade was welcome by people out walking. It dropped the temperature and made being outside manageable. Neither Ursula nor Eric minded the heat and were looking forward to the car getting back into the sun.

Andrea reached the end of a street, so full of parked cars that the Range Rover could only just drive through, and turned left. Ursula could see a large LCD advertising board in the distance. Its bright images flickered constantly and it looked out of place against the old buildings. From the shady streets they entered a small tree-lined lane which divided a town park in two. Children played happily amongst the trees, chasing each other with water pistols. Adults lounged in the sun, dressed only in bikinis and swim wear. They moved only to bronze one side of their bodies and then the other. Dogs stayed in the shade cast by bushes and trees, their tongues hanging out of the side of their mouths as they tried to cool down.

Eric ignored them all. He was deep in his thoughts and this was just another home for him. Ursula, on the other hand, was glued to her window, trying to take in as much as possible. Neither of them had looked out of the front window at the villa they were approaching. It belonged to the time of Mozart and looked untouched by the decades that had followed him. Tall, gabled windows and finely decorated awnings dominated the front of the building. In its centre was a sweeping staircase which rose up to a finely crafted wooden door on the first floor.

Andrea looped around a spluttering fountain and parked at the bottom of the staircase. At this moment Ursula laid eyes on her new home. Her jaw hit the Range Rover floor and she thought that there must be some kind of mistake. Sighing as if bored, Eric lifted his eyes from his lap, glanced at Ursula and then at the villa.

Without addressing Ursula he uttered, almost as a throw away comment, "We only have the ground and first floors, the second floor and attic space belong to some Austrian aristocrat."

Only the ground and first floor! thought Ursula but she did not say anything in case she seemed over excited. It was still more than she had ever imagined or even dreamed of. She sat, stunned into silence.

As Andrea removed the suitcases from the boot a loud clunk woke Ursula from her thoughts. She looked up to see that Eric was already bounding up the curved staircase to the front door. Feeling as if she was walking on air, Ursula got out of the car and followed.

None of the steps were cracked or broken, there was no litter covering the ground and no graffiti on the walls. They were no longer in Saint-Denis. For a moment Ursula felt glad about this and then she was consumed with guilt at thinking such a thing.

The wooden doors were heavy but swung open silently on well-greased hinges to reveal an entrance hallway the length of a bowling alley. A Persian rug dominated the floor and above it a large chandelier reflected drops of sunlight around the room.

Silently Andrea came up behind her. "Downstairs is the lounge, kitchen, dining room, pantry, library and study," she explained. "On this floor we have the bedrooms and bathrooms. Your room is at the end opposite Eric's."

They walked down the hallway, past closed doors and a descending spiral staircase, to a white door with a brass handle. Andrea pushed it open with her foot to reveal Ursula's room. It was the same size as her grandparents' entire flat. A large comfortable looking bed stood in the centre surrounded by wardrobes, a desk with a laptop and video phone, well-padded armchairs, a plasma TV on the wall and a library of books. Ursula had never seen such a room and she was dumbstruck. Despite this feeling of awe she felt the villa was missing something but she couldn't think what.

When Andrea left Ursula sunk into the bed and the answer slowly dawned on her. There was no life to the villa; in spite of its size and splendour, it was dead. No music blasting in from open windows, no smells of Mémé's baking, no raised voices from next door and no revving of car engines below. From outside she heard a train whistle and a screech as it came to a halt. Maybe I just have to give it a chance, she thought and hopped down from the bed to tell all to her grandparents via the videophone.

In the opposite bedroom Eric had thrown his jacket on to a boxing glove bean bag next to a giant chess set and gone straight to the window. It was one of many homes but he loved this house and he especially loved the view from his window. After pulling back the velvet curtains he opened the tall window and stood admiring the vineyard and city beyond.

The grapes were now visible on the vines and would need to be picked in the next week or so. Baskets of juicy green fruit would then be squashed and turned into wine, continuing an annual tradition that began in 1353 when Charles IV had first planted the vineyard.

Even though he was only a child his parents allowed

him one mouthful of wine each year. The thought of his parents made Eric feel suddenly empty. It made the bulging vineyard seem empty and the villa feel empty. There was no sound from downstairs. No singing from his mother or the noise of card playing from his father. Eight months! At that very moment it really did feel like forever. However, once the PPP had cried off back to Paris his parents would rush back. Eric was certain of this. A plan had formed in his mind during the journey from the airport. Once he was alone he would execute it.

After a Caesar salad lunch, on the terrace overlooking the vineyard, Andrea offered to take them into town to buy school materials and clothes. Placing a hand on his brow and rubbing his temples Eric complained of a headache. He asked Andrea to get him whatever he needed, excused himself from the table and went to lie down on his bed.

Ten minutes later Eric heard the Range Rover roar into life and drive away. Without wasting a second he left his bedroom and ran down the hallway to Andrea's room. Even though he knew they had left he still crept into her room on tip toe.

No matter how many times he entered Andrea's room, and he had visited many times since he was born, he still found it odd. The walls were white, the thin wardrobe was white, the desk was white and the iMac was white. It did not contain a bed and never had; Andrea had always claimed she preferred sleeping on the floor. This minimal approach to furniture made his task much easier. All he had to do was find a key.

Sliding back the wardrobe door he was greeted by a row of rock band T-shirts, black leather trousers and matching jackets. He expertly searched the pockets but found nothing. The desk was also empty but underneath it, hidden under a metal bin, was a white safe. A panel on its door contained a touch pad with the numbers zero through to nine and a mini LCD screen displaying four asterisks. Eric did the maths in his head. Ten different digits for a four digit code would mean ten times ten times ten times ten or ten thousand possible combinations. Andrea's shopping trips normally lasted three hours or one hundred and eighty minutes or ten thousand eight hundred seconds. Therefore if he could input one code every one point zero eight seconds he should be in the safe before they returned. He pressed zero zero zero zero with the speed of a machine gun, his fingers a blur over the touch pad. Nothing happened. He moved onto zero zero zero one and kept going. Three and a quarter minutes later the safe was open. The code was his birthday and he kicked himself for not trying obvious codes first.

Eric first found a leather-bound book and then a map of southern and eastern Europe. The map was covered in scribbles and the book was bursting with scraps of paper trying to escape. Next to them was a piece of rock and the keys he was searching for. Eric grabbed them and ran downstairs. He sprinted into the kitchen past the lunch dishes in the sink and through the door at the rear. The pantry was a small windowless room which was always cool and smelled so tasty it always made him hungry. Pickles, wines, conserves, preserves, cured meat and smoked fish lined the walls but Eric was looking for another food item - one that looked real but was never to be eaten. Eric felt his heart begin to pound in his chest.

About one metre from the ground, in the corner shadows of the room, was a large Hungarian salami. It was next to an old shelving unit which contained nothing but dust. The salami hung from a string on a nail. However, when Eric removed the loop from the nail the salami did not move. Eric put both hands on top of the salami and pushed down. It swung outwards from the wall and he could hear cogs grinding. The empty shelving moved away from the wall and Eric felt that his heart was ready to jump out his chest. Suddenly he felt cold but he also knew that he was sweating.

Behind the shelving unit was a steel plated door. Eric slid the key into the lock and turned. The lock mechanism groaned, gave way and opened. The door was made of concrete twenty centimetres thick, and had four chunky pins that moved when the key turned. Perspiration ran down Eric's brow into his eyes and his hands began to tremble. The last time he had seen this door open he had been six. Not knowing what had lay beyond it, he had entered and the door had closed behind him. It had been Andrea's day off. For eighteen hours he had been trapped but his parents had not noticed. It was Andrea who found him; cold, hungry, thirsty and wet through.

Scarred by his memory, and worried that Ursula and Andrea may return sooner than expected, he retreated back upstairs quickly. The keys were put back, the safe locked and he returned to his room feeling much better. A little while later he heard the front door open and two sets of footsteps entered the villa.

After knocking lightly on the Eric's door Andrea entered. She touched his brow and commented that he was 'clammy'. They talked briefly and, once satisfied that Eric was feeling better, she left. Through squinting eyes Eric watched as she was replaced by the PPP.

Ursula stood in Eric's doorway, wary of going any further into his bedroom.

"Are you feeling better?" she asked, looking at her feet.

"Yes, thank you," mumbled Eric clenching his eyes shut.

There was a long silence, neither of them knew what to say next.

"Do you want to show me..." started Ursula

"Shall I show you..." began Eric.

They both finished by saying, "Around?"

"Yes," they said in chorus.

Eric rose from his bed with only one thought on his mind.

"How about upstairs first and then downstairs?"

suggested Ursula, feeling uneasy but unsure why.

"An excellent idea," replied Eric. He had been thinking the same thing.

When they got downstairs Eric led Ursula straight to the kitchen and into the pantry. The large concrete door was still open as he had left it and nothing had been touched. Andrea had not been down here yet. Drops of sweat formed on his brow and goose-bumps appeared over his arms. At the same time Ursula started to feel genuine fear but did not know why.

"This is our cellar," announced Eric, tripping over his words as he said them. "We have pinball machines at the bottom of the stairs in there and a table tennis table. Do you want to play? I would."

He stood by the doorway and beckoned Ursula in. Everything he had said was a lie and for a second or two Ursula did not move. The situation did not feel right, she did not feel right, but Eric seemed to be making an effort. In the end she nodded and approached Eric.

"After you," he said inviting her through the open doorway with an outstretched arm. "There is a light five metres in, could you turn it on please, I don't like the dark."

Cautiously Ursula entered the very dim passage. She wanted to impress Eric with her lack of fear and so walked tall without turning back. Every footstep she took seemed to reduce the faint beam of light entering the cellar. Before she had walked five metres there was a loud slam like a bass drum being struck. The door shut and she was plunged into darkness.

Outside the door Eric pulled the salami up, watched as the shelving unit closed against the wall and then walked out of the pantry and back to his room, whistling.

Ursula waved her hand in front of her face. She could not see it. She shouted but knew no one would hear. Strangely, now that she was alone, she no longer felt scared. A wave of calm washed over her and she waited patiently for her eyes to adjust to the pitch blackness.

Gradually her eyes started to make out shapes and, about twenty five metres ahead, she could see white light in the outline of a rectangle. It was not bright but it was enough to beckon her forward. Gingerly, she placed a foot forward into the black and began to walk. Every few paces the corridor would turn slightly and she brushed against the cool brick walls. The faint outline grew stronger, acting as a beacon and pulling her forwards. When she arrived at the light she discovered it was around a door and actually came from the room beyond. Relying on touch, rather than sight, she moved her hands around the door until she found a stiff metal handle. She pushed it down. The door squeaked on its hinges and slowly opened. Instantly the light went out and Ursula stood, once more, in darkness.

She pushed the door fully open and stepped through to the other side. A chilly blast of air pushed its way past her and down the corridor. Below she heard a low whirring sound which dominated the whole room.

"Hello," she shouted out, "Eric!"

Her words echoed in the darkness. This room was large - far larger than any of the rooms upstairs. Ursula couldn't see how big but it was definitely bigger than any subway she had walked through.

Cautiously she put a foot out. It came down on the edge of an irregular stair. She stepped down and then again. Taking only small careful steps she negotiated the stairs. There was no handrail and she sensed that there was nothing on either side of the stairs. With each step that she took she counted. At seventy-one there was no stair. It seemed she had reached the ground or a platform or a floor. She stepped forward then took another step and then another.

Suddenly her foot hung in the air, the floor had disappeared and she found herself off balance, unable to stop herself from toppling forward. Rather than fall like a stone she pushed off with her other foot, sprung away from the invisible platform and somersaulted in the air. She was still falling but, when she came out of the spin, she was falling feet first. Before she hit the ground she hoped she would sense it and bend her knees to protect herself. She never had to. Unexpectedly, two petite but strong arms caught her.

"I'll take you back upstairs," said Andrea matter-of-factly, as if nothing had happened.

Keeping hold of Ursula she walked back up more than seventy-one stairs, through the doorway where Ursula had seen the light and along the corridor to the thick concrete door. After placing Ursula back on the floor she pushed something on the wall and the door opened. Bright light streamed into the darkness temporarily blinding Ursula. Andrea pushed her gently into the pantry.

"The cellar is out of bounds," said Andrea and closed the door between them.

8

BACK TO THE DESERT

KNOCK, KNOCK.

The noise from the lion door knocker echoed through the house.

KNOCK, KNOCK.

Professor Schwarzkopf stirred from his sleep and tried to figure out what had woken him. A few seconds later he had his answer.

KNOCK, KNOCK.

"Henry! Martha!" he croaked.

Nobody replied.

KNOCK, KNOCK.

He put out a wrinkled hand and fumbled for the reading lamp. Light filled the room. He fumbled some more, found his oval framed spectacles and put them on his pointed nose. The wind-up alarm clock, a retirement present, pointed to twelve minutes past three.

"Who the blazes would call at this hour in the morning?" he said to himself, clearly irritated.

"Henry! Martha! The door!" he shouted loudly.

The exertion forced him into a coughing fit which took him a while to contain.

KNOCK, KNOCK.

"Don't worry," he grumbled, "I'll go."

Professor Schwarzkopf lifted off the heavy sheets and got out of his empty four poster bed. He was a man who had been shrunk by age. His striped pyjamas swamped his bony frame and his veins could be seen clearly on his hands, feet and head. Whereas his body had shriveled, his skin had not and gave him so many wrinkles that his face looked like a prune. Across his almost bald scalp were a few remaining black hairs. Whenever anyone commented on his lack of grey he would reply, in no uncertain terms, "I came into the world a Schwarzkopf and I will leave this world a Schwarzkopf." It was a reply that normally killed the conversation dead.

After putting on a pair of tartan slippers and matching dressing gown he shuffled downstairs.

Henry and Martha arrived at the front entrance at the same time. "Sorry, Professor," they apologized, "we were asleep."

"So was I," Professor Schwarzkopf grumbled. He put his spectacles on his head and his eye to the peep hole.

Two big men in dark suits with shoulders that looked padded, stood on the brightly lit porch. One of them reached into his pocket and took out a plastic wallet which he thrust at the door. Professor Schwarzkopf looked briefly at the three blurred letters and stepped back from the peep hole. After a long, resigned sigh he sent Henry and Martha back to bed and opened the door. Without a word he led the two men into his study.

The study was his favourite room in the house. A large mahogany desk dominated the room and upon it was a small flagpole, flying the stars and stripes, and a plain, free-standing picture frame. Above the desk, hanging neatly on the emerald green wall, was an enlarged photograph of himself shaking hands with an ex, and now deceased, President. Neatly arranged on the other walls were other, smaller picture frames. Some held photos of him receiving awards, others held certificates or letters signed by important or powerful people, and the rest were designs for new and old inventions. Under these frames and around the desk were three red leather arm chairs with high backs. Two were placed symmetrically in front of the desk and a larger one behind. Professor Schwarzkopf sat in this one and invited the two men to sit. They declined and stood between the chairs with their hands clasped behind their backs. The taller man opened his mouth to speak but Professor Schwarzkopf cut him off.

"Do you know how long I've lived in this country?" he asked picking up the flagpole. Before the men could reply he slammed the ornament back on the desk and answered, "sixty two years!" He ran his fingers around the base of the flagpole. "And do you know how long I have lived here? In Vienna? In Fairfax County?"

He looked at the them with eyes as alert as when he had first arrived in America and he dared them to speak, "Twenty nine years! Before that I worked night and day for thirty three years doing exactly what was asked of me and I helped turn this country into THE world power!" His voice was raised and he looked like a head teacher telling off two naughty school boys, "And all I asked for in return, when I retired, was a little peace and quiet. But have I got it?"

The two men looked at each other with wide, questioning eyes. They had been told to go to the Professor's house, collect him, brief him and transport him. They had not been told what to do in the event of finding a cranky old man. Unable to think of an appropriate answer and unable to think of a way to shut the Professor up that did not involve shooting him, they remained silent. Hoping that, like a hurricane, he would blow himself out.

"No, I haven't got it," roared Professor Schwarzkopf. "Every few years some new jocks drag me out of my house and my peaceful retirement. Another problem to be solved, another national emergency, another job you cannot handle without my advice. Well I won't be here forever you know!"

He paused, his lungs were empty, and he was forced into another coughing fit which turned his face red and made his veins pulsate.

The two men looked at each other again, both wondering what it would do to their chances of promotion if the Professor died. It wouldn't look good on their records, that was for sure. They stepped forward to help but Professor Schwarzkopf put out a wrinkled hand to stop them approaching. From below the desk he picked up a metal bin and spat. A phlegmy globule flew through the air and landed in it with a moist splat. One of the men visibly retched.

"The least you can do is show me some respect!" ordered Professor Schwarzkopf.

Confused, the men replied, "Professor?"

"Well you could tell me what this is all about."

The slightly taller man spoke, "With all due respect, Professor, you haven't..."

Professor Schwarzkopf interrupted, "Don't you 'all due respects' me. A small summary would have been enough, a sentence or two, even one word. So, in one word, tell me what this is all about."

"With all due..."

"There you go again. One word, that's all I ask."

There was silence. The two men looked at each other and the one who had been doing the speaking ummed and erred before saying, "Roswell."

Fear and excitement ran down Professor Schwarzkopf's spine in equal measure but his face remained unchanged and he continued to look annoyed. "That's more like it. It wasn't so hard, was it?" He paused before asking, "I take it I'm coming with you?"

The men nodded slowly.

"I thought as much. Why else would you disturb me in the middle of the night. There are two leather suitcases in the cupboard in the hallway. They are packed with everything I may need. Please take them to your car. I will join you in fifteen minutes. Dismissed."

Unable to think of a reply, the two men left the study. Professor Schwarzkopf leant over the desk and held his head in his hands. In front of him, in the plain picture frame, a black and white photo of a young woman gazed up at him.

"You're never far away Ingrid," he told her and after kissing the photo he left.

In the black unmarked Cadillac Professor Schwarzkopf only spoke twice. The first time he asked if he could open the windows as the car was stuffy. The driver responded by turning the AC on. His second question concerned where they were going.

"We were going to Langley but we've just been informed to take you straight to the airport. You will then board a private jet which will take you to Roswell, New Mexico."

For the rest of the journey Professor Schwarzkopf stayed silent, lost in memories from many years ago.

The near hurricane winds tossed the twin prop Boeing 247D around in the air like a rag doll. After a battle between the pilot and the gusts, which the pilot almost lost, the plane touched down on a military airfield just outside Washington D.C. He, a young Professor, stepped out from the plane with nine others, walked down the unsteady staircase and almost kissed the ground the moment he stood on it. The year was 1945 and his plane was one of thirteen involved in Operation Paperclip. He felt remarkably fortunate to be there. World War II had just ended and by all rights he should have been dead.

The Americans placed him in a small room, in a holding house, in a pleasant little town called Vienna. On entering the town he read aloud the sign, 'Welcome to Vienna, Fairfax County, Inhabitants 1016, Have a nice day.' Only a few of the other scientists on the bus could read English and he had helped with translating when he was needed. He was the youngest scientist in the group and had learnt English at the Humboldt Universitat zu Berlin while studying Physics and Physiology. His English accent was weak but his knowledge of the language was very strong.

After a week of staring at mustard coloured walls, in a house he was not allowed to leave, he was visited one afternoon by two men. Major Jesse Marshall was a squat man with army regulation length hair and a head that retreated into his shoulders whenever he spoke. Agent Cavett was taller, his hair was slicked back with Bryl cream and his head remained aloof. His sharp chin pointed up while his eyes looked down and all his movements were angular and calculated.

Agent Cavett stood by the door with his arms crossed. Major Marshall pulled up the one chair in the room and motioned to him, the Professor, to sit on the bed opposite.

Major Marshall was friendly but questioned him, without any breaks all afternoon, about his work with Victor Schauberger. Agent Cavett took out a small notebook and a pen and wrote down all his answers.

"Had he worked with Victor Schauberger? What had he worked on? Had he used liquid vortex propulsion or LVP? Did he understand the concepts behind it? Did he use LVP in a flying disc craft, otherwise known as a Foo Fighter? Had he done some of this work in Czechoslovakia, outside Prague? Did he and Schauberger send an unmanned flying disk craft measuring six feet in diameter to a height of forty-five thousand feet, in only three minutes, on 19th February 1945?"

During the interview he puzzled over why they were asking him questions to which they already knew the answers. At the end they discussed the physics behind LVP and how it could be used to accelerate objects. Then he was asked a question which would change his life, and thinking, forever. "Could you replicate this technology here?"

Following a brief pause for thought he answered, "If I had the right people to work with me...yes, I could do the same work here."

The next day he was flown from Vienna, Fairfax County to Roswell Army Airfield, 509th Division, New Mexico. He was not to return for over thirty years.

Getting off the plane at Roswell was like walking into a wall of hot dry heat. New Mexico was largely a desert state and the earth was baked hard and barren. The land was made up of rocks, sand and little else. Pathetic looking bushes, barely green in colour, were scattered around, their roots desperately searching for water under the sun-cracked ground. Ragged mountains rose up around various parts of the state and rivers, if they had not dried up, trickled rather than flowed. People, like greenery, were scarce and most of them who lived there worked for the army. In other words, it was perfect. Perfect for conducting secret experiments in flight, away from curious eyes.

Within one week Professor Schwarzkopf had the team he requested. Ted from Stanford, Archie from Yale and Ingrid from Europe. He worked closely with all of them but especially Ingrid, who he found much more open to his ideas than the others, and much more attractive.

It was a hot July day in 1947. There was no wind in the sky and, according to the weather balloons, no sign of change. The flying disc, measuring a little over eight metres in diameter, was wheeled out of Hangar 84 and along the runway. It was followed by a select group of spectators. Major Jesse Marshall was there, along with more senior Army and Air Force officers. Bringing up the rear was a bear of a man who, at that point, he did not know. Only those who were needed had been invited.

After twenty one months of hard work they were ready to launch a manned prototype. Ted and Archie had agreed to pilot the flying disk on its maiden flight. He could still remember their expectant faces as they sat in the centre of the metallic saucer. Ted scrawled 'Roswell's Foo Fighter' around its centre, like on a fighter plane, and then a plastic dome was bolted down over their heads.

Archie started the flying disk and then he, the leader of the project - the professor - counted them down from ten through his awkward headpiece. On five the three legs supporting the saucer were retracted and it hovered, swaying ever so slightly above the ground. On three it began to spin, going faster and faster. On zero it shot into the sky so quickly that half the people in the crowd thought it had vanished. He received only eight seconds of speech through his headphones.

"Geez Professor, this thing goes some," reported Ted.

Followed by Archie exclaiming, "Oh my God! What is..."

Then there was nothing, only static.

At first he assumed the two way radio headset had been unable to cope with the speed and distance and had shut down. Two minutes later he saw bits of debris raining down from the sky, towards the desert and around the military base. He didn't need to see anymore to know that something terrible had happened. The saucer had exploded or, and this seemed a crazy idea at first, it had hit something.

A few seconds later, weaving drunkenly through the bits of flying disk, they saw a silver dart shaped craft. As the bits of debris hit the desert, and sent plumes of sand into the air, the dart flew like a silent rocket, just above them, and into the distance. No plane could have matched its speed but two P-80 Shooting Star fighters, which could fly at almost one thousand kilometres an hour, were sent to follow it. Parts of the disk continued to fall for a further two minutes and he held Ingrid as close as he could. All he could think about was Ted and Archie, whom he knew had been killed. After the last visible piece had hit the barren terrain troops were sent to locate and retrieve all pieces of debris, and to hunt for any survivors. The bodies of Ted and Archie were never found.

Before nightfall the massive floor of Hangar 84 was littered with remains of the disk. Later, as the sun set behind the mountains, the silver dart arrived. An observant troop of soldiers had found it forty five miles, or about eighty kilometres, away in a place called Corona. It had been hidden in the shadow of a very large rock. A little while later the Roswell Sheriff, George Wilcox, along with a ranch hand, Max Badham, arrived at the Army Airfield. In their possession they had a piece of twisted metal from the flying disk. Around it was wrapped a curled sliver of silver. The professor's collision theory now had concrete proof. His Foo Fighter had hit the other craft, an unidentified flying object, the silver dart.

The loss of their two colleagues brought Ingrid and him closer together. A blossoming romance became an engagement which quickly led to a loving marriage and, throughout all, a strong professional partnership . Badham's piece of twisted metal had convinced everyone there that evening that there had been no fault with the flying disk. The disaster had been caused by a simple collision which nobody could have predicted. Attention quickly turned from the pieces of debris to the silver dart.

Orders from Washington were clear and direct.

1. What is it?
2. Where has it come from?
3. How can we make use of it?

The answer to the first question seemed easy enough, it was a ship of some kind. From the way it moved across the sky it could best be described as an aeroplane crossed with a rocket. However, there were no windows, no obvious means of propulsion, no lights, no tail and no wheels. It looked like a piece of flint on a medieval arrow head and was made up of triangles - two on top, two on the bottom and two smaller ones at the rear - six triangles joined seamlessly together. From tip to 'tail' it measured five metres, four metres across the 'wing span' and was three metres high. Only one imperfection could be located on the craft. Underneath its tip an area of silver looked thinner, as if it had been stretched to a point where it was almost see through. The size of this area could have matched the Badham piece if stretched.

The second question was much harder to answer. It didn't belong to the Army, the Air Force or the Navy. If it had been one of the allies from World War II, especially the Brits, they would have known. In fact, it was highly unlikely to be from any of the nations involved in World War II and those who weren't involved did not have the resources to build such a craft. Of all the countries in the world the Soviet Union seemed most likely. However, he felt that the Soviets were too busy with Berlin and the Eastern European countries to send spy craft to America. With all other possibilities exhausted, he was left with two options: either it was someone's private project untracked by governments or it was not from the Earth.

Rumours had been circulating around the base, since the crash, of mysterious bodies which had been found with the silver dart. Some of these had come from reports in the local paper, the Roswell Daily Record, and included rough sketches. Others had come from eye witnesses who claimed to have collected two non-human forms from an area near-by.

He and Ingrid ignored all the rumours. Instead they concentrated on the third question, 'could it be used?' The answer lay in whether they could open the silver dart and investigate what it contained. They approached the problem scientifically, trying out theory after theory.

Knocking the silver dart by hand, hammer or battering ram did not even cause a dent. All liquids from water to oil through to molten iron simply ran off it. Blow torches and flame throwers failed to mark it. X-rays, ultrasound, sonic waves and the music of Glenn Miller did nothing. Bullets bounced off it, grenades failed to detonate and, though the army wanted to place a small nuclear device underneath it, Ingrid and he successfully advised against this.

Their attempts had taken more than six weeks. While

they found their lack of success both baffling and exciting the government took a dimmer view. One morning they were summoned to General Grant, the chief on the base. His office was airless and buckled blinds kept most of the sunlight out. General Grant asked them to sit and tell him what had happened. Luckily for them the General was also an amateur scientist. On hearing about their failed attempts he scratched his chin and thought.

Finally he said, "Then I had better grant you clearance," and handed them two passes marked, 'Access all areas.'

Major Marshall escorted him and Ingrid out of the General's stuffy office and away from Hangar 84. They crossed the burning hot runway and continued towards a disused bunker jutting out from a rocky desolate hillside. Inside, it was empty. Bricks and rocks had been combined together to build a small but functional room in case of air attack. On the bare slabs of rock names had been chiseled by soldiers who had wandered in. At the back of the bunker, where the light had been swallowed by the darkness, there was a wooden door. If Major Marshall had not led them to it they would not have noticed it was there. He opened it and the three of them entered a cage elevator. It descended rapidly, stopping with a jolt after Ingrid had quietly counted forty seven seconds.

They were marched out of the lift into a bright white corridor. Major Marshall led them down the passage, took a left, a right and a left again around the underground maze. He stopped at a room with a sign which read, 'Laboratory B - Top Level Security Clearance Personnel ONLY'.

The lab's metal door opened slowly and a scientist exited. He gave them each a white suit which covered them from head to toe, a mask for their mouth and a pair of goggles. Pushing the door open, he beckoned them in.

"Professor, we're here," the sudden voice broke Professor

Schwarzkopf from his memories.

The Cadillac had pulled up beside an unmarked, black Falcon 7X jet. The car's rear door was opened and Professor Schwarzkopf was helped out onto the warm tarmac. As he got out he marveled at the jet. He was filled with pride and, curiously, a sense of wonder at one of the many things he had helped to invent. Admittedly he had not designed the cigar fuselage and tipped wings, but his work had influenced the position of the wings and the three engines were bound to rely on his propulsion research and findings.

His baggage was handed to another, even bigger man, whose bulk had been squashed into a suit, and Professor Schwarzkopf followed him on board.

The interior was luxurious. Dark wooden cabinets with glass fronts stood opposite the entrance. Bottles of high quality bourbons and whiskeys, glasses, tumblers and fine china crockery rested securely on special shelves. Beside them were two comfortable looking chairs sat opposite each other with a small table between them. Further down the plane, towards the tail, were four large airline chairs, in cream leather and with wide, wooden arm rests. They were arranged in a circle, fixed to the floor and all facing inward. As Professor Schwarzkopf walked towards them one chair spun casually around and a thick cloud of cigarette smoke followed.

"Hello John, it's been a long time," greeted Agent Angel, "too long."

Professor Schwarzkopf froze and stared at Agent Angel. He was unsure as to how to respond. "You're supposed to be dead," he finally said.

"You know how stories get exaggerated," replied Agent Angel with a smile.

"But I was invited to your funeral, it was somewhere in Europe."

Agent Angel shook his head from side to side slowly. "Things were becoming difficult, shall I say. Anyway, the subject is closed." He lifted his hand to signal the end of that conversation and as he dropped it again he asked, "How long has it been since I saw you last, John?"

There was a long pause while Professor Schwarzkopf stared at the man who had come back from the grave. "Thirty three years I believe Buddy," he eventually replied, "and you still insist on calling me John rather than Johan."

"That long John, well doesn't time fly?" said Agent Angel with a touch of menace. "Please, have a seat, we'll be taking off as soon as you are buckled up."

Professor Schwarzkopf sat opposite Agent Angel and took a long look at him. Apart from going grey and acquiring soft wrinkles he had hardly changed in the years since they had last met. His body was still the size of a bear, he still looked to be covered in hair and he still seemed as strong as ever.

"Death obviously suits you, Buddy. You're looking well. I assume you're retired," commented Professor Schwarzkopf, suddenly painfully aware of how old he must look.

"I'm not retired John, could never find the time."

"But I thought all government employees had to retire at a certain age. Especially when they are supposed to be dead!"

"Depends if you work for the government or if the government works for you," replied Agent Angel with a twisted smile and a wink.

Not knowing what else to do, Professor Schwarzkopf laughed.

Their conversation stopped until the plane was at altitude. Agent Angel lit another cigarette during the ascent and Professor Schwarzkopf contemplated the man in front of him, whom he had thought dead. He was worried by what he saw.

When the plane leveled out both men were served, for old times' sake, bourbon on the rocks. Professor Schwarzkopf took one mouthful and as the cold liquor hit the back of his throat he was forced into another coughing fit. Agent Angel watched with interest, the tumbler of whisky resting in the palm of his hand. After the coughing had finished Agent Angel began to speak.

"In the last thirty three years I have not changed John and, from what I hear, nor have you. We're both too long in the tooth and too set in our ways. I know you, and you know me, so I am just going to get straight to the point. Five days ago we rendered, or should I say recovered, a craft from Romania. It was silver in colour, looks metallic and has no signs of an entrance on it. Ring any bells?"

Professor Schwarzkopf's shoulders drooped, "You know it does, you were there too, many years ago."

"Well this one is definitely not extra-terrestrial, it was jettisoned from the European Space Station some years ago but it is almost identical in every other aspect."

He stopped, swirled the dark liquid and ice-cubes around in the tumbler and waited for his words to sink in. He did not have to wait long.

"The European Space Station blew up over ten years ago."

"I know. A most unfortunate accident. Thank the Lord no one was on board at the time."

"But if it was that long ago why has it taken until now to find it?"

"It's a big planet, John, things get lost. And funnily enough those flakey Europeans knew nothing about it."

Professor Schwarzkopf thought about the enormity of the discovery. Another silver craft, sixty years later. Why? There must be a reason. Why did Agent Angel need him? The question spread across his face in puzzled wrinkles and Agent Angel answered it before he asked.

"We want you to open it." He stubbed out his cigarette and in one movement lit another one.

Leaning forward in his chair and staring Agent Angel straight in the eye Professor Schwarzkopf asked, "Why me? With all your technology surely you can do it?"

"We can't and you opened one before..."

Professor Schwarzkopf interrupted, "That was over sixty years ago Buddy, and you know as well as I do, that it wasn't me that got it open, it was Ingrid."

"But you were there, you saw her do it," he paused. "If anyone knows, you do. She was your wife."

"Let me think about it," but he knew that he didn't really have a choice.

"Take all the time you need. We have a while before we land."

Professor Schwarzkopf tried to relax back into this chair as more memories came flooding back to him.

The white suited scientist had led Major Marshall, Ingrid and himself into a white tiled operating room. It was sparkling in its cleanliness. Two metal operating tables stood in the centre and upon them, covered in white sheets, were two child sized bodies.

"Don't worry," reassured the scientist through his mask, "they are quite dead. Come closer, have a look."

But Ingrid had stopped; she was frozen. She did not approach the table and just stayed near the door, staring at the covered bodies. "They're not dead," she announced in a whisper and left as quickly as she could.

He followed, and Major Marshall followed him. The sheets on the operating tables had not been touched.

They found her waiting nervously by the lift. She was pacing up and down biting her nails, repeatedly touching her forehead and refusing to talk. As Major Marshall opened the caged door she pushed past him and stood with her back to the two men.

By the time they arrived back on the surface her hands had returned to her sides. She was less agitated and a look of determination had appeared on her face. When they left the bunker and emerged into the day light he felt it was safe to talk to her again.

"What did you mean down there?" he asked, holding

her hand lightly.

"Women's intuition," she replied, kissed him on the lips and walked off assertively towards Hangar 84.

It was probably the most memorable kiss he would ever receive.

Behind him, Major Marshall sniggered, "Broads, I'll never understand them."

Ingrid was in Hangar 84 when he caught up with her. She was in the area shielded by temporary wooden boards, sitting on a fallen gas cylinder, at the tip of the silver dart. Her eyes were closed and her head was bowed. He laid his hand gently on her shoulder but she shook him off and said nothing. Seconds turned into minutes which became hours. She did not move and he just stood and watched her.

After seven hours he uttered the words he would come to regret. "I'll go and get you a drink."

When he returned with two cups of steaming hot coffee the silver dart was open. Ingrid was standing beside it. He could not work out if she looked victorious or defeated.

"We'll be landing soon gentlemen," said a voice over the jet's speaker system, "better buckle up."

Professor Schwarzkopf made sure his seat belt was fastened and faced Agent Angel. "Why are we going back to Roswell, Buddy?"

Agent Angel blew out some cigarette smoke and smirked, "The place is so full of UFO nuts that even if someone did see something nobody would believe them. But don't worry no one will see anything."

"I didn't mean that, I meant why are we going? Why now? Why me? Why you?" Professor Schwarzkopf looked and sounded tired.

Staring intently at the Professor, Agent Angel replied seriously, "Because whatever was inside that silver craft could change our way of life forever."

9

PRAGUE ANGLO-INTERNATIONAL SCHOOL

The day before school began Eric and Ursula found they had something in common, something they could finally agree upon.

It was Sunday evening and they were eating a late dinner out on the terrace. The sun had started to set and the vineyard, which they overlooked, was bathed in glorious orange. Moths fluttered madly around the terrace lights and crickets could be heard serenading each other around the vines. Andrea placed a selection of salads on the table in front of the children, who were trying to ignore each other. Since the cellar incident they had not communicated. Even when Ursula got her revenge, by pouring the contents of the compost heap over Eric in his bed, they said nothing. Normally the only communication at dinner time was with Andrea, whom Ursula had come to trust and whom Eric relied on.

They ate in silence and then Eric, hunched over his food, grumbled to himself, "I hate going back to school."

Ursula, who was staring at the train track at the bottom of the vineyard, replied through a mouthful of salad, "So do I."

"I can't do what I want," continued Eric.

"I get told what to do," followed Ursula.

"And when to do it."

"And how to do it."

They both paused, playing with their food absentmindedly and watching a passenger train pass by.

"The worst thing of all is..." began Eric.

"...I can't just be free," finished Ursula.

The train chugged out of sight and they were pulled back to reality. For a split second they looked at each other and then went back to eating.

When they arrived at school the next morning Andrea dropped them at the main entrance. Eric ran off, to rid himself of Ursula, as Andrea drove away. Ursula stood alone on the brick path looking up at the building. It was in a different world to her old school. For a start it was definitely not old. Her Parisian school had existed for over sixty years; it was in need of repair, was dirty and covered in graffiti. This school looked brand new. The school sign glistened in the sunlight and the yellow paint looked fresh.

Children were arriving at the front of the building every few seconds but none had walked to school. Instead, they were dropped off by adults driving Jaguars, Mercedes, BMWs and other expensive looking cars. All the children were dressed the same as Ursula. They wore black trousers or skirts, red polo necks and blue V-necked sweaters, which were taken off the moment they got out of the air-conditioned cars. They all hurried past her into the school while Ursula stood and stared. She felt she was watching a car show, not that she had ever been to one. After watching a Rolls Royce drive by a 'normal' car came around the corner, it was a small green Škoda. Back home it would have seemed quite new, and a target for car thieves, but here it just looked out of place.

The Škoda stopped right beside her and three similar looking girls piled out, laughing and joking. All three of them were smaller than Ursula.

"Hello," said the oldest looking one, approaching her, "are you waiting for someone?"

"Er, no," replied Ursula, and not knowing what else to say, said, "I'm new."

"I'm old," said the girl, "and my name's Molly."

She had long hair, a pixie nose and introduced the other girls.

"This is my sister May," she pointed to the girl with wavy shoulder length hair. "And this is my cousin Millie," and she pointed to the other girl, who had a bob cut.

All were the same height, about a head shorter than Ursula, all had the same light blond hair and the same skinny bodies.

"Hi," replied Ursula, "I'm Ursula."

With the introductions over Millie led into them into the school building. They were met by a tall man in a straw coloured suit, matching hair and a huge grin.

"Welcome back girls," he greeted, and turning to Ursula said, "and welcome to you, Ursula."

"Hello," replied Ursula, surprised that he already knew who she was.

"Anyway I'm Mr Ball and I'm the Head teacher," he waved a clipboard in front of them. "Now then, where are you all going? Let me see."

He tapped a chewed biro on his clipboard and flipped through pieces of typed paper. "Ah ha, jolly good, got it."

Looking up from his clipboard he continued, "Millie you're in Year 2 with Miss O'Gara and May you're in Year 4 with Mr O'Shea. The luck of the Irish for you two then," and he winked.

May and Millie skipped off happily to their classes and Mr Ball flipped through his papers again.

"So, Ursula and Molly, I have two treats for you. The first one is that you're both in the same Year 7 class and the second is that you're going to the Welsh valleys and you will have Miss Evans as your form teacher."

Miss Evans was like a beach ball, short and round with a bright smile and matching ginger hair. They found her in a new cupboard, with a tin in her hand, looking at a poster of Johnny Depp. The poster had been roughly stuck to the inside of the door giving the impression of a pupil's locker rather than a teacher's cupboard.

"Biscuit?" she asked, in her soft Welsh accent, as the two girls approached. Without giving them time to answer she thrust a crumbly digestive into their hands.

"This is Johnny," she explained, placing a loving finger on the poster. "You may gaze on him whenever you need but you cannot, on any account, touch. Okay?"

"Okay," replied the two girls, neither of whom were much interested in Johnny Depp.

"Now then, I don't know about you but I hate the start of the school. It scares the willies out of me. I haven't slept a wink and I feel rougher than a badger's behind."

All of a sudden she stopped, her nose started to twitch like a hungry squirrel and she commanded, "Stand back!"

She curled up like a tightly wound spring and then unwound, in a flash, with an almighty sneeze that sent her flying backwards into the cupboard. The door slammed shut. All around the school staff, pupils and parents said, "Bless you, Miss Evans."

"Where was I?" asked Miss Evans, emerging from the cupboard and wiping her nose. "Oh, I know. We were about to have a bit of a chin wag. Pull up a pew and let's have a natter."

In the space of one minute Miss Evans had become Ursula's favourite teacher ever. They sat down on red chairs and the three of them talked as the rest of the class arrived. During their chat Ursula was happy to discover that the school year would be busy with productions, sport matches, talent shows and, the icing on the cake, a trip to Pompeii. She was even happier to discover that Eric was in the other Year 7 class and they wouldn't be sharing many lessons.

Once everyone had arrived they were lined up at the class door.

"We are going on a tour of the school for those of you who are new, and for those of you who are too dopey to remember what it looks like. When we have finished I will award house points to anyone who can tell me how many…" Miss Evans paused and touched her nose, "…I know, how many security cameras are around the school?"

The school was much bigger and brighter than Ursula's old school. Multi-coloured display boards covered the walls of the long corridors and in numerous cosy classrooms. The gym was the size of eight Badminton courts, the theatre was round like Shakespeare's, the roof on the school was glass and there were security cameras everywhere.

When they had finished their tour and had arrived back in class, Miss Evans repeated her question, "How many security cameras?"

Ursula was sitting beside Molly at the front of the class underneath an interactive whiteboard. She had not seen one before and stared at it, trying to avoid answering the question. She knew the answer but stayed quiet. From previous experience she knew that other children, and the teachers, did not like a 'know-it-all'.

"Seven," answered one boy confidently.

"Three," shouted another.

"Eight," joined in Molly.

"We're getting warmer, some good answers there," and Miss Evans looked at Ursula with a smile. "You're very quiet Miss Benjamin. Come on, have a guess."

"Sixteen," answered Ursula very quietly. She had thought about lying but wanted to try to make a good impression.

"Oh come on, Ursula, be confident," encouraged Miss Evans.

"Sixteen," repeated Ursula loudly.

"Well done, have a biscuit," and she threw the tin into Ursula's arms.

The class clapped and Ursula relaxed. She turned around to thank them and Miss Evans told her to pass the tin around.

"Right then," said Miss Evans pulling a loose thread

out of her skirt, "next question. Who can tell me where they are?"

Ursula didn't mean to do it but she blurted out the answer without thinking, "main entrance, main reception; the art, languages and science corridors; two in the Primary school plus two at the Seniors entrance; two in the car park and five in the playground."

A hush fell over the class and Miss Evans kneeled close to Ursula and said quietly, "There is only one other person in school who is as observant as that."

Ursula could guess who it was.

"Did you notice anything else?"

Suddenly Ursula felt she had done wrong and clammed up. Miss Evans put a hand on hers and reassured her that she had done nothing to be worried about.

"Come on, tell us what else you noticed?"

"Tell us Ursula," shouted a boy from the back.

He was echoed by four or five children saying the same. Ursula could see them, out of the corner of her eyes, leaving their seats and coming closer to her table. All the class were soon around her, hiding her from the outside world.

"Tell us Ursula, please," asked Molly.

Unused to all this attention she stumbled over her words at first, "Well, er, there are, er, four security guards, the main entrances and primary entrances are controlled by a buzzer system, the car park has an electronic gate and there is a two metre high fence around the whole school."

Miss Evans stood up, "Blow me down with a fart! You know what this means don't you?" she said to the whole class.

They nodded, all part of a secret which Ursula did not know.

"It means there is nowhere in school where you can have a secret cigarette or snog!"

The class laughed.

"Be serious," said a stocky boy, whose voice Ursula recognized from before.

"I think we need to ask some more questions," said a girl with piercing eyes who was looking right at Ursula.

"Good idea," complimented Miss Evans and, kneeling back down, said kindly, "Ursula, this is not a serious test but it is a sort of test. A bit like smelling your socks to see what pair is least stinky so you can wear them."

One by one the children put their hands up and asked questions.

"What is the capital of Mongolia?"

"Ulan Bator," replied Ursula.

"How do you spell achievement?"

"A, c, h, i, e, v, e, m, e, n, t."

"What is one thousand seven hundred and sixty five divided by seventeen?"

"One hundred and three point eight, but I don't know the rest."

"What is thirteen times forty one?"

"Five hundred and thirty three."

With each correct answer the children's faces became more and more excited and expectant. After the last question Ursula's new classmates' enthusiasm had rubbed off on her and she was feeling excited herself.

Miss Evans repeated what she had said earlier, "You know what this means don't you?"

All the children nodded.

"After three years in school it looks like Mr Eric Meyer finally has a rival."

All the children cheered.

That night, on the video phone, she told her grandparents what had happened. They were pleased she had had such a good first day but she was warned about Eric.

"If this boy has been used to being the best for so long he is not going to take kindly to being challenged by you," warned Granddad Benjamin.

"*Oui, c'est vrai,*" agreed Mémé, and they were right.

In the first few weeks of term the children were tested in every subject. Ursula never told anyone her scores but everyone seemed to know them. They also knew when she had beaten Eric, when she came close and when they were equal. She was way ahead of anyone in her class but no one seemed to care as long as she was better than Eric.

It soon became very clear to her that when Eric had arrived at the school his talents and skills were welcomed by everyone. In fact when Ursula talked with other children about Eric's first two years in school, nobody had said a bad thing against him. Many children told her that at first everyone had liked him and the teachers had loved him. This was in sharp contrast to now. Ursula watched the teachers with Eric. It was obvious from the way they talked to him that they no longer liked him, called him arrogant and probably felt threatened by him.

On a few occasions Eric and Ursula's classes were merged. In Ursula's opinions Eric asked interesting questions but the teachers brushed him away or ignored him. Other children thought he was showing off or were jealous of him. Outside the classroom more children were jealous of Eric's sporting ability but everyone wanted to be on his team. If you were on Eric's team you won, if you weren't you lost, it was that simple. From Molly, May and Millie, Ursula discovered that the children were willing her to beat Eric in anything and everything. Unfortunately, it was very obvious to both her, and Eric, that the teachers wanted the same.

Eric's frosty way with Ursula had already reached freezing point and she began to worry what he might do to her. If trapping her in the cellar was his first attack what would be his second?

As the seasons changed Ursula began to feel a little more relaxed about Eric. Summer faded away, autumn came and went, and green trees lost their leaves almost overnight. The vineyard turned into a graveyard of brittle vines and Prague lost its colour. Despite this Ursula was feeling happy. School was good and for the first time in her life she found learning fun and being in a classroom comfortable. She did not have to pretend to get things wrong, as she did in her old school, she was well liked by her classmates and she had formed close friendships with Molly, May and Millie. Eric refused to acknowledge that Ursula existed. He would not talk to her, look at her or recognize the fact that she was alive. His attitude suited Ursula fine.

By the end of the first term there was snow outside and the temperature never rose above zero. It was the first time in eight years that it had snowed before Christmas and during PE lessons they had to stay inside. In one lesson, at the start of December, their muscular PE teacher, Mr Tait, announced that they were to have a contest between the two Year 7 classes. More importantly, for Eric and Ursula, this meant against each other's classes. Individual pupils faced off in different events and winners scored points for their class. Ursula was, unsurprisingly, paired up against Eric. As the two classes sat on the gym floor Eric glared at her.

The final contest was to be Eric against Ursula in the rope climb to the ceiling. Two ropes hung close to each other and underneath them were placed red crash mats. Eric and Ursula took their positions at the bottom of the ropes and the children sat around the mats. Ursula's class was cheering her, and shouting her name, but as she turned to the other class she realized they were doing the same.

Nobody was shouting for Eric and she looked across at him. His eyes were full of tears but his face was full of anger. For a moment she felt sorry for him but these thoughts quickly disappeared as he mouthed, "No one really wants you, Parents' Pet Project."

On the teacher's whistle the two of them shimmied up

the rope to the top of the gym faster than a monkey. Ursula touched the cold metal beam the same instant as Eric. She looked down and was happy to see that she was quite high up. The PE teacher, who did not like draws, called them down and made them race again and again and again. After the ninth stalemate the end of lesson bell rang and they were allowed to stop. The classes drifted off to the changing rooms and Mr Tait followed them. Ursula sat on her crash mat breathing deeply and looked across at Eric.

He was laying, spread-eagled on the mat, facing the ceiling with this eyes closed. It was the first time Ursula had actually looked at Eric without worrying about the consequences. He looked sad and strangely old. His face was screwed up in anguish, not pain, and he looked almost wrinkled. He even looked as if he was going grey around his ears but Ursula dismissed this as a trick of the light. Eric shook his head, as if shaking off an unpleasant thought, and moved one hand so the palm faced upwards. She was shocked to see that it was scarred red from burns and the thin skin looked as if it could break and bleed at the slightest touch. She had never seen this before and whispered softly, "I'm sorry Eric."

Eric jumped up muttering, "You will be," and stormed off to the changing rooms.

That night Ursula locked the door to her bedroom. She took off her clothes, put on a yellow night shirt and got into her warm bed. The curtains had not been drawn and she sat for a while looking out of the window. High up in the sky she could see the moon, its white light reflected in the snow on the roof tops and on the ground. The moon beams entering her room filled it with a ghostly glow. From the bedside table she took her hair brush and pulled it through her black hair. As she did this she tried to forget about Eric. After one hundred strokes she had done just that. She placed the brush back on the table and lay her head down on the pillow, sending fallen hair into the air. They drifted slowly towards the floor, black and silver strands glistening in the moon light.

The week after the rope contest was the worst Ursula had ever had in school. Eric was far too clever to say, or do, anything hurtful to Ursula with all the video cameras around. Instead he bullied her by doing nothing. At least nothing she could tell the teachers about. In their shared lessons he would sit near Ursula and, when the teacher wasn't looking, stare at her. During break times he made sure that where ever Ursula went, he was near her, watching her. At lunch times he sat opposite her, his brown eyes fixed upon her. Lots of children thought Eric had a crush on her and, when he was near her, kept away. Molly, May and Millie told Ursula to ignore him and not to rise to it. She followed their advice but his constant menacing attention made it difficult to relax and she soon found that she was short tempered with her friends.

On the last day of school, during the Christmas party, Ursula left the classroom to go to the toilet. Eric followed her down the corridor. In front of the toilet door she paused and Eric stopped right behind her. She could feel his breath on her neck. It was the last straw, she had had enough and spun around to confront him. Their noses were almost touching and their eyes met.

"Go away, Eric," Ursula said calmly, trying to avoid using words she had heard before fights in Saint-Denis.

"Why?" Eric replied, equally as calm.

Ursula decided she was going to be completely honest, "Because you are always there, everywhere I go. I can't escape you, I can't move without someone commenting about you being there, I am losing friends, it's awful, you're suffocating me and I've had enough."

Eric smiled, it wasn't malicious nor sinister nor nasty. It was a smile of triumph.

"Good," he said bluntly, "now you know what it feels like." Without saying anything more Eric walked happily away.

10

OPENING

Apart from feeling hotter New Mexico had hardly changed in the thirty years since Professor Schwarzkopf had left. It was still like living in an oven, was still barren and was still a place for only the most hardy of humans. Roswell, on the other hand, had changed. To keep the town from dying its residents had turned to tourism to bring in much needed money. They had cashed in on their fame, or infamy, and the town had become a UFO and Alien theme park but without the rides.

Professor Schwarzkopf was in a black Yukon with Agent Angel. The AC was on full blast and the inside of the car was so cold that Professor Schwarzkopf was almost shivering. His request to have the AC turned down had been refused by the driver, a young man with a slight Eastern European accent whom Agent Angel called Mihai. He was driving them along the sleepy main street of Roswell at the legal speed limit, trying to avoid any unwanted attention.

They had been collected from a small private airport, which Agent Angel delighted in saying secretly belonged to the government. He would not say where they were going to as this information was classified. Professor Schwarzkopf was pretty certain that they were heading for the Army Air Field, 509th division.

Through the cigarette smoke and the car's dusty windows, Professor Schwarzkopf gazed out on to places he had fond memories of, places that still existed but had been corrupted by time. The diner where he and Ingrid ate steak every Friday night, on heavy crockery with solid metal cutlery, had become the Warp Speed Fast Food Joint. Its billboard advertised alien burgers and fries in paper boxes with novelty plastic forks on worn plastic trays. The small family run hotel, where they had spent their wedding night, had become the Martian Motel. Crisp white sheets and fresh flowers in a vase by the bed had been replaced by 'UFO Interior Rooms.' Lastly, the cinema, which had been their escape from the world of the base, was now the official 'Roswell UFO Museum.'

A tear ran down his cheek along the lines of his wrinkles.

"Why did we stay here so long together?" he asked himself.

The answer followed his question the moment he had asked it, "Because they were making more scientific discoveries every year than all the other scientists on the planet, and enjoying doing so."

His next question he could not answer, "Why did I stay so long after...?"

Parts of the Army Air Field, 509th division, had been open to tourists for a few years but the majority of it was still a functioning base. 'UFO Veterans' gave tours around those areas that were no longer 'no-go' areas and this included Hangar 84.

Near the entrance to the base Professor Schwarzkopf saw a large sign stating, 'Hangar 84 Tours HERE!' Three solitary men, one in a black 'Close Encounter of the Roswell kind' T-shirt, the other with a 'I survived Hangar 84' flag and the last wearing a red cap embossed with UFO, stood below it.

The car drove past the base, continued onto a lonely highway further out of town and into the barren wasteland that best resembled a desert. Mountains grew bigger as they drove on and sandy rock rose up beside the road. As they approached a lonely cactus the driver slowed down and carefully checked his mirror. Once he was satisfied that nobody was behind them he sped up towards a line of bill boards by the side of the road. Each one of them was the size of a cinema screen and all had similar messages. 'Visit Roswell', 'Come to the capital of UFOs' and 'Welcome to Alien Country.' Around them were adverts for cigarettes, fuel-guzzling cars and electric goods that no one really needed. The driver took a black credit card from his pocket and pressed it. He slowed down again and pulled off the road. The car bounced over the uneven ground as they approached the bill boards. A door, previously invisible, slid open underneath a gigantic picture of an alien and the Yukon drove through it. Looking through the rear window, Professor Schwarzkopf watched as the door shut behind them. In the front of the car Agent Angel had not taken his concentration away from his cigarette.

They were now driving along a rough track between two rocky banks, towards the jagged mountains. The Yukon was hidden as it bumped along, unseen by anyone on the road, as if it had simply vanished from the highway.

After half an hour they reached the foothills and the banks were replaced by sharp rocky inclines on both sides of the jeep. A little further along they reached a road block manned by two soldiers in desert fatigues. On seeing Agent Angel the dry and branchless tree trunk that blocked the road was lifted. They drove under it, slalomed through five concrete filled oil barrels and were away. The narrow road turned a corner and all at once they were on a large plain surrounded on all sides by mountains. The road became a very long runway, much longer than a normal one, and Professor Schwarzkopf knew he was back on an air force base.

At the end of the runway, he could see soldiers marching and jeeps driving around purposefully. Some soldiers, who were obviously off duty, were drinking long, cool drinks underneath camouflage nets and outdoor air conditioning units. It amazed Professor Schwarzkopf to see how much energy was being wasted by these units when soldiers could simply sit in the shade. As they drove closer to the soldiers it dawned on Professor Schwarzkopf that there were no buildings. No offices, no sleeping quarters, no hangars, only the camouflage nets. It wasn't until the jeep drove towards the bottom of a mountain that he realized why. The base was underground.

Thirty metres above the end of the runway was a long overhanging rock which hid an enormous entrance into the mountain. It prevented the entrance being seen from the air, in spite of its size. The Yukon slowed down, drove into it and disappeared into the mountain. After a few hundred metres it pulled up beside a rocky wall and stopped. Professor Schwarzkopf opened his door gingerly, a vague feeling of excitement beginning to grip him, and got out.

The vast space in which he now stood was a hangar, at least three times larger than Hangar 84. Five Raptor jet fighters stood on the far side of the hangar, missiles gleaming below their slick wings. Mechanics crawled over the jets, like ants on a sticky sweet, busily checking the fuselage and jet engines. In the centre were two sinister looking Aurora jets, the fastest fighter planes in the world. Professor Schwarzkopf knew that they could reach speeds of Mach 6, two kilometres a second, but officially they did not exist. These storm grey planes were triangular in shape, and obviously had their roots in technology discovered in Roswell in 1947. Beside the Aurora stood three Black Hawk helicopters and behind them was a sealed off area. Tall, blank screens shielded something that was obviously not for public viewing, from the rest of the hangar.

Beside a temporary door in the screens were two soldiers, guarding the entrance. Professor Schwarzkopf knew what they were protecting. As he looked at the guards he realized that they had no American flag on their desert fatigues. Carefully, he looked around the hangar, at the mechanics and soldiers, but he could not see a flag anywhere. They all seemed American; over the banging of tools and firing of jet engines he could definitely hear American accents. They also seemed very confident and...and...

There was something else but he couldn't put his finger on it. Something that reminded him of the last time he was at Roswell.

Agent Angel came up behind Professor Schwarzkopf and woke him from his thoughts with a hefty slap on the shoulder. "It's good to be back, isn't it John!" and lit another cigarette.

For a moment Professor Schwarzkopf said nothing, he just looked around, "I don't know yet, Buddy."

His comment was ignored as a soldier in a plain uniform approached. He saluted the two older men and gave two white, clip-on badges to Agent Angel. Agent Angel put one on his suit and passed the other to Professor Schwarzkopf.

"It doesn't look like much but this could keep you alive," said Agent Angel.

He paused to let Professor Schwarzkopf think about what he had said.

"It gives a different heat pattern to your body. We have a heat monitoring system over the whole base. If you are wearing one of these things," he tapped his ID badge with his cigarette, "you'll appear as a white blob on our computers. If you are not wearing it you'll appear red or orange or yellow, depending on your real temperature. Within fifteen seconds of us spotting this you'll be staring down a barrel of an automatic weapon."

"I'll wear it," replied Professor Schwarzkopf. There was nothing else to say.

"Swell," applauded Agent Angel and slapped Professor Schwarzkopf hard on the back again, "come on, I'll show you to your quarters."

He led Professor Schwarzkopf away from the Yukon towards a door that resembled a submarine hatch. It was embedded in a wall behind the helicopters and had a metal wheel in its centre rather than a handle. As they walked, Professor Schwarzkopf tried to find something on the clothing of any soldier which indicated their unit or regiment or rank. Nothing was visible except the white badge. All the uniforms had been stripped of anything that would make the soldiers easy to identify.

"You'll find the facilities have improved since we were at the Army Air Field, 509th, John. In your room..."

Professor Schwarzkopf interrupted, "Is this part of the Army Air Field, 509th base?"

"No."

"A military base?"

"Not technically," replied Agent Angel mysteriously.

Professor Schwarzkopf, who was used to working in secret, was unflustered by this response and asked, "Then whose base is it? Who am I working for? I assume that it is a government base and I am working for the government?"

"Yes and no."

Professor Schwarzkopf stopped, pulled back Agent Angel and faced him. He did not appreciate Agent Angel's ambiguous answers and Agent Angel did not appreciate being touched.

"On the plane you said we know each other too well, you said we're too long in the tooth, we should get straight to the point and other baloney. Well let's get to the point now. What does 'yes and no' mean, Buddy? Who exactly am I working for?"

"You're working for me," Agent Angel answered directly.

"And, in other words, I'm working for...?"

"The Office for Strategic Services."

Professor Schwarzkopf tried not to look too shocked but his mouth still fell open like a hungry fish, "The OSS!

The OSS ceased to exist before I arrived in this country. It was replaced by the CIA."

"You're right, John" agreed Agent Angel. "I don't want to bore you with details but publicly you are right. In September 1945 President Truman disbanded the OSS. But, well how I should put this?"

He finished off his cigarette, threw it on the floor and crushed the butt under his foot. "You see, we felt our great nation needed an agency that no one knew about."

"But it's impossible to keep an organization secret," stated Professor Schwarzkopf firmly. "Politicians, military leaders, department chiefs, they would all need to know. There would be leaks, people would find out. You know that as well as I do."

Taking a fresh cigarette packet from his pocket, Agent Angel asked, "How do you stop leaks, John?"

He did not wait for a reply. "You make sure everything is water tight and secure. And how do you do that? I'll tell you."

He leant forward and whispered in Professor Schwarzkopf's ear, "You make sure the Heads of the Army, Navy and Airforce, CIA and FBI, the Secretary of Defense, Secretary of State and the President are all your guys. One team playing for you or, in this case, me. As I said on the plane, I don't work for the government anymore, the government works for me. And everyone here knows it."

Despite the pleasant temperature in the mountain hanger, Professor Schwarzkopf felt a chill run down his back.

"Let's walk and talk," suggested Agent Angel and moved away.

Professor Schwarzkopf joined him, "But this base isn't invisible, people must be able to see it?"

His throat itched and, unable to contain it, he broke into a fit of coughing. When he had finished Agent Angel answered the question.

"You always did ask lots of questions, John. I guess that's what made you such a damn good scientist."

He paused, as if he was about to tell a bed time story to a small child. "This base is in the middle of a desert state. It was built while you were still at Roswell and I bet you didn't even know."

Professor Schwarzkopf shook his head, "But what about passing planes or wandering tourists or Google earth or spy satellites, surely someone must have seen it?"

"No planes are allowed in this air space because of the Army Air Field base at Roswell and any that do come this way are instructed to turn around before we blow them out of the sky. Tourists don't walk into a desert, and over mountains, in hundred degree heat. We control Google Earth, in fact we control the internet. And lastly, spy satellites ignore this area because all the false UFO sightings have made it a joke. You wouldn't believe how many people send remote control, home-made UFOs into the sky around here in an attempt to become famous. Especially when they receive anonymous money and instructions on how to do it."

They arrived at the door and as Agent Angel turned the wheel to open it Professor Schwarzkopf asked, "One last question. What about the media; TV, radio, newspapers?"

The door opened and Agent Angel answered, "News is controlled by very few people, the media moguls, you should know that. Control these people and you control the news. Any minor local news channel or newspaper can easily be discredited if you get the nationals on to it."

They walked through the doorway and into a halogen lit passage. Agent Angel led Professor Schwarzkopf a little way along to a closed door. As Professor Schwarzkopf stepped towards the door it slid open.

"From the outside it will open for you, and only you, but you must be wearing your ID badge," said Agent Angel by way of an explanation.

The two men entered a small but well contained room.

It was like a ship's cabin; a computer dominated a small desk and Professor Schwarzkopf's two suitcases had been placed next to his bunk.

"Have a rest, John," urged Agent Angel strongly, "you'll be collected at o-eight-hundred hours for a full briefing."

Before Professor Schwarzkopf had a chance to ask any more questions Agent Angel left and only the smell of his cigarette remained. The door slid silently shut and Professor Schwarzkopf lay down on the regulation size bunk. He felt tired but his head was buzzing with so many thoughts that he could not rest. In less than a day he had met a man he thought was dead, an organization he thought was part of history was very much part of the present, and he had returned to a place he thought he would never see again. Perhaps the thought that most worried him was the one involving Agent Angel. If what he said was true Angel was the most powerful man in America, which in turn made him possibly the most powerful man in the world and a man whom Professor Schwarzkopf had never fully trusted. Another cold chill crept down his spine and he began to cough.

The briefing room was big enough to seat twelve people at six desks. At the front of the room was a large whiteboard and a computer screen. Standing beside them, slightly hunched and holding a pointer like a sword, was Jean Kurtz. She was an average looking woman with average build, average face and average hair. She was, in Professor Schwarzkopf's opinion, truly unmemorable. Jean was one of five scientists on the base and perhaps, felt Professor Schwarzkopf, the one with least social skills. It was a struggle to listen to her loud whiney voice and watch her 'I know everything' attitude but he did his best. He suspected that Jean had been given the briefing job to get her out of everyone else's hair for a while. She spoke for almost an hour but Professor Schwarzkopf could summarize her speech in four short sentences.

Firstly, the 'new' silver craft appeared to have the same properties as the 'old' craft. Secondly, it came from the European Space Station. Thirdly, the USA knew it had landed in Europe almost ten years ago but its exact location was only discovered recently. Lastly, they couldn't open it. In other words nothing in the briefing was new to him.

Jean spoke to Professor Schwarzkopf as if he was a child and when she asked if he had any questions he almost put his hand up. Instead he simply asked if he could see it.

The two soldiers stopped laughing as Professor Schwarzkopf and Jean Kurtz approached the screened off area of the hangar. Instantly their faces became serious, they scanned the ID badges and then let the scientists pass.

Immediately behind the entrance there was a preparation chamber which felt like being in a room-sized plastic bag. The chamber contained white body suits, surgical masks and plastic socks which hung neatly on free standing coat stands. Professor Schwarzkopf, much to the annoyance of Jean, walked straight past them, and towards a door that was zipped shut.

"We'll contaminate the craft," she whined.

"I didn't contaminate it in 1947 and I won't contaminate it now," answered Professor Schwarzkopf gruffly, as he unzipped the door and stepped through.

The screens were dark and imposing, and it was like walking into a funeral parlour. Along the far screen was a table, but instead of flowers and photos it had a computer and a microscope. A selection of technical equipment lay against the other screens like urns and in the centre of the space, like a coffin, lay the craft.

It was a lot smaller than the 'old' dart and looked more like a shell found at the seaside than a dart. Professor Schwarzkopf looked slowly around it.

"This wasn't designed to fly," he muttered to himself quietly.

Jean, who was hovering by his shoulder like a shadow, overheard. "I'm sure you're mistaken, whatever makes you think such a stupid thing?"

Professor Schwarzkopf bit his tongue and tried to answer politely, "Because my craft, the 'old' dart was just that, a dart. This is different, it is all curves. My dart was all triangles so it could speed through the air. This looks to me like a shell, no not a shell, but a..., a.... a pod, a seed from that, that tree..."

He paused, unable to find the word, "I'm sorry my English still has gaps even after all these years, I don't know the names of all flora and fauna. It looks like the end of a seed that floats down from the tree like a helicopter."

"The Sycamore tree," stated Jean as if the answer was hardly worth her breath, "but surely professor, the Sycamore has a wing which turns it into a helicopter. There is no wing here."

Professor Schwarzkopf stopped pacing around the silver pod, "That doesn't mean it couldn't grow one, as and when it needed it."

He put out his hand slowly, appreciating the moment, and then knocked his knuckles against the pod's hard surface.

"With all due respect, Sir, I do not..."

To stop Kurtz saying anymore Professor Schwarzkopf placed his hand in front of her mouth.

"Don't you 'with all due respect' me. If you have a question or a statement you ask it or say it. But you do not patronize me. I may be old, but I still have all my faculties, and I have much more experience in this area than you," and he began to cough.

Jean Kurtz looked annoyed and uttered under her breath, "It's just a machine, Professor."

The coughing gradually stopped and Professor Schwarzkopf answered, "Is it?"

That night, as he lay on his narrow bunk, the same

thought came back again and again. A thought that bothered him very much: the truth. The truth was that there was nothing he could physically do to open the pod and he knew it.

The next day he tried to find Agent Angel to explain that he would be of no use. Instead he discovered that Agent Angel had left the base and would return when the pod was opened. In other words, he could not leave until the job was done.

During the course of the next few weeks he passed all the information he had about the 'old' dart, and his past experiences with it, to the other five scientists he was working with. He told them all he knew except for the most important detail - he had not opened the dart, Ingrid had. He preferred to say that he thought it had opened by itself.

While he was passing on information the other scientists ignored this detail but by the middle of October he had nothing more to tell them. The pod refused to open despite using all the latest technologies that were available.

In November they had access to a powerful laser which could cut through anything on Earth. After a week of pointing the green beam at every square millimetre on the pod, they had to accept that the laser would not penetrate it. Relationships between the scientists and Professor Schwarzkopf became strained and conversations were short. Meetings and discussions on the best way to move forward became longer and longer but less and less was said. Professor Schwarzkopf started to feel that, unless there was a miracle, the pod would not open. Every possibility that he, and the other scientists, could think of had been exhausted. They had tried a logical and systematic approach but privately he thought the only thing that could open the pod now was luck.

By December, almost three months after Professor Schwarzkopf had arrived, the respect from the other scientists had all but vanished. As he had feared nothing he could physically do would open the pod. He knew that they were doubting his intellect and his 'aged' mind. Following a pre-lunch meeting one day the five scientists, led by Kurtz, challenged him openly. She harshly questioned his memories, knowledge and skills while the others stood behind her nodding uncomfortably in the background. He knew why they were worried. They had been told that Agent Angel would be visiting before the end of the year and they had no results to show him. Professor Schwarzkopf felt sorry for them. They lived in a 'now' society where they could do everything, and get everything, at the touch of a button. However, despite feeling this, he had still been hurt by the things that had been said.

After their rant they went for lunch and left the Professor to his thoughts. He sank down onto a chair next to the pod, buried his head in his hands and closed his eyes. His mind filled immediately with memories of happier times and images of his beloved Ingrid. If she were here she could open the pod, he thought. She had been the only person on the planet who knew how it could be done and she wouldn't tell a soul. Not even her husband. He chuckled to himself; she always was better at keeping secrets. The happier thoughts were replaced by sadder ones. He wished she could still be with him, he wondered what it would have been like to grow old together and he regretted that they had never had any children. The one thing that he really missed was her determination to finish anything she started and to inspire him to do the same. He heard the faded memory of her voice encouraging him, lifted his head from his hands and opened his eyes.

The pod was open.

The reaction of the scientists, when they returned after lunch, was mixed. Kurtz congratulated him without meaning it and could not hide her distrust of the

Professor. The other four were amazed, then extremely apologetic, and then excited by the task ahead. Professor Schwarzkopf saw in them Ingrid and himself, sixty years younger, energized by their work.

The inside of the pod was very different from the dart. In the centre of the pod was a cherry red object that best resembled a bed. It was made from a material that obviously had not been seen on earth before. The 'bed' was the same size as a baby's car seat but it moved as if alive. The scientists soon discovered that if they put their hand on the 'bed' the material would wrap itself around their hand, cocoon-like, leaving it warm and snug. If the scientists put a non-living item on the material it would do nothing. Their next discovery was that the material could expand to accommodate different living things bigger than itself. To test this they experimented with the base's dog, an Alsatian called Ben.

From wet nose to fluffy tail Ben was three times as long as the 'bed'. The mild mannered dog was picked up and gently placed the onto the 'bed', much to Kurtz's dismay. Ben lay down and the scientists watched with interest. Within a few seconds the bed began to grow upwards, around Ben. He began to whimper but was told sharply, by Kurtz, to stay where he was. In less than a minute it had covered all of him except his eyes, ears, nose, mouth, and funnily enough, his bottom. His whimpering stopped, his tongue hung out of his mouth and he looked perfectly content. At first the scientists were pleased by this discovery but when they tried to get Ben out they cursed themselves for putting him on the 'bed'.

It was impossible to pull the red material away from the relaxed dog. They tried using their hands and tools but, like the craft itself, the material was impossible to get into. In the end it was decided that, if they could not get in, Ben would have to get out. A very large bone was acquired from the mess hall and waved in front of Ben's mouth. Saliva dripped from his jaws, the material pulled back from his body, Ben jumped out and the 'bed' returned to its original state.

Surrounding the 'bed' were multi-coloured tubes, wires and probes, which could have easily come from Earth. The engine or propulsion system was virtually identical to the dart, but much smaller, and based on technology apparently from another world. The on-board computer looked quite dated on the outside. However, when it was opened up they found electronics that companies were only just including in their most expensive and up-to-date machines.

After three weeks of studying and dissecting the pod the scientists, supported by Professor Schwarzkopf, concluded it was an alien/human hybrid craft - a machine built using both alien and human technologies. When Agent Angel visited the base, Professor Schwarzkopf told him of their findings.

"Interesting," he said without showing the slightest bit of interest whatsoever, "now tell me, what was in it? Whatever was in it is dangerous and it ain't there now. As I told you before, John, it is a danger to our way of life. Of that I am certain."

Over the next few days they searched everywhere in the pod looking for evidence of a living thing, cursing the fact that they had put Ben inside and ignoring Kurtz's moaning. Every hair, speck of dirt and bit of dust that they could find, was analyzed to see if it contained DNA - the building blocks of life. It took them two and half days to rule out every hair Ben had shed. A day to dismiss every skin cell and hair dropped by the scientists, and another half a day to rule out the dirt and dust. On the sixth day, at the end of one the tubes which had been checked once before, Professor Schwarzkopf found a white flake, barely bigger than a full stop. He was pleased that his old eyes had not failed him but his find also stirred deeply buried and unpleasant memories. Sixty years previously he had discovered a similar sample - a sample that he had always regretted finding. He hoped the same would be not true of this white flake.

The flake was placed on a glass slide and put under the microscope. Professor Schwarzkopf sat at the table and stared at it though the eye piece. He did not recognize it and asked the others to have a look. Doctor Karima Khan, a specialist in human biology, stated straight away that it was a piece of dried saliva. The computer, connected to the microscope, ran tests and the scientists waited. Suddenly the word 'testing,' which had been blazing across the screen, vanished and it was replaced by two words, 'Human DNA'. No sooner had they appeared than they disappeared, to be replaced by one word, 'Error'. They flashed up on the screen repeatedly, 'Human DNA. Error. Human DNA. Error. Human DNA. Error.'

Dr Khan took the slide into her lab to run further tests. Her findings matched those of the computer: it was Human DNA but there was something wrong with it. Something she had never seen before.

On the seventh day Professor Schwarzkopf and the other scientists took a break. They had done what had been asked of them, and after working almost twenty hour days they were exhausted. Their last remaining energy they used up on a party to celebrate, which Kurtz attended only briefly.

The following day, feeling slightly worse for wear, they met Agent Angel in the briefing room. He was sat on the front row looking serious and expectant. Professor Schwarzkopf had been elected to lead the briefing despite Kurtz's protests. Nursing a sore head, he stood at the front of the room. He spoke about the discoveries they had made without using the whiteboard or computer and his only prop was the sealed slide of saliva. Occasionally the other scientists supported what he was saying but for the most part they just listened. Near the end of his speech his lungs started to give up and every other sentence was broken up by a bout of coughing. Agent

Angel's cigarette smoke did not help.

After the presentation Agent Angel and Professor Schwarzkopf changed places. Professor Schwarzkopf placed the slide carefully on the desk in front of him and Agent Angel stood, domineering, beside the white board. While flicking his cigarette ash onto the floor he thanked them all for their hard work.

"Did you find anything else? Any data files or documents?" he asked.

The scientists shook their heads, the computer on board would not reboot and the files were irretrievable. Unhappy with their answers, Agent Angel dismissed them all except Professor Schwarzkopf. Kurtz loitered in the corridor outside.

"I'm glad I pulled you out of your humdrum retirement, John," he said, sitting on chair next to Professor Schwarzkopf.

"It's been interesting," replied Professor Schwarzkopf honestly.

"Good, I'm glad, because I may have need of you again."

"When?" asked Professor Schwarzkopf, moving uncomfortably in his seat.

"I don't know," replied Agent Angel, taking a drag of his cigarette before continuing, "but you go home now and rest. I'll get my boys at the lab onto this."

He picked up the slide, "Consider your job here done. Go and pack. A driver will be waiting to take you when you are ready."

He directed Professor Schwarzkopf towards the door, "See you around John, and thanks again."

He held out his hand and the two men shook.

Professor Schwarzkopf left the room feeling slightly uneasy. He followed Kurtz down the corridor and was passed by six men who looked like marines. They all looked the same: closely shaven heads, dressed in black soldier's gear and built like tanks. He watched as they entered the briefing room, one by one, in neat file.

"Team Omega, reporting for duty, Sir," said one of them in a regularly drilled voice.

The six men stood rigid, with their arms by their sides, squashed behind the chairs in the briefing room. The room seemed to have shrunk since their arrival.

"At ease, Team Omega," ordered Agent Angel.

In a synchronized move their shoulders dropped, their arms fell behind their backs and their feet parted.

"Your mission is to find out who this DNA belongs to." Agent Angel waved the slide in front of them. "They are a threat to our national security. Once you have found him or her then you will make sure that they are never again found by anyone else. Ever!"

"Yes, Sir," chanted Team Omega.

"Dismissed."

11

CHRISTMAS CHEER

The sun rose to reveal rain washing the Christmas day snow away. Eric did not want to get out of bed. His Christmas wish was to sleep for the rest of the holiday and to wake up the day before school began. The villa was empty except for himself and Andrea. However, as Andrea was always doing something else which did not involve him, it felt like he had it all to himself. No matter what he did, in any of the large rooms, he felt alone. If he played cards it had to be patience. If he played chess his opponent was the computer. When he picked up his guitar there was no band to play with nor an audience to perform for. When he turned on his games console he had to select 'one player.' He was alone, alone, alone. He almost wished that Ursula was there. In many ways he had started to get used to having her around, not as a friend but more like a bad smell which, once gone, you notice is missing.

Wearily he opened his eyes and looked around his bedroom. At the end of his bed was a big, bulging sack. Obviously his parents had instructed Andrea to put it there while he was asleep. He had been told that Father Christmas never visited him when he was three years old. Rather than a pleasant surprise, the sight of the presents emphasized even more the fact that his parents were somewhere else in the world. Without him.

Every year he enjoyed opening his Christmas presents with his parents. It was the one family 'thing' they were good at, probably because it involved spending money.

On Christmas morning he would be allowed to open only one in his bedroom. His father would then lift his sack and carry it downstairs. Eric, hand in hand with his mother, would follow. In the lounge, under the pine tree, they would open all their other presents, steal chocolates from the green branches and flick the sparkling baubles. But not this year.

There was a knock at the door and Andrea entered. Andrea fulfilled many roles for Eric and many of these were as a substitute for his parents. Unfortunately she was not his parents and though she was always there, reliable and trustworthy, this was one role she could not play. She was also not particularly excited by Christmas, or any celebration for that matter, which did not help. Her clothes reflected her lack of interest. Rather than something special she was wearing her usual black leather trousers, matching jacket and another rock T-shirt, this time for a band called 'Sunshine'. In her hand she held a small gift and an envelope.

"Merry Christmas, Eric," she greeted, attempting to sound enthusiastic.

"And to you," replied Eric gloomily.

Andrea passed a precisely wrapped present to Eric and waited.

"I think you will like it," she said.

Eric sat up in bed and, taking his time, peeled back the Christmas paper. He had a feeling that he knew what it was. Underneath the wrapping he found what he expected, a T-shirt with a picture of four men with fake rabbit heads.

"They are my new favourite band," Andrea said, pointing to her T-shirt. "They are very cool."

"Thank you, Andrea," replied Eric, "that is very kind of you."

"Also, I was told to give you this," and she handed Eric the envelope. "I will now go and cook you a large and special Christmas breakfast. We are flying to Switzerland at eleven. You can open your presents there."

Eric watched her walk away. She did not carry his sack of presents and had not held his hand.

With a sense of dread Eric turned the envelope over in his hands. On the front, written in his father's familiar scrawl was his name: Eric Meyer.

Ursula looked uneasily at the envelope in her hand; something about it felt wrong. She did not recognize the messy handwriting and the stamps were in Dubai. Neither she nor her grandparents knew anyone from Dubai. She put the envelope to one side and decided to open it last.

They were all sat on Ursula's yellow bed - Ursula, Mémé and Granddad Benjamin - and were all intrigued by the foreign envelope. Christmas morning had been lovely, just what Ursula had wished for. They had always celebrated Christmas on the 25th, rather than the 24th like the rest of France. Normally this was through choice but this year it was a necessity as she had only arrived home the night before.

Celebrating on the 25th was Granddad Benjamin's doing. His anglophile father brought him up with Christmas on the 25th and that was where it was going to stay. He rarely put his foot down, especially when going against his formidable wife, but on this he was not going to budge.

Before the sun had risen Ursula had been woken by Granddad Benjamin poking her in the shoulder with a roughly wrapped present. Ursula thought that Granddad Benjamin was more excited by Christmas than she was. By the time she was fully awake and sitting up in bed, Mémé had also entered her small bedroom. Sweet smells of cinnamon and ginger wafted into the room with Mémé and filled their noses. Carefully, she placed a plate of homemade Christmas biscuits onto the bed.

The three of them took a biscuit each and, wishing to enjoy the taste for as long as possible, slowly bit into them.

In one bite the taste of Christmas filled their mouths and tiny bits of biscuit sprinkled onto the bed. At any other time of the year Mémé would have had a fit at crumbs on the bed but on Christmas day she turned a blind eye.

Granddad Benjamin continued to prod Ursula with the present until she took it from him. As she unwrapped it she felt she knew what the paper was hiding. The card game she had been imagining, fell from the paper and into her lap. It was called Mugins. They read the instructions carefully, dealt the cards and played until the sun rose, while eating the delicious biscuits. After the last one had been eaten Mémé handed the mysterious envelope back to Ursula.

Using his Swiss army knife, Eric slit open the envelope. Inside it he found a card with flashing LED lights on a snowy Christmas tree. As he cautiously opened it, 'Oh Tannenbaum' started to play in horrible tinny beeps. Immediately Eric slammed it shut, pulled the wires out from the card's battery and silently opened it again. His father's messy handwriting took up one side of the card and a concerned Eric began to read.

Dear Eric,

We are having a wonderful time sailing around all these nice hot countrys and we are now in Dubai. At times the seas can be very bouncey but your mother has learned what to do and is staying in bed. I am pleased to be writing that it is infrequently that she is doing this.

We are writing and wishing you a very Happy Christmas. You're mother and me we were worrying you will be alone during the holiday but we have solved this problem.

Eric stopped reading. He knew what his father, in his imperfect English, was going to write next.

Ursula paused, took a deep breath and, translating into

French for Mémé, read on.

To keep Eric company we would like to be inviting you to our winter chalet in the mountains in Switzerland. We would like you to arrive on the 26th December and stay until after the New Year. Andrea has been arranging all the details and if you agree we would be very welcome to have you staying in out chalet. Natrually we will be paying for all your taxi and flights for the three of you.

Please phone Andrea to be confirming and we wish you a Happy Christmas and Merry New Year.

Unsure of whether he was happy, sad, angry or all three, Eric read on.

Lots of love,
Papa and Mama xxxxx

"Fantastic!" said Granddad Benjamin gleefully, almost jumping for joy.

"*Incroyable!*" added Mémé.

"We had better pack," suggested Granddad Benjamin.

"And phone that lady," reminded Mémé.

Ursula remained silent. Her grandparents had already forgotten the numerous video phone calls she had made to them on the subject of Eric and the problems she had with him. The thought of spending any more time with him did not appeal in the slightest.

"But Granddad," she said, trying to find an excuse as to why they couldn't go, "you're not well, what if anything happens to you?"

"You're right, I'm not well," he replied with a smile, "but I am much better. That lovely girl Andrea paid for me to see a specialist. The doctor said she could help me and she has put me on some new medication. It was uncomfortable at first but since then I've felt much better. Isn't that true, Marie-Thérèse?"

He looked at his wife for support.

"*Oui, c'est vrai,*" she answered. "He even helps me with the cleaning now... which means I have to do more cleaning afterwards!"

Ursula looked for another means of escape, "But Mémé, you would have to leave your flat for at least a week."

"*Ce n'est pas un problème,*" she replied. "When you were here you were our eyes and ears to the outside world, but since you have been away we go outside regularly. It is not so bad; the news makes the modern world seem a scary place but actually it is fine."

Ursula knew she had lost. Also she did not want to stand in the way of her grandparents and a free holiday. To the best of her knowledge they had never had a holiday, ever. When she won the puzzle competition three months earlier, and left them, they had not stood in her way. Therefore she would not stand in their way now.

"Good," she lied, "what a great Christmas surprise!"

Great, thought Eric, what a surprise! Closing his eyes, he tried to fall back to sleep, but mixed emotions and daylight kept him awake.

Ursula had only flown twice in her life. The first time was to get to Prague and had been an interesting journey. The second time was to return to Paris from Prague. Andrea had sorted out everything for her at the airport but flying alone had been as dull as dishwater. She did not consider herself an experienced flyer; however, compared to her grandparents, she was an expert. Consequently she found herself in charge of getting the three of them to Switzerland.

During her time away both her grandparents seemed to have changed for the better. For a start they were now much keener to spend time outdoors, which made leaving the flat a lot easier than she had expected. As they walked to the taxi Ursula worried that her grandparents newfound joie de vivre was due to the fact that their granddaughter was out of the way in Prague. It was true that Mémé worried less about Ursula now but she also worried far less about Granddad Benjamin too. The new medicines he was receiving had improved his life immeasurably which, in turn, had improved hers.

The taxi arrived before dawn and the ride was fun. Mémé and Granddad Benjamin were glued to the windows like two children, talking about everything they saw and making comments on how much Paris had changed since they were young. Ursula enjoyed listening to them and heard stories she had never been told before. The taxi left the centre of Paris and headed for the airport. In the car the conversation changed. They were excited about seeing the airport, the planes and, for the first time in their lives, flying.

As they entered the airport Mémé and Granddad Benjamin took out their new passports. Andrea had helped to get them while Ursula was away, in case they needed, or wanted, to visit her. This trip was the first time they were to use them and they were both on edge. In the queue for the check-in they kept looking at their passport photos, trying to memorize their photo booth poses. Both were worried that the check-in man was would not recognize them as the people in the photos, unless they looked exactly the same. They had even worn the same clothes, just to be on the safe side. Unfortunately Granddad Benjamin was smiling like a demon on his photo and Mémé looked like she had just sat on a drawing pin on her photo.

Anxiously, Ursula's grandparents handed over their passports to the bored looking man at the check-in desk. He didn't even look up at them. With his head bowed he took the passports, opened them quickly and then looked up at Granddad Benjamin and Mémé. To his surprise he was confronted by a smiling demon and an old woman who had sat on a pin. Without blinking an eye he thanked them, handed back the passports and tried to hide the fact that he thought he was dealing with a family of lunatics. This became harder with each security question he had to ask.

"Did you pack these bags yourself?" he asked in solemn French, as Ursula put three suitcases onto the scales attached to his desk.

Mémé looked shocked that she should be asked such a question, "Do I look like someone who would ask somebody else to pack my bags? I may be old but I still have all my faculties young man. Anyway, who would I ask? Someone from..."

Ursula interrupted. "Yes."

The man looked at his list of questions and then at the length of the queue. In his mind he weighed up the amount of time it would take to ask each one against how many people would miss their flights. He thought he could probably ask two more. "Has anyone asked you to carry anything on the plane for them?"

"Like what?" asked Mémé.

This was not the answer he had expected. "Er, like anything."

"Do we look like porters?" asked Mémé. "Do we look like the kind of people who would carry other people's things for them? Do we..."

Ursula interrupted again. "No."

The check-in man, rapidly losing his patience, asked his last question, "Have you packed any of these items?" and he showed them a list of prohibited items.

Mémé took her glasses from their case and balanced them delicately on her nose. She picked up the list of items and studied it carefully. After looking at every item and, oblivious to the tutting behind her, she passed the list back to the check-in man.

"Young man, are you having a joke? Why on earth would we take explosives, hand guns and swords! Do we look like criminals?"

"I'll take that as a no," he said, thrust the tickets into their hands, pressed the conveyor belt button and wished them a pleasant flight.

Mémé watched the bags trundle away on the conveyor belt and screamed, "Jerome, he's taking our bags! Do something!"

Before Ursula could explain, Granddad Benjamin stumbled onto the moving conveyor belt, fell over and promptly disappeared from view in pursuit of the bags.

Two giggling policeman carrying very large guns, accompanied Mémé and Ursula to the runway. They found Granddad Benjamin on a trolley, surrounded by bags being placed in the cargo hold of the plane. Once the three of them were on the aircraft the rest of the journey was, fortunately, much less eventful. In fact, Granddad Benjamin's loud yippee on landing was the most interesting part of the flight.

Geneva airport was very busy. The arrival lounge was full of people carrying skis, snowboards and big bags full of winter clothes. Towering above them all, was a very tall man holding a board with their names on it. He whisked the Benjamins out of the arrival lounge, into a Range Rover and drove them out of the airport. Within a few minutes they were on the motorway and on their way to the Meyer's chalet in the Swiss Alps.

The drive along the Swiss motorway was the most memorable Ursula had ever done, not that she had been in many cars. Snow covered mountains, that touched white fluffy clouds, rose high above them on either side of the motorway. Below was Lac Léman, stretching as far as the eye could see, a glistening lake in the winter sun. In places the motorway pierced mountains and disappeared into numerous tunnels. In other places it gripped the side of the mountain like a shelf on a wall.

After they came off the motorway they drove through a small town and then onto a narrow mountain road. It twisted and turned, passing wooden chalets and snowy trees as they drove upwards. Occasionally they heard cow bells ringing from inside old, hay covered barns and they saw animal tracks in the snow. Ursula would not move from the window and kept looking down at the small town below. With every bend in the road the town became smaller and smaller. Finally, the driver steered the car round a particularly tight bend and a plain sign welcomed them to the village of Champex.

In the centre of the village tourists and locals skated on a frozen lake shaped like the number eight. A few guest houses sat on its shore with chalk boards advertising comfortable beds and home cooked food. Further away, scattered around the lake and clinging to the slopes of steep mountains, were picturesque wooden chalets.

The Range Rover turned off the village road and onto a slushy track. They passed through thick, snow covered pine trees before arriving in a clearing. On one edge, surrounded by trees, was a large chalet. The driver slowed down and stopped near the front entrance.

Wide stone steps led up to the door; underneath them were piles of neatly arranged logs. Close by, they could see Andrea and Eric sawing through an old dead tree trunk. Ursula jumped out of the car and into the snow. It was freezing, much colder than she anticipated. She waved to Andrea who was wearing only a T-shirt, her leather jacket and trousers, and seemed not to notice the chill.

Andrea put the saw down and came over to greet the Benjamins. She ushered them out of the cold and into the chalet. Eric, dressed in his dark blue ski clothes, ignored them. He picked up an axe and began to chop the trunk into log sized pieces.

By lunch time Ursula had searched the whole chalet. She had discovered that all the walls, ceilings, floors, doors and furniture were made of wood. Mountain scene paintings, of varying quality, were dotted around the bedrooms. Under-floor heating ensured the chalet stayed warm. The biggest room in the chalet was multi-purpose and contained a dining room, kitchen and a lounge. In the middle of the room were two fat sofas placed either side of a thick woolen rug. Dominating the room was a burning log fire with the skull of a deer above it and a Plasma television beside it. On the opposite wall, floor to ceiling windows gave impressive views of the picturesque village, the frozen lake and the imposing mountains.

The worries that had been playing on Ursula's mind disappeared. Eric obviously felt the same as her and was keeping his distance. Her grandparents loved it and to see them so happy made Ursula feel much more relaxed. Even the appearance of a sullen looking Eric at dinner could not dampen the mood.

The table sat six, three on either side. Eric sat on a middle seat, spread himself out silently daring anyone to sit beside him. Granddad Benjamin and Mémé dared.

"Hello," greeted Granddad Benjamin. "I'm Jerome," and he put out his hand.

Eric reluctantly put out his hand and replied sulkily, "Eric."

"Nice to meet you, Eric." Pointing to his wife he said, "and this is my beautiful wife, Marie-Thérèse, but you had better call her Madame Benjamin or Mémé or she will probably hit me."

A strange thing then happened: for a fraction of a second, Eric almost smiled. Before his smile became noticeable he got a grip on himself, his face returned to a frown and he turned to Mémé.

"Bonjour," Eric greeted sullenly.

He put out his hand but Mémé completely ignored it and instead gave him a big hug. Eric did not have time to escape and did not know what to do.

Mémé held him close and whispered in his ear, "You poor boy, how could your parents leave such a lovely boy alone for so long?"

She let go and Eric was even more confused. His head was spinning, this was not part of his game plan. Before he had a chance to say anything Mémé thrust a homemade Christmas biscuit into his mouth and a present into his hands.

Eric's eyes bulged and, spraying crumbs everywhere he mumbled, "Merci."

"Don't talk with your mouth full, Eric, I'm sure you have better manners," scolded Mémé, wiping the crumbs off the table and into her hand.

"*Je suis desolé,* Madame Benjamin," replied Eric and shot more crumbs over the table.

Ursula's mouth dropped open. Her grandparents had made Eric, who never spoke to her, speak more in three minutes than she had managed in three months. What's more, he had spoken French without complaint and had even exhibited manners, a characteristic Ursula thought he did not possess.

"And you can close your mouth too," Mémé told Ursula. "We brought you up to be a young lady not a goldfish."

At this comment something remarkable happened. Eric laughed. More crumbs were flew over the table which sent Mémé into a fit which, in turn, caused Ursula to start laughing. Granddad Benjamin began to mimic his wife as she picked crumbs off the table, and this made the two children laugh even harder. Only the arrival of Andrea at the table, carrying four plates of Rösti, briefly calmed everybody down. She was thoroughly confused by what had just happened and the moment she returned to the kitchen Eric and Ursula couldn't help but laugh even more.

In spite of their shared laughter Eric and Ursula did not talk to each other over lunch. They joined in the conversation, with Granddad Benjamin and Mémé, but did not exchange any words directly. After everyone had finished eating Andrea cleared away the plates and served some Christmas stollen.

"Are you going to open your present?" Granddad

Benjamin asked Eric expectantly, pointing to the small box which had been forgotten during the laughter and meal.

"Er, I'm not sure, maybe I should wait until after dessert," replied Eric in French, looking nervously at Mémé.

"You open it when you want, mon cheri," said Mémé.

Ursula felt as if she had just been slapped around the face, how could Mémé call Eric mon cheri?

'I'll open it now then," decided Eric and tore off the wrapping paper. Inside he found a little book of Sudoku puzzles and a box of magic tricks.

"Ursula loves those puzzles, so we thought you would too," explained Mémé.

"Thank you," said Eric gratefully, "that's very kind of you."

"You're very welcome," said Ursula's grandparents together.

You're very welcome, thought Ursula to herself, after all the things Eric did to me, and I told you about, how can he be very welcome? She smiled weakly but on the inside she was sulking. If she could have reached him, she would have kicked Eric under the table.

Following lunch, the five of them went for a walk around the lake. The sky was bright blue, snow crunched softly under foot and whenever they opened their mouths their breath sparkled in the cold air. Ursula looked at her grandparents, they looked younger than when they arrived. Granddad Benjamin even wanted to try out an exercise station they passed but Mémé stopped him.

While walking around the lake they passed eleven more exercise stations, each different, which formed a circuit. Andrea explained that they were part of a local summer exercise called Parcour Vita. It consisted of twelve different exercise 'events' that worked the heart and the muscles.

"How long does it take to do them all and run round the lake?" asked Granddad Benjamin.

"A healthy adult will do this course in forty minutes," Andrea answered.

"But I've done it in thirty eight minutes," boasted Eric with a smile, walking between Ursula's grandparents.

"Well done," congratulated Granddad Benjamin.

Unable to stop herself Ursula blurted out, "Then I could do it in thirty seven minutes."

The smile on Eric's face disappeared the moment Ursula opened her mouth.

"I think it is highly unlikely either of you could beat a time for adults," said Mémé, daring either of them to say differently.

They both did. At exactly the same time.

"You will have to prove it then," Granddad Benjamin told them. "Tomorrow morning you can race around the circuit and the person who comes first gets three of Mémé's homemade Christmas biscuits."

"Jerome!" exclaimed Mémé.

But it was too late, the two children had already agreed

12

THE RACE AROUND CHAMPEX LAKE

The next morning the temperature in the mountains rose slightly. Dark clouds blew over the village and they hung menacingly above the lake. The laughter of the previous day's lunch was forgotten and both children withdrew into themselves. As normal they wouldn't speak to each other but now they kept away from the adults too. Mémé tried to stop the race but her husband felt strongly that it would do the two children some good to settle their differences.

When the children left the chalet, followed by Granddad Benjamin, it was snowing heavily. Large flakes filled the sky and made it difficult to see too far ahead. Eric didn't care about the cold and walked quickly away from the Benjamins. Ursula, wanting to prove that she was equally as fast, kept up with him. This left Granddad Benjamin far behind, bringing up the rear at his own, rather slower pace. Squinting through the falling snow, he watched the two children. He could just make out a dark blue blur as Eric and a yellow blur as Ursula. They were both getting further and further away from him and did not look likely to slow down.

"Slow down you two," shouted Granddad Benjamin, his words muffled by the snow.

They did not stop until they were out of the clearing and hidden amongst the thick pine trees. Eric made sure Granddad Benjamin could not see them and then pulled Ursula under the snow laden branches.

"This is the deal," he began, his eyes scowling at

Ursula, "when I win, you will agree to disappear back to Paris and your horribly poor little life forever."

Ursula stared back and, standing firm, replied, "When I win you will agree not to talk to my grandparents unless I give you permission and you will never be nasty to me ever again."

She held out her hand and Eric took it strongly. Their fingers wrapped around each other and they squeezed as hard as they could. Only when Granddad Benjamin appeared under the trees did they let go. They waited for him to reach them and then Eric immediately started to talk to him. Despite her best efforts Ursula could not interrupt the conversation. Every time she tried to join in Eric would speak over her, Granddad Benjamin would reply and she was forced back into silence. Ursula fumed. Snowflakes that landed on her face melted instantly and she was forced to walk behind the two of them. Their conversation only stopped when they reached the start line, the start of exercise circuit.

Granddad Benjamin stood in front of them, beside a wooden board showing a Parcours Vita map with a red line that marked the route.

"Welcome to the first Eric and Ursula Champex Championship," he announced. "When I say 'go' the two of you will run around the lake, visit each of the twelve exercise stations in order and do the exercises that we saw yesterday. The first back here is the winner and will get to eat Mémé's delicious homemade Christmas biscuits."

Eric looked at Ursula and silently mouthed, "When I win, you are history."

Flicking her head back, Ursula pretended to laugh.

"Now, do you solemnly swear not to cheat?" asked Granddad Benjamin.

"I do," they replied.

Stepping away from the path, Granddad Benjamin scraped a start/finish line in the snow. "In that case, on your marks."

Eric and Ursula squatted down at the line.

"Get set."

They rose slightly.

"Go!"

The two of them shot away from the line and Granddad Benjamin clicked the start button on the stopwatch Andrea had given him. By the time he looked up from the stopwatch they were already far away. It has been a number of years since he had seen racing children and he was surprised at the speed of Eric and Ursula. With every step they took, snow flew into the air and they soon vanished into a thick white mist.

They were neck and neck as they reached the first station. After hopping over the ten logs, which the exercise demanded, they ran on to the next station still neck and neck. It was a pattern that was to be repeated over the next nine stations. From doing twenty star jumps to one hundred press-ups to fifty sit-ups, they would not be separated.

Eric was fuming. In all of his sports competitions no child had ever been able to match him physically and he was not going to lose now to a girl. Ursula was furious. If she could outrun a policeman why couldn't she do the same with this spoilt little rich kid? They sprinted off the lake path, into the dark forest and towards the eleventh station.

It was made up of four thin, long logs, placed in a square shape half a metre above the ground. It was a simple exercise that tested balance and the two children jumped onto it at the same time. However, instead of going the same way around the square they chose to go in different directions. They negotiated the smooth slippery logs with confidence and sped around the first half of the square. As they approached the half-way point they were both aware that they were heading for a collision but neither wanted to stand down.

Let's play chicken, thought Ursula.

You WILL get out of my way, thought Eric.

Rather than slow down they dug their heels in and sprinted as fast they could towards the other. Just before they collided head-on Eric leapt into the air and Ursula leant backwards into a skid. She was almost horizontal as she slid underneath him. Eric somersaulted above her and was about to land back on the log when a gust of wind blew. It was barely noticed by the two children but, unknown to Ursula, it blew her hood into the air. Silently it hit Eric's foot and enveloped it. Eric could do nothing, he was pushed off course and his trapped foot missed the log. He fell towards the ground and Ursula was dragged with him. They fell heavily on top of each other and a great plume of dusty snow exploded into the air.

"You stupid, stupid girl!" Eric yelled in Ursula's face as she lay on top of him.

"Don't call me stupid, you idiot, it was your fault," Ursula shouted back, trying to get off and away.

"It is a good job your parents aren't here to see such a..." Eric never finished his sentence. A handful of snow was thrust into his mouth and he started to choke.

"Shut up about my parents!" Ursula screamed, and ran off.

While spitting the snow out of his mouth Eric jumped to his feet and sprinted after her.

The last station looked like ten sets of parallel bars. They were positioned under pine trees, in a small clearing, and stood two metres above the ground. The aim of the exercise was to travel from one end of the bars to the other, without touching the ground, by swinging from one bar to the next.

Ursula was already hanging from the fourth bar and swinging towards the fifth when Eric reached the station. He jumped up onto a rock and sprang towards the bars like a tiger. His leap took him past the first bar, then the second, then the third and towards the fourth. But he wasn't aiming for the bars.

He hit Ursula from behind with all his weight. The momentum pushed Ursula's whole body up towards the bars and she clattered into them with a loud crack. The wooden structure shuddered and when her knees crashed into the sixth bar it dropped to the ground with a dull thud. Ursula gripped her bar tight. Eric grabbed her around the waist and locked his fingers together so he would not fall. They swung, joined together, as the snow swirled around them.

"Let go!" shouted Ursula.

"No," replied Eric into the back of her padded ski jacket.

Ursula clenched her fingers around the bar, gripped even tighter and shook her body in an attempt to get Eric off. All that fell were snowflakes from her shoulders.

"I mean it, Eric," she warned.

Her words fell on deaf ears. Eric was not going to let go. All he wanted was to get Ursula back for what she had done to him. With difficulty he unlocked his fingers, pushed his left hand into her stomach and stretched up to her shoulder with his right. He took hold, his left hand quickly followed and he hung from Ursula's shoulders like a baby monkey on its mother's back.

"Get away from me," yelled Ursula.

She refused to let go of the bars, to be beaten by Eric, but her shoulders were beginning to scream from the additional weight.

Pulling himself up so his head was behind hers, Eric whispered in her ear, "You're now feeling how I have felt since I met you."

"And you are about to feel how I have felt since I met you," replied Ursula threateningly.

Her response was unexpected. She let go of the bar with her right hand and her whole body lurched to the left. This came as such a surprise to Eric that he lost one of his grips on her. Frantically he tried to reclaim it but as he struggled Ursula punched him hard on the top of the head.

Gloves softened the blow but it still hurt. He pushed away from her, spun round and caught the bar behind.

The snow was falling much harder now and visibility had become very poor. Cross-country skiers on a path less than a stone's throw away could not see the fighting children and the snow deadened all sound.

Without Eric pulling her down Ursula felt considerably lighter and was filled with a burst of energy. In one fluid movement she pushed her legs out, and up, towards the hole where the sixth bar had been. The backs of her knees wrapped around the seventh bar and she let go of the one she was holding. Her shoulders relaxed, she swung upside down, and in the next moment she was through the hole and standing on the bars.

Meanwhile Eric had quickly worked his way back to the first bar, pirouetted around it, launched himself into the air and landed perfectly on the bars opposite Ursula.

"Where are your mummy and daddy?" sneered Eric.

"That's funny, I was thinking the same thing about you!" replied Ursula. "At least mine have an excuse. Yours just don't want you!"

Before Ursula had finished her sentence Eric had jumped at her, feet first. His karate kick hit her in the chest as she said, "you," and propelled her backwards onto the bars. Eric bounced off and leapt onto a branch of a pine tree above her. Heaps of snow fell from the tree and covered the fallen Ursula. Only her mouth could be seen as she strained to regain her breath. Warm air melted the snow around her lips and blew it away from her nose. Slowly she sat up, still wheezing and looking shaken.

Eric felt a sense of satisfaction as he looked down on her from the tree. He had obviously won and now the PPP would leave forever and he could continue his life as normal. He turned away from her and looked for the best way down. The branch, which he was standing upon, was almost three and a half metres above the ground and he preferred not to jump the whole way down. A little way below him was another branch which would be easy to...

Suddenly he could see nothing. Ursula had launched herself at him like a cobra in for the kill. His eyes were covered by a yellow blur and two arms wrapped themselves around his head, squashing his skull like a vice. Unable to see, and thrown off balance, Eric slipped off the branch and fell. Without any choice in the matter, Ursula joined him.

The bars of the wooden exercise station shook as the children bounced off them, falling like rag dolls over the side and continuing downwards towards the ground. Fortunately a deep snow drift gave them a softer landing but they were already both badly winded from the collision with the bars.

They lay beside each other, half buried in snow and breathing deeply. They were exhausted and, either from the cold or the fight or both, felt numb all over. Neither spoke nor moved. Apart from their flickering eyes they looked dead. The heavy snow started to settle on their faces but they remained still and silent. Five, ten, fifteen minutes passed and nothing changed. Finally Eric broke the silence.

"How did you do that?" he asked quietly.

"Do what?" murmured Ursula.

"Hold on to the bar, while I was on your back."

"I don't know," she paused, thinking about their fight. "How did you jump on that branch after kicking me?"

"I don't know either."

Silence returned as they relived the fight and what had happened. Overhead, a lone Robin perched on the branch they had fallen from and twisted his head rapidly searching for something. It looked lost and lonely, amongst the large trees, with no other birds around. As the two children watched they heard the tweeting of another bird. It flew over their heads and perched itself on the branch. It was another Robin. The first Robin calmed down, rubbed his chest playfully against the other and together they flew off.

Gingerly Eric stood up and offered Ursula his hand. She took it and he pulled her up. Without rushing, they walked back down to the lake and towards Granddad Benjamin.

"How do you feel?" asked Ursula.

"Tired, a little bruised. And you?"

"The same."

"But we fell from...," he paused, "and..."

He became lost in his thoughts and his sentences remained unfinished.

"I know," Ursula spoke slowly, considering every word as she said it, "Eric, do you think we're different?"

Eric stopped and looked Ursula straight in the eye. His quiet answer was almost lost amongst the heavily falling snow.

13

RECOVERY

On their way down to the lake Granddad Benjamin had been left behind by Eric and Ursula. On the way back their positions were reversed. Every fifty metres or so he had to stop and wait. Eric and Ursula were walking like mourners in a funeral procession. Their heads drooped, their bodies hunched and their feet dragged in the snow.

"You two took much longer than you said you would to finish the course. Are you both okay?" Granddad Benjamin asked as they trudged towards the chalet.

"Tired," they replied together.

Granddad Benjamin would not have minded such a leisurely pace if it had not been for the weather. The snow storm had become much worse and had turned into a full blown blizzard. The snow was falling so thickly that it was difficult to see which way to go. At times the snow was as hard as hail and stung as it was blown into them. At other times it was like walking through cold cotton wool. Low clouds hung like a dark veil over the village and street lights had turned on automatically. Luckily Granddad Benjamin had a very good sense of direction and by following this, and the street lights, he led them back towards the chalet. However, due to the bad weather and the children's extremely slow pace, it was taking forever.

Eventually they reached the clearing in front of the chalet. By this time Granddad Benjamin was literally leading them. Eric and Ursula had almost ground to a complete stop under the pine trees and only by pulling them would they move.

Mémé was waiting by the front door when they arrived. Even though she was very concerned she hid it behind a calm exterior.

"Who won?" she asked, a little too enthusiastically.

"No one," mumbled Eric, barely able to stand.

"It was a draw," whispered Ursula, leaning against the open door way.

"*Ce n'est pas important.* I think the best thing to do now is get you out of those wet clothes and then you can have a rest."

Sleepily the two children nodded in agreement. With Mémé's help they fell out of their sodden ski suits and then crawled up the wooden stairs, dressed only in their thermals. Mémé watched them go through worried eyes.

"I'll call you for lunch shortly," she said warmly.

The moment the two children were out of sight she turned to her husband and gave him such a telling off that it was a wonder she didn't start an avalanche.

Delicious smells filled the chalet before dinner. The aromas of fragrant French onion soup, honey roasted pork and sweet carrots, wafted up to the children's rooms. Granddad Benjamin was desperate to eat and could hardly wait for Eric and Ursula to bound downstairs and join them at the dinner table. They didn't.

Mémé called up the stairs, "Ursula, Eric, *mes cheris, à table.*"

Nobody came.

"I'll go and get them," Andrea offered, and left the kitchen area.

Eric's room was right at the top of the stairs. It was a good size but not huge. The bed was high above the floor and a rope ladder had to be climbed to reach it. Eric was nowhere near it. Instead he was lying on the floor of his room. His torso was draped over a train set, his legs on a guitar shaped rug and his head on the wooden floor. His arms and legs were bent into the most uncomfortable sleeping position Andrea had seen since Eric was a baby.

Gently she shook him but he did not respond. She tried again but harder. Nothing. Then again and again and again. The most she got out of him was a short grunt. Andrea knew when she was beaten. Carefully she lifted Eric up. Held him above her head and walked towards the bed. She dropped him on to the high mattress, put the duvet over him and left the room.

Next door was Ursula's room. It had been furnished simply, with a thick white rug, a wooden wardrobe, a chest of drawers and a single bed. Beside the bed was Ursula's open suitcase and, fast asleep, Ursula. Unlike Eric she had managed to reach the bed but hadn't quite managed to get into it. Her lower body rested on the floor, her upper body on the bed and one arm hung limply over the suitcase. As Andrea approached she could hear Ursula softly snoring. Placing her hands on Ursula's feet she tickled. Nothing happened. She tried the same thing under Ursula's arms but again there was no reaction. Admitting defeat, Andrea put her hands around Ursula's waist and lifted her into bed.

The elder Benjamins ate lunch alone and then dinner as well. When they went to bed four hours later they peeped into both rooms. The two children were still fast asleep and hadn't moved from where Andrea had put them.

By the next morning the blizzard had blown over. All tracks outside the chalet, both human and vehicle, had been covered by fresh snow. Snow drifts taller than people rested like sheets against the chalet. The drifts even reached the windows on the first floor. Andrea opened the windows before making breakfast, and brushed away the snow.

The sweet aroma of pains au chocolat and croissants soon woke Granddad Benjamin from his sleep. He joined Andrea in the kitchen dressed in an old tracksuit that he occasionally slept in. Shortly after Mémé entered, her hair full of pink curlers and wearing a matching pink dressing gown. She had not slept well. All night she had been tossing and turning, worried about Ursula and Eric. On two occasions she had got out of bed, entered their rooms and stayed until she could hear them breathing. Due to her lack of sleep she was not in the best of moods and almost forgot to wish everyone bonjour.

"I'm very worried about the children," she said, sipping a steaming coffee which Andrea had given her. "If they are not awake in the next hour we will have to call for the doctor."

"Don't worry, Mrs Benjamin," assured Andrea, "I can look after them."

"But they have been asleep for over eighteen hours!"

"Maybe they just needed a long rest to recharge their batteries. I know how they feel sometimes. I am sure they will be down soon and you will have nothing to worry about."

Right on cue Eric ran into the room like an express train.

"I'm starving," he declared, looking at the adults.

"So am I, what's for breakfast?" asked Ursula, skidding through the door and stopping beside Eric.

Nobody moved. Granddad Benjamin simply stared, Andrea looked intrigued and Mémé shakily pointed at their heads.

Eric and Ursula turned to face each other and only then saw what had caused the shocked silence. Around their ears their hair had turned completely white.

14

THE THAW

It took a few days for Mémé to accept that Eric and Ursula, in spite of their white hair, felt fine. She finally relaxed on New Year's Eve. The sun was shining brightly, the sky was brilliantly blue and the snow sparkled as if it was covered in diamonds.

They had all walked to the bottom of the ski slope so the children could do some bum boarding. Watching Eric and Ursula run up the slope, sledge down as fast as they could and then repeat this for nearly two hours, convinced Mémé that they were alright. Granddad Benjamin, however, was still watching his every step. Only when Mémé scolded the children for removing their hats and unzipping their ski suits did Granddad Benjamin know his wife was feeling better. It also meant that he was off the hook, which pleased him. He wasn't feeling that bad anyway; in fact, he felt quite smug.

Since the race Eric and Ursula's icy relationship had started to thaw. He had no idea what had happened on that day but he was pleased he had suggested the race which had helped. There was still some way to go before they would be friends, if ever, but at least they now recognized each other's existence. Even as he watched he could see evidence that friendship would not happen overnight. The two children were running up the slopes side by side, and zooming down on their sledges at the same time but they weren't playing together. They were playing beside each other and that was a big difference.

His next plan, he decided, would be to change this.

That evening they had a small party in the chalet. Just before midnight, carrying mugs full of thick hot chocolate, they went outside to the clearing. Andrea moved away from them all and with a long burning stick set off fireworks to celebrate the New Year. Rockets whizzed up into the black above them, multi-coloured explosions danced around the sky and red, blues and greens reflected in the snow.

Raising his mug of hot chocolate into the air, Granddad Benjamin proposed a toast. "To new friends."

His words were repeated and they chinked their mugs together. A final firework exploded above them and Granddad Benjamin's smile shone like the full moon.

Eric, Ursula and Granddad Benjamin spent the whole of New Year's Day morning in their beds. As usual Andrea was nowhere to be seen. Mémé, on the other hand, was everywhere. She spent New Year's Day morning as she did every year, waking early and cleaning. Her view was that the New Year should begin the same way you want it to continue. For her that meant being tidy, clean and well organized. Normally Granddad Benjamin ignored his wife's tradition, as he lifted his legs out of the way of the vacuum cleaner. This year however, he had to agree with her and also wanted it to start the way it should continue. With this in mind he got out of bed just after two o'clock in the afternoon and set out to find a chess set.

In the living room, behind one of the sofas, was a dusty games cabinet which Mémé had not yet reached. Crouching down, he opened the doors and searched through the crammed shelves until he found a black and white board and a box full of chess pieces. He placed them on the coffee table between the two sofas and arranged the pieces into a chess puzzle. Once this was complete he sat back on the sofa and waited. He could feel the warmth of the log fire on his face and gazed happily at the burning embers. His plan would work and he felt positive about Ursula and Eric's future relationship.

Before too long Eric came into the room. He was still wearing his pyjamas and his blond hair was so ruffled that it looked as if he had slept in a barn.

"Good afternoon, Eric," greeted Granddad Benjamin jovially.

"Er, good afternoon," replied Eric through a yawn.

After getting himself a bowl of cereal Eric sat on the sofa opposite Granddad Benjamin and in front of the chess set.

"What are you doing?" he asked, spooning Muesli greedily into his mouth.

"I'm trying to solve this chess puzzle," explained Granddad Benjamin. "White has to checkmate black in three moves. It is black's move."

Putting his bowl on the edge of the coffee table Eric leant forward and looked at the board.

"Do you play chess, Eric?"

"Oh yes, I'm the best in my school," he said casually.

"In that case you may have a chance to solve this."

Stretching out his arm and playing with the pieces, Eric replied, "I would be surprised if I couldn't do it."

Granddad Benjamin watched Eric as he made the required moves. His hands sped over the board so quickly that it was like watching a normal film speeded up.

"There you are," said Eric, "isn't this the end game between Topalov and Kramnik?"

"Well done, I think you're right," complimented Granddad Benjamin. "Would you like to play a game?"

By the time Ursula entered the room, in her orange dressing gown, Granddad Benjamin and Eric were happily chatting and finishing their fourth game. The first three had been won by Eric and this one was about to go the same way. Admittedly Granddad Benjamin had let him win the first one but after that Eric won without help. He was good, maybe even better than Ursula, thought

Granddad Benjamin.

"Morning Granddad," greeted Ursula, not seeing nor hearing Eric.

"Actually it is four o'clock in the afternoon, darling," replied Granddad Benjamin.

"I know but it doesn't feel right getting out of bed, staying in bed clothes and then saying 'good afternoon'. Even if I was woken earlier by Mémé. Why does she have to clean every New Year's day? It's not even our home."

"Your grandmother likes to start each New Year afresh, she throws out the old and brings in the new."

"Oh," murmured Ursula, taking a vanilla yoghurt from the fridge and joining Granddad Benjamin on the sofa.

Only then did she see Eric. She greeted him and then hastily put a spoonful of yoghurt in her mouth. Eric looked up from the chess set, shyly wished her a good afternoon and then turned this concentration back to the game.

Holding back a smile, Granddad Benjamin focused on the chess game. His King was not in a very good position but he still thought he had a small chance. This illusion was shattered in an instant by Ursula.

"You've lost, Granddad," Ursula told him bluntly and snuggled up against his shoulder.

"Thank you for your support," laughed Granddad Benjamin putting his arm around her.

Out of the corner of his eye Eric looked on enviously. Maybe Jerome and Mrs Benjamin could convince his parents to come back, he thought.

Ursula was right about the game and within four moves Eric had won again.

"Thanks for the games, Eric," said Granddad Benjamin. "You're too good for me."

"Thank you as well. Can we play again?" he asked eagerly, setting up the pieces for another game.

Slowly, Granddad Benjamin shook his head, "I had better stop there, a man can only take losing for so long."

A look of genuine sorrow appeared over Eric's face. "Please," and throwing his Queen off the board said, "I'll play without my Queen, that will make it much more even."

Since he had learnt to play chess he had only played serious and silent chess with his father, against the computer and in competitions. Playing social games had been such a pleasant surprise that he wanted to do it again.

"That's a very kind offer and later I will happily accept but now, to be honest, I need to go and take my medicines." Carefully he unwrapped himself from Ursula and stood up.

Eric sat back heavily on the sofa and looked really upset. It was the second time Ursula had seen Eric looking miserable and once again she felt sorry for him.

"I could play you," she suggested.

"Great idea!" agreed Granddad Benjamin. "She's much better than me."

Unfortunately the idea didn't improve Eric's mood. The race around the lake dominated his thoughts and he did not want to repeat it.

Looking up at Granddad Benjamin he said, "But we'll try to beat each other and it will turn nasty."

Ursula was thinking the same, "Eric's right."

Picking up the Queen and placing it back on the table Granddad Benjamin spoke to them both gently. "We all want to win. If you set out to win something that is very different from setting out to beat someone." He stood up again and his knees creaked loudly. "If you are worried about it turning 'nasty', as you say then why not play a less serious game of chess? Have you ever played Suicide Chess?"

The two children shook their heads.

"Good. I am sure you will both like it. It is a simple game which turns chess upside down. All you have to do is lose by losing all your pieces," and clapping his hands together he left the room.

Gradually the look of sorrow on Eric's face faded and was replaced with one of interest.

Ursula moved off the sofa and sat closer to the chess board, on the thick rug. "You start," she said.

Their first game confused them so much that, apart from the occasional, 'your move,' they said nothing. Hands skated across the chess board moving pieces into positions they would normally avoid and as both of them started to lose, they began to smile. In the end the game resulted in a draw.

Keen to lose, rather than win, they reset the board and played again. Halfway into the game they started to discuss strategies and ways they could possibly lose. Unsurprisingly the second game ended in another draw.

During the third game Ursula told Eric how Granddad Benjamin loved all games and had taught her chess when she was four. Eric explained that his father only played two games, poker and chess, both of which he insisted that Eric learn.

Ursula had only played poker once. A year ago, Granddad Benjamin had tried to teach her. During her one and only game Mémé had asked what they were playing. When Granddad Benjamin had replied 'poker' she had lost her temper completely. In one movement she swept the cards and matchstick chips off the table and banned Granddad Benjamin from ever teaching, "immoral betting games," to Ursula again.

Eric laughed. His father obviously had a very different view of poker. They decided that if Eric's parents and Ursula's grandparents ever met, they would try to keep the conversation away from poker and betting.

Inevitably, with so much conversation, the third game of Suicide Chess also ended without either of them losing.

For the fourth game they decided they would both make a real effort to lose but no matter how hard they tried they just couldn't do it. Before every move they became more and more aware that they knew exactly what the other was about to do.

As they approached the middle of the game Eric asked, "What am I going to move next?"

His hand circled over his remaining pieces like a hawk but did not rest on any of them.

"You're going to move your rook from A8 to A4," Ursula replied confidently and she was right.

Before each of their remaining moves they asked each other what their next move would be. Every time they guessed correctly. By the end of the game Eric was making Ursula's moves for her and Ursula was making Eric's moves for him. Needless to say the game ended in a draw and, surprisingly, a fit of giggles. As they rolled around laughing, pieces from the game were knocked off the coffee table and scattered all over the rug and the floor.

"*Mon dieu!* I tidied here!" exclaimed Mémé as she entered the living room, and found two giggling children rolling on the floor and chess pieces everywhere.

"Do not worry yourself, Marie-Thérèse," assured Granddad Benjamin, following his wife into the room, "they will tidy up, won't you children?"

They managed to nod between laughing and gradually calmed down. Crawling on their hands and knees they retrieved every piece apart from two. Eric's King and Queen seemed to have disappeared. Together they searched under the coffee table, lifted up the rug and looked under the sofa cushions, but the pieces could not be found. Just as they were about to give up Ursula saw them in front of the burning fire, hidden amongst a small pile of logs. She picked them up and gave them to Eric.

Without any warning Eric's smile suddenly vanished, his face dropped and the chess pieces fell out of his hand. At the same time Ursula felt something was wrong, very, very wrong. But before she could put her finger on what it was, Andrea ran into the room and turned on the plasma screen television.

15

BREAKING NEWS

"Breaking news," announced the news presenter. His angular face showed signs of excitement and his toupee looked as if it was about to fall off his head. "We are getting reports of a large explosion somewhere in the Persian Gulf. As yet we do not know much else but when we do you will hear it first on this news station! Onto other news now. Landslides in..."

Andrea, who had been standing very close to the log fire, stepped in front of the plasma television screen, "We must assume the worst," she said coldly and left the room.

Eric sat staring into space, as if he had been turned into stone. The Benjamins continued to watch the news but nothing more was said. Only on the hour did Eric move, and that was to face the television again.

"You are watching the news live at five with me, Campbell Windsor. Good afternoon. Coming up: widespread flooding across Peru, forest fires in Australia and a freak tornado hits California. But we begin with our main story this hour." He paused and shuffled his papers. "It has been reported that at 7.37 p.m. local time a large explosion approximately fifty kilometres north-east of Dubai rocked the Persian Gulf. It was witnessed by the crew of the cargo vessel 'Gulf Steam.' We are going live now to Captain Sharma of the Gulf Steam."

A photo of a large cargo ship appeared on the screen and underneath was written, 'Captain Sharma speaking live on satellite phone.'

"Hello Captain Sharma, can you tell us what you witnessed?" asked Campbell Windsor.

After a short time delay a well-spoken Indian gentlemen began talking. "Good evening. We were on a course from Dubai to Mumbai across the Persian Gulf when a vessel appeared ten kilometres away on our radar. We hailed the ship to warn that we would be passing quite close to them and to be aware of our wash. We received no reply. We repeated this warning a number of times more but without receiving any acknowledgment. It is prudent in these situations to err on the side of the caution. As we were moving considerably faster than the smaller vessel, which appeared to be bobbing about aimlessly, I cut our speed from twelve knots down to six. At 7.36 p.m. we were hailed by a hysterical woman. Amongst a great deal of commotion we just made out the words, 'help us!' This was instantly followed by a large explosion, which we witnessed far away on the horizon, in front of the Gulf Steam. We have just arrived at the last recorded coordinates of the other vessel but so far we have found nothing. Absolutely nothing. All debris has oddly, already sunk to the depths of the ocean and there are no signs of survivors. However we will continue looking."

The picture of the container ship was replaced with the news reader, "We are now going live to Dubai, to our reporter there, Angus Nichols. What can you add Angus?"

A pale, ginger haired man wearing a beach shirt over his large belly filled half the screen. Expensive yachts stretched out behind him and towering above him was a building shaped liked a luxury cruise ship. People were walking around aimlessly between boats, as if in a daze.

"Well Campbell, I'm here at the Dubai Yacht Club and the Dubai Creek Marina. I've spoken with the coastguard and the Dubai Ports Authority here and they're not hopeful. They have confirmed that a yacht left the marina here this evening heading for Mumbai but as yet they will not release any further information."

"How is this news being received around the marina?" asked the news reader.

"That's a good question and you can probably see the answer in the people that are walking behind me. As we all know Dubai attracts the rich and famous of the world but this does not mean they are any less of a community. Like any community the news is traveling fast. People are taking stock, checking on their friends and business partners, and there is a noticeable but quiet sense of relief when they find them."

"Are there any theories about what has happened?" asked Campbell, tidying his notes.

"It is difficult to say as yet, as it is still unclear who the actual victims are. However, a little earlier I did manage to speak to Jolanna Corn, the US Secretary of State, who is about to embark on a series of peace talks around the Middle East. She stated firmly, and I quote, 'This has all the hallmarks of a terrorist attack committed by a cowardly group and designed to keep the world an unstable place for us all.'"

Angus Nichols signed off and Campbell Windsor opened his mouth to speak. Before he had a chance to say anything Mémé had turned the television off.

"There is no point in us continuing to watch this for the next hour," she said, standing next to the television.

"Marie-Thérèse is right," agreed Granddad Benjamin, from the sofa opposite Eric, "until news people know the facts they will consider all kinds of theories. Most of them wrong."

Mémé sat down beside Eric. "We don't even know who owned the yacht that exploded yet."

Eric turned to look at her. His eyes were blank and empty. In a distant voice he said quietly, "It's bad, Madame Benjamin."

From the other side of the coffee table Ursula agreed with him.

"We know nothing yet, let's not jump to any false

conclusions," said Mémé smartly.

"Marie-Thérèse is right again," added Granddad Benjamin placing a pack of cards on the coffee table, "rather than sit here moping let's play a game of something."

Reluctantly the two children agreed. For almost an hour they played Rummy, but it felt like the longest game in the world. The two adults talked constantly but Eric and Ursula rarely joined in. Eric, unsurprisingly, offered only one word answers to any question he was asked. For the rest of the time he was sullen. He looked as if he was concentrating on the game but his mind was elsewhere.

At six o'clock Eric stood up, switched on the plasma television and sat back down next to Mémé.

The intro music began and the camera slowly zoomed in on the news reader, Campbell Williams. Once again he was looking serious while trying to contain his excitement.

"Our top story this hour: The Meyer family are missing, presumed dead. Other news: European Scientists discover signs of possible life on Mars but NASA dispute these claims and landslides in...

Mémé turned from the television to Eric. He was staring intently at the screen, his eyes glazed over with tears. His body was stiff and when Mémé put her arm around him he did not move.

"It has been confirmed that the luxury yacht, 'Queen of Hearts', exploded in the Persian Gulf fifty kilometres off Dubai earlier this morning. The 'Queen of Hearts' was owned by the Meyer family, one of the richest families in Europe, who are rumoured to be worth just under half a billion Euros. Martin Meyer, his wife Maria and their son Eric are all missing, presumed dead."

The news reader faded from the screen and was replaced with a black and white photo of Eric's father. A compassionate voice spoke over a series of old photos and some poor quality, eighties television footage of a poker game against a moustached man.

"His chips have been cashed in, the game is over and Martin Meyer, probably the best poker player in the history of the game, has left the green velvet table of life. But for many followers, and players of poker, he died almost twenty years ago.

In 1984, at the tender age of sixteen, Martin Meyer arrived on the international poker stage and was quickly nicknamed 'the kid'. For the next seven years he dominated every tournament he played in, winning over twenty five million dollars in the process. However in the summer of 1991, after bitter disagreements with the organizers of what would have been the biggest poker game in history, he vanished from the world of poker and out of the spotlight. Thus he became known as the Bobby Fischer of poker.

For the rest of his life he shied away from public performances, remained hidden from the media and, some would say, became a recluse as he dedicated his time to running the Meyer foundation and investing his millions.

In 1993 he briefly hit the news again when he married the Latin beauty and Miss World, Maria Torre. It is said that her influence changed the face of the Meyer Foundation.

Initially the foundation invested money into projects as diverse as cures for the common cold, extra-terrestrial locating, real estate, the European Space Station, vehicle design, robotics, materials, training dolphins, satellites and their biggest earner, computers and the internet. For a brief spell Martin Meyer had been a consultant at CERN, the European Centre for Particle Physics Research, where he had met Tim Berners-Lee, the father of the internet. It is reported, though not confirmed, that a large number of dot com businesses began with Meyer money and still earn millions for the foundation each year.

In 1997, a year after the virtually secret birth of their son Eric, the Meyer Foundation shocked the world of business and closed down as an investment company. All employees were give lucrative redundancy payments and not one original member of staff remained. It reopened, in name alone, as a charitable organization but its staff are invisible, its benefactors unknown and its donations kept secret. However, it is believed that millions each year go to worthwhile causes worldwide.

Since he disappeared from the public eye, and up until his untimely death, there are strong rumours that Martin Meyer continued to play poker at secret locations around the world and played regularly on the internet.

Over the last twenty years the Meyers have guarded their privacy in the same way that Martin would have guarded a winning hand. Rumours have spoken louder than facts and nothing about them is known for certain.

For these reasons Martin Meyer will be remembered as a sixteen year old poker player who took the card playing world by storm and, during a period of seven years, blew it away. His wife Maria will be remembered as a former Miss World. A woman of such profound beauty and stunning looks that she took the world's breath away. With their death of their son, the Meyers have no surviving relatives."

Eric stood up like a robot, switched off the television and walked back towards the sofa. He stepped painfully on a chess piece, the Queen from the earlier game, and almost fell. Like a volcano he suddenly erupted. He kicked the Queen with such force that it shot through the air like a bullet and cracked a pane of glass as it hit the window. Falling on his knees in front of Mémé, he smashed his fist against the coffee table so hard that it broke in two. His hands dropped by his sides, he suddenly looked unsteady and then dropped into Mémé's lap. She put her arms tightly around him and he burst into tears.

Ursula was shocked and clung hold of Granddad Benjamin. For what seemed like forever no one moved and the only sound was Eric's sobbing.

Suddenly Andrea entered the room. "We must go now!" she said forcefully. "Pack your bags. We leave in ten minutes."

16

REPORTING BACK

It was dark in the Persian Gulf. The moon was barely a crescent and the slim strip of light was swallowed up by thick mist. Two large search lights, operating from the deck of the 'Gulf Steam', criss-crossed the open water. Apart from the occasional plastic drinks bottle they found nothing. There were no remains of the yacht, 'Queen of Hearts', and no survivors. The crew had been searching without any luck for two hours and their search had also been conducted in near silence. If they could not see anyone in the water then they hoped they would still be able to hear them. They heard nothing except the waves lapping against the hull of the ship.

The silence was finally broken by the ship's loudspeaker. It seemed far too loud and disrespectful given the circumstances.

"This is Captain Sharma. The Dubai coast guard will be here soon with an international team led by the Americans. We have been thanked for our efforts and asked to continue toward our destination. Please turn off the search lights and return to your stations. We shall resume our journey in five minutes."

The crew did as they were asked. With the search lights off it was as if a black shroud had suddenly wrapped itself around the ship. Clinks and rattles echoed across the water and with a low roar the ship's engines started up. Painfully slowly, the ship sailed away from the site of the explosion. Their rescue mission had failed.

Just above the water level, attached to the hull with magnetic grips, were six large figures dressed in all black wet suits and with blacked out faces. They were almost invisible; white barnacles beside them were easier to spot, despite being a fraction of the size.

"This is Team Omega reporting in," said one of the black figures.

"Please report," said Agent Hoover, from the comfort of his air-conditioned observation room.

"Target has been destroyed but no sign of the boy. I repeat, no sign of the boy."

Agent Hoover picked up the phone and relayed this information to his boss.

Agent Angel was furious and roared back, "Search every port, every shipping record, flight reservations, immigration lists, border crossing reports, passport control data! Put out a warrant, use Interpol, do what it takes, but FIND THAT BOY!"

17

RETURN TO SAINT DENIS

Outside the chalet was a red Toyota Subaru. The paintwork was scratched, there was a small dent above the left wheel, the French number plates had faded and it was badly in need of a wash. Andrea was loading the bags into the boot when Eric, accompanied by the Benjamins, left the chalet.

His shoulders were drooped and his head bowed low. Silently, he got into the rear of the car with Mémé and Ursula, while Granddad Benjamin sat down in the front. Andrea checked that the chalet was locked, pressed a button on what looked like a television remote control, jumped into the car and wheel spun away.

The Subaru skidded through the trees down to the lake. All the tourists were inside, out of the cold, which suited Andrea fine as she sped onto the lake road and drove past a line of parked cars. Every car was empty except a lone American car: a black Chrysler. As she drove out of the village it pulled out and, with no lights on, followed at a safe distance.

It wasn't until they reached the motorway that Eric spoke and he asked mournfully, "Andrea, why aren't we taking the Land Rover?"

"Because this car is faster."

"What is this car? I've never seen it before."

"This is a Subaru and it is probably the fastest mass-produced car on the market. Your father keeps a number of different cars."

"My father kept," corrected Eric sadly and fell silent again.

Within two hours they were approaching the Swiss/French border. Signs on the road announced that the border crossing was only five kilometres away but Andrea took the slip road off of the motorway.

"Where are we going?" asked Granddad Benjamin and pointed back towards the motorway. "The border is that way."

"I know Mr Benjamin, but I do not think it would be a good idea to present Eric at a major border crossing. According to the news he is dead and I do not want him to suffer any awkward questions."

"That's very kind of you," said Mémé warmly, but Granddad Benjamin did not share her view.

During the journey he had watched Andrea regularly check the mirror, slow down without any reason and speed up when it wasn't necessary. He was sure Andrea was being something but she was definitely not only being kind.

They passed Geneva Airport and Andrea turned the car down a deserted road that ran parallel to the runway. Frost covered fields ran to the airport fence on one side of the road and large bare trees hugged the other. Andrea slowed down to a crawl and looked into her mirror.

"The road is icy," she said to justify the speed but then kept her eyes on the rearview mirror.

There was no car behind and, satisfied with this knowledge, she sped up. From the way she was driving it was as if she had grown up in the area. Without using the Galileo satellite navigation system, she speedily negotiated the car around the maze of country roads until the border was in sight. Once more she slowed down.

The crossing was marked by a small hut in the centre of the road. Signs requested that drivers slow down but the hut appeared empty. As they drove through, Granddad Benjamin noticed Andrea's hand did not leave the gearstick and she checked the rear-view mirror every few seconds. After crossing into France her hand returned to the steering wheel and she seemed less concerned with what might be behind her.

The rest of the journey passed without incident and it was almost two in the morning when they arrived back in Paris. Andrea drove them straight to Saint-Denis. Rain drizzled down from the bleak sky and piles of rapidly melting grey slush lined the sides of the roads. Andrea parked the car beside a wall topped with broken glass and they all got out, stiff from the journey. Down the road, just out of sight, a black Chrysler parked behind an abandoned Citröen.

Wearily, the Benjamins took their suitcases from the car. They made their way through the broken doors of the block of flats and into the graffiti covered lift. Andrea looked neither tired nor sleepy and supported Eric who really didn't know where he was or whether he was awake or asleep.

"It is late, can we stay the night, please?" asked Andrea, before the lift doors closed.

"Of course," replied Mémé, holding back a yawn, "it may be a squeeze but I'm sure we can manage."

Eric and Ursula were almost asleep when they entered the small flat. After changing into their pyjamas they were led into Ursula's room and were put top-to-tail into her little bed. They were asleep before Mémé and Andrea shut the door.

In the living room Granddad Benjamin was sitting at the table, his head in his hands, thinking. Wrinkles caused by old age and by his new worries stretched up from his brow to his bald head.

"Thank you for letting us stay," said Andrea to Mémé, "it is late and, like Ursula, Eric is already so tired. I am not sure he could have managed a journey across town as well."

"It's the least we could do after all the things you have

done for us."

The two women sat down together on the zebra coloured sofa.

"Do you mind sleeping here on the sofa, *ma cherie*?" asked Mémé, despite the fact that there wasn't anywhere else for Andrea to sleep.

"It will be fine," replied Andrea, testing the cushions with her hands.

Granddad Benjamin lifted his head from his hands and twisted round to face them. His brow was still wrinkled and he looked concerned. "Before you go to sleep, can I ask you what is going on?"

Mémé almost fell off the sofa and spluttered, "Jerome! You can't ask such a question."

"I don't mean to be rude Marie-Thérèse but something is wrong, and if we can I would like to help. It wouldn't be the first time we've helped a lonely child."

Andrea looked up at him. Her face was impossible to read. "What do you think is going on?" she asked.

"I think the boy is in danger."

"You are correct," answered Andrea.

Beside her, Mémé gasped.

18

BACK FROM THE DEAD

Winter sunlight broke through the gap between the thin, yellow curtains. The narrow beam split Ursula's room neatly in two and, as the sun rose, gradually moved towards the bed. It wasn't long before the beam covered Eric's head. He moved out of the glare and opened his eyes. They were tired and bloodshot. Underneath them large, grey sacks made him look as if he had been wearing mascara that had run. He wasn't sure if he had slept or not during the night. At times he had felt numb and distanced from himself but he wasn't sure if he had actually been asleep. All night his thoughts had been dominated by one thought and one thought alone. His parents were dead.

His parents were dead. Four simple words that changed his life forever. With the new day it didn't seem possible. Just a bad dream. A nightmare. Something that couldn't be true.

Eric looked around him. If it wasn't true then what was he doing in this pokey little room with its old, glass-topped desk and wardrobe covered in magazine cuttings. By his feet he heard a sleepy sigh. Raising his head slightly he looked down the bed at Ursula, who was fast asleep. Only the top of her head down to her nose was above the duvet and her face was covered by her long black hair. Gently Eric pulled the duvet towards him to reveal the rest of Ursula's head. Before the duvet had reached her mouth she grabbed at it in her sleep, wrapped it around herself and turned onto her front.

The sudden movement pulled the bedcover off Eric's chest and revealed Ursula's feet. The skin on her soles was much lighter than on the rest of her feet. It looked so thin that Eric feared it would tear if touched. Surrounding this skin was a bright red scar.

Curious, Eric placed his hands next to Ursula's feet. He looked from his palms to her soles and back again. The thin skin and scarring on his palms were almost the same as on Ursula's soles. Not wanting to wake her, Eric very lightly touched Ursula's feet. She did not move. The skin felt the same as on his palms. Beginning at her heel he delicately traced the scar with his finger. As he neared her toes Ursula started to fidget, mumble and then sleepily laugh.

The laughter brightened up the bedroom and helped him, for a few seconds, to forget his troubles. He continued to playfully tickle her until she shot up in bed. Her eyes were vacant, staring through Eric, but she still uttered, 'help me!' and then fell, literally, back to sleep.

Those two words, 'help me,' put memories of his parents, and his mother in particular, back into his mind. Last night when Captain Sharma had said them on the news they had barely registered. However, now they echoed in his head like a ball bouncing around an empty room.

"Amongst a great deal of commotion we just made out the words, 'help us!'"

How could there have been a great deal of commotion? thought Eric. A commotion means noise and is implies many people. Yet only two people were supposed to be on the 'Queen of Hearts', his mother and his father. Eric doubted that they had invited anyone else onto the yacht. His father liked his privacy and as long as his wife or a pack of cards were near, he was happy.

Another question popped into his head: how did the yacht explode? Yachts don't suddenly explode! Especially one which was checked and serviced monthly by a dedicated mechanic at its moorings in Monte Carlo.

The more Eric thought about it, the more troubling the events of the previous day became. Before he knew it his sadness had been replaced by a simmering anger. This explosion had not been an accident, it was something else. Somebody wanted them dead. Somebody had killed his parents. Silently he promised himself that he would avenge their deaths.

By now Eric was wide awake. Rather than lay in bed and listen to Ursula sleeping he decided to get up. As quiet as a mouse, he tiptoed out of Ursula's bedroom, down the narrow corridor and into the bright living room.

"Good morning, *mon cheri*," greeted Mémé, popping her head out of the kitchen. "Have a seat and I'll bring you some breakfast."

Eric sat down at the white formica table and looked around the room. The television looked like an antique, the sofa looked like it had been rescued from a rubbish dump and a glass cabinet proudly displayed a collection of Kinder egg toys, glass animals and a wind-up clock standing on a CD. It was like nowhere he had ever seen but, to his surprise, Eric realized that he didn't care what the room looked like.

From the kitchen he could hear Mémé softly singing in a language he did not recognize. The sweet smell of pastries wafted from the oven and teased his morning hunger. By the time Mémé placed two homemade croissants and homemade strawberry jam in front of him his stomach was rumbling. She kissed him on the forehead and sat down heavily beside him, her behind spilling over the sides of the seat.

"How are they?" she asked, as he took a bite of jam covered croissant.

The pastry melted in his mouth and the strawberry jam tickled his taste buds.

"Delicious, *merci*," Eric answered, before he had even swallowed.

"It's always a pleasure, but don't speak with your mouth full," she scolded.

A flake of pastry rested on Eric's cheek. Mémé softly flicked it off and, in one movement, stroked the side of Eric's face. Her plump fingers felt warm and comforting.

"You're a good boy Eric Meyer," she said and then, out of the blue, added, "don't worry, I won't let anything happen to you."

Before Eric had a chance to reply Andrea entered the living room. Her unzipped leather jacket revealed a Rammstein T-shirt but apart from this there was no difference in her appearance. In her hands she carried two bags from an expensive designer clothes shop, which she dropped onto the floor. Underneath both arms were thick piles of newspapers which she placed on the table, with a thud.

"I have some bad news, Eric," she announced.

More bad news, thought Eric, but he did not say anything.

Flicking through the newspapers she said, "You are dead around the world, from Australia to England."

She sat down opposite him and Eric couldn't work out if she was joking or not. Lifting the first newspaper he read aloud the paper name and the headline.

"El Pais. Family Dead in Explosion!"

Strangely the headline had no effect on him. It was as if, overnight, he had stopped feeling, as if these stories were not about him. Even the second paper was fine.

"Das Bild. His biggest bluff? Is Martin Meyer really dead?"

Eric looked through a few more.

"Hindustan Times. The Beauty World Mourns. The Australian. 500 MILLION on the table? Who will take the pot? De Telegraaf. Their chips are down. The International Herald Tribune. Terrorists Attack Families - No One Is Safe!"

Granddad Benjamin entered the room in his jogging

bottoms and an old T-shirt. He was followed by Ursula who still looked half-asleep. There was no room at the table so they sat on the itchy sofa.

"I have read all the articles and not one paper reports that you are alive. It is the same on the TV, radio and, I assume, the same will be true on the internet but I have not checked this yet. This is a difficult situation we find ourselves in," explained Andrea in her usual calm voice.

"Why?" asked Eric, taking another bite of his croissant.

"Because it is much harder to bring someone back from the dead than to kill them," Andrea replied.

Mémé and Granddad Benjamin hoped that Eric and Ursula had not noticed what Andrea had said. For a moment there was silence.

"Kill? You said kill," they both observed.

Following a short cough to clear his throat, Granddad Benjamin joined in the conversation. Eric was reminded of his father.

"I think it is best if we are honest with you. Andrea believes that the explosion on the yacht was not an accident."

"Nor do I," replied Eric and Ursula together.

Eric continued, "And I'll make them pay."

"I do not think that this is a good time for revenge," remarked Andrea.

Mémé tutted, "It is never a good time for revenge."

Andrea moved away from the table and went to the window overlooking the balcony and the rest of les banlieues. In one quick movement she closed the patterned curtains and then returned to the table.

"You are still in danger Eric. The whole worlds thinks that you are dead. For anyone who knows that you are still alive you are therefore easier to kill. It is easier to cover up the killing of someone whom everyone believes is already dead."

Briefly Eric closed his eyes to think about what Andrea had said and when he opened them again he asked, "So what can we do?"

From her right pocket Andrea pulled out a polaroid camera and packets of film. She placed them on the table. From her other pocket she produced a tower of envelopes. Eric picked up the first few and thumbed through them. The first envelope was addressed to Eric's school. All the others were addressed to a major newspaper or media network around the world.

"Every envelope has an identical letter, read one," Andrea told Eric.

Pulling back the envelope lip, Eric removed and unfolded a letter. It had been written in English, in Andrea's precise script, using only capital letters. He read it aloud, translating into French for Mémé.

TO WHOM IT MAY CONCERN,

MY NAME IS ERIC MEYER AND I AM ALIVE. I AM PERFECTLY SAFE AS I WAS NOT ON THE YACHT WITH MY PARENTS. HOWEVER I FEAR THAT THEY WERE KILLED AND THAT I MAY BE NEXT.

AS PROOF THAT I AM ALIVE, PLEASE FIND ATTACHED A PHOTO OF MYSELF HOLDING MY PASSPORT AND TODAY'S NEWSPAPERS.

I AM BEING LOOKED AFTER AND I WILL BE RETURNING TO SCHOOL SHORTLY.

I WOULD APPRECIATE BEING LEFT IN PEACE AT THIS DIFFICULT TIME.

YOURS SINCERELY, ERIC MEYER

Eric thought about what was written as he folded the letter and put it back in the envelope.

"There are two things I don't understand," he began, "firstly why tell the newspapers and media networks? They will try to find me and once they do they definitely won't leave me in peace. They'll be everywhere, I won't be able to escape them. If I am in danger we will be telling and showing everyone where I am."

Granddad Benjamin shuffled on the sofa and smiled. "Think about it Eric, you're a clever boy. While journalists and people with cameras are watching you, you will be safe. Nobody will try to harm you while the world is watching."

Eric did not look convinced but he understood the reasoning.

"What was your second question Eric?" asked Ursula from the sofa, bringing her knees up to her chin.

"I don't understand why we don't just send an email, it's a lot quicker than sending letters."

Andrea answered, "Your father knew much about the internet and the way it works. More than most people knew or even suspected. He taught me all he knew and then I expanded on this using my own knowledge and skills. Many people and organizations monitor the internet. Large super computers will be searching for any traffic over the internet with the key words, 'Meyer.' If we send an email it will be picked up the moment we send it, as will the location of the computer that sent it. If we send letters we have more chance of journalists finding you first."

With Eric's questions answered they put all the newspapers on the floor. Eric lay upon them with his passport in his hand and Andrea, standing on a chair, took a stack of polaroids.

The mood in the flat was strange. Everyone, except Andrea, seemed a little on edge and a little gloomy, but at the same time there was an air of excitement. After the photos had been taken Andrea threw Eric and Ursula one of the shopping bags each, which she had brought in earlier.

"What is this?" asked Ursula, looking surprised.

"In one week it is Eric's twelfth birthday and in ten days it is yours. We decided you should get a birthday present each," explained Andrea.

Inside the bags were a pair of black wheelie shoes each, a yellow designer hoodie for Ursula, a dark blue designer hoodie for Eric and matching beanies.

An hour later Eric and Ursula, in their new clothes, were in the red Subaru with Andrea. The Benjamins had wanted Eric to stay indoors but Andrea insisted that, as Eric's guardian, he would stay near her. Ursula went with them, after convincing the adults that she would be good cover for Eric as no one was looking for two children. In truth, she just wanted to get out of the flat for a while and try wheeling around on her new shoes.

Andrea parked the car outside Serge's post office on the busy rue Paul Baudry. Before they left the car Andrea instructed the children to wear their beanies and put their hoods up. She wanted to make sure that Eric was not spotted on the post office security cameras and recognized. The two children did as they were told and got out.

Down the road a black Chrysler parked behind a meat van. A man in a red cap got out and watched them enter the post office.

The post office had changed since Andrea last entered it. It was brighter and there was no sign of grey. The eight counters had been replaced with new, modern ones and the old glass replaced with new safety glass. Above the counters a roof had been added, so that no one could jump over the glass and, above this, the high domed ceiling had been repainted bright white. A ledge, joining the walls to the ceiling, had been decorated with the post office horn emblem and long strip lights hung down above the customers.

Five elderly people stood in a queue waiting to get their savings. Behind them two butch builders were holding a large parcel and three mums exchanged stories by their prams. Around the room were six large display boards showing the history of the postal service. They were in the shape of a crescent moon, starting at counter one, arcing out towards the entrance and then arcing in to finish at counter eight. In the centre of the post office was a glass display case housing some very rare stamps. Standing beside this was Serge.

He looked more alive than when Andrea had seen him last. The last few strands of hair had been shaved off and his polished bald head gave him more style. He stood tall, wore a casual shirt and a smart pair of trousers. He looked much younger.

After greeting each other with kisses on the cheek, Serge explained how he had fallen down the drain, broken both legs, fallen in love with the nurse who looked after him and was now happily married to her. Eric and Ursula left Serge and Andrea to chat and wheelied off to look at the displays and the history of the post office. They both felt that anything was more interesting than a love story.

Serge was so engrossed in his tale and Andrea was listening so attentively that neither of them noticed the two dark suited individuals enter the post office. They were wearing plastic masks of ex-French presidents, Chirac and Mitterand, and each was holding a gun.

A shot was fired into the ceiling and the babies started to scream.

"Everyone on the ground," shouted Mitterand and everybody did as he ordered.

Behind a display board, hidden from the men, Eric and Ursula looked at each other with wide eyes but otherwise they did not move.

"Bonjour tout le monde," began Chirac approaching the glass cabinet containing the stamps, "allow me to introduce ourselves. My name is President Chirac and my colleague here is President Mitterand. We are here because we have an interest in stamps. We are keen collectors but unfortunately we are missing some to complete our collection. By an amazing stroke of luck these stamps are right here. Once our helpful manager," and he kicked Serge in the ribs, "deactivates the alarm on the cabinet that will summon the police we will take our stamps, leave and nobody will get hurt."

Chirac picked up Serge from the floor and walked him towards his office door, beside the display board where Eric and Ursula were hiding.

Mitterand stood by the entrance to the post office, brandishing his gun like a trophy and warning people not to move.

Eric and Ursula stood like statues. The footsteps grew louder as Serge and Chirac walked towards them but they still did not move. Ursula was sure her heart would give them away, it was beating so hard that it thumped against her chest like a drum.

Serge approached his office. Nervously, he took out the keys from his pocket and with shaking hands opened the door. He entered and Chirac followed with his gun aimed squarely at Serge's head. Neither of the two men spotted the children outside the open door.

Without a sound Eric and Ursula lifted their toes, leant back, and, using the wheels in their heels, rolled towards the wall.

From inside the office they heard jangling keys and Serge's quickened breath. There was a small crash as the keys dropped to the floor and then the sound of Serge scrambling to pick them up.

"You're wasting my time," barked Chirac and everyone in the post office heard his boot crack against Serge's ribs, followed by Serge whimpering.

"Turn the alarm off now! Or you'll get more of that," threatened Chirac.

"It will only take two minutes," replied Serge panting.

Ursula's heart was still racing but she was starting to think that the only people who could do anything were herself and Eric. Eric looked tense and was deep in concentration.

Next to the glass cabinet, in the centre of the post office, Andrea was lying on the floor. Slowly, barely noticeably, she turned her head towards the displays in search of Eric and Ursula. Below the boards she could see the children's shoes and in the office she could see...

Suddenly a leather boot stomped on the ground right in front of her face.

"And what is your name beautiful?" asked Mitterand menacingly, tapping her forehead with his boot.

"Andrea," she replied calmly.

"You sound very relaxed Andrea. You are not trying to be a heroine are you?"

"No," she answered calmly again.

"Then why are you moving? When I said, DON'T MOVE!"

He screamed the last two words in her ear and then pressed his boot down on her head.

"It you move again little Andrea I'm going to crack your head open like a nut in a nut cracker."

Behind the display board Eric became more tense. The look of concentration passed from his face and was replaced with a look of action. All the emotion of the last two days welled up inside him and he was about to burst. Eric had already lost his parents, he was not going to lose Andrea as well. Ursula looked at him with pleading eyes but she knew it was too late and that he would need her help. Without exchanging any words they agreed to act.

Purposefully, Eric walked in front of the office door and stood opposite Ursula. Chirac immediately jumped out the office and pointed the gun directly at Eric.

Before Chirac had a chance to do anything Ursula kicked him up the backside as hard as she could. He spun round like a wild cat and Eric booted him in exactly the same spot. He spun around again and was met with a karate kick to the groin from Eric.

Chirac doubled over and collapsed onto the tiles behind the display board groaning in pain. Instantly Ursula jumped onto the hand holding the gun. The moment Chirac let go Eric kicked it into Serge's office.

"What's going on? Chirac, talk to me!' ordered Mitterand.

Apart from some feeble groans there was no response.

Stepping off the injured Chirac, Ursula motioned upwards to Eric. She then turned, sprinted towards the end of the display board and wheelied quickly towards the next one. Confused by the sudden movement Mitterand fired a shot to where Ursula had been. The bullet hit the wall and sprayed fragments of brick over the floor like confetti at a wedding. Meanwhile Eric had jumped silently onto a very narrow ledge above him and was starting to creep up behind Mitterand.

Ursula sped between another two boards. Mitterand fired another shot but a fraction of a second too late and it smashed a small hole in the wall. Her heart was racing, she had run out of boards, there were no more. In front of her were only the glass fronted counters.

Without having time to think, she sprang up onto the counter, bounced against the wall and accelerated out into the open like a Formula One driver on a green light. Mitterand took aim and as he fired Ursula jumped onto the roof above the counter, laid down and disappeared from view. The safety glass cracked but didn't shatter.

"Come out or I'll shoot someone," roared Mitterand.

Directly behind and above Mitterand was Eric. He launched himself at the thief like a guided missile. His feet smashed into Mitterand's back, sending his gun into the air and propelling him forward. At the same time Ursula jumped down from her hiding place. She grabbed hold of a hanging strip-light as she fell, swung forward and landed with two feet perfectly in Mitterand's face. He collapsed to the ground in a moaning heap.

By the time Mitterand and Chirac had their breath back, Serge had one gun and Andrea the other. The two criminals were placed roughly against the counter by the builders and guarded by a ring of mean looking elderly people and furious mums with prams.

Before anyone had a chance to thank the children, Andrea placed her letters and the right amount of money on the counter, gave a gun to a mum, grabbed the two children and left. They had been in the post office less than four minutes.

In his darkened room, his face lit up by countless screens, Agent Hoover clapped. "Impressive stuff," he said to himself, looking away from the screen marked rue Paul Baudry and continuing his search for the solitary child, Eric Meyer.

Back in the car Ursula was shaking, almost uncontrollably, and Eric was almost rigid. They both looked exhausted and moments after Andrea pulled away they fell asleep.

The roads were busy but Andrea weaved through the traffic like a racing car driver. Hoots and beeps from other drivers followed the red Subaru but she hit no other vehicle. Without stopping she drove out of rue Paul Baudry, away from Saint-Denis and onto the motorway out of Paris. Just after entering Germany she filled the car up with unleaded petrol and phoned Ursula's grandparents to explain what had happened. Mémé took some calming but otherwise they both understood what Andrea was doing. Eight hours later the red Subaru arrived at the villa in Prague. The children had slept the entire journey.

A fresh layer of dusty snow covered the driveway and shone brightly in the car's headlights. However, once the car had stopped and the lights were off the snow became grey. The moon was covered in thick cloud and the lamp outside the villa was not working.

Andrea got out and opened the back door. The car interior light flickered on to reveal the two sleeping children. Behind their ears, towards their neck, more white hair had appeared and subtle wrinkles had etched crow's feet around their eyes. Andrea picked up Eric, carried him to bed and then did the same with Ursula.

Once she was sure the children would not wake up she went back outside, locking the villa behind her. She took absolutely everything out of the car and piled the things tidily beside the front door. After making sure no one was watching she got in the car, drove ten minutes away, parked in a grubby street next to the railway line, left the keys in the ignition and walked away. On the way back to the villa she passed a black Chrysler. Unlike the other cars in the street the engine was still warm. Andrea didn't notice.

19

PURSUED

The next day the children woke to a dull sky which promised rain rather than snow. Over a breakfast of porridge Eric and Ursula kept glancing at each other's white hair and crow's feet. Neither knew what to say about their changing appearance and so it wasn't mentioned. Instead they tried to talk about what had happened in Serge's post office but every time they brought it up Andrea would change the subject. Much to the children's annoyance Andrea had also informed them that they would be returning to school the following day. The icing on the cake, however, was when she took both their mobile phones, crushed the SIM cards underfoot and then returned the phones without any explanation.

Just after breakfast the front door bell rang. Andrea sent Eric and Ursula to their rooms, which was in keeping with her odd behaviour, and went to answer it. When her back was turned the two children opened their doors and, laying on their stomachs, peered out to see who it was. A shifty looking man with a long nose and a dirty coat asked, in Czech, if he could speak to Eric Meyer. In fluent Czech Andrea responded by informing the man that he was on private property, was trespassing and that she would phone the police if he did not leave.

"So, he is here?" asked the man expectantly.

Andrea slammed the door in his face and walked back along the corridor. Eric and Ursula slid like snakes back into their room.

For the next hour the doorbell rang every few minutes or so. Under orders from Andrea, nobody answered it and the children began to feel as if they were under siege.

"And don't look out of the windows either," she told them. "I don't want you to be seen. Stay in your rooms."

This was not greeted favourably by the children, who wanted to see what was going on. However, given Andrea's strange mood, they did as they were told.

After half an hour Eric crawled into Ursula's room. She was sitting on her bed reading. He grabbed her foot and pulled her off the bed and onto the floor.

"What are you doing?" Ursula asked in a loud whisper.

"Shhh!" replied Eric, put his finger to his lips and then beckoned her to follow him into his room.

Eric's room was a mess. The bed, the boxing glove bean bag, the desk and the floor were covered in toys. They seemed to have been flung around the room by an explosion. The centre of the blast looked to be the wardrobe, which ran the length of his room, as there were more toys on the floor in front of it than anywhere else.

"What happened?" Ursula asked.

"I was trying to find something."

"What?"

"A spy kit. It's here somewhere but I can't find it."

Ursula looked at the floor and, from under a teddy bear, pulled out a yellow box with the words 'spy kit' written on it in big letters.

"That's where it was. Well found," said Eric, taking the box from Ursula and opening it.

Inside were toy spy gadgets, including a mini camera, a disguise, a listening device and walkie-talkies. Eric ignored them and rummaged to the bottom where he found a periscope. It was about half a metre long, yellow like everything else in the box and shaped like two Ls joined together.

"This is what we need. We can look in here and see what is going on above us," he explained. "Come on, follow me."

Eric tiptoed out his room and walked down the corridor towards the front door. Ursula followed but tapped him on the shoulder after only a few paces.

"What about Andrea?" she whispered in Eric's ear.

"Don't worry, she's downstairs somewhere. I think she's in the cellar, she spends a lot of time down there for some reason," and he shivered.

At the front door Eric turned left and went into the room beside it. Once through the door he crouched down on to all fours and crawled towards the window. Ursula followed him slowly, she had not been in this room before. The velvet curtains were almost closed and there was not much light in the room. A large Turkish rug dominated the floor and what she could see of the furniture, which wasn't much, looked very heavy and very old. Every piece - armchairs, sofa, bookcases, a table and a writing desk - was covered in plastic sheeting. The whole room looked like it should have been in a museum.

Eric crawled under the curtain and sat facing the wall. Ursula joined him. Carefully, he raised the periscope so the top of it rested against the window and then looked in the viewing panel.

A shifty looking man was standing at the end of the driveway, on the public road through the park. The trees around him had spindly trunks and no leaves on the brittle branches. In his long coat, the man blended in with his surroundings. He was holding a cigarette in one hand and mobile phone in the other. In between puffs he would speak into this phone, finish a call and then make another one. Hanging around him were another twelve people. After a few minutes a large green Skoda screeched to a halt beside him and a photographer jumped out. Within an hour four more reporters had joined him.

During the rest of the day Eric and Ursula kept coming back to the room to spy on the people outside. By the time darkness fell there were twenty four reporters and photographers huddled together under the bare trees.

Overnight rain fell from the skies and washed the snow, the reporters and the photographers away. Before the children left the villa for school, Andrea did a quick sweep of the driveway, to check that nobody was still lurking around. Once satisfied, she collected the Range Rover from the garage, pulled up in front of the building and then, with two toots on the horn, signaled for Eric and Ursula to get in the car. Despite not wanting to go to school both children were looking forward to returning to some kind of normality. Eric was worried that other children would ask him questions about the news reports over the Christmas holidays, but Ursula had promised to help him out if she was around. In the Range Rover they chatted happily about the new term. There was a degree of warmth between them which definitely had not been there on the first day of the school year.

Andrea drove silently and did not join in the conversation. She had other things to think about. These became clear as they turned into the narrow school road. It was often congested but this morning it was full of expensive looking vehicles beeping their horns impatiently, moving at a snail's pace bumper to bumper. When they finally neared the drop off point the reason for the traffic jam became clear.

The reporters and photographers had moved from the Meyer property to the school. They had been joined by two television crews and all their vehicles were partially blocking the road - a situation which none of them seemed to care about. The shifty looking journalist with a dirty coat and long nose, was talking seriously to a serious looking woman in a brown woolly hat, a nodding photographer in a red baseball cap and a few others. The television cameramen, weighed down by their cameras, sat upon a low wall while their frontmen stood around making sure they looked smart for when they went on air. The rest of the reporters, including two built like tanks, hung around in small separate groups, fiddling with their dictaphones or notebooks.

"Are they all for me?" cried Eric in disbelief.

"I am afraid so, Eric. Now listen to me. When I stop the car, open your door, get out and do not get back in the car until the journalists are almost on top of you," Andrea instructed.

She stopped fifty metres from the drop off point and hoped the traffic in front of her would clear. As Eric jumped out of the car it did. Ursula giggled at Eric standing uncomfortably beside his door and waited to see what would happen. Behind the Range Rover other parents, seeing a gap open up, started beeping their horns angrily. The noise attracted the journalists' attention and as they turned they saw Eric. Within a second they became a herd of stampeding cattle and charged at him. Just before they reached him he climbed quickly back into the Range Rover, Andrea accelerated up to the drop off point, Eric and Ursula jumped out and quickly darted into school. As the car door closed behind them cameras flashed and shouted questions fell silent.

Mr Ball, the head teacher, was standing in the main reception wearing his usual straw coloured suit. His arms were behind his back and he was watching the events outside as if he had seen it all before.

"Welcome back. A busy term ahead for you two. You have tests, the school show and a trip to Pompeii all coming up I believe," said Mr Ball.

"Yes, Sir," replied the two children.

Before they went to class Mr Ball turned to Eric. "Journalists are tenacious beasts young man. Once they smell blood they won't give up the hunt. I hope you have the stamina to outrun them, the resolve to ignore them and the intellect to out think them."

For the first four days Eric, supported by Andrea and Ursula, exhibited all these qualities. By the fifth day he ran out of stamina. He was tired of playing the same cat and mouse game wherever he went. By the seventh day his resolve was all used up. He was sick of having journalists stalking him; he just wanted to be left alone and could no longer ignore them. By the eighth day Eric had had enough of being a prisoner at school and at home. That evening they had celebrated Eric and Ursula's twelfth birthdays but Andrea had refused to throw a party. Neither Eric nor Ursula were in the mood to celebrate anyway and, even if they had held a party, none of the other parents would have sent their children. On the ninth day Eric used the only quality he had left, his intellect, and escaped. The escape had not been planned but Eric saw his moment and took it.

It was the last lesson of the day, PE, and as they were getting changed Mr Tait popped his head into the changing room and unexpectedly announced that the Year 7 classes were going on a cross-country run. In Mr Tait's opinion, the 'conditions were perfect for a bit of a jog.' The sky was clear, the snow had melted away and the ground, rather than being icy, was simply hard.

All the Year 7 children trudged into the gym and sat on the multi-coloured floor. They were all dressed in their tracksuits, woolly hats and gloves, and looked miserable. Nobody wanted to go on a run.

'We'll go the normal route. Not too far," explained Mr Tait happily.

Most of the children groaned but Mr Tait ignored them.

"Just follow me out of the gym, through the gate at the back of the school, into the park, down to the river at Modrany and back again. Easy! Any questions?"

Eric saw his opportunity. "Mr Tait, I've left my gloves in the changing room, can I get them please?"

It was a bare-faced lie but Mr Tait didn't doubt his star pupil for a second.

"If you must, but you'll have to catch us up. I'm not waiting for you."

"No problem. I'll be with you before you reach the path."

"A challenge, Mr Meyer? We'll see about that. Come on everyone let's go," and Mr Tait sped out of the gym followed by all the other children.

Eric took his time, went back into the smelly changing rooms, packed his bag and then returned to the empty gym. After a few minutes of stretching he pushed open the fire door at the back of the gym and stepped out into the cold. There was no one around. All the children were in lessons, the herd of journalists were at the front of the school and the car park next to the gym was quiet. Eric began with a fast walk over the playground, broke into a jog across the football pitch, sprinted out of the back gate and into the tree covered park.

There were many paths through the park. The main one led gently down to the river beside a trickling stream and was covered in crumbling tarmac. This was the path Mr Tait would have taken. Eric followed it at first, skipping over pot holes and jumping over larger cracks as he went. After a few hundred metres a thin, well-trodden path appeared on his right. Hanging branches provided a canopy over it but they were too low for adults to go under. Eric ran down this path. The mud was hard and easier to run on than the tarmac. Within a few minutes the main route was out of sight and all he was surrounded by were bare trees. For the first time in over a week he felt free and happy. There were no journalists, no photographers and no one to bother him. Eric now understood why his father had been so keen to protect their privacy and for the first time appreciated his father's decision.

At one point he heard his classmates but fortunately he didn't see them. This was the first time he had ever skipped school and did not want to get caught before he had actually taken full advantage of it by treating himself to something. As he neared the river he sensed that Ursula had spotted he was missing. Her initial fears soon passed and her concentration turned away from Eric.

The park would have ended right on the Vltava river if a four lane road and tramline had not been built there instead. Eric crossed the road and waited at the tram stop. A thin layer of sweat covered his face and his cheeks were rosy from the run. A plan of action had formed in his mind. He was now officially skiving and as he was in trouble anyway he wanted to do something to deserve a punishment. With this in mind he decided to go into the city centre, lose himself amongst the thousands of tourists and buy an ice cream at the best ice cream shop in Prague.

A red and white tram soon arrived and he got on. All the seats were taken by elderly people and other adults were clinging on to the hand rails. Faced with no choice Eric decided to tram surf all the way to the Old Town area of Prague.

Old Town square was bursting with tourists. Hundreds stood by the six hundred year old astronomical clock, waiting for the skeleton to strike four o'clock and the apostles to move. Big groups of Japanese lined up in an orderly manner to take photos of the twin towered Tyn church, numerous school groups stared dutifully at the architecture and other tourists just hung around taking in the atmosphere as the sun set.

Getting lost amongst the tourists was easy, but escaping them was almost as hard as getting away from the reporters. Fortunately Eric knew his way around the smaller, cobbled streets and alleys well. There were always less tourists on them and he was soon at his favourite ice cream shop.

A bell jingled as Eric pushed the old door open. In front of him, glistening like a frozen paint palette, was a white counter jammed full of tubs of freshly made ice cream. Forest fruits, pistachio, mint, caramel, banana and more fought for Eric's attention. In truth he wanted them all; however, after much deliberation he chose chocolate and coconut. The young lady behind the counter skillfully balanced his two scoops on top of a wafer cone and Eric paid his money.

Outside the shop it was almost dark. The sun had not quite set but the closely packed old buildings reduced the fading light in the narrow lanes. A group of Italian tourists had noisily gathered in front of the shop, gesticulating wildly. Fearing that one of them may accidently knock his ice cream, Eric cut through them and walked happily into a cobbled alley between two old hotels.

The alley was thankfully free of tourists. There were no shops on it, no cafes and no street entertainers. It was empty except for an old street lamp which cast weak light over the peeling walls.

Eric stood against the cold metal of the lamp and admired his creation. Despite the short walk it had not melted and still looked as delicious as when it was served to him. As he brought the cone towards his mouth someone bumped sharply into his back. The ice cream was sent spiraling into the air and landed with a splat on the cobbles.

"I'm sorry," apologized the man in English. "I was in a rush and didn't look where I was going."

Eric did not look at him. His eyes were fixed on the messy pile that was his ice cream. At that moment it was all he wanted and all he needed. Everything else had been lost to him. Even though he knew it was only an ice cream, and in spite of himself, his eyes welled up with tears.

"As I said, I'm really sorry, it was my fault. Please don't cry, I'll give you the money to buy another one. How much was it?"

Through sniffles Eric told him the price and the man rummaged through his pockets.

"Here you are, and a bit extra," said the man and Eric blindly held out his hand to receive the money.

Without warning, strong fingers gripped Eric's wrist and a needle painfully pierced his vein. He tried to shake free but it was no use. He was held tightly until the syringe was empty.

The world around Eric became muffled, he felt dizzy and couldn't focus. The last thing he saw was the red splodge of a cap on the man's cloudy head and then he passed out. Before Eric hit the cobbles the man caught hold of his arms, slung him on his back and walked away calmly. Apart from two grey rats feasting on Eric's ice cream the alley was deserted again.

"Is he okay?" Andrea calmly asked Ursula as they drove home.

"Yes, he's fine."

"How do you know this?"

Ursula thought long and hard before replying. "I don't know, I just kind of feel it."

"And you are sure he is fine?"

"Yes, I'm su..." Ursula stopped. "No, something's wrong."

20

WHO ARE YOU?

A low rumble like a minor earthquake woke Eric and then faded away. He had no idea what time it was or where he was. The only thing he did know was that his head hurt. It hurt a lot. It hurt as if someone was using it for a drum solo. At least wherever he lay was now quiet. Very, very quiet. With his ears not needing to work and his eyes closed, his nose was working overtime. Unfortunately, wherever he was smelled damp and musty. The smells forced their way up Eric's nostrils and made him feel sick. Cautiously he opened his eyes but the bright glare from a nearby light made his head even worse. He closed them again quickly and let out a dull groan.

Where was he? He tried to establish what he already knew. He was under a blanket and curled up in the foetal position. Neither his hands nor feet were bound so he stretched out. By feeling around he worked out that he was on a particularly uncomfortable sofa but without being able to see he couldn't add much to this. Once again he tried to open his eyes but the glare was too much and he had to close them.

From behind his head he heard footsteps. They sounded hollow, as if the floor underneath was empty.

"Are you okay or still feeling as if you have been in a boxing match?" asked the same voice from the alley.

The man's English was perfect but had a slight accent. Eric could not say whether he sounded slightly American, Russian or north European but he definitely was not

English. He sounded concerned but Eric remembered that he had also sounded concerned in the alley way. So concerned, in fact, that he had stabbed him with a needle and drugged him unconscious.

"I imagine you've got a thumping headache. I must apologize on that account. It was the lesser of two evils I'm afraid. I was going to use chloroform but I had a change of heart after fears that I may choke you."

"You're very considerate," Eric croaked sarcastically.

"Here, sit up."

Two strong hands gripped Eric under the armpits and lifted him into a sitting position. His head pounded more than ever now that he was vertical.

"Drink this. Within ten minutes you'll feel as good as new," and a mug of fizzing liquid was placed in Eric's hand.

Eric did not move. This man had already drugged him, what was to say that he wouldn't now poison him?

"To be honest I doubt I would drink it if I were in your position either," said the man, as if reading his thoughts, "however you're not bound, nor gagged, nor blindfolded, so I'm hardly going to poison you. Admittedly it is going to taste rather foul but it will get you back on your feet in next to no time. You have lost natural body salts and sugars. This will put them back."

The mug was removed from Eric's hand, he heard the man drink a mouthful and then it was given back. Suspiciously, Eric raised the glass to his mouth. Fizzy bubbles tickled his lips. The liquid tasted both sweet and salty. It also tasted horrible.

"Drink it down, it will help. Honestly," and the man walked away.

Against his better judgment Eric followed the man's advice. Within ten minutes his pounding headache had eased and he was feeling much better.

In the distance he heard a low rumble again. The sofa he was sat on began to vibrate and the rumbling noise filled the room. Eric wasn't certain but he thought it sounded like a metro train had just passed underneath him. Fortunately it had no effect on his much improved head.

Tentatively, he opened his eyes. The light was bright at first but he soon became used to it and looked around. He was not sat on a sofa as he had suspected but on three joined seats with the arms broken off. They were threadbare and looked as if they belonged in a theatre. Resting up against them were Eric's bag and coat. Opposite him were another set of seats and, to his left, a rusty desk lamp sat on an old popcorn maker. It was the only light and the rest of the place was in semi-darkness. Beyond these, Eric could just make out rows of similar seats. They were in a large auditorium and on the back wall, faint light crept through a small rectangular opening.

Eric stood up carefully and his head spun at first. Behind him a tall and wide pleated curtain was draped across an entire wall. It had been made from purple satin but in places moths had feasted to reveal a white background.

"Good stuff, you're up," said the man's voice from the shadow. "Tell me, what do you think of my temporary abode, the Kino Alfa? I admit that as cinemas go its halcyon days are long gone but at least no one bothers me down here."

He emerged from the dark and walked towards Eric. In his hands he was holding what Eric first thought were revolvers but turned out to be two hot dogs. He gave one to Eric, who noticed that the man's fingernails were very bitten.

"I thought you might be peckish," said the man and sat down.

He was dressed in jeans, a tight red T-shirt which emphasized his muscles and a red baseball cap. His face was covered in thick black stubble, peppered with grey, and Eric thought that he looked in his forties. Running across his right cheek, from his mouth to the top of his right ear, was a long pink scar where no hair would grow. However, the most striking features on his face, in contrast to the unpleasant looking scar, were his sky blue eyes. Last year Eric's art teacher had told him that eyes are the windows to the soul. If that was true then Eric felt he was not in danger. For some reason the man also seemed familiar. Eric was sure he had seen him before but he didn't know where or when.

"Who are you?" asked Eric accusingly, in between bites of his hot dog.

"How rude of me. Let me introduce myself. My name is Doctor Alexander Johansen, but you can call me Alex. Most people do."

"What kind of doctor drugs and kidnaps a child?" demanded Eric, spraying bits of sausage over the floor.

Dr. Johansen moved forward in his chair. "If you would allow me to correct you? Firstly, I am not a doctor of medicine. Secondly, I have not, I can assure you, kidnapped you. You are here for your own protection. I am protecting you. Consider me your guardian angel."

Eric looked for the nearest exit. "Protecting me? I don't think so! Well, if you are not kidnapping me I'll go. I can look after myself thank you very much."

Without looking back Eric stood up, jumped off the stage and made his way, in the dark, to an exit at the rear of the cinema.

Dr. Johansen watched him leave but before Eric reached the door he shouted after him, "Let me ask you one simple question Eric Meyer, who has just turned twelve but actually his birth date is incorrect. What kind of fool leaves the safety of his home and school when he knows, and has been told, that he is in mortal danger?"

Eric stopped dead in his tracks beside Row J. He did not like being insulted and shouted back, "I am not a fool!"

"Then come back here and let me tell you the truth about your past," suggested Dr. Johansen, biting his nails.

Slowly, Eric looked from Dr. Johansen to the exit and back again. Part of him badly wanted to leave and be back with Andrea and even with Ursula. However another part of him was intrigued by what Dr. Johansen had said. Confident that he could outrun this man, Eric walked back towards the cinema screen and sat down opposite Dr. Johansen.

All the screens in Agent Hoover's viewing room were focused on Prague. Every few seconds he scanned the countless LCD displays but without any success. The room stunk of cigarettes and behind him Agent Angel lit yet another one. He had been pacing and chain smoking since his arrival, one cigarette after another after another after another. The smoke was becoming unbearable for Hoover, who could not leave his swivel chair. In the corner, at the rear of the room, a sinewy figure breathed in the cigarette smoke contentedly.

"It's been four hours now. Why can't we find him?" Agent Angel's voice was calm which, in Agent Hoover's experience, was not a good thing. It was like the lull before a storm.

"Geez, I can't answer that, Sir," replied Agent Hoover. "We had him and then BAM! The kid just vanished."

"Status report from the elementary school," ordered Agent Angel breathing out more smoke.

Without turning from the screens Agent Hoover answered, "Agents Alpha and Beta have checked it out. It's clear. The kid ain't there."

"The house?"

"Agents Gamma and Delta report nothing, Sir. It's clear."

"In that case, have you gathered any intelligence on the Elf and the Street Kid?"

He pointed a sausage sized finger to the displays covering the right side of the wall. Three photos covered seventy five screens. Underneath the words 'suspects' were a photo of Andrea behind the wheel of the Range Rover and another one of Ursula in the playground. Below them, and imprinted with the words 'TARGET', was the polaroid shot of Eric taken at the Benjamins.

"Nothing to report," replied Agent Hoover after checking his computer.

"Nothing to report! How can there be nothing? We control the internet and can access any database on the planet but we can't find a damn thing on this Elf and street kid! Have you accessed the school records?"

"We're trying to, Sir, but the encryption code they use is proving mighty hard for our boys to crack," Agent Hoover did not like giving his boss bad news so added, "But Agent Beta heard another kid call the black girl 'Ursula'."

Raising his hands in the air in mock prayer, Agent Angel said sarcastically, "Well thank the Lord." As he brought them down he smacked Agent Hoover hard on the back of his head and ordered, "Status report on the town!"

"Agents Ypsilon and Zeta have finished an in depth search of the area outside the ice cream store, where we saw the kid last, but have nothing to report.

"Damn!" roared Agent Angel. "We were so close. He was in our grasp."

The dinner table felt strange without Eric, thought Ursula. Admittedly they had not had many civil meals there together but it was still strange without him. Things had improved between them since the Christmas holiday and they both recognized that.

Andrea had not said anything since they arrived home and disappeared until dinner. While Ursula ate, Andrea sat thinking. Only when Ursula had almost finished did she break the silence.

"Do you feel anything from Eric now?" she asked.

"Not really," replied Ursula, her mind preoccupied with

the vegetable pizza she was eating.

"Stop eating, please, and concentrate."

Ursula did as she was told and tried to focus on Eric. At first there was nothing, but gradually she started to feel something. It wasn't positive but neither was it negative.

"He's okay," she paused and focused more. "He's confused but okay."

"Good. Eat all your food, you will need it. After dinner you are going to find Eric."

Ursula swallowed the piece of pizza she had just put in her mouth and tried not to choke. "Me? How am I going to find him? I don't know where he is."

"Yes you do," corrected Andrea and touching Ursula's head said, "all you have to do is use this."

The cinema was not warm. Eric put his coat back on but Dr. Johansen seemed to be quite content in just his T-shirt.

"So, what are you going to tell me?" asked Eric irritably.

"All in good time, but first I need to prepare you."

"You're not going to inject me again!"

Dr. Johansen smiled. "No, no, no. I need to prepare you mentally."

"And you're not going to hypnotize me either," Eric replied quickly.

"If you would just hold your tongue for a second it would give me the opportunity to explain."

Eric said nothing. He was not used to being told to be quiet by a stranger.

"Thank you. I know that you are a clever boy but I doubt you have learnt what I am about to tell you. As far as I know Psychology is not a subject which many schools teach. At least, not at your age Eric. Psychologists have a concept called 'self'. This was first proposed by a Viennese psychologist called Heinz Kohut. Self is 'who' or 'what you are'. Your 'self' is shaped by your experiences and the people around you - your family, teachers and friends for instance."

Eric felt that Dr. Johansen was either very clever or was just pretending to be very clever.

"As you grow older your sense of self will change. For example, from a baby to a child, a child to a teenager and so on. The best definition I have read was from a lady called Hazel Siromani who said, 'self is a process of uncovering, discovering and rediscovering different layers to reach the core of your very being.' Normally this happens over an entire life time and the process of discovery is a gradual one. Are you with me so far?"

Eric looked as if he was being patronized, "Yes. We are who we are because of the people around us and what we find about ourselves by doing things. That's hardly rocket science."

"I agree, rocket science is a completely different kettle of fish and we may get onto that later." Dr. Johansen paused and thought about what to say next. Even though he had given this moment much thought it still worried him. "To cut a long story short Eric, you are not who you think you are and you're about to discover some layers that will change your view of yourself. Quite heavy stuff for a twelve year old. Are you sure you want me to continue?"

Eric nodded, he was becoming bored with Dr. Johansen's monologue.

"In that case, let us begin with your name. Originally your name was not Eric and you were sadly devoid of any surname. You were simply called 'Adam'."

Eric felt himself beginning to smile at this absurd comment and raised this hand to cover his mouth.

"Your birthday is also completely wrong because, odd though it may sound, you don't actually have one."

Behind his hand Eric tried to hold back a laugh but failed. Dr. Johansen could not help but notice and stared at Eric while biting his fingernails.

"It is unfortunate that you find this amusing. I am not

being frivolous with my comments. This is not a game. Do you think it was a game for the agency that killed the couple you called your parents?"

"Who killed my parents?" asked Eric, the smile instantly wiped from his face. He wanted to lash out at this crazy man in front of him. "What's that got to do with anything?"

"I'll tell you," Dr. Johansen leant forward and stared intently into Eric's eyes, "the same people who killed mine. And you are looking at one of the very few people on the planet who knows more than diddly squat about them." Now that he had Eric's full, undivided attention, he continued. "They are an American government organization called the OSS. An organization which, officially at least, has ceased to exist for over sixty years. I know this for many reasons but probably of the most interest to you right now is that I have been one of their main targets for about ten years, even though I doubt they have ever seen my face." He ran a finger subconsciously down his scar, almost caressing it. "But now, alas, I am no longer one of their most wanted. They are more interested in someone else and that is why you are here. They are after you and I cannot allow them to reach you."

Hidden behind parked cars, on a road outside the Meyer villa, a shadow whispered, "This is Agent Gamma, suspects are leaving the villa. We are in pursuit."

Once Ursula had her seat belt on, Andrea sped off. The Range Rover kicked up pebbles on the driveway and left two deep tracks. It accelerated on to the tightly packed streets and towards the centre of the town. From underneath a broken street lamp two black motorbikes powerfully roared into life and followed. Andrea spotted them on Peace Square, as she drove around the tall brick church. There was nowhere for the motorbikes to hide. The road was empty and as she slowed to let a tram rattle past they appeared in each of her wing mirrors, stalking like vultures near a wounded animal.

"Where are we going Ursula?" There was no urgency in Andrea's voice.

In the back of the car Ursula had her head down and her mind was focused solely on Eric.

"That way," she said and, without looking up, pointed to the right.

Andrea looked in her mirror and followed the way Ursula was pointing. She continued to follow her directions until they reached Wenceslas Square.

The long square was busy with people despite the late hour. Bright shop fronts lit up people's faces as they swayed towards clubs and bars. They were moving quickly in the cold and were keen to be back inside as the light snow had turned to drizzle.

Andrea drove round the square twice but Ursula was confused. They decided to try on foot instead and parked in a side road.

Underground nightclubs with loud music stretched out along the street where they parked. After getting out of the car, Ursula found it hard to concentrate. Big groups of Englishmen, swearing loudly and fighting amongst themselves, waited outside club entrances until scary looking bouncers let them in. Andrea put a protective arm around Ursula, who had dropped her head again, and led her the short walk onto Wenceslas Square.

Sitting at the top of the square, like a judge overlooking the courtroom, was a grand museum and guarding it a statue of King Wenceslas on his horse. Unlike the tourists, Ursula and Andrea moved away from them. Fifty metres behind them, the two Agents followed.

Half-way down the square Ursula felt Eric's presence become stronger. Beside a shop selling crystal she walked into a wide passageway and away from the square. Then, next to a milliners, full to the brim with expensive ladies' hats, Ursula stopped and lifted her head. As she looked she saw a shop packed with stamps and, nearby, the silhouettes of two men in the passageway's entrance.

They began to walk toward them and came into the light. Both were in black leather, similar to Andrea, and both were still wearing their black helmets.

"I'm sorry Andrea, I can't do this," Ursula said, bowing her head again.

Andrea did not reply. She put her arm around Ursula and led her away from the two men, past the sealed up entrance to Kino Alfa and out of the passageway's far exit.

"You look as if you've had a turn. What is it?" asked Dr. Johansen with concern in his voice.

Eric had turned pale and it took him a while to reply. "A warning."

"A warning! What kind of warning? There's no one here."

Eric explained, pointing to his head as he did so, "I sometimes know what Ursula is thinking and she is afraid."

This answer did not help Dr. Johansen feel any less confused. "Who is Ursula?"

"She's my Parent's Pet Project. They published a puzzle that was meant to be difficult, but I didn't think so, in the world's newspapers. She solved it and left Paris to join me in Prague. She claimed that she did it in less time than me but I don't believe her."

Dr. Johansen leant back on his seat and pulled his fingers to his mouth. His face was pained and he began to bite his nails again while staring straight through Eric.

Removing his fingers briefly from his mouth he asked, "This Ursula whom you talk about. If I were to meet her I imagine I would find someone who is about your age, possibly a very close birthday and… the same skin colour as you?"

"No," replied Eric, "I think her family were originally from Africa."

The seat creaked as Dr. Johansen flung himself back into it. His teeth were chattering over his fingernails like a typewriter. He looked consumed by worry and almost desperate.

Abruptly, he stopped. "Unfortunately, like attracts like and fate has conspired against us. We need to get back into your villa without being seen. Pick up your things, it is time to leave."

Dr. Johansen drove his black Chrysler into a street far away from Eric's villa. The road was empty of people but so full of parked cars that they could not find a parking space. By the time they found one it was way past midnight but at least they knew they had not been followed.

The night was very dark. Heavy clouds blocked out the moon and the stars. Apart from the rumble of the occasional train the area was silent.

"Is there a way into your villa which cunningly avoids going through the front door?" asked Dr. Johansen, as they stepped onto the cobbled pavement and the freezing puddles left by the melting snow.

Looking around himself Eric tried to work out where he was. The buildings looking down on them were all over one hundred years old. Some had towers, others had gables and none were the same. Eric was not sure where he was until he saw a small square, with a lonely tree, at the top of the road. Without answering the question he walked off in that direction. Dr. Johansen followed him. His eyes flitted between Eric and dark corners where somebody following them could easily hide. If Eric wanted to escape this would be the perfect time, but he didn't. His kidnapper now wanted to break into the Meyer villa to see Ursula and, though he wouldn't admit it, breaking into his own home fascinated him. At a large white gate under an unstable looking arch, Eric stopped.

"Behind here is a park," said Eric, his breath visible in the cold night. "If we get into the park we can make our way to the vineyard fence, climb over it, get into the villa's vineyard and then onto the terrace. From there we can get into the villa through the gardener's entrance. It's covered in ivy and well hidden. We can get in there."

Eric moved away from the gate to a wall in need of repair. Before Eric could climb up, Dr. Johansen pulled him under a street light. His face was yellow and strained under the light.

"When we have scaled this wall, lead the way but do so silently. If I tap you on the shoulder you must freeze instantly. The villa is under surveillance but currently the OSS don't think you are there which, in many ways, makes it the perfect place to be. That is, if we remain hidden as we enter. It would be prudent to keep them in the dark by staying in the dark."

Eric did not like being ordered and shook himself away from Dr. Johansen. "I don't know you but I do know where I am. You had better keep up with me because I won't wait for you. And, for your information, since my parents were killed the whole world has been watching me so it is hardly something new for me."

With that said he turned away and looked at the wall. Many bricks were missing, or were chipped, and it looked like a badly painted chess board. Seeking out his first handhold he approached the wall, found it and scaled the three metres of brick like a spider. In a few seconds he was on the other side. Dr. Johansen was beside him in an instant.

On the road side of the wall the street light had bathed everything in yellow light. On the park side there was no light and Eric and Dr. Johansen were plunged into darkness. Their eyes slowly adjusted and what they could see, which was not much, was in various shades of grey. The path they stood on was light grey, the trees grey and, beyond the vineyard, the villa was silhouetted black against the dark grey sky. Below them, in the opposite direction, a long train rumbled by.

Eric ran off through the trees and bushes towards the vineyard. He could not see well but managed to duck and swerve around all the branches that blocked his way. Behind him Dr. Johansen painfully hit most of them. Just as Eric reached the wire fence around the vineyard, Dr. Johansen placed his hand strongly on Eric's shoulder and pulled him down into a crouch. Eric's shook the hand off but before he had a chance to say anything Dr. Johansen placed his hand over Eric's mouth and pointed to below the villa.

Supporting the terrace and at the top of the vineyard was a high wall. Eric looked along it but stopped when he reached the centre. Leading majestically from the vineyard to the terrace were two diagonal staircases, and hidden beside the last step were two figures. They were almost invisible and would not have been seen from the villa's windows or from the terrace. They were a little over two hundred metres from where Eric and Dr. Johansen were hiding. Eric wrote the letters O, S and S in the air, Dr. Johansen nodded. The two agents were moving their heads in wide arcs, obviously checking the area. Before they looked in Eric's direction Dr. Johansen dropped down onto his belly. Eric copied him.

The ground was cold, hard and in places there were still snow. Moving like snakes they approached the wire fence and moved along it until they found a place where it was not touching the earth. Without making a noise Dr. Johansen lifted the wire fence upwards for them to crawl under. When he let go it curled back down. He tried again but the same thing happened. He tried lifting it higher but the fence was attached to metal poles and would not move further.

Dr. Johansen considered his options. To make a gap big enough for them both to get under would mean ripping the fence from its posts. This would be noisy and would attract unwanted attention. If they attempted to climb over it instead they would be seen by the OSS agents but, looking along the fence, there were no other ways in.

The silence was broken by a train screeching to a halt.

Immediately Dr. Johansen yanked the fence upwards. It shook and rattled but the train covered the noise. The resulting gap was big enough for them both to slide through and by the time the train had finished braking they were in the vineyard.

Eric stopped moving when he reached the end of a row of vines. He looked towards the men. They had gone. From behind Dr. Johansen tapped him on the leg. He was clearly agitated and urgently motioned Eric to lead on. Once again Eric scanned the area around. The men were nowhere to be seen. The terrace overlooking the vineyard was empty, there was no one against the walls below it and the staircases, where they were heading, were free.

Raising himself onto all fours, Eric scampered off like a monkey, with Dr. Johansen close behind. He was just reaching the other end of the row when two large figures stepped out in front of him. Instantly, Eric stopped, fell onto his belly and rolled into a shallow ditch under the vines, scratching himself as he did so. His trousers started to feel wet and then freezing water pinched at his skin. The cold crept up his body, daring him to shout out in shock but he clamped his lips tightly shut.

"Where was it?" asked a man with a rough New York accent.

"Down by the fence," replied his buddy. "Definite movement."

"Probably two kids making out."

"Yeah, probably, but we better check it out. And stay low. We can't be seen, this is still a covert operation remember."

"You don't have to remind me of protocol," replied the New Yorker, sounding slightly annoyed. "Come on, let's go." Despite their body size, the men's footsteps were as light as children's as they walked away.

When he could no longer hear them Eric rolled out of the ditch and quickly crawled towards the staircase. His teeth were chattering and his legs stung from the cold.

At the bottom of the two marble staircases Dr. Johansen motioned Eric to stop and remove his shoes and socks. Their bare feet made no noise as they bounded up each step but the polished stone was bitterly cold and chilled their feet to the bone. They didn't stop moving until they had sprinted across the open terrace and were hidden behind the ivy clinging to the villa. Next to a solid wooden door was a pair of old wellies. Eric reached inside one, pulled out a key and used it to let them both into a pitch black room.

The room smelt of earth, fertilizer and fermented wine. Dr. Johansen closed the door behind them and Eric felt around in the dark, trying to find a light switch. Suddenly a cold hand covered his mouth and gripped him tightly. Metal brushed against his cheek and he felt a gun.

A few seconds later the light sparked on to reveal a small windowless room with garden equipment lining the walls like weapons and bags of fertilizer piled on the floor amongst the demijohns.

"Well done, that's much better," said Dr. Johansen, as he fiddled with the door's lock, his back to Eric.

But Eric could not reply and his eyes were fixed on the small firearm pointing towards the door.

"What's up? The cat got your tongue? It's time to rejoice. We made it," and he turned around. His mouth fell open like a fish and his eyes widened. At the same time Eric was released and the gun fell limp.

"Hello Andrea," greeted Dr. Johansen.

"Alexander," replied Andrea and she almost sounded surprised.

21

PROFESSOR LARSEN'S STORY

"You know each other?" asked Eric, not believing what he was hearing. He jumped away from Andrea as if she had suddenly given him an electric shock. Andrea and Dr. Johansen nodded.

"And you knew he was going to kipnap me?" asked Eric, pointing accusingly between the two of them.

His jeans were sodden and he was shivering as he spoke, both from the cold and from anger. He felt betrayed.

"I have not spoken to Alexander in thirteen years, five months and eighteen days," replied Andrea, putting the gun in her pocket.

"We had lost contact," added Dr. Johansen, a little too quickly for Eric's liking.

"I'm not surprised," said Eric to Dr. Johansen. "You're mad and Andrea's the sanest person I know."

He turned to Andrea, "You should have heard the things he told me. He's a crazy man."

"Go and get changed and meet us in the lounge," Andrea replied. "I'll make you a hot chocolate."

The lounge was decorated in keeping with the age of the building. Landscape paintings hung on the emerald green walls and a faded Persian rug covered most of the floor. Around the rug were three Edwardian leather sofas and in the centre of it a mahogany coffee table, upon which was a steaming mug of hot chocolate.

Ten minutes later Eric entered through the heavy door,

looking less tense than he had been in the gardener's storeroom. He had changed into his cotton pyjamas and a white dressing gown. He stood in the doorway, looking in, and trying to understand the relationship between Andrea and Dr. Johansen. They were sat on one of the sofas talking. At one end was Dr. Johansen, his face switching between excitement and fear as he spoke. Andrea sat at the other end, just listening and without any signs of emotion.

Eric walked sleepily across the rug towards the coffee table. He was enjoying the soft feel of the threads between his toes. He took his mug in two hands, shot a displeased glance at the adults and lay down on the sofa opposite them.

"It is very late, Eric," Andrea began, "I would like you to drink your hot chocolate and then go to bed."

"I'm not tired," answered Eric, between yawns, "I want to hear him tell you what he has told me." He lifted a finger from the mug and pointed it angrily at Dr. Johansen.

"There's no need," Andrea replied calmly. "I already know what Alexander has told you. You do not need to worry about it now."

"How do you know?" asked Eric slowly, fighting to keep his eyes open while yawning.

Before she could explain, Eric was fast asleep. The mug resting on his chest rocked gently up and down as he breathed.

The next morning Eric woke up to find himself back in his own bed and Ursula sat on the boxing glove bean bag watching him.

"What are you doing here?" he asked sharply.

"I was worried about you and you've got more white hair so I think I was right to worry," replied Ursula, bringing her knees up to her chin.

She was wearing her favourite ripped jeans and the new hoodie she had received in Paris. Even though she was the same height as Eric, he felt that she looked smaller this morning. Worry has shrunk her, he thought.

Eric regretted being so sharp with her and tried to make up for it. He had never known another child to worry about him before. Perhaps this is what friends do, he thought.

"I'm fine thanks, how are you?" he asked politely.

Ursula uncurled herself on hearing these words, grew to her full size and bounced up on to the end of Eric's bed. "I don't know really. I guess I feel confused... and excited... and worried."

"Er, why?" Eric was not used to conversation in his bedroom in the morning, it was not something that happened that much.

"I knew where you were last night. You were in the Kino Alfa, the old cinema, weren't you?"

Eric nodded.

"And I knew you were sort of okay until you left and then I started to worry about you and then I fell asleep."

"So?"

"So? We can read each other minds. Can't you see?"

Yawning, Eric thought about it and replied, "Yesterday when I escaped from school you were worried about me then, weren't you?"

"Yes."

"But then I tried to send you a good thought and you felt okay then."

Ursula smiled.

"And is this why you are excited and confused?"

"Yes," replied Ursula still smiling.

"So, why are you worried?"

The smile disappeared from Ursula's face in a flash, "Because I can't find Andrea. I haven't seen her all morning."

It was like a rocket had gone off beneath Eric and he exploded out of bed. The duvet, other bed covers and pillows flew to all corners of the room. He grabbed a pair of jeans, pulled them on, put on a T-shirt, and headed for the door.

Under his breath he was muttering, "I should never have let him in. I should have never have let him in."

The two of them went first to Andrea's room. It was empty and looked as if it hadn't been used, which was not that unusual. They then searched the other rooms on their floor of the villa but they were also all empty, so they went down to the lounge. Apart from Eric's mug, left on the coffee table, there was no sign that anyone had been there. The kitchen was also empty but, on entering the pantry, they discovered the cellar door open.

Strolling forward, Ursula looked down the dark passageway, but Eric stood well back. Beads of perspiration were forming on his brow and he was nervously moving jars of jam on a shelf.

"There's a light at the end coming through a half open door. If we run down the corridor we can reach it in only a few seconds. I'll go first and then all you have to do is look at me," suggested Ursula.

For a moment Eric did not move but then the thought of losing Andrea overcame him and he placed his hands on Ursula's shoulders. "Let's go," he whispered in her ear.

They sprinted down the dark passageway. When they reached the door Ursula opened it fully and they stepped cautiously into the room beyond.

They stood on a very high platform at the top of a cave. Beside them was a rock face and coming out from it were steps leading down. Each one was a piece of rock and, even though they all had flat tops, none were the same size or shape. In front of them, hanging from the rock ceiling, was a circular floodlight which bathed the floor in bright light. All the other sides in the room were covered, if not entirely, in walls made from terracotta brick. The walls curved dangerously over rounded rocks faces and looked very unstable.

The floor of the large room looked like polished marble and was covered with piles of strange looking objects. Some were as small as a mobile phone and others were as big as a car. Some looked like guns and others like hairdryers. Many looked like rockets, a few looked like vehicles, but most looked like junk. There were so many it was hard to take them all in.

Step by step, as quietly as they could, Eric and Ursula descended the rock staircase. A dull whirring noise, barely noticeable at first, became slightly louder with each step they took. By the time they reached the floor it was the same volume as a car engine ticking over. Away from the stairs and behind the scattered objects was a doorway in the brick work. The noise was coming from behind the doors.

They tip-toed through the objects and into another room with brick walls. It was much smaller than the first one, about the size of an average kitchen. One side of it was taken up with two large screens, nine smaller ones and a computer the size of six fridge freezers. Lights flashed behind glass doors, metres of multi-coloured cables joined up countless circuit boards and six fans whirred noisily, keeping everything else cool.

Standing in front of the computer, staring at one of the large screens, were Andrea and Dr. Johansen. They were watching the flickering image of a grey haired lady.

Falsely, Eric coughed, something he had inherited from his father, and the two adults turned around. Dark bags were visible under Dr. Johansen's eyes and both he and Andrea were wearing the same clothes as the previous evening.

"Good, you are up," said Andrea and paused the image on the screen.

She turned to Dr. Johansen and pointed towards Ursula, "Alexander, this is..."

His tired eyes lit up and he put out his hand. "Ev..."

"Ursula," said Ursula, talking over him.

"Of course. Ursula," he said her name slowly as if each syllable was new to him. "A very real pleasure to make your acquaintance."

Eric stepped between them and nodded towards the screen, "Who is that?"

Neither Andrea nor Dr. Johansen spoke and instead looked from one to the other. Eric recognized this behaviour from his parents. They did it when they wanted to avoid telling him something.

"Telling them is against my instructions," Andrea told Dr. Johansen.

"I think we have debated it enough," he replied seriously. "It is best that they find it all out now. From what you have told me it is obvious that they have started to piece together some of their story already."

In the corner of the room were two swivel chairs. Dr. Johansen fetched them both, placed them in front of the screen and beckoned the children to sit down.

"This will answer your question," Andrea said and pressed play.

Eric and Ursula sat down silently. Each could feel the other's worry as well as their own.

Black and white lines criss-crossed the screen and replaced the woman. They flickered some more and then the woman appeared and began to speak. She looked to be in her seventies or eighties. Her hair was silver and tied back neatly away from her face, which was covered in smooth wrinkles. Her eyes were her most striking feature, they were sky blue and as bright as a child's.

When she spoke she did not rush, as if each word brought a new thought into her mind or awoke a distant memory. Even though she looked content and peaceful she also seemed sad and tired.

"This is disc one of four. Both pods contain identical discs. Disc one is a history, an autobiography if you like. Disc two details my research with supportive data. Disc three explains how I spliced together DNA, the building blocks of life. And Disc four goes into depth about how I created life."

Andrea stepped forward and pressed pause. "There are actually five Compact Discs, Professor Larsen added another after this. However the fifth was corrupted and I cannot get it to work no matter what I try." She pressed play again and stepped back.

The grey haired lady continued her story. "It is of the most urgent importance that none of these discs fall into the wrong hands. It would be better for the world if they were destroyed than for this to happen. I do not choose my words lightly.

"My name is not Professor Larsen but that is what I am known as. For reasons that will become clearer later I had to change it for my own protection. From the late nineteen forties through to the early sixties I worked at a top secret military base in the USA with my husband. We were in charge of dissecting an alien craft and using its technology to further our own. At first we worked closely together but in 1961, with the craft's possibilities exhausted, we were handed separate assignments. Mine was in the relatively new field of cybernetics and artificial intelligence. In simple terms, I was given the job of creating the world's first robot using the alien technology. My husband was moved into the field of biology and physiology.

"We were government scientists and sworn to secrecy. For this reason we never discussed our work in our own quarters, or anywhere else for that matter."

She paused and ran her fingers over her hair until she was happy that it was still in place. For a moment her eyes lost their shine and became vacant, as if something inside her had died, and then she continued.

"One morning in 1966 I felt sick and did not go into the lab. By the afternoon I felt much better and decided to busy myself at home by tidying our quarters. After finishing every other room I decided to clean my husband's study, a room I rarely went into. Unlike me he always brought his work home. It was what he lived for and what eventually took his life away. On top of his desk was a file marked 'OPERATION MULATTO. TOP SECRET'. Curiosity got the better of me and I sat down to read it. The documents detailed plans to create a separate and superior race of beings who would, initially at least, be soldiers. They would be fitter, stronger, smarter and able to communicate between themselves without words if necessary. To build such an army they were experimenting with joining together alien/human DNA to create Identical Hybrid Beings or IHBs. I simply called them Hybrids. I was shocked and appalled. It went against everything I believed in but, as I was not meant to see these files, I said nothing.

"Two or three days later my husband brought his Director back for dinner. After a few bourbons had loosened his tongue, the Director talked at length about his vision for the future. A future in which the USA was the only global superpower, unchallenged by the rest of the world, with its own superior army. I looked over at my husband. He had drunk too much and his eyes had glazed over.

"After the Director left I quizzed my husband on what had been said about superior power. His eyes were animated, sparkling even, and after another glass of bourbon, he probably said much more than he meant to. I still remember his words to this day. 'Imagine a world where everyone is fitter, stronger, healthier, cleverer and no one is different. No poor people, no sick people, no needy people. A new era. Isn't that something to aim for, a leap forward in human evolution orchestrated by science.'

"Maybe I should have said something there and then but, regrettably, I said nothing. Fear held my tongue. I couldn't say a word. I didn't see a new era. I saw a catastrophe for humankind. Evolution takes millions of years. To mess with it in this way was against the very meaning of life. We evolved until we could breathe on land, we evolved thumbs until we could pick up objects and use tools, we evolved an advanced brain until we ruled the planet and we all evolved differently. No two humans are the same, not even twins, and it is this difference that makes us human and keeps us advancing or evolving. A race of Hybrids who are all identical would not be a step forward in evolution. It would be a step backwards. If they succeeded in creating an army of genetically engineered soldiers what would be next? Who is to say that it would stop there? Would they then create different hybrids to fill different roles? Hybrid police or scientists or fruit pickers or accountants, each of them with a life mapped out for them before they are even born. It would be like Aldous Huxley's Brave New World."

She stopped talking, closed her eyes and took a deep breath. When she opened them again she pulled a metallic bag from off camera. A clear tube protruded from one end and she placed this in her mouth. After a few gulps she let go of the bag. Slowly it floated away.

"I'm sorry. I am preaching and speculating. Speculation is guesswork, it is not Science. I will return to my story and the facts." She paused and looked apologetic. "It was at this time that I discovered I was pregnant. I wanted to bring up a child in a world full of diversity and colour. Not a world dominated by one global power and full of Hybrids. My next actions were not thought out, each was impulsive and each act led to the next. I began a chain of events which, once started, I was unable to stop.

"I had been feeling unwell for a while and one evening I used this to my advantage. We had already agreed that I would leave the base for a few days to recover and had been granted permission by Major Marshall by the two days previously. The evening before I was going to leave I packed one suitcase with my essential belongings and alien DNA I had taken from the labs. I had a second suitcase which I filled with explosives I had stolen from the stores that afternoon. I told Major Marshall I had to leave early and needed to say goodbye to my husband. Major Marshall was extremely busy but he was also understanding, and even drove me by jeep to the old hangar. The time was just after six when I arrived and I had made my husband promise to leave before this. The underground lab was empty and I quickly placed explosives set the timer and left. Fortunately Major Marshall had not waited for me so I walked out of the old hangar and into the dessert away from the base. I never returned and never saw my husband again.

"Only twenty years later did I discover, at least to some degree, what had happened that night. The explosion had indeed stopped my husband's work and he was moved from this assignment to creating engines, rockets and missiles instead. At the time I had no way of knowing that I had been successful. A secret explosion, underground, and on a secret base was never going to make the public news.

"For nearly two years I disappeared off the radar. From the USA I travelled to Canada then into Alaska, across the ice into the Soviet Union, down to the Ukraine as it is called now, into Moldova, Romania, Hungary, the then Czechoslovakia and finally fleeing into Austria and Western Europe. Times were harsh, especially after giving birth, but behind the Iron Curtain I was an enemy of the United States of America, with secrets to sell, and this made me a very dear friend of the Soviets.

"As I mentioned I had no way of knowing if my husband's work had been destroyed or not. Eating away at the back of my mind was one thought and one thought alone. What if they were still working towards the creation of their Hybrid army? And if they were, how could they be stopped? Over the following years I debated with myself, almost daily, the best response to these questions. In the end, when I arrived back in the West, I felt I had no choice but to follow a similar course of action myself. If they were to create an identical army of Hybrids to help them take over the planet then I would create two unique humans who could help defend it. Two people who would be made up of the greatest human beings on the planet.

"In justifying this to myself I argued that these two may assist the next stage of human evolution but this would not be for certain. They would not be a leap forward but rather the scientific equivalent of giving evolution a helping hand. If Darwin was right, as I feel he was, nature would decide whether this next stage would live on or die out. The survival of the fittest.

"Over the next few years I collected the genes and DNA from many great and talented people. On days when I was not trying to splice them together I worked on creating a test tube baby. All my research was conducted in complete secrecy. Only two others knew what I was doing but I am one hundred percent certain that they will not share this information with anyone else unless it is essential.

"In the early nineties the person I was running from found me working at the European Space Operations Centre. He wanted me to come back to the USA and, when I refused, I feared for my life. If my visas and travel patterns were to be believed, I vanished into India. In fact I had moved not more than one hundred kilometres away, to a place that was impossible to find on Earth.

"I moved into Space and have been living here, on the European Space Station, for a number of years. Mostly I am alone." She paused, lost in thought. "I refuse to go back to Earth. The European Space Centre tolerate me and my whims because some of my work here provides a large percentage of their funds each year. Truthfully, I know I am an embarrassment to them - a cranky old lady who refuses to come back down to Earth. For this reason my existence is barely mentioned within the centre walls in Germany and never outside. John Glenn travelled into space at the age of 77 and he is applauded as a hero. I travel into space at 78 and I am spoken about in hushed whispers.

"Really, I should be grateful. The peace, solitude, closer proximity to the sun and environment here have allowed me to complete my research and make discoveries I could never have made on Earth."

She stopped talking and stepped out of the camera shot. White plastic walls, covered with faint flashing lights, were revealed. Floating around in front of them and leaking tiny droplets of water was the bag from which she had drunk earlier.

A large white blur filled the screen and then Professor Larsen appeared back in shot. A broad smile had appeared across her face, her eyes were warm and she looked as if she had suddenly blossomed. She placed two small objects far too close to the camera and let go. They were very blurred and all that Eric and Ursula could make out on the screen were two splodges of colour, one blue and one yellow.

"These little wonders are Adam and Eve," she announced proudly.

Gradually the small blobs floated away from the camera and came into focus. They were two smiling babies. One had beautiful ebony skin, black hair and was obviously a girl. The other was a pale boy with blond hair.

Black and white lines filled the screen, the CD stopped and quietly ejected. Written in its centre was a small number one.

Eric and Ursula did not move.

22

TIME FOR SOME EXPLANATIONS

Silence.

No one spoke. No one moved. Even their breathing seemed quieter and only the whirring of the fans could be heard.

Behind Eric and Ursula, Dr. Johansen began to shuffle nervously from one foot to the other. Beside him Andrea stood like a statue, waiting patiently for someone to speak.

One, two, three minutes passed and still not a word was uttered. More time ticked away and the silence became deafening.

Eventually Eric spoke, his voice strong and a little too forceful to be fully believable. "I don't care. Really I don't. This explains a lot and I don't care that they were not my real parents. They were hardly 'real' parents anyway, when they were alive."

"Genetically speaking it is highly probable that they were a fraction of your parents," said Andrea. "Both Mr and Mrs Meyer donated their genes for you and Ursula."

On hearing her name Ursula joined in the conversation. She spoke softly. "Does this mean that they were partly my parents as well?"

"Them and a number of others, yes."

"So is that why I am here? They knew who I was all along."

Dr. Johansen moved so he could face Ursula. His fingers were in his mouth and subconsciously he was biting his nails. He stopped as he began to speak. "I am unable to say with definite certainty as I never had the pleasure of meeting Mr or Mrs Meyer. However, I am almost certain that they knew nothing about you." He turned to face Andrea. "Would you agree with that Andrea?"

"Yes. That is true."

"Nobody on Earth knew of your and Eric's existence, except for Andrea and myself. However, until last night, rather surprisingly, neither of us knew that the other knew. We had both been kept in the dark by Professor Larsen. If there had been any problems on the Space Station or if your safety had been compromised in any way, you were to be sent back to Earth in specially constructed capsules or pods. We each had been given the co-ordinates of one of these pods and assumed that you would travel together. Alas, that was a mistaken assumption."

He paused and fought to keep his fingers away from his mouth. "When the OSS discovered Professor Larsen's whereabouts on the space station, they sent her a well-wrapped present of a guided missile that was almost invisible to radar," the sarcasm in Dr. Johansen's voice was impossible to miss.

"Moments before the Space Station exploded she jettisoned the two of you towards Earth. Andrea set off for her coordinates but when she arrived at the location she found nothing, the cupboard was bare. By analysing the data and comparing it with her knowledge of the explosion, plus a meteor storm around this time, she was able to pinpoint a different location. I had to do the same. Andrea found Eric and I found Ursula. When we each discovered only one of you, we assumed that the other needed, and had to be, located as soon as possible. We have independently spent more than a decade fruitlessly attempting to find you and to retrieve the two missing pods, before the OSS. I located Eric's pod in Romania but I had a run in with the OSS. It was not my first and unfortunately will not be my last." He stroked the scar on his cheek. "Until sixth months ago, when I saw Eric at a gymnastics tournament in Paris, I had assumed that he was dead. Andrea had believed the same to be true of Ursula until luck, or fate, brought her to the Meyer doorstep."

"Do my grandparents know?" asked Ursula, her voice almost cracking.

Dr. Johansen started to chew his fingers again. "Your grandparents know nothing except that they discovered you in a shopping trolley, in a rather grotty underpass in Paris. I had placed you there, Madame Benjamin found you and I walked away."

The moment he had finished Ursula jumped up from her chair and stepped towards the open doorway. "I want to speak to my grandparents."

"Not yet," Dr. Johansen told her, placing a warm hand on her shoulder. "You need time to think about this and I recommend quite strongly that you take your time. Mr and Mrs Benjamin are good people. They have brought you up and taken a great deal of care over you. In all the ways that matter, they are your grandparents. I am wholly convinced that someday, when they felt you were old enough, they had planned to tell you. Let us not upset them and disturb this happy equilibrium just yet. Please sit back down."

Ursula did as she was asked, but only because she had been brought up this way. Andrea joined Dr. Johansen in front of the children.

"On the Compact Disc that you have just been watching Professor Larsen said, 'This is disc one of four. Both pods contain identical discs.' She then continued to say, 'It is of the most urgent importance that none of these discs fall into the wrong hands.' I retrieved all five Compact Discs from Eric's pod, and Eric himself, when I found him. Unfortunately Alexander did not do the same when he found Ursula."

Dr. Johansen opened his mouth to protest but Andrea cut him off before he could say a thing.

"I am not judging you Alexander. Please do not take this personally. I am fully aware that the pods fell at different locations than we had been expecting. I am also aware that you were confronted with problems which I did not face."

Raising his hand, like a child asking to speak, he said, "Most certainly. Eric's pod had the good fortune to land in a field, situated on the edge of a small town in Romania. You were able to work at a leisurely pace and retrieve everything you needed in your own good time. Ursula's pod landed in the middle of one of the most popular tourist destinations in Europe. I did not have the good fortune of time and had to work hastily. I did what I was told to do - I retrieved Ursula. Then, with a great deal of effort, I moved the pod from a rubbish pile, where it had landed, to the edge of a hole a few metres away. I tipped the pod into this hole, and pulled it into an ancient Roman tunnel at the bottom of the hole, and then I covered it over. I had a screaming child, I had to work fast through the night and it was very dark. However, I do still remember where the hole is located and it will not be difficult to find it again."

"As I said, it was unfortunate," repeated Andrea.

Dr. Johansen stepped towards the computer screen. There were four clear cases next to it in a pile, each containing an almost blank looking CD. He picked them up and carefully looked at each one in turn as if searching for something.

"Why is it unfortunate?" asked Eric.

"Because he only took Ursula. He left the five Compact Discs in the pod. As Professor Larsen says, 'It is of the most urgent importance that none of these discs fall into the wrong hands. It would be better for the world if they were destroyed than for this to happen. The wrong hands in this case would be the OSS. We need to retrieve the discs before they do. What is more, none of us have watched disc five yet, and it is probable that this is the most important disc of the five as it is not mentioned on the other four. Andrea's disc five is corrupted."

One by one, Dr. Johansen put the CD cases back down. He sighed deeply as he let go of the last and his shoulders drooped. Reluctantly he turned back round to face the others and smiled falsely.

"Where did you find my pod, Dr. Johansen?" asked Ursula.

"Italy," replied Dr. Johansen, "or to be more precise, in Pompeii."

Eric almost jumped from his seat, "Pompeii? That's a coincidence! Our class trip is to Pompeii."

Dr. Johansen looked at Eric, shook his head and pointed to Andrea.

"That is not a coincidence. The Meyer Foundation are sponsoring the trip. I convinced your late father, Mr Meyer, to do this last summer. Your pods fell to Earth on the night of the 24th December at the same time as an Uroid meteor storm. Between ten and one hundred lumps of rock, from the Ursa Minor system, fell each hour. I did not know how long Ursula's pod took to fall to Earth nor did I know where it was scheduled to land. I had to track down every meteorite that fell over a sixteen hour period in order to find it. Up to June last year I had investigated one thousand and two possible landing sites. Each one contained a meteor and only sixty three percent of these were over ten grams in weight. At this time I discovered the site in Pompeii and I was ninety eight per cent certain it was Ursula's pod. I had organized the funding of the school trip to provide cover for me while I searched for the pod. Since this time Dr. Johansen, has confirmed the pod is there," explained Andrea.

Dr. Johansen cut in, "You could have just picked up the telephone and given me a call."

"I could not. We had been given a clear instruction not to contact each other."

Fixing his eyes on Dr. Johansen, Eric remarked, "I am

pretty sure that kidnapping me, breaking into my house with my help and knowing Andrea was here means you can't really be trusted to follow instructions that well."

Dr. Johansen adjusted his red cap and looked hurt. "Only because I was concerned for your well-being. I could have left you to be killed but I felt compelled to help."

Eric did not know what to say to this and looked at Andrea. "Can I say two things?" He did not wait for an answer, "Firstly I would like to clarify something. All we need to do is find the pod and the five CDs before the OSS does?"

"Yes."

"Secondly, this room is a not very comfortable and the noise of the fans is getting on my nerves. I was wondering if we could move upstairs to the lounge?"

Before they entered the lounge Andrea made them all wait by the oak door. The curtains were open and winter sun shone through the net curtains into the room. At her normal pace she approached the windows and glanced outside. Once satisfied, she drew the flowery curtains tightly shut and beckoned everyone to sit down.

The two adults sat in the same place as the night before, at either end of the leather sofa. Eric sat on the same sofa also but this time he was wide awake and sat upright. His face was tense and it was obvious he was still thinking about everything he had learnt since the previous evening. Ursula sat down on the other sofa, lost in her own thoughts. Her mind was somewhere else, slowly digesting, piece by piece, the news she had just heard.

"What do we do now?" asked Eric, getting to the point immediately.

He leant forward, his eyes glued on Andrea, waiting for a response.

"We retrieve the pod and the CDs," answered Dr. Johansen. "This is unfortunately what we must do. And to do this we must travel to Pompeii. It's as simple as that."

"I understand that," Eric spat out, rolling his eyeballs, "but I asked what do we do now?"

Despite discovering more about Dr. Johansen, Eric was still angry at being stabbed with a syringe and, as he saw it, kidnapped.

Dr. Johansen thought for a while before replying, "We wait until the trip and then we go too."

Andrea added more details. "The OSS do not know that you and Alexander are here. We must make sure that this does not change. They will not look for you in this house. We will continue to pretend that Eric is missing and use the media to convince the world of the same. Meanwhile Ursula and myself will continue as normal."

At the mention of her name Ursula looked up. She hadn't looked as if she had been paying attention but added, "I'll just tell everyone at school that we don't know where Eric is and we are very worried. I can lie."

"Our trip isn't until the start of April. That's almost ten weeks away!" Eric's voice was becoming progressively louder, "You mean I have to stay in this villa for seventy days and I CAN'T GO OUT?"

"Don't worry Eric, never mind. I'll bring you comics and other treats to keep you occupied," said Dr. Johansen, trying to make him feel better.

Andrea shook her head, "Oh no, you will not. The same rule applies to Alexander, too. Both of you must not leave the villa."

Dr. Johansen's mouth fell open and he shot forward, "But..."

"No 'buts', Alexander. My initial instructions were to protect you. I was then given additional instructions to protect Eric. They are my instructions, if I have to protect you from yourselves I will do this as well." There was no uncertainty in Andrea's voice. The instructions she had been given she would follow to the letter.

Both Eric and Dr. Johansen knew Andrea well enough to know that once she said she would do something, she did it. In their experience no amount of persuasion would make her change her mind.

"Over the next ten weeks I will find a way to get the two of you to Pompeii without being seen and you will construct a plan that will enable us to retrieve the Compact Discs and the pod," she said.

"Easy," announced Eric.

"I do not predict it will be easy," contradicted Andrea. "The OSS know the pod is in Italy. They know it is in the region of the Amalfi coast. They will have already sent a team there to search for it. Even if they do not suspect Ursula or myself, they will still become suspicious when we arrive in Pompeii. It will not be long after we arrive that more of them will join us."

Silently, Ursula stood up and headed for the window. Her feet hardly lifted from the floor as she walked. She opened the curtain slightly and peeked through the slit. Without turning from the curtain she whispered, "Eric and I are different. We're different from every single person outside this window. We're different from every other single person on the planet."

Dr. Johansen bit his nails and looked down at his feet, suddenly fascinated by the carpet. Andrea looked from him to Ursula but before she could reply Eric spoke.

"But you knew that," he told her softly.

Ursula moved from the window and stood behind the sofa she had been sitting on. She gripped the leather and leant forward, using the sofa's back to support herself. "I didn't know we were different. I just thought we were. Thinking something and knowing something are not the same." Her fingers tightened around the sofa and she asked, almost pleading, "What do we do now?"

Dr. Johansen stood up and walked towards Ursula. He sat down on the sofa in front of her and placed his hands warmly upon hers. "You do nothing. You're unique and we don't know how your lives will progress but this is equally true for every other person on the planet. There is no reason for you to change. You are still the same person as you were when you woke up this morning. And that is all you need to worry about for now."

"I need to know more about this street kid," said Agent Angel pointing a sausage sized finger at the picture of Ursula, "and I need to know it now. What have we got?"

Ducking as he answered, Agent Hoover replied, "Nothing Sir. We still can't break into the school's database. Our guys in the lab say they've never seen such a complex encryption code."

Agent Angel took a draw on his cigarette, inhaled the smoke and, as it slowly entered his lungs, he thought over what Agent Hoover had said. "That strikes me as strange, what do you think, Hoover? Am I way off base here?" and silently he moved to behind Agent Hoover.

"No, Sir, it's mighty strange, Sir."

"Good, I'm glad we agree on something," he replied calmly and then barked, "NOW TELL ME SOMETHING I WANT TO HEAR, YOU USELESS KLUTZ!"

Before Agent Hoover could duck again he had been slapped hard on the back of the head. Through clenched teeth he replied, "Our Enquiry Team have landed in Naples, Italy. As you well know Sir, these pods are made from a material which cloaks them from our satellites. So our Enquiry Team are just going to have to do their hunting on foot or in a four by four. It isn't the best situation but our Space boys have predicted that its trajectory would have meant it landed within a twenty mile radius of Naples. The Enquiry Team have an expected retrieval time for the pods of sixteen weeks. But, with me scanning the screens for anything unusual and reporting it to them, we should be able to cut that down to ten weeks."

"Good, maybe you have a use after all," said Agent Angel and ran a finger softly down Agent Hoover's ear. "With the boy missing we must have the contents of that pod instead. It's taken a long, long time but we are finally nearing the end of our search. I think I can just wait another ten weeks."

Agent Angel patted Agent Hoover hard on the back. "Prove to me you're not a klutz, Hoover. Stay vigilant, liaise with our boys on the ground and find me that God damn pod!"

23

THE PRISON SENTENCE ENDS

For as long as he could remember, Eric had hated the end of winter. The snow was grey and had turned to slush, the skies were grey and the grey rain came down. Spring was on its way and the delights of summer were just around the corner. However, the fact that they were close just made it even worse; so close yet so far.

This year Eric hated it even more. He was stood in his room peeking at the world, through a thin gap in his curtains. It was Sunday evening and even though the sun was setting the light was brighter than at any point during the day. The grey clouds that had thrown down rain for two weeks solidly had begun to separate. They drifted across the horizon like gigantic ships, leaving open patches of sky. Golden light spilled through the gaps, making buildings shine as it touched them. Oh, how he wished he was outside.

Moving away from the curtains he approached a Formula 1 calendar on his wall. A sleek red racing car dominated the page and printed on top were the days of the year, listed out under each month.

In the middle of January he had taken a thick red marker and drawn a big cross over one of the dates. He had repeated this at the end of each day since then, each cross marking another day of his house arrest, a prisoner in his own home.

From his pocket he pulled out the marker and put a cross through the 6th of April. This was the last day of the sentence forced upon him by Andrea. A luminous green circle ringed the 7th, the date of their freedom. His time under house arrest had seemed to last forever.

The two weeks until the end of January had passed reasonably easily. It was like being on holiday and, as he felt he had not experienced a truly relaxing Christmas vacation, he had welcomed the break. He had read, played on his computer, learnt a few more songs on guitar and had come to terms with a lot of the events that had happened. During this time he had stayed out of the way of Dr. Johansen, or Alexander, as he was now called.

When freezing February came, however, Alexander kept bothering Eric. He would ask Eric if he needed something or wanted anything or if he would like to play a game, any game... any game at all.

It was about this time that Eric started looking forward to Ursula coming home from school. Even though he wouldn't admit to it, Ursula's arrival home was more often than not the highlight of his day. They would talk together, play tricks on the adults, practise reading each other's minds and chase each other around the house like two lively kittens. The best part of his entire imprisonment was Ursula's half-term holiday when he had a week to spend with her.

Once Ursula had returned to school Alexander started to bother him again. Within a few days Eric lost his temper with the man who had kidnapped him. He said a number of things he shouldn't have and called Alexander a baby for biting his nails. Alexander tried to say nothing back but in the end he called Eric a spoilt brat who didn't appreciate how much people cared for him.

It had not been a pleasant experience for either of them but it had cleared the air. Over a cup of tea Eric apologized for the things he had said, Alexander apologized for 'kidnapping' him and they agreed to start afresh.

Alexander began to teach Eric, as he was not in school.

When they weren't learning, Eric discovered a chess opponent who was not easy to beat and a drummer who was happy to beat out any rhythm for Eric's guitar. To work off their energy Andrea installed a small gym in one of the spare rooms. As well as running on the treadmill, rowing and pushing weights, Alexander taught Eric some more martial arts, other than kick boxing. They also, and most importantly, worked on a way to recover the CDs and pod without being detected by the OSS or anyone else.

Over the following weeks they studied maps and internet sites of Pompeii, proposed countless plans and then found ways their plans could be foiled by the OSS. They worked well together, bounced ideas off each other and were finally able to select the best plan.

Even though they were both irritable at being stuck indoors, they tried hard not to take it out on the other. This was probably the reason why they had spent the last three days of their sentence apart and in their own rooms. Gradually they had both become a little stir crazy and were feeling like bears in a cage.

Eric looked at the calendar again. The green circle around the 7th shone like a bright star. The plan was ready. Tomorrow they would be free.

24

ESCAPE TO POMPEII

Before the sun rose, everyone in the Meyer villa woke and got ready. Eric walked to the window and peered outside. As he looked he thought of the rhyme he had been taught at school, 'red sky at night, shepherd's delight.' It was true. This morning the outside looked glorious, the sun was bright and the sky clear. A wonderful day for his first day of freedom. He put on black jeans and a dark blue sports top and went down to the kitchen.

Alexander was already there. His salt and pepper stubble had been stylishly trimmed and he was wearing a crisp V-necked T-shirt along with his trusty red cap. Like Eric he was full of nervous energy and the two 'prisoners' talked happily about their planned escape.

Ursula joined them in the kitchen soon after. She was still half-asleep and looked scruffy in her favourite ripped jeans and an orange cardigan that her grandmother had knitted her. Andrea did not join them in the kitchen.

Once breakfast was finished they all went up to the hallway where Andrea was waiting. She was dressed, as usual, in leathers but this time had a Hives T-shirt on.

Arranged neatly on the floor were two rucksacks and three large identical black hold-alls. Andrea lifted one of these and one rucksack while Ursula took the other rucksack.

Outside the villa it was still a little chilly but the blossoming trees and daffodils that lined the driveway had not withered. The bags were put into the back of the

Range Rover and Andrea returned to the house to collect the remaining two hold-alls.

While she was gone, Ursula cart-wheeled to the front of the vehicle and picked up some stones from the drive. When she stood upright again she looked extremely upset. Her face was tense and her eyes were filling with tears. She jumped up and down, her fists clenched tightly around the stones and her eyes fixed on the trees fifty metres in front of her. Without warning she started to scream and threw the stones at a point just beyond the trees. As soon as she had used up the ammunition in her hands she picked up some more and threw them, then some more and more and more. Her screams has turned to words and she yelled over and over again, "Leave me alone! What have you done to Eric?"

Meanwhile, Andrea placed the remaining two bags in the boot of the Range Rover.

Beyond the trees Ursula thought she saw some movement but kept screaming, yelling and throwing stones anyway.

"Ursula, do not do that. It is time to go," snapped Andrea.

After unleashing one last stone Ursula left the scene of her outrage and, with a huff, got into the car. Andrea followed and they immediately drove off.

Two large men were hiding behind a tree near the Meyer villa. Nearby were randomly scattered stones which they had ducked away from when Ursula had thrown them.

One man put his finger to his ear and spoke, "This is Agent Delta. The street kid has gone wacko and the two birds have flown the nest. We are in pursuit."

From a distance it looked as if a soft breeze had just blown the leaves on the tree. Behind it the men had gone. They left only footprints.

Within ten minutes Andrea was on the motorway and heading to Prague airport. Outside the car window the countryside whizzed by and Ursula watched the fields come and go. She had calmed down and was smiling to herself.

"Time to check, Ursula," instructed Andrea.

Ursula turned away from the window, pulled the arm rest down and placed her head beside a slender gap to the boot. "Hi Eric, hi Alexander, are you comfortable?"

From two of the hold-alls came a muffled response in stereo, "Hi Ursula. No."

Ursula giggled and faced the road.

As she checked her mirror to look at Ursula, Andrea saw two black motorbikes in the distance, slaloming between cars. She announced loudly, 'We are being followed. We will stick to the plan. I still do not believe they know anything about Eric and Alexander."

Fifteen minutes later the Range Rover pulled into a space in the multi-story car park opposite Prague's Terminal 2. Andrea and Ursula jumped out the moment the hand brake was on. Ursula took a rucksack, Andrea took a hold-all and they walked briskly out of the car park, towards the terminal building. In front of the entrance they strode past two helmeted motorcyclists, who watched them as they entered, and then drove away. Waiting in the terminal was the rest of the PAIS school party; Andrea and Ursula were the last to arrive.

Two hours later the flight to Naples, complete with thirty one children, Miss Evans, three other teachers and Andrea, took off.

Alexander looked at his watch, which was not particularly difficult as it was squashed right up against his nose. The flight had left and he announced quietly that it was time to go. He undid the zip of his hold-all and beside him Eric did the same. Every muscle in their bodies screamed as they moved. Painfully, they tried to remove themselves from the bags. Their heads appeared first and Eric used his periscope to check that the car park was empty. It was. Alexander managed to reach the boot and flipped a switch to open it. They rolled out of the bags, out of the car and landed with a thud and a groan on the tarmac.

They worked as fast as they could and filled the two hold-alls with items that Andrea had hidden inside the Range Rover - a tent, ropes, harnesses and more. When the bags were packed they put on a polyester dress and grey wig each, locked the car and hobbled off with the bags like two very old women. They did not need to pretend. Instead of Terminal 2 they headed towards the Freight Terminal. Gradually their legs came back to life, their backs straightened and their necks lost their kinks. By the time they entered the building they were walking normally again.

Large cardboard boxes, wooden tea chests and plastic covered packages littered the vast hanger of the freight. Forklift trucks scooted around them, picking up pieces and moving them to the aircrafts outside near the runway.

A yellow path had been painted on the concrete floor and a dark arrow pointed them towards a portacabin office situated next to the furthest wall.

Sitting beside the door, on an upturned box, was a grey haired gentlemen reading Le Figaro. When he noticed Alexander and Eric walking towards him he carefully folded his newspaper and, without rushing, stood up. "Greetings gentlemen, I trust you have had a successful journey thus far," he said and placed his newspaper under his arm.

Alexander replied first, "Well I am not sure my spine will ever straighten fully again but, as luck would have it, we weren't followed here. So, it has indeed been successful."

Eric had turned red and blurted out, "I'm sorry about what happened on the plane last time we met, Captain Hudson. I've changed since then."

A warm smile raised Captain Hudson's salt and pepper moustache slightly and he nodded slowly. "I know you have Eric, Ursula has been very complimentary about you. Now onto other things. I have arranged everything here for our departure. May I suggest we move on tout de suite, as they say in French! I believe time is of the utmost importance and we can talk during the journey."

Without rushing, he led them out of the freight terminal. His plane was standing close to the door and stopped Eric dead in his tracks the moment he saw it.

"Are we flying in that?" he asked incredulously, gazing at the twin prop, high wing plane in front of him. "It's an antique!"

"Apart from the engines cutting out every half an hour and the loose propellers, it's more than air shape."

Eric's mouth dropped open and Captain Hudson laughed. "Don't worry. This craft is a N262 Frégate, built in France in 1968 and the first plane I ever flew. When she was taken out of service by l'Armée de l'Air I was able to purchase her and she has served me well since then."

"It looks like it should be in a museum," said Eric, following the adults towards the plane.

"Your father thought she was a wonderful old bird," said Captain Hudson in a throw-away manner.

"My father!" Eric stopped dead again. "You knew my father?"

"Oh yes. I knew your father for many years and was deeply saddened to hear of his untimely death."

"He was murdered," stated Eric angrily.

"It would not surprise me young Mr Meyer. Your father had many enemies and they were unfortunately rich or powerful or, in most cases, both. He was a good man but he was more comfortable with cards than with people and did not always leave a good impression. It was why we agreed that he would disappear from the public spotlight."

"You helped him with this?"

"I did, and not long after I met you for the first time. You were only a few weeks old so I would be very surprised if you remember me."

"What?"

"Come on. If we have time I will tell you more on the plane," replied Captain Hudson slowly winking. "Let's go! My co-pilot is waiting."

Eight hours later, and after one long fuelling stop in Slovenia for both the plane and the people on board, they landed at a small, forgotten airport just outside Naples. It was almost dusk but the temperature was considerably warmer than in Prague.

The plane came to a standstill next to a large shed with a corrugated iron roof. Somebody had written 'arrivals lounge' over its doorway in spray paint but there was no one around. Parked next to it was a dark green Fiat hatchback, with a trailer, which Andrea had organized for them. Eric and Alexander agreed to meet Captain Hudson back at the plane in two days' time, at ten in the morning, and then they drove off.

The PAIS school party had arrived six hours earlier, unpacked their bags and eaten a quick snack. After lunch they began a guided tour of the main sights of Pompeii.

Ursula had never been so close to the sea nor to such an historical area. As she stood on a slope leading into the ancient Roman city she didn't know where to look. If she looked out from the entrance she could see the sea glistening only a few kilometres away. If she looked to her right or left she could see buildings older than she had ever seen before. And if she looked above the entrance she could see Mount Vesuvius, the volcano whose fury had brought about the end of Pompeii. Green shrubs and trees grew on the low slopes and out of the grey lava beds that rose towards the summit. Near the top there was nothing but loose volcanic stone. Occasional wisps of smoke blew from the hidden crater. To be so close to such a powerful beast, Ursula found both nerve-racking and exciting.

She could have gazed at Vesuvius or the sea for much, much longer but her Year 7 peers were walking off and

Miss Evans was calling. Trailing behind them, and keeping a careful eye on Ursula, was Andrea.

The weather was perfect: blue skies, fluffy white clouds and a warm, comfortable temperature. They spent the rest of the day touring the ancient city but it was impossible to walk around it all. The cobbled roads on which they walked were thousands of years old and had grooves where Roman carts had been pulled down them. Occasionally, large stepping stones in the road blocked their path. Their guide explained that these were for people to cross the road without stepping into the free flowing sewage. When she said this everyone immediately jumped onto the stones.

All the houses beside the roads were still standing and it was hard for Ursula to believe that they were 2000 years old. They looked as they had been abandoned ten or maybe twenty years but not two millennia. The interiors of the houses contained beautiful mosaics showing Roman Gods and customs, and well preserved rooms.

Down one of the streets they found an ancient theatre. The stone seats were still in a perfect C shape in front of the stage and small lion statues marked the aisle between them.

On the edge of the city they visited the amphitheatre, the home of the city's gladiators and staged battles. Ursula stood in its dusty centre and imagined being a gladiator. She pictured thousands of Roman spectators surrounding her and waiting for the Emperor to give his thumb up or down to decide her future. She wondered where her future lay. Would she ever return to Saint-Denis? Would the relationship with her grandparents change? Would she have a normal life like other people? These thoughts and more passed through her head as they walked back towards the centre of Pompeii.

On their way they made a brief stop to look at the Castellum Acquae, where water had entered the city. While they stood there a group of large and loud American tourists, doing a Pompeii tour, joined them. Ursula noted, with some concern, that two of the group spent most of the time looking at her rather than the Castellum Acquae. This had not been missed by Andrea who, by the time they left, had already sent a photo of them to Alexander, via her phone.

That night, as she lay in her hotel bed, Ursula recalled all the fantastic things she had seen that day. Meanwhile, Eric lay next to Alexander in their two man tent, unable to sleep, thinking about what the next day would bring.

25

UNDER OBSERVATION

"Status report," commanded Agent Angel, his voice echoing in the bunker. He was dressed in black army fatigues which were warm as well as waterproof. It was damp underground and years of dripping water mixed with rusting metal had made the solid concrete walls look as if they were stained with blood. Two small but powerful orange floodlights lit up the area and made the walls look even more gruesome. The tunnels had been built after World War II and had not been used since the early nineties. Over ten years of neglect could be sensed with every inward breath. If this had been an OSS facility there was no way it would have been left to fall into disrepair, thought Agent Angel. But one man's loss is another's gain and now they were there they were going to make the most of it.

Eighteen hours earlier a skeleton crew of trusted OSS operatives, all dressed in the same black fatigues, had boarded the plane from the USA to Europe. They consisted of cooks, technicians, doctors, strategists, soldiers and scientists, including Jean Kurtz. Agent Hoover had stayed back to monitor the situation from his observation room.

"Status report," boomed Agent Angel for the second time. His voice echoed further down the forgotten tunnels and it was not friendly. Agent Angel did not like being kept waiting.

"We are good to go in ten," answered a techie running

between computer equipment and a generator.

Silently, Agent Angel counted down from ten. When he reached zero the generator rumbled loudly into life and the computers turned on one by one.

He didn't waste time congratulating his team for their hard work. "Patch me through to Hoover."

In front of him an operations centre, consisting of computers, surveillance apparatus and communications equipment, was now functional. A little further down the tunnel stood an artillery rack, full of everything from grenades to sub-machine guns to rocket launchers. Side tunnels had been turned into temporary living quarters and, a kilometre away at the tunnel entrance, were his own private OSS army, guarding their location. He was not impressed with the OSS teams' achievements in such a short space of time and with so little sleep. He expected it and anything less would not have been good enough.

Hoover's chubby red face appeared on one of the five screens.

"I've been off the radar for two hours now, Hoover. Tell me what's happening and make it fast."

Agent Hoover swallowed hard. "Professor Schwarzkopf is on his way, Sir. ETA eleven hours. Team Omega are all in position in Pompeii. They are keeping the Elf and Street Kid under close observation. They are currently watching the two of them digging not far from the Vesuvian gate, on a square north of the Forum. Our Enquiry Team are continuing to investigate the possible location of the remaining pod.

"Send them home!" barked Agent Angel.

"But Sir, they haven't completed their mission."

"Don't argue with me Hoover. We know the pod is in this area and suddenly two of our suspects turn up. That's neither a coincidence nor divine intervention. They'll lead us to the pod and then Team Omega will take it from there. Now send the Enquiry Team back home, watch those screens like a hawk and send us all the feed we need."

"Yes Sir," answered Agent Hoover, relieved to end the conversation.

The four blank screens suddenly flashed on. Each showed the same scene but from different angles - a party of brightly dressed school children happily digging.

They were in a large open area between two small villas, a cobbled street and a toilet block. Red and white tape prevented tourists from entering their dig site although many stopped to watch the students as they walked past. A dark skinned girl was standing in the centre of the PAIS school group, surrounded by her peers. She was gazing from the sea to Vesuvius and back again.

Ursula could not decide if being an archaeologist was either really interesting or really boring. It was like having lots of turns in a lucky dip box but without really knowing if there were any prizes left. The only thing she was certain of was that it was dirty work. All the students were covered in dust and none of their multi-coloured clothes were clean. It was also hard work and she was thankful that it was not yet the height of summer.

They had each been given a trowel, or small spade, and a paint brush. They had been told to dig a bit, move their dirt a bit and brush a bit. Most of the children could follow these simple instructions though some secretly wondered why they couldn't just use a digger instead.

As Ursula sat back down to dig again she caught site of the two American tourists she had seen the previous day. They had been joined by four more. They were big and looked the same size as American footballers but they were not wearing any padding. Baseball caps advertising teams she had never heard of, and wrap-around sunglasses, hid their faces. They were wearing Bermuda shirts so bright that everybody's eyes were drawn to the patterned material. The 'tourist' in the Cub's cap looked straight at Ursula and flashed her a smile. It was not friendly. Ursula faked a smile back and returned to her work.

From a bench near the children Andrea took another six photos and sent them to Alexander via her phone.

Alexander and Eric looked for all the world like father and son enjoying the delights of Pompeii. They were both wearing Italian football shirts and matching caps. Eric was carrying a miniature football which he would throw up in the air and catch. Both were holding audio guides to their ears and occasionally they would stop and look at a plan of Pompeii they had bought at the entrance. Alexander was also holding a Nordic pole in his hand and, since the morning, he had developed a limp.

At certain points on their tour they would stop, type the appropriate number into their audio guide and then a voice would tell them some historical information. Unlike other tourists their tour was not a circular route. Instead it took them in a straight line from the Marine Gate along the Via dell'Abbondanza to the spot where Alexander had found the pod twelve years previously. On the way they pretended to be interested in the Basilica, the House of Amarantus and the House of Loreius Tiburtus, so as not to attract unwanted attention. However, they had only two goals: firstly, to find the pod and secondly, to make sure the OSS did not find them.

At the last major villa on the road, Alexander stopped Eric and they both walked inside. It was called the House of Venus in the Sea Shell. There was a small group of Spanish tourists wandering around but otherwise it was empty. Alexander led Eric to the rear of the house and stood in front of the beautiful mosaic which gave the house its name. They put the audio guides close to their ears but they were not turned on and instead Alexander spoke.

"Behind this house is a field containing a few trees and bushes. This is where Ursula's pod landed. Fourteen years ago this area was being excavated, when the archaeologists discovered a tunnel dug by Roman looters over nineteen hundred years ago. Ancient tunnels often mean all the best artefacts have already been removed and it is my understanding that, after a hurried look, the archaeologists abandoned their excavations and moved on. Pompeii is a vast dig site and archaeologists are not as patient as is to be believed. As you already know, I pushed the pod down this hole, covered the hole with timber that was laying around, covered this with mounds of dirt and then left. It is my sincerest hope that it has been left but..."

The Spanish group filed past the mosaic in front of them and Alexander stopped talking.

When they had gone Eric asked, "Are we still going ahead with our plans?"

"Yes," replied Alexander trying to sound confident. "Let's go."

It was almost eleven o'clock and there were many tourists walking around. Alexander checked his phone to make sure none of them were OSS agents and then left the House of Venus in the Sea Shell. A group of German tourists talking loudly strolled past them and they joined the back of their group toward the Sarno Gateway.

Eric was throwing his ball up in the air and catching it, waiting for the sign from Alexander.

"Throw the ball to me, son," instructed Alexander jovially, after a few seconds.

"Okay Dad, I'll make it a big throw," replied Eric skipping to the other side of the road. He looked at Alexander and threw him the ball, which sailed over Alexander's head, over a waist high, ancient wall and into the field behind.

"Oh, Dad, my ball," said Eric disappointed, bounding over to Alexander. "That's my favourite one."

"Don't worry son, I'm sure we can find it."

And they both leap-frogged over the wall and into the field beyond.

After much thought Ursula had decided that excavation was actually quite enjoyable. About twenty minutes earlier Molly had found a piece of ceramic. Normally, a bit of smashed plate would not have interested Ursula but this piece was different. This piece had been used by Romans, had experienced a Volcanic eruption and had been buried under ash, pumice and earth for nearly two thousand years. Their tour guide, who was also an archaeologist and their dig manager, explained that it was indeed Roman and that there was sure to be more. The children's enthusiasm for the dig increased tenfold with this comment.

As Ursula looked around her she could see that all her classmates were busy chatting and digging, trying to find more pieces. Beyond them, roughly circling their group, were six American tourists in loud Bermuda shirts. They seemed to have an unhealthy interest in the school group and one person in particular.

If they are here, thought Ursula, they are not with Eric and Alexander, and that's perfect. She focused hard and sent this thought to Eric.

Eric smiled and told Alexander that the OSS were still with Ursula as the two of them continued to hunt for his ball. Nobody gave them a second glance. The tourists were far more interested in the historical sites than a father and son looking for a ball in an overgrown field.

After a quarter of an hour a severe looking Pompeii guide asked them what they were doing. Alexander replied, in bad Italian, that his son has lost his ball. The guide relaxed, asked them not to be too long and walked away.

"Where did you bury it?" asked Eric. "We can't spend much longer here, another guide will turn up and ask the same question."

"I know," replied Alexander, becoming tense, "but it was at night and it was over ten years ago and it was dark. A degree of patience would be appreciated."

Another fifteen minutes passed and, apart from the ball, nothing else had been found. They that staying any longer in the field would make people suspicious and left.

As they walked back along Via dell'Abbondanza Alexander said brightly, "Let us concentrate on the positives. Judging by the amount of vegetation I think it is safe to conclude that the area we have just searched has not been used for a number of years. If this is the case then I think we can also rightly assume that the pod is still there, under the surface."

"You're right," replied Eric gloomily, "but if we are realistic we can say that Plan A has failed. Now we have to go with Plan B and we both know that Plan B's success is down to faith or luck and is more dangerous."

"Needs must, needs must."

They walked on in silence. Taking his phone from his pocket, Alexander texted Andrea the letter 'B'.

Deep in the pocket of her leather jacket, Andrea's phone buzzed. She looked at the message. The time was 11:43 a.m., or seventeen minutes until Plan B could begin. She was sat on a bench near the dig area and beside her was one of the black hold-alls. Among the throng of children Ursula was happily digging and chatting to Molly beside her. A few children away Miss Evans was busily digging with the three other teachers, her face bright red with the effort.

"Miss Evans," shouted Andrea.

"Yes dear," she answered, pleased with the excuse to have a short break.

"It will be lunch soon."

Even though she was talking with Molly, Ursula noticed the single letter in Andrea's sentence.

"Oh yes," replied Miss Evans, looking at her watch. "We'll stop at twelve and then go to the restaurant."

At twelve, as good as her word, Miss Evans brought the dig to a halt. She gathered the children around her and complimented them on their work. The six OSS agents took a step forward.

"Well done, good digging. Now it is time to go to the restaurant for some food."

Ursula put her hand up, "But Miss Evans I'm filthy. I can't go into a restaurant like this."

"I really don't think it matters that much, but I guess that it would be a good idea if we all went into the toilet block and freshened up."

"But Miss Evans," Ursula whined, "I'll still be filthy. I can't wash my clothes as well."

Molly joined in, "We'll be thrown out of the restaurant and we'll get dirt in our food. We should have bought some spare clothes."

Some of the other children joined in and soon most of the year group were grumbling.

"Boys and girls!" shouted Miss Evans above the ruckus. "The restaurant is quite used to dirty archaeologists and, to be fair, there really isn't much else we can do about it."

"Miss Evans," said Andrea, walking towards the group with the hold-all, "maybe I can help. In his spare time the late Mr Meyer liked to excavate and he always took spare clothes for lunch. When he became involved in this trip he instructed me to have some spare clothes ready for all the children."

From the hold-all Andrea produced a brown, long sleeved top, khaki trousers, sunglasses and a wide brimmed khaki hat. "There is one set of these for each child and each piece has the PAIS logo on it. Consider them a gift from the Meyer foundation. One size fits all."

The children cheered and Miss Evans thanked Andrea for her kindness before organizing the classes. "Okay Year 7, please form an orderly line and then go into the toilets to wash and change."

Behind the toilet block, their backs against the wall and listening carefully, were Eric and Alexander. Eric had changed out of the Italian football shirt and cap. He was now wearing a bright red T-shirt with a colourful target painted on the front.

"Time to rumble," announced Alexander, quietly giving Eric a bunk up to the small toilet window, into the boy's section of the block.

"Good luck," he wished as Eric disappeared from view, "I'll see you later."

"You better," whispered Eric from inside.

The Year 7 children had not formed an orderly line, in fact they had stampeded like elephants towards Andrea. At the front of the queue was Ursula. After she had been given her bag of clothes and was walking towards the toilet block Andrea appeared to have difficulty in removing the rest. Once Ursula was inside, the clothes came out of the hold-all easily and quickly. The children grabbed theirs and piled towards the block too. In just over a minute all the children were inside getting changed.

Andrea motioned to the adults to join her. The four teachers stood in front of her with their backs to the toilet block while Andrea rummaged inside her hold-all, looking for the teacher's T-shirts. All the time she had one eye on the outside of the toilets.

From the boy's entrance, Eric stepped out and stood there looking around. He did a visual sweep of the area and made eye contact with each of the six OSS team members.

In his surveillance room back in the States, Agent Hoover almost fell out of the chair he was wedged into. He didn't need to report the news to Agent Angel as the OSS chief was watching the same feed.

"It's the boy!" roared Agent Angel, his voice booming down the tunnels. "It's the boy! Get that boy!"

Team Omega scrambled across the dig site towards Eric, who sprinted away like a one hundred metre champion, but then they stopped.

Ursula could feel that Eric was scared as she climbed out of the toilet window. She did not feel too differently herself. Alexander was waiting for her and the moment her feet hit the ground he put Eric's Italian football shirt and matching cap on her. She took his hand and together they walked quickly away.

The sudden appearance of Eric, and his sprint away,

had put Team Omega into two minds... to follow their order and the boy, or stay with the girl? Rather than pursue him they stood, momentarily, wondering what to do. Their heads moved between the toilet block, where they knew Ursula was, and the fleeing boy.

Agent Angel, roaring down their earpieces, brought an end to their indecision. "What are you doing? Agents Alpha, Beta and Gamma get the boy! Go, go, go, damn it! Agents Delta, Ypsilon and Zeta stay with the other two suspects." He then turned his attention to the operatives in front of him and Agent Hoover back in America. "When the girl comes out of that john make sure you keep every available camera and satellite on her and find me that boy too."

By the time the teachers had their new T-shirts and had turned around, the toilet area had returned to calm. Eric was nowhere to be seen and there were only three tourists left in Bermuda shirts. As the teachers entered the block themselves, thirty identically dressed children left and mingled outside. The long-sleeve tops were too long and covered the children's hands, the hats flopped down to their shoulders and the sun glasses were large. However, no one seemed to care.

Neither the three remaining agents, the operatives in the bunker nor Agent Hoover could work out which child was Ursula. Even as they followed the children to the restaurant they were unable to pinpoint her.

Andrea calmly picked up the hold-all and followed the three agents plus the children to the restaurant. The dig site was now empty and as she walked across it no one noticed her.

Down at the field, next to the House of Venus in the Sea Shell, Ursula and Alexander were busily searching for the pod. It had taken them twelve minutes to get there and they thought they had only about another twelve minutes before the OSS realized that Ursula was missing.

"Just relax," Alexander encouraged Ursula, "walk

around and see if you feel anything. If a diviner can use a stick to find water underground, why can't you find your pod?"

"I'll try," she answered, "but I'm not feeling very relaxed."

"Is Eric okay?"

Ursula focused her mind on Eric. "Yes, he's fine. He's in the girl's toilet at the restaurant, he lost the OSS."

"Then there is nothing to worry about. Come on, concentrate on that pod."

In rapidly decreasing circles Ursula moved quickly across the field; Alexander walked behind her.

Shortly after she had started, she stopped. "It's here, below me, I can feel it."

Lifting his Nordic pole high above his head Alexander brought it down hard and fast into the ground. The point of the pole had been specially sharpened. It broke through the top soil with ease, pierced timber and then met no resistance. Falling to his knees Alexander dug around the pole with his hands. After twenty centimetres or so he reached the wood.

"You're right," he said gleefully. Quickly he refilled the hole and, taking a small phial of liquid from his pocket, sprinkled its contents around the hole.

"What's that?" asked Ursula.

"It will be seen by UV light, it will help us find the spot later. If you can't find it again, that is. Come on, let's go."

They jogged to the wall, jumped over and walked out of Pompeii via the Sarno gateway.

About the same time as they were leaving the three OSS agents in the restaurant realized that Ursula was not there. They were sat at a plastic table together drinking colas and watching the children.

Agent Delta put his finger to his ear and said, "The street kid has vanished. I repeat, the street kid has vanished."

The three agents paid for their drinks and left.

Agents Alpha, Beta and Gamma had not fared any better. They had run after Eric but, by the time they began their pursuit, he had already disappeared. Since then they had run around half of Pompeii trying to locate him.

Agent Alpha put his finger to his ear and said, "The boy has vanished. He's somewhere in Pompeii but we don't know where."

Lunch had been eaten and the children were eager to return to their digging. Miss Evans was sat on a table with Andrea and the other teachers. She stood up and, pointing at each child, counted. There were thirty children.

"Oh my goodness," she said to the other teachers and Andrea, "we appear to be missing one."

Looking up, Andrea said helpfully, "I think I saw Ursula going to the toilet. I will go and have a look."

In the girl's toilet, waiting in a cubicle and putting on the same outfit as the other children, was Eric. The clothes had been hidden there, and Andrea knew exactly which cubicle to approach.

"Are you here, Eric?" asked Andrea as she entered.

"Yes," he replied somewhat sulkily.

Andrea went back into the restaurant, where she found the children lining up and ready to leave. At the back of the line was Miss Evans and Andrea approached her. "I am afraid that Ursula is not feeling well," she explained, "I will take her back to hotel."

"Oh, what a shame. I'll leave her with you then, thank you," and Miss Evans told the children to go.

As the Year 7 children and teachers walked out of the restaurant Eric came out of the girl's toilet. His head was held low so no one could see his face under the floppy hat and he clutched his stomach. Andrea put her arm around him and they followed the PAIS tour group at a safe distance.

At a crossroads the Year 7 children headed left towards the dig site. Eric and Andrea turned right and headed for the Marine gateway and out of Pompeii.

"How can we lose both our target and one suspect? Or, to put it another way, how can we lose two kids?" roared Agent Angel at everybody.

No one dared respond.

"Run back all the video recordings we have," he ordered. "I want to know how the hell this happened!"

26

THE MISSING POD

Pompeii was virtually silent. The ancient streets were empty, the tourists were all tucked up in bed and the sleepy security guards were sat in their hut waiting for the next shift to arrive. High above Pompeii the full moon cast a ghostly light over the ruins. The city's only permanent residents, rats, hid in the shadows, scuttling between buildings and looking for scraps of food. Vesuvius loomed menacingly on the horizon, a dark shadow on a grey night, but the rats ignored it. They had already survived one eruption and would live through a second when it came.

Not too far away from Vesuvius, past Pompeii and squashed against the coast, was the city of Naples. A yellow glow, of street lights hung warmly over the peaceful city and made it clearly visible to boats way out to sea. For now its residents slept but in two to three hours' time they would wake up and the city would come busily to life.

A Fiat, with trailer attached, drove out of Naples towards Pompeii. The roads were empty and it was not long before it came to a stop on a tiny lane near the east side of the ancient city. The silence made the noise of the engine louder and the rats looked up until it was switched off.

Four people quietly got out of the car. In two rucksacks and a hold-all, they carried ropes, spades, pocket torches and other things they may need. All of were dressed in black and wore climbing harnesses, but only one was dressed in leather.

"Let's go," whispered Alexander. "The security guards are changing shifts now. We have about one hour until their rounds take them to this spot and about one hour until sunrise."

He led the way to the Sarno Gateway, followed by Eric, Ursula and lastly Andrea, who carried the hold-all. The gateway had barely survived the eruption and, despite being partly rebuilt by archaeologists, it still looked as if it was about to fall down. Broken and missing bricks made excellent hand holds. In a few seconds they had all climbed over and were standing in Pompeii. Rats, lurking where sewage had once flowed in the streets, quickly fled into the doorways. Moonlight reflected off their eyes as they watched the four intruders walk along the Via dell'Abbondanza.

At the field where the pod was buried, Alexander removed a special laser pen from his pocket. Ultra-violet light shone from its tip and he hastily scanned the field. Near its centre the beam picked out the liquid he had spilt earlier, glowing purple. The four of them approached the spot, dropped the bags on the ground, took out their spades and began to dig. No words were exchanged.

When they reached timber they put their spades down and felt their way along the planks until they found the ends. There were fourteen pieces in total and all of various widths, but they only removed the middle four.

Eric and Ursula quickly removed the ropes from their rucksacks, threaded them through their harnesses and knotted them correctly. Andrea and Alexander then took the other ends and knotted a figure of eight around their harnesses. Beside the hole, the children nodded that they were ready. Andrea and Alexander made sure they were stable and firstly Ursula, and then Eric, was lowered into the hole.

Above the ground the moon provided pale light but below the surface it was pitch black. Eric took a pen torch from his pocket and turned it on. Ursula did the same.

The hole was uninteresting. Closely compacted dry earth walls were revealed by the small spotlights and it was just big enough for the two of them to be lowered without clattering into each other. There was evidence that the walls had begun to collapse inwards and as they bumped into the wall great clumps of soil fell. After three metres or so they reached the floor. A tunnel, only big enough to crawl down, stretched out before them.

Ursula ignored it, knelt down and started to brush dirt from the floor to discover what lay below her. If the pod was here, and she felt that it was, then they would be standing right on top of it.

Eric was not feeling good. He was breathing quickly and sweating. This reminded him too much of the cellar passageway back at his villa in Prague. Bravely, he tried to calm himself down by using deep breaths and bent down to the powdery ground to help Ursula. Before he began to dig he shone his torch along the tunnel and a smiling skeleton was suddenly spot lit by the beam. Unable to stop himself Eric screamed, scrambled back to Ursula and started to hyperventilate.

Straightaway, Ursula stopped and pointed her torch at Eric. His forehead was dripping with sweat and his chest rose and fell at an alarming rate. The rope that was secured to Eric's harness dangled between them. She took hold of it and tugged twice. The rope became tense and slowly Eric began to rise towards the surface. Ursula followed him with her torch and then pointed it back towards the floor. Out of the corner of her eye, she noticed a flash as the torchlight reflected off something shiny.

Where Eric had scrambled away from the tunnel his heels had dug deep into the earth to reveal what looked like smooth metal. It has to be the pod, thought Ursula, and bent down to look. As she did so she glanced up the tunnel and came face to face with the skeleton. Nervously she began to laugh, looked away and started to reveal more of the pod. Every now and again she looked up to make sure the skeleton had not moved.

After a few minutes of brushing away the dirt, into the tunnel, she had revealed almost a square metre of the pod. A few minutes later she had uncovered all the ground below her. She sat on the edge of the tunnel with her back to the skeleton, scanned the pod with her pen torch and thought about what to do next.

Two things struck her. The first was that the pod was buried and therefore stuck in the ground, which made it impossible to remove before sunrise. The second was that there was no visible door to enter the pod by and retrieve the discs.

There was nothing she could do except try and get into the pod. First she stroked it, trying to find a lip or a hole which she could force open with her fingers. There was nothing, so she banged on the surface with her fist. Nothing happened. Her only other option was to jump up and down on it. She did this, but once again nothing happened. Defeated, she sat back down at the tunnel entrance. Her harness suddenly tightened and she felt a short sharp tug. It was one of their signs and it meant be quick. How could she be quick when nothing was happening, she thought, and dropped her head, wishing the pod would open.

There was another sharp tug and she looked back at the pod. At the end of her feet, a circular opening just big enough for her to fit through, had appeared. Without wasting any time she leapt onto her belly, held the torch in her mouth and leaned her head into the pod. The unsteady torch beam made it difficult for her to see clearly. However, she saw what looked like a red bed, some wires and then the beam reflected off something. She stretched into the pod and ran her hands over where she had seen the reflection. Her fingers felt around a small, slim circular object, and then another and another and another. As she searched for the fifth she felt the harness tighten and then she lifted off the ground. Desperately she tried to pull herself back, and clawed at the pod, but she was rising too rapidly. In her hands she held four discs, numbered one, two, three and four. Once again disc five was out of reach, she thought, except, except...

She had seen it somewhere but she couldn't remember where. Carefully she slipped the four discs into a small wallet, strapped to her chest underneath her loose black top. Just before she was pulled out of the hole she looked back down at the pod. It had resealed and there was no sign of the opening.

With fast moving fingers Andrea unclipped Ursula from the rope and threw it on the floor.

"What's happening?" asked Ursula, her voice sounding loud in the silent city.

Andrea did not reply, she just pointed to the lane and towards Naples. In the distance Ursula could see two sets of car headlights speeding towards them, slashing the darkness into strips.

Andrea broke into a run back towards the Sarno gateway. The hold-all she carried swung wildly in her hand. Ursula understood the urgency of the situation and followed. Eric and Alexander were already at the gate and climbing over. The headlights were getting closer and Ursula ran faster. Just before the gate she stumbled on a loose cobble, her left foot twisted painfully underneath her and she slammed into the crumbling brick. Fear kept her going and, using only her arms, she pulled herself up the tall gateway. At the top she could see the other vehicles; they were not far away, and she jumped down to the other side instinctively, as if she was jumping between buildings back in Paris.

Ursula hit the ground hard and, though her right leg cushioned most of the impact, her left foot could not support her weight and buckled. Pain screamed through her body and she collapsed to the floor, rolled forward and then stopped. As she looked up she saw Andrea climbing into the Fiat and heard the car engine fire up. Coming quickly up the lane towards them were the headlights of the other two vehicles. She knew she wasn't going to make it, she couldn't stand up.

Fear and a sense of failure gripped her but before she could start to cry the Fiat's rear door opened and Eric sprung out. He sprinted towards her, placed his hands under her armpits and lifted her into a standing position.

"I'm not leaving my PPP behind," he said strongly.

The headlights were almost upon them but with Eric's help she managed to hop to the car. The headlights were right behind them now and lit up the Fiat. Ursula jumped onto the back seat, Eric followed and, without waiting for the door to be closed, Alexander sped off.

"This is Yukon One. We are in pursuit," said Agent Ypsilon, fixing his sights on the Fiat in front, and he pushed the accelerator down.

"This is Yukon Two. We will retrieve the pod," said Agent Beta, and he stopped his jeep where the Fiat had been parked.

From past experience, Alexander knew that driving at speed, with an attached trailer, was not easy. Even though the trailer was empty it pulled the rear of the Fiat out with every bend and caused the car to skid. The last thing he wanted was to crash and kill them all.

Eric fought to close the door and just as he managed it Andrea ordered them to put their seat belts on.

It was a task easier said than done. The lane was uneven and full of pot holes, and the car skidded at almost every turn. This made it hard for the children to stay in one place long enough to put their seat belts on. An added difficulty for Ursula was her ankle which throbbed painfully. Every bounce or skid sent her clattering into either Eric or the door, and shot further pains up her leg. Despite trying desperately to hold them back, tears welled up in her eyes.

Alexander looked at the speedometer - eighty, eighty-five, ninety kilometres per hour. They were accelerating but their pursuers were easily keeping up and getting closer by the second. Alexander looked briefly into his rear view mirror. The Yukon was so close he could see the perfect, white toothed smiles of the three people inside.

"This is Agent Ypsilon. We are on the bandits' tail. Awaiting instructions. Are we looking for closure or seizure?"

Deep in the tunnels Agent Angel paced up and down in front of the screens. A fat cigar, rather than a cigarette, sat comfortably between his large fingers. From a camera fitted inside the Yukon he could see the trailer, the Fiat and the bobbing heads of the four thorns in his side. They were obviously smart, they had proven that with their little vanishing act from Pompeii, but he was smarter still and the current situation proved that.

His pacing was not due to fear or worry but excitement. He loved the thrill of the chase, the prey in sight and the wait before the certain kill. However, in this situation it could be more beneficial if the prey was brought back alive. After careful consideration he stopped and took a long drag of his cigar.

"I just love the smell of victory in the morning," he said quietly to himself and then gave his orders. "Render the boy and bring him here. Dispense with the Elf, the Street Kid and Red Cap. They are just collateral damage."

"Yes, Sir," answered the three members of Team Omega in Yukon One.

This was the kind of order they liked to hear. As far as they were concerned the Fiat in front was going nowhere. It was slow anyway but the trailer made the chase even easier. Like chasing a deer with a broken leg, reflected Agent Zeta, winding down his window. In his hand he held the OSS regulation revolver. Taking careful aim, he fired and deliberately sent his first shot over the car.

In the back of the Fiat Ursula and Eric ducked down.

"They're shooting at us, really shooting," exclaimed Eric in disbelief.

Without panicking Andrea looked back at them, "But they are not aiming directly at us. They are simply trying to scare us. It is OSS protocol. It means we are more valuable to them while alive."

"Andrea's correct," said Alexander, spinning the steering wheel and skidding around a tight bend. "If they wanted to hit us they..."

He was interrupted by the sudden explosion of his wing mirror. Broken shards of glass scratched against the window and fell onto the road. Before they had a chance to say anything, Andrea's wing mirror was shot off the car and crushed noisily under the rear wheels.

"They have excellent aim, which proves that if they wanted to harm us they would have done so by now," stated Andrea so calmly that it was hard to believe they were on a tiny lane, in the dark, in a high speed chase, being fired upon.

Alexander was not as calm as Andrea and rushed his words. "They can't get past us, it is an old ploy. They're trying to scare us. I'm going to drive into Naples and try to lose them. If we do we can still make the rendez-vous with Captain Hudson."

He then spun the car hard to the right and onto a two lane road towards the yellow glow of the city. There were not enough cars on this road to slow them down but there were enough to put an end to the OSS's shooting.

"Stay with them Yukon One but do not engage," instructed Agent Angel, and took a triumphant drag from his cigar.

Both vehicles soon reached Naples and dropped their speed as they entered the suburbs. The OSS Agents were in no rush and were happy just to wait, safe in the knowledge that 'amateurs' always make mistakes.

It was still dark and most of Naples had not yet woken up. The narrow, disorganized streets were packed with parked cars and piles of rubbish lay on street corners. The rubbish collectors were just beginning their rounds and they were joined by fruit sellers driving into the city. Random lights began to flick on from the tightly packed apartment buildings and a few people stepped onto their balconies to smell the salty sea air.

"Where are we going, Alexander?" asked Ursula. Her voice was strained and she sounded in pain.

Alexander checked his mirror. The Yukon was still there and the men inside were still smiling. "We are going to drive around Naples until she wakes up and then, at rush hour, we're going to leave the car and lose the OSS on foot."

Eric understood very well that this was not the best plan. When Alexander and he had covered this situation during their imprisonment they had both agreed it was a last resort and nothing else. There were too many things that could happen, it was too risky and the Naples road layout was terrible to say the least.

No sooner had he thought this than a diversion sign appeared and forced Alexander into following another route. A few minutes later they were unwillingly driving up a small hill and heading out of the city. Behind them, Alexander was certain he could see the OSS rubbing their hands in glee.

The long, straight road they were on had thick concrete barriers down its centre; it was impossible to do a U-turn, and return to the city. They had no option but to continue onwards, heading towards Vesuvius.

The volcano loomed ahead of them. As the sun rose an orange glow, pulled it out of the darkness turning it into a beacon. It was a beacon Alexander would rather avoid. Once he was on the narrow mountain roads he knew he would have no choice but to drive to the summit and a dead end. The way up was also the only way down.

The single lane road became two lanes and the central concrete barriers ran out. Alexander pressed his foot hard on the accelerator and their speed crept up from sixty to seventy, eighty, ninety. Before they hit one hundred the Yukon overtook them with ease and screeched to a halt over both lanes directly in front of them. Two guns were trained on their Fiat.

Alexander had no option but to yank the wheel hard to the right. The Fiat and trailer skidded across the entire highway and onto a much narrower road. Alexander sighed with relief and then swore. They were on the road that led up to the volcano. He checked his mirror to see if he could turn back, but the Yukon was already behind them.

There was no need to go so fast on the windy lane. Nobody could overtake easily and Alexander dropped down to a safer speed. Trees growing beside the road stopped whizzing past and came into focus. The darkness was slowly lifting and the orange glow of dawn made driving easier.

"There's nowhere to go," stated Eric, from the rear of the car.

"Up," replied Andrea matter-of-factly.

"And that is where we are going, whether we like it or not," said Alexander.

Ursula said nothing. The pain from her ankle had taken over her senses and she could not concentrate on anything else, no matter how hard she tried.

"What is the plan?" asked Andrea.

Alexander glanced briefly at Eric in the rear-view mirror. He looked as lost as Eric felt.

"We don't have one," answered Eric sheepishly.

"Being chased up a sleeping volcano at dawn by the OSS was not a scenario we anticipated," added Alexander, ramming the car down into third gear. "The best plan, as far as I can see, is to outrun them on foot when we reach the top."

Silence gripped the car and then quietly Ursula spoke, "I can't outrun them. But we could release the trailer.

That would slow them down and give us a chance."

Her idea was greeted with enthusiasm and Eric promptly unclipped his seat belt. He shuffled towards Ursula, pulled the back of his car seat down and crawled into the hatchback boot. Despite the car turning left and right around the narrow bends he managed to wedge himself so he hardly moved.

"There should be a clip just at the bottom of the boot door, flick it but hold the boot door with your other hand or it will fling open," advised Alexander. "If this is going to work, it has to be a surprise."

Driving close behind them was Yukon One and half of Team Omega. They knew from their preparations that the road was a dead end and that the Fiat had nowhere to go. They decided to dispose of the adults first and then seize the boy but they were undecided on what to do to the girl. However, there was no one around and they did not anticipate any problems.

Eric gripped hold of the boot door with his right hand and found the metal clip with his left. As he pulled it up he had to strain to keep the boot door closed. Slowly he let the door open to a gap just big enough for his hand. Wind, mixed with unpleasant fumes from the car's exhaust, blew into Eric's face and made him wheeze. Through the opening he could see the handle which would release the trailer. His hand slipped through and found the cold metal lever. At the same time the Fiat hit a bump and the boot door slammed down on his arm. Eric bit his lip until he drew blood but he kept his hand where it was. Using all the strength he could muster he pulled the handle up. Nothing happened.

"It's not working!' he yelled and the boot door slammed painfully onto his arm once more. He swallowed his cry.

"There will be a pin," shouted Alexander.

Eric felt around near the handle until he found it. His arm was hurting, sapping his energy, but he pulled the pin as hard as he could. It would not budge. He pulled and pulled but it simply wouldn't move. The car hit another bump and as the door came down onto this arm he felt the pin give a little. He pulled it up and the trailer came loose.

Neither Agent Ypsilon, who was driving, nor the other agents noticed that the trailer was no longer attached to the Fiat. By the time they realized, they were too close and it was too late. The trailer hit their right head light, as they tried to swerve around it, and they were forced off the road. Agent Ypsilon hit the brakes just before the Yukon, plus trailer, smashed into a group of young trees. The agents looked up to see the Fiat disappear from view. Thrusting the jeep into reverse Agent Ypsilon tried to separate from the trailer but it had somehow become attached to the Yukon. He drove forward and back but the trailer refused to move. Only when he crashed it back into a tree did it come off. The Yukon did a wheel spin and roared away, continuing upwards in their pursuit of the Fiat.

The Vesuvius car park was situated about one hundred metres below the summit of the volcano and was on a slope. It was the furthest point accessible by car and, except for a parked van, was deserted. To reach the summit visitors had to walk past a wooden ticket office, through a chained entrance and up a steep path.

The Fiat skidded to a halt under a tree, sending gravel spinning into the air and drawing a half-circle on the ground.

"Get out! Head towards the summit!" shouted Alexander.

Eric jumped out of the boot first and then sped round to the rear door to help Ursula. She put her arm around his shoulders and they moved as fast they could towards the entrance. They did not look back. The path up to the summit was covered in loose pumice and was difficult to walk on even in full health but for Ursula it was even harder. Eric provided much support but it was still difficult to keep a steady footing. Apart from the noise of the Fiat's engine ticking over, everything was silent.

After a few minutes Ursula realized that Alexander and Andrea were not with them, nor were they following. With Eric's help she turned round to look back down at the car park.

The Fiat was accelerating towards the road which led back down the volcano, when the Yukon sped around a corner towards it. The Fiat continued to speed up and, just outside the car park entrance, they collided with an almighty smash. Steam floated up from the crumpled bonnets and they could see two large cracks on the Yukon's windscreen.

Neither Eric nor Ursula spoke. Instead they turned away from the scene and headed up the path as fast as they could. The sun had risen higher in the sky, the sunlight was becoming stronger and, despite tears in their eyes, it was easier to see where they were going. When they reached the summit they turned around to survey the crash below and frantically tried to locate Andrea or Alexander. They were nowhere to be seen. The same was not true of the three OSS Agents who were walking unsteadily past the wooden ticket office. Revolvers were being waved back and forth by the agents but their hands were too unsteady to fire a shot. Ursula did not want to hang around and motioned Eric forward.

The view from the summit would have taken Eric and Ursula's breath away if the preceding events and climb had not already done so. They could see Naples and the sea glistening beside it. The Amalfi coast stretching away from them, fields that looked like they had been crocheted together on a blanket, lonely villages and Pompeii. From where they stood all were miniature, shrunk down to the size of models.

Wincing in pain with every step, Ursula pulled Eric towards the crater. A small chain fence stopped them from getting too close and, when they saw the crater, they understood why. It was a massive circular hole with sheer rock and earth walls. If you toppled over the edge you would not be coming back, thought Ursula and she moved on, taking Eric with her.

"We have to get back down again," Eric said, looking away from the crater towards the volcano's slope.

"I know, but we can't go the same way. They're following. We'll get to the other side of the crater and then go down. But I need a short break first."

"Let's head for those," suggested Eric, pointing towards a high pile of sharp looking rocks half-way around the crater. "We won't be seen there."

As they walked, puffs of steam rose from the sleeping volcano and a soft grinding noise could just be heard. Neither of them really noticed, their eyes were fixed on the rocks and when they reached them they collapsed.

Just above Eric and Ursula the dawn sun was shining brightly and its rays started to revive them. They basked in the warm sunlight as they sat against the rocks and, after a few minutes, were ready to move. Eric stood and helped Ursula up. Her left ankle felt better and she was able to put more weight upon it. When Eric offered to support her she declined at first but then placed a hand on his shoulder.

They took another look at the crater. A large cloud of steam rose up from the depths and floated past them. Slowly they continued on. Neither of them spoke. They trudged in silence around the summit to the other side of the crater and the furthest point from the OSS. Occasionally they looked behind them but no one was following.

27

TO THE AIRPORT

"What shall we do now?" asked Ursula, looking at the green countryside stretching out far below them.

Eric did not answer but gazed out in the same direction. He was certain that he could see, on the horizon, the small forgotten airport where he had landed only thirty five hours earlier. It seemed like a lifetime ago.

"We can't go back to the car," he finally said. "We must head for the plane. Alexander and I agreed that we would rendez-vous there if anything happened. Captain Hudson will get us out of here."

"Eric," began Ursula hesitantly, "I think Alexander is okay. I can feel that he is fine."

Eric concentrated hard on Alexander and, like Ursula, felt the same. Worryingly, neither of them could sense anything from Andrea.

With slightly lighter hearts they looked into the distance at the walk that lay ahead of them. It would take them down the volcano and through the countryside but first they had to get down from the summit.

The steep slope was covered in small pumice stones, like a carpet of marbles, and there was no path down it. They lost their footing in the first few steps and only Eric, digging his heels into the volcanic stones, stopped them rolling all the way down. It did, however, give them an idea.

Instead of trying to walk down they crouched onto their right legs and put the other out in front of them.

Ursula draped her injured left leg over Eric's shoulder to protect it and then they pushed off with their hands. They began to slide slowly down the volcano, as if on an invisible sledge. They picked up speed as they slid but Eric controlled this with his front foot which he used as a brake. Great clouds of dust followed them as they descended and, from a distance, it looked like a small eruption or an avalanche.

The slope came to an end two hundred metres below the summit. Eric and Ursula ground to a halt upon a large pile of pumice stones which they had pushed down the slope. They had been so focused on the countryside further afield that they had taken little notice of what lay below them. If they had seen their destination they would have stopped but the dust cloud shooting up around them had blocked their view.

They were standing at the bottom of Vesuvius's first crater: The crater that had exploded two thousand years previously and sent stones and ash fifteen kilometres into the sky towards Pompeii. After the gigantic explosion it had healed itself and the gaping hole in the earth was no more. The ancient crater was the size of ten football pitches and was surrounded by sheer cliff faces, as high as a six floored building. Boulders and rocks as big as houses, some almost the same shape, lay next to rocks the size of footballs. Scattered amongst them were tall trees and round spiky bushes.

"We go straight," said Eric confidently, pointing forwards.

"I know that," replied Ursula, "but that's easier said than done."

There was no direct route the way Eric was pointing. A family of rocks and boulders, all of different shapes and sizes, blocked their path. For a few minutes they just sat, looking at their options and appreciating the morning sun. No matter what way they went they would have to climb round or climb over huge lumps of stone.

From behind they heard the pitter-patter of stones rolling down the slope and then stones began to rain down on them. They jumped up and moved a safe distance away. Ursula's ankle felt stronger and she felt pleased until she looked back up the volcano. A short distance from the summit, running towards them, were the three OSS agents. Two of them had open wounds on their foreheads but they no longer looked drunk.

Ursula stood transfixed, looking at their pursuers and only when Eric pulled at her arm did she turn away.

They sprinted off in the direction Eric had been pointing to, using the smaller boulders as steps up to the bigger ones. Some of the boulders and rocks were uneven, some were smooth, some were very jagged and some contained holes. Skillfully, Eric and Ursula ran around them, over them and leapt between them like mountain leopards. Not once did they stop and look behind them but they could sense that the agents were getting closer.

The rocks and boulders were becoming further apart and the jumps between them were growing in distance. They landed safely on a flat rock the size of a tennis court and sprinted across it. Ursula was leading, her ankle feeling much stronger, but as she neared the edge she skidded to a halt. Eric did the same.

In front of them was a gap of over five metres. A large curved boulder lay on the other side about a metre lower than them.

"You won't make it," Ursula said, desperately looking for another way down but failing to find one.

Eric scoffed and he continued to disagree as they ran back the way they had come.

Suddenly an OSS agent appeared on another rock in front of them. "Stop!" he yelled and waved a gun threateningly at them.

"It looks like I will have to prove you wrong," Eric told Ursula, spinning around.

He sprinted away from her, and the OSS agent,

towards the gap. Faced with no other choice Ursula followed.

Eric leapt a second or so before Ursula and flew through the air towards the next boulder. His feet hit it first but he landed on a steep curve rather than the flatter top. He lost his balance and began to topple backwards, his arms flailing wildly above him.

Ursula saw him starting to fall when she was halfway into her jump. Instantly she dropped her right hand and, as she reached the boulder, she caught hold of Eric. Their fingers clasped tight around each other and Ursula pulled Eric on to boulder where she landed on top of him.

"I told you that you wouldn't make it," she said looking down at Eric.

"You didn't give me a chance to get my balance," he replied with a cheeky smile.

However, his thoughts said something different and Ursula knew he was extremely grateful.

There were no more large rocks or boulders for them to jump onto and they had almost reached the ancient crater's cliff face. They were too far away to jump directly onto it and too high up to jump down safely. To make matters worse the boulder was too smooth to climb down. They were stranded. As Eric looked over one of its sides he saw a leafless fallen tree leaning against the boulder.

"Over here," he shouted.

When Ursula saw it she was not impressed. "It's only resting against the boulder, it won't take our weight."

A gun shot echoed around the crater and they looked up to see the agent pursuing them about to make the jump on to their boulder.

"I don't think we have much choice," remarked Eric and gently lowered himself on to the fallen tree trunk.

It moved slightly but held his weight.

"Come on," he urged Ursula.

Hesitantly, Ursula joined him. The moment she stood on the tree it dropped a few centimetres. The two of them held their balance and, like tight rope walkers, pigeon stepped down the trunk.

"It's just like doing the beam in gymnastics," said Eric smiling.

The moment the words were out of his mouth the tree dropped half a metre, leaving Eric and Ursula standing in thin air. They dropped back onto the tree, their feet slipping underneath them as the tree rolled but they managed to hold their balance. They were still too high for a safe fall.

"Since when have beams moved?" asked Ursula pointedly after catching her breath.

Eric did not reply. Gently they stepped forward but with every step the tree dropped a little further. Each time they held their balance. When they were closer to the ground they jumped. The tree crashed to the ground at the same time, scattering brittle branches around them.

The OSS agent looked down from the top of the boulder. There was no way to jump down and no way back. The two children looked up at him and were tempted to smile but they didn't. For a moment he considered ignoring orders and just shooting the kids for the trouble they had caused. On reflection, he decided that Agent Angel would then shoot him and fired a shot above their heads instead. The children turned and fled towards the side of the crater.

At the base of the sheer cliff face Eric and Ursula stopped to look up. It looked like a multi-tiered cake, with six layers of solid rock, earth and earth with stones. Each layer was about the same height as a floor on a building and none looked particularly easy to climb.

We have to go up, thought Ursula.

"Race you," challenged Eric. He wasn't joking and immediately started to climb.

Ursula just looked at him and also began to climb. Why do you have to turn everything into a competition? she thought.

"Because that's what boys do," Eric replied, speeding up, but Ursula was already ahead of him.

After climbing past the first two layers they both sensed danger below them. They looked down and were greeted by a smiling OSS agent pointing a gun between the two of them.

"I don't want to have to shoot the two of you," the agent yelled in a southern states accent.

"Then don't," shouted back Eric and tried to catch up with Ursula above him.

The spot where she was about to put her hand suddenly exploded, showering her in shards of rock and earth.

The voice below yelled up again. "When I was a kid I was brought up to have some respect for grown-ups, and to call them 'sir' and 'ma'am', mister smart mouth. You'd better be remembering that or the next bullet hits your girlfriend. Now come back down here the two of you before you fall and hurt yourselves."

Ursula looked down at the agent but made no attempt to descend.

Eric smiled and, imitating the agent's southern drawl, replied, "I'm pleased you are thinking of our safety 'sir' and 'ma'am' but if you want us you'll have to come and get us."

As soon as Eric had finished speaking the agent began to climb.

Ursula was still ahead Eric but around halfway up they reached a layer of crumbling dry soil. There were no hand holds or foot holds and the only way to get past it was to find stones or fossilized roots that were wedged securely in the earth. This slowed them right down. Roots they tried to hold on simply fell out, stones they put their feet on gave way under their weight and the ones that held did not feel very safe.

At all times they made sure they had at least three points of their body, either two feet and a hand or vice versa, secure against the cliff face. One mistake was all it would take for them to fall and, at three floors above the ground, they did not want to do this. Their caution, and reduced speed, allowed the agent to catch up with them. By the time Ursula had climbed over this layer the agent had reached it and Eric was still on it.

"Stop right there," ordered the agent.

He lunged for Eric's foot and only narrowly missed it. Eric tried desperately to find another hand hold to lift him out of reach but each stone he grabbed at fell out of the earth the moment he tested it. Below him the agent had a secure footing on the rock layer and was not having the same problems as Eric.

The agent's second lunge was successful and Eric's foot was held in a vice-like grip. Eric said nothing but, without turning to look at him, Ursula knew he was in trouble. Eric shook his foot as hard as he dared but the grip just got tighter. The stone supporting Eric's other foot was beginning to loosen and his right hand hold was creeping out of the soil.

Urgently, Ursula looked around her, there was nothing she could throw at the agent and she could not go back. Throw stones Eric, she thought, and looked down. Eric was clawing at the earth trying to find stones he had not already dislodged. At the same time he was still shaking his left foot, trying to lose the agent. Only having two body points next to the cliff face was very, very dangerous climbing and Eric knew this as much as Ursula.

No matter how hard he looked he could not see any more stones. Eric placed his right hand back on the stone that was creeping out of the earth. He moved it quickly up and down until it came free. The agent was still below and with all the strength Eric could find he launched the stone at him.

The stone hit the agent right between the eyes. The force was so great and the shock so unexpected that he let go of the cliff face and fell backwards. He landed with a loud, unpleasant thud on a spiky bush which cushioned his fall. Ursula heard obscenities being screamed at them but she knew the agent was not going to risk chasing them again.

Eric did not hear anything, he had other things to worry about. He was swinging wildly and about to fall himself. The only possible hand holds were above him and out of his reach. With no other option he sprang from his one foot hold and leapt upwards. His fingers felt around a stone and gripped it. His other hand did the same and, as he kicked at the earth, he found two foot holds as well. They held and Eric lay flat against the cliff face, his heart beating so hard that he thought it would force him off. When it had slowed down he joined Ursula and together they climbed the remaining half of the cliff face.

On reaching the top, and flat ground, they both lay down and looked up towards the sun. They were both breathing hard and lost in their own thoughts. As their breathing returned to normal Eric faced Ursula, pointed to himself and declared that he was the winner. Ursula simply laughed.

It took a while for their energy to return and when they stood up they felt better. They were on the edge of a forest and headed towards it.

The sun was still rising and the trees cast long shadows over the ground. Where the sun broke through, the rays scattered as if reflected off a mirror ball. Birds danced through the light singing the dawn chorus, and animals could be heard scavenging through the dry leaves that littered the floor. Roots had broken through the surface and, with Ursula following, Eric led a path through them. It was not long before Eric noticed that Ursula was falling behind, so he stopped and waited for her to catch up.

"What's wrong?" he asked.

Ursula looked embarrassed and replied meekly, "I need the toilet."

"You need the toilet? You don't get Indiana Jones or Spiderman or James Bond escaping the bad guys and then needing the toilet."

Ursula stepped up to Eric, looked him straight in the eye and said forcefully, "That's because they're not real."

"Okay, okay, go up against that tree over there and then we can move on," Eric told her, waving at a Maple tree close by.

Ursula bit her lip, why are boys so stupid, she thought and went off to find a bush.

"I heard that," Eric shouted after her.

He was stood in a small clearing surrounded by Neapolitan Maple trees weighed down by leaves. It was shady under the trees and Eric moved to the centre of the clearing where the sun shone through. Underneath his feet was fine pumice dust and he started to write his name on the ground. His father used to complain that he was always waiting for his mother, and now Eric knew what he meant.

The E was finished and Eric began to scrape the R. As he was approaching the curve of the R he felt that something was really wrong. He abandoned his writing and ran off to find Ursula. On the ground he could see her shoe prints clearly and they were easy to follow.

Behind a scrubby bush the prints stopped and next to them were much larger and heavier shoe prints. As quietly and as quickly as he could Eric followed them. After a few hundred metres he reached an old lava flow, bisecting the forest like a grey river. Walking across it, with Ursula held tightly under one arm and hand over her mouth, was another OSS agent. Eric waited until they had crossed back into the forest beyond, and then sprinted over the solidified lava.

The other side of the forest had Cork Oak trees as well as Maples. They had grown so close together that only pinpoint beams of sunlight managed to break through from above them. A little way in front of Eric the OSS agent had stopped and pinned Ursula at arm's length against a thick tree trunk.

"You can hit me all you like young lady," said the agent menacingly, pushing his fist harder into her chest, "but if you bite me again I swear I will snap you like a twig. Do I make myself clear?"

Ursula tried to reply but she felt her ribs were about to break and her lungs would burst.

"Do I make myself clear?" he asked louder.

"Crystal," shouted Eric, leaping through the air and smacking the agent with a well-aimed kick to the head.

The fist holding Ursula in place fell away and she climbed up the tree as quickly as a monkey.

"Why you little..." began the agent.

Before the sentence was finished Eric hit the agent hard in the stomach and jumped out of reach. The agent let out a sadistic laugh and, removing a revolver, pointed it at Eric. "I knew you would come after your little girlfriend. By rights you should be dead, killed with your dear ma and pa when their little boat blew up. So I am sure my boss won't mind much if I bring you back in pieces too."

Eric watched helplessly as a finger wrapped around the trigger. A fraction before it was pulled, Ursula jumped from the tree and onto the revolver. The bullet scattered leaves as it hit them and the revolver spilled onto the ground. In one movement Eric dived forward, grabbed the gun and threw it as far away as he could. He was on his feet again before the agent had fully taken in what had happened.

Above Eric was a low hanging branch which he jumped onto. He quickly climbed up further and out of the agent's reach. On the ground below him he could see Ursula scuttling backwards like a crab, away from the agent. Eric looked in the direction she was going. A short way from her was a branch about three metres above the ground. Eric willed Ursula to head for it and did the same.

Ursula followed Eric's instructions and led the agent towards it. When she was directly below she stopped and the agent looked down at her with a smile on his face.

"You win," said Ursula, resigned to defeat, and slowly stood up.

As soon as she was on her feet the agent took hold of her and gripped her so hard it hurt. Ursula responded by screaming and fighting to escape.

At the same time Eric launched himself silently at the branch above them. It was a perfect leap, he gripped it tightly and spun around as if on the parallel bars. When he reached the top of his spin and was upside down, he froze, changed his hands and flipped through one hundred and eighty degrees. He was now directly above the agent and began his swing back downwards. He brought his knees in close to his chest and as he neared the agent he kicked them out as hard as he could. Both his feet hit the agent's jaw with a crunch and sent him flying backwards. Eric landed on the earth perfectly, as if at a gymnastics competition. The agent hit the ground with a crunch and did not move a muscle.

"Time to go," said Eric, and taking Ursula's hand they quickly walked away.

For the next four hours they walked under the shady trees. Dry leaves littered the ground and small plants with sharp branches broke through the surface. They had to trust their instincts that they were heading in the right direction because they could only see trees and there were no viewing points. The branches above them were thick with leaves and neither of them had the energy to climb a tree in order to see where they were. Ursula's ankle had begun to smart again and they were both very tired.

Gradually the grey volcanic soil turned browner and the vegetation thinned out slightly. Apart from the occasional bird they saw no one, but the thought of an OSS agent lurking behind any tree kept them on edge and made for a tense journey. Only when they saw a wire fence topped with barbed wire did they relax slightly. Beyond it, almost hidden behind more trees, they could see a runway.

By the time Eric and Ursula had climbed over the fence into the forgotten airport they were covered in small scratches and exhausted. They broke through the remaining trees and there, sat at the end of the weedy runway, was Captain Hudson's plane. The old twin-propped craft gave them a boost and they began to feel more positive as they walked towards it.

The door was open and three small steps led inside but to the two battle-weary children it felt like many more. Inside the body of the plane, draped across the worn leather seats, were Andrea, Alexander and Captain Hudson. They were deep in serious conversation but this stopped the moment they saw the children.

"What happened?" asked Alexander, obviously concerned.

"Nothing much," replied Eric, collapsing into a chair.

"We just ran into the OSS, that was all," added Ursula, joining him.

"And we won," stated Eric proudly.

Captain Hudson stood up and went to the plane's door. He brought in the steps, closed the door and walked quickly to the cock-pit. Before he sat down in his pilot's chair he said, "Put your seatbelts on. We will be leaving immediately."

All four of them did as they were told and then Eric asked Alexander and Andrea, the same question, "What happened to you?"

"We saw the crash," said Ursula turning in her seat so she could see the others. "We thought you were in it."

"Nothing much happened," sighed Alexander, "we just set the car rolling, jumped out, hid in the trees and watched it happen. I have no desire to be in a car crash, I can assure you. It was Andrea's idea."

They turned to face Andrea. She was neither smiling nor grimacing and did not look as if this was anything extraordinary. "Do you have the discs?" she asked Ursula, putting her hand out.

"Yes," replied Ursula with a smile. She touched her chest, where they were hidden in the wallet, and suddenly the smile vanished from her face. Frantically she undid her seat belt and she placed her hand urgently under her black top.

"They are not there, are they?" guessed Andrea.

"No," replied Ursula starting to cry, "they must have fallen out somewhere."

"They can't have done," said Eric in disbelief spinning in his seat to face her. "We spent so long planning this, check again."

Ursula did as she was told but no matter how carefully she checked the CDs still weren't there.

Unable to contain his emotions Alexander punched the seat next to him. "Then we put ourselves in danger for nothing!" Once he had calmed down he added, "We must hope that the OSS do not find them."

For a moment no one spoke. The plane's engines became louder and they began to accelerate along the runway.

When they were in the air and her sobs had stopped, Ursula answered, "It wasn't for nothing. There were only four CDs in the pod - numbers one, two, three and four."

"I'm sorry Ursula but it was for nothing. The OSS now have the pod, they may have also found the discs and we are still missing disc five. It was all for nothing," replied Alexander, looking depressed.

"No, it wasn't! Down by the pod I remembered something. Until now I haven't had time to tell you. I know where CD five is."

"Where?" asked Andrea in a business-like tone.

"It's at my grandparents. In the cabinet in the living room, next to my Kinder egg toys and Mémé's glass animals."

Without warning Alexander started to laugh. At first it

was snort of disbelief but as it grew it became more real. The hiding, the planning and the danger all seemed suddenly ridiculous. Eric and Ursula joined him and the three of them soon had tears running down their faces.

Andrea seemed to have missed the joke and waited patiently until they had all calmed down. "We are going to Paris to retrieve this disc and we shall stay with Mr and Mrs Benjamin. It will be cramped but safe."

When she had finished speaking she undid her seat belt and walked towards the cock pit to instruct Captain Hudson of their new destination. She was with him for a less than a minute but when she returned both Eric and Ursula were fast asleep.

28

VICTORY OR DEFEAT

Deep underground Agent Angel had watched the boy he was hunting and the street kid slide rapidly down the volcano and his OSS agents follow them. His cigar had been squashed underfoot on the floor and he was holding a cigarette again. Using a satellite he had been able to follow the children until they walked under the trees in the forest and then he lost them. It was out of his hands and he had to wait.

He felt helpless and that made him furious. The Enquiry Team had been sent back to the States, Yukon One was out of contact and Yukon Two was engaged in retrieving the pod. Angrily he rammed the cigarette into his mouth and took a long drag. No one at the Operations Centre dared speak in case he took out his aggression on them.

The silence was broken by Agent Beta, on the loud speaker. "This is Yukon Two. We have achieved our objective. We have located and extracted the pod. I repeat we have the pod."

"Good," bellowed Agent Angel. "At least I can rely on some of Team Omega to get the job done. Anything else to report?"

"Yes, Sir. Outside the Sarno gate we also found four CDs in a wallet. Shall we bring these as well?"

Agent Angel clapped his bear-like hands in glee and extinguished his cigarette between his palms. "Oh yes, Agent Beta. Guard them with your life, they are as important as the pod. Proceed to the forest east of Vesuvius, locate and assist the other Yukon Team in their assignment and then proceed here. What is your expected ETA at field base?"

"If we have to locate the other Team Omega agents first then I would say approximately twelve hours, Sir."

Agent Beta was as good as his word. Just over twelve hours later Yukon Two drove off a ferry, into a tiny port town, on a small Mediterranean island called Viz. He drove straight towards the centre of the hilly island along rarely used roads, past untidy vineyards, scrappy looking orchards and dry fields. Occasionally the Yukon drove past grey brick buildings that looked either abandoned or just neglected. The sun beat down and, even with the air conditioning on full blast, it was still warm inside the jeep as the six Team Omega agents were squashed together like sardines in a can. Behind the Yukon was the Fiat's trailer and upon it, wrapped in thick tarpaulin, was the pod.

Agent Beta steered the Yukon onto a lane that led up the biggest mountain on the island and within ten minutes they were at the OSS field base. The Yukon was parked under scrawny trees and a camouflage net placed over it. The trailer was unhooked and Team Omega pushed it and the pod towards the tunnel entrance.

Standing in front of the entrance and dressed in his black Army fatigues was Agent Angel, slowly smoking a cigarette. If he was happy with Team Omega's achievements he was hiding it under a thunderous expression. Next to him stood Jean Kurtz, who was dressed the same. On her face was a look of excitement, as if she has been running a marathon and had just seen the finishing line. The last person standing there was Professor Schwarzkopf, wearing a khaki suit dating from the sixties and a blue handkerchief tied around this neck. His eyes were fearful and he looked very uncomfortable. This was clearly a place he did not want to be.

Team Omega stopped in front of them, saluted and

Agent Beta carefully handed the CDs to Agent Angel. He glanced at them and his expression lightened before passing them on to Kurtz.

"Get your team onto these immediately, Kurtz. I want a full report on everything you know when we arrive back at Roswell."

Kurtz took the CDs and skipped down the tunnel like a child with a new toy. She was followed by Team Omega, pushing the trailer with the pod, and a reluctant Professor Schwarzkopf.

Agent Angel came up behind him and slapped him on the back. "You look down John, but you shouldn't be. It's a good day for America. We now have both pods in our possession, plus the data CDs that our intelligence officers said we would find. On top of all this we have managed to contain the very real danger to our way of life."

A cold chill passed through Professor Schwarzkopf's body. There was a look of genuine shock on his face and he began to cough. After he had finished coughing he said, "When you first told me about this danger I assumed you meant weapons or technology or information that could kill. You didn't tell me that the danger was the boy we saw on Vesuvius earlier."

Agent Angel did not rush to reply. He first took a long, last drag from his cigarette, dropped it on the cold concrete floor and crushed it underfoot. "Until you opened that pod for me we didn't know either. A tiger cub may be cute too, but once it grows up it'll rip your throat out in the blink of an eye. Don't worry about him, John. After the Yukon Two team collected those wasters from Yukon One they told me which way the boy and the Street Kid were heading. I had this information passed onto the Italian authorities and I'm sure they've picked up the two of them by now. They'll look after the kids until we can ship them over to the States. He's a special kid, we'll be hospitable and keep him safe. Like a tiger all he needs is a little training and to do what his master says."

"What about the girl?"

"If we can use her we will. If not then..." He let his words hang in the air. "Anyway, now we have the pods and the CDs I am not even sure that we need the boy anymore either. I think we have enough without him to achieve our objective.

Professor Schwarzkopf did not feel any better and asked, "What objective is that, Buddy? Something new that I've missed since my retirement?"

"Oh no, John," Agent Angel replied shaking his head. "This is one that we discussed at length one night at your quarters many years ago. If I remember correctly we shared a bottle of Bourbon and ate some of your lovely wife's delicious meatloaf."

Professor Schwarzkopf thought about that evening many years ago and tried to remember what had been said. The memory came back with a shock and he stammered, "Identical Hybrid Beings?"

"The very same."

"I thought you abandoned that idea a long time ago."

"Oh no, we've had some setbacks over the years but I'm confident we can correct this in the near future," said Agent Angel enthusiastically, opening a new packet of cigarettes.

On hearing these words Professor Schwarzkopf began to cough violently. He had blocked this memory from his mind for a reason. Within a week of their last discussion on IHBs, his personal world had fallen apart and Ingrid had left him. He saw it as a curse and could not share Agent Angel's enthusiasm. Instead, he chose to remain silent and followed the pod further into the tunnels.

The Italian police arrived at the forgotten airport three minutes after Captain Hudson and his four passengers had taken off. By this time the plane was flying towards the sun and was impossible to see. The police ignored it anyway. They were looking for two children not an aeroplane , so they searched the small airport but discovered nothing.

Back in their messy little Police Station in Naples they filed a report, put it in their metal filing cabinet and then went out to a nearby cafe for an espresso.

29

REUNION

The children stayed fast asleep for the entire flight to France. When they hit a storm over Switzerland strong winds rocked the plane and threw it around but the children did not wake. Even when they landed in Paris, bumping along the runway before coming to a standstill inside a cavernous hangar, they did not stir.

The two sleeping children, plus Andrea and Alexander, stayed inside the plane after landing, while Captain Hudson fetched his car. He drove his metallic pink people carrier right up to the plane's door and Alexander carried Ursula off while Andrea brought Eric. The two children were placed onto the back seats but they remained fast asleep and did not even murmur. Once Alexander and Andrea were in the car Captain Hudson drove away.

It was warm in Paris, the sun was shining, trees were full of blossom and the roads were reasonably quiet. After less than an hour of driving, and following Andrea's directions, they arrived back at Saint-Denis.

The children were finally woken by Andrea forcefully shaking them. The white hair around their ears had spread further and the crow's feet around their eyes were more noticeable.

Mémé took a last bite of her lunch and stood up from the white formica table. She was wearing a yellow apron over a bright coloured frock and her hair was in curlers. Her husband was still eating, scattering baguette crumbs over his '*Allez Les Bleus*' T-shirt and black trousers. Mémé took his plate into the kitchen before he had finished eating and began to wash up. When the knocks on the front door came her hands were covered in soap suds and she instructed her husband to go and answer it.

On seeing Ursula at the door Granddad Benjamin had to stop himself from crying. His eyes went red and he fought to hold back the tears as he held his Granddaughter tight. Ursula then hopped off to surprise Mémé. Granddad Benjamin gave Eric a welcome hug before politely kissing Andrea on the cheeks and then shaking hands with the two strangers - Alexander and Captain Hudson.

Like her husband, Mémé was over the moon to see Ursula again and was also delighted to see Eric and Andrea too. She politely welcomed Captain Hudson and Alexander, whom she was sure she had seen somewhere before. Within an hour she had warmed to both men and her suspicions had been confirmed - she had indeed seen Alexander before.

During this time Ursula and Eric told Mémé and Granddad Benjamin all that had happened to them since Christmas. In places Andrea and Alexander joined in, either adding bits to the narrative or correcting a number of exaggerations. Captain Hudson listened to the story, as absorbed by it as the Benjamins. He found it curious how his own fate seemed to be linked in some way to the Meyer's.

The living room was cramped with seven people but with the children, plus the Benjamins, squashed up on the itchy sofa and the three other adults at the table, they all had a seat. Mémé had provided them all with tea and homemade biscuits and there was a warm, safe feeling in the room.

When they got to the part of the story involving Ursula, the pod and her grandparents finding her, the three Benjamins were left alone in the living room. The other four stood on the balcony, amongst the plants, and gazed out across les banlieues.

It was not long before they were beckoned back into the room. All three Benjamins had shed a tear, but they were tears of relief and gratitude rather than of sadness. Their heart-to-heart, and the truth behind Ursula's past, did not divide them but brought them even closer together.

When the children had finished telling their stories Captain Hudson wiggled his moustache and said, "The last two days have been most illuminating. When I saw grainy images of men land on the moon it changed my world forever. I did not think that would happen to me again but I was wrong. My life changed beyond measure when I met Martin Meyer many years ago and has changed again now I have met his descendants. The information you possess is valuable, and so are the four of you." He pointed to Eric, Ursula, Alexander and Andrea.

"Use the information wisely and plan your futures with great care and precision. If you need me at any point I will always be at your service," he stood up, bid everyone farewell and Mémé saw him to the door.

"It was a pleasure to meet you Madame Benjamin. I apologize for my departure but if I do not go soon Cécile will be thinking I have a girlfriend," he said, slowly winked at her and then left.

Mémé returned to the living room and refilled all their teas, except Andrea's which was untouched. She sat back down between the children and put her arm around both of them. Ursula knew that Eric was happy for the first time in many months and she felt the same.

"I believe this is where we add our piece of the story," began Granddad Benjamin. "We always wanted a child but for reasons only God knows it never happened. We hoped and prayed but as the years passed, and we aged, we came to accept our childless fate."

"Then one night," continued Mémé, "I was walking home down a poorly lit underpass with an old shopping trolley in it. It was cold and it had been raining. There was nobody out, but there was a man lurking near the entrance to the underpass who was watching me. I tried to go as quickly as I could because he put me on edge."

"Sorry," apologized Alexander, "I didn't mean to scare you. I didn't think you had seen me."

Mémé gestured with her hand that it was nothing and went on. "As I got near to the trolley I heard crying. I was worried about the man," she corrected herself, "Alexander, watching me but I stopped anyway. Laying in the beaten up trolley, wrapped in thick woollen blankets, her little nose poking through a gap, was the most beautiful baby. The moment I picked her up she stopped crying. A voice echoed down the underpass, 'she's yours, take her.' When I turned to speak the man had gone. So I did as he said and took Ursula home. After peeling the blankets away I removed her strange silver baby clothes and found, laying her against her chest, a compact disc."

"We didn't know what it was," said Granddad Benjamin standing up. "We have never been very good with technology but we kept it anyway. As it was with the baby we thought it might be important."

He approached the glass cabinet and opened the doors. Near the back, behind Kinder toys, glass animals, china ornaments and underneath a wind-up clock was a CD. Carefully he removed it and handed it to Ursula. She turned it over in her hands trying to find a number. Next to the hole in the centre, faded by sunlight and Mémé's cleaning, was a very faint number five.

"It is number five," she said excitedly and passed it to Andrea.

"Do you have the laptop I gave you?" Andrea asked the Benjamins.

They both looked suddenly very guilty.

"It was very kind of you to give it to us," answered Granddad Benjamin, "but technology is a young person's game and we're a bit too long in the tooth for something new. To be honest we've been too scared to turn it on. Will it still work?"

Andrea shrugged, "It is not a problem, but do you still have it?"

"Oh yes," replied Mémé, "I put it in Ursula's bedroom. It is on her desk."

"Alexander and I will go and watch the CD. The rest of you can stay here."

The three Benjamins were happy for this to happen but Eric argued until Granddad Benjamin said that he wanted to talk to him. Andrea and Alexander left the living room with the disc and went into Ursula's bedroom.

When they had left, Granddad Benjamin pulled up a white formica dining chair and sat in front of the sofa. "Ursula and Eric, I would like to tell you something and then I would like to ask you something. My grandfather was the chief of his village on the plains of the great continent of Africa. One day he told my father that he was special, that he could change the world, and asked him what he would do. My father thought carefully about these things and after careful deliberation decided to leave the village of mud huts and start a new life in the town. Many years ago my father told me that I was special, that I could change the world, and he asked me what would I do. I puzzled over this problem for weeks and then finally decided to leave hot and dusty Africa and start a new life in France. I now turn to the two of you and say, you are special, you could change the world, and I ask you a very important question, what will you do?"

Eric and Ursula were lost for words.

30

THE END IS NEAR

Apart from a clean set of pastel yellow sheets on the bed, Ursula's room had not changed since Christmas. Every week Mémé would go in to wipe the dust away but she did not touch or move or take away anything. It was Ursula's room and she was not going to change that. Occasionally, when he really missed Ursula, Granddad Benjamin would enter, sit on the bed and recall fond memories. Like Mémé he would not touch anything and would only leave his imprint where he sat on the bed.

The door creaked open and Alexander and Andrea entered. Straightaway they noticed the perfectly made bed with the ruffled end where Granddad Benjamin chose to sit. On the glass topped school desk they saw the laptop. It still looked brand new and had obviously not been touched. Alexander flipped open the screen, pressed the on button and the slim computer whirred into life. Andrea inserted CD five and they both sat down on the bed to watch.

Professor Larsen appeared on the screen but she looked different from the other CDs. Her composure had gone and she looked frantic. Her grey hair had not been brushed and untidy strands fell over her face. There were bags below her bloodshot eyes and the white gown which she wore had been buttoned wrongly.

In her arms she held Eric and Ursula, who were dressed in silver baby-grows and looked fast asleep. Professor Larsen talked rapidly, gently rocking the babies as she did so. It was difficult to make out her garbled words at times but Alexander and Andrea still understood what she was saying.

"This is Professor Larsen and this is an additional compact disc to my original four. I do not think I have long and therefore, I must be quick. They have found me, and because they have found me, I must pass on my fears. These are fears that have come from my observations and inferences. Some people will dismiss them as the mad ramblings of a space sick old lady. I assure you, they are not, and despite my current appearance my thinking behind these is clear and logical. My three fears are these...

"Number One. In the fall of 1947 I accompanied Professor Schwarzkopf and Major Marshall into a secret laboratory far below ground at Roswell Airforce base in New Mexico. We were taken down white washed corridors to a sterile white tiled room. Inside it, on two metal tables, were two child sized bodies covered in white sheets. They were extra-terrestrial beings, or aliens, from the dart shaped craft which had crashed. Other scientists believed that they were both dead. I do not believe this was true. I am certain that at least one, maybe both, was still alive. Its body may have seemed dead but its mind was not. The moment I pushed the heavy doors open and entered I felt as if my own mind had been seized. It was as if someone was hypnotizing and analyzing me at the same time. It tried to take control of my mind and read my thoughts. I fled before it achieved its aim.

"Over the following years I have come to some conclusions regarding our alien visitors. None of these are based on fact, only observations, and I hope that they are simply the result of my over active imagination.

"The crash between our Foo Fighter and the alien craft in 1947 was a tragic accident. However, I do not believe the alien's location was an accident. New Mexico is a hot, dry, barren and ragged area of the world. In many respects it resembles other, non-gas planets, more closely than anywhere else on planet Earth.

"Many scientists are now beginning to believe that originally there was no life on Earth and that you cannot create life from nothing. Therefore life had to be introduced to our planet. A theory has been proposed that a meteor storm crashed into the Earth bringing life in the shape of single-cell organisms and maggot like creatures. From this 'accident' we all evolved. On Mars, rocks have been recently discovered that contain tiny tunnels as if made by a tiny, maggot like creature. It is my assumption that the same meteor storm which hit the Earth also hit Mars and other planets too. It is possible, though not probable, that life evolved on other planets too. In an infinite universe it is hard to believe we are on the only planet capable of supporting life. But different worlds have different environmental conditions and therefore life could evolve differently and at different rates. On some worlds this could be slower than on Earth but on others it could be faster. Likewise, some alien races, if there are others, may be technologically behind us while others may be light years ahead of us.

"I have said before that the role of science is not to speculate and I will try to avoid this. I shall therefore report the facts. In the last sixty years especially we have witnessed huge technological advances and with them our lifestyles have changed. All these advances require energy. We are using more and more fuels and also wasting more and more. The energy we use has come from using the rapidly vanishing natural resources underground as well as massive deforestation. The results of this have been increased carbon dioxide in the atmosphere, global warming and an increased temperature on average of between one and half and two degrees. This does not seem like much but it has meant increases in storms and their power, loss of biospheres and species, an increase in lands that we can no longer use and a loss of coastal lands. In short we are becoming a more extreme planet and in this respects much more similar to other planets in the universe.

"The questions I want to ask are: what if another race has advanced quicker than us? What if they destroyed their world the way we are destroying ours? What if they are looking for another one? And what if a hotter, more extreme world, is their idea of home?

"My second fear also goes back to Roswell. In 1966, after discovering Operation Mulatto and the plan to create Identical Hybrid Beings or Hybrids, I fled New Mexico and America. However, before doing so I returned to the underground labs for only the second, and last, time.

"I stole alien samples and other items I thought may be useful to me. As I mentioned on another compact disc, I also destroyed everything else.

"My fear is that my efforts were in vain. Agent Angel does not give up easily and will not be beaten. He has set a goal and will not stop until it is achieved. He will still want to create his Identical Hybrid Beings, his cloned army, and have a 'super army for a super power.' I may have delayed him but I have not stopped him, of this I am certain. If I can achieve his goal, albeit on a smaller scale and on my terms, then so can he."

Professor Larsen stopped and looked down at Eric and Ursula like a mother with her new born infant. "My last fear concerns my Adam and my Eve. Before beginning my research on humans I conducted preliminary studies on rats. For a number of years I achieved nothing with these studies but then slowly, painfully slowly, I made breakthroughs. Two years ago my research on rats was successful and I managed to create a 'test tube' rat."

Suddenly a loud beeping noise drowned our Professor Larsen and her face filled with panic. She left the camera for a short while and the beeping stopped. When she returned she was crying.

"I must be quick, I do not have much more time. The average life span for a rat is three years or thirty six months, and is equivalent to the average life span for a human of seventy two years. I noted that for the first three months of my rats' lives they were normal. At around three and a half months they started to develop, what I can best describe as, abilities beyond that of an average rat. However, each time this happened they visibly aged. None of my rats lived beyond six and a half months. In human terms this means that my Adam and my Eve will not live beyond their thirteenth or fourteenth birthdays."

The beeping began again but it was faster and louder. Professor Larsen leant forward, mouthed the word 'sorry' and then the screen went blank.

EPILOGUE

THREE MONTHS LATER

Agent Angel was stood in the observation room next to Agent Hoover, looking at thousands of screens which monitored the world. The last twelve years of his life had been devoted to finding those pods, this room had been built to do just that, and now his aim had been achieved.

In his hand he held a half-smoked cigarette which was slowly burning down to the butt, sending spirals of smoke around the room. A thin sinewy figure lurking in the shadows at the back of the room breathed in the smoke through two tiny mouth-like nostrils. At the same time, Agent Hoover tried to blow the smoke away from his face.

The Italian police's failure to take hold of two children aged only twelve years old had made Agent Angel furious at first, especially when he found that they had both come from the pods. He arranged for the policeman involved to be discharged but now, three months later, he had come to accept it. After all, he reflected, they now had both pods and all four discs. From this point of view the mission had been a success, even if the second pod was still not open.

An electronic bell rang inside the room and Agent Hoover looked down at the image on his computer. It was a woman dressed in a white lab coat.

"It's Jean Kurtz, Sir, shall I let her in?" he asked.

Agent Angel nodded and Agent Hoover pressed the switch to buzz her in. Steady footsteps echoed dully around the room as she approached Agent Angel.

"What is it, Kurtz?" asked Agent Angel.

She spoke slowly in her confident whiney voice but Agent Hoover could tell she was worried about what she was saying. "We've analyzed all the data on the four CDs and put it against our own. I can assure you, Sir, that we've checked and rechecked our findings countless times. However, no matter how we look at it we can't create Identical Hybrid Beings using Professor Larsen's research alone. I'm sorry."

Agent Angel crushed the lit cigarette in his palm and asked, "What are you telling me, Kurtz? That we can't move on? That it's the end of line? That I have to finally abandon my dream after forty years? A dream that began before you were even born!"

Jean Kurtz shuffled from one foot to another. "No, Sir, I am not saying that at all. We can still achieve the objectives of Operation Mulatto."

"How? And your answer better be a good one."

"We need DNA, Sir," she paused. "We need at least one of those two children. They are the key."

ABOUT THE AUTHOR

I'm the author of the 'Adventures of Eric and Ursula' series of books. Book 1 is out now, Book 2 will follow in 2013 and the Books 3and 4 will follow later.

I began writing 'An Extra-ordinary Beginning' while waiting for the birth of my son. Funnily enough it took exactly nine months to write. After he was born this book collected four years of cyber dust on my computer before I rediscovered it.

Over the last fourteen years I have written, and directed, plays for children that have been performed in the UK, Romania, Sri Lanka, Switzerland and Czech Republic.

For an older audience I wrote the films 'Seagulls' and 'your baby disappeared'. 'Seagulls' was shown at the Brighton Film Festival. While 'your baby disappeared' premiered in Prague in 2011.

When I am not writing I enjoy spending time with my family and continuing to teach children in an international school.

CONNECT WITH ME ONLINE

Website www.winchad.com
Twitter @adwinch
Facebook adwinch
Email winchad@hotmail.com

PREVIEW OF BOOK 2

SURVIVAL INSTINCT

Electricity was in the air and dark storm clouds were gathering on the horizon. They blew menacingly over the city while the Benjamins and Eric tucked into their dessert.

Eric finished eating and walked to the window. He was wearing grey shorts, a black, long-sleeved T-shirt and his new trainers. Against the backdrop of the coming storm he was almost camouflaged. Ursula joined him; dressed almost identically.

Are we still going to do this tonight? thought Ursula.

Of course, thought Eric, the storm will provide even better cover for us.

Behind them Mémé cleared the dishes from the table and took them into the kitchen for Granddad Benjamin to wash-up. She stood behind him like a parrot perched on his shoulder, telling him what to do while Granddad Benjamin carried on regardless, apparently deaf to the 'correct way' of washing-up. However, when Ursula asked if she and Eric could go out onto the roof to watch the storm he replied, "Yes" immediately.

"But only if you take your rain coats and umbrellas," added Mémé and went to fetch them. She returned with a black travel umbrella, a large 'Roland Garros 1982' tennis umbrella and their water proof jackets which she made them put on straight away.

"Are you sure you'll be okay?" she fussed. "I worry when you two are up there."

"We know," answered the children together.

"We'll be fine," reassured Ursula. "The worst that could happen is that we get wet."

"And I love storms. I can watch them for hours," added Eric.

"As long as you're back down here before bed time, I trust you."

The last three words stabbed Ursula right in the heart. Her grandparents had brought her up to be honest and on the rare occasions that she wasn't, it hurt.

Eric slipped out of the living room and sprung up onto the balcony wall. No matter how many times Mémé had seen Ursula and now Eric do it, her heart still skipped a beat. She remembered clearly the first time she had seen Ursula up there. Ursula had been five years old and she had shouted to Mémé to leave the kitchen and come and see. Mémé had entered the living room and seen Ursula tight-rope walking on the balcony wall.

"Ursula! No!" she had shouted and ran towards the balcony, her arms outstretched.

Ursula had stepped back, lost her footing and disappeared from view. Mémé ran to the wall and looked over the side but there was no trace of Ursula. Then Ursula's smiling face had appeared from the balcony below and Mémé nearly had a heart attack. This was the first time that Mémé had considered that her granddaughter was not quite like other children. The idea had crossed her mind on many other occasions since then but she tried not to dwell on it.

Ursula joined Eric on the balcony. They threw their umbrellas above them and in one coordinated and fluid movement they leapt up to the roof; gripped it tight and then swung themselves upwards.

Once on the roof they could see that the storm clouds had covered Paris. Behind them the Stade de France had turned on its floodlights and lit up the sky.

"Are you sure you want to do this?" asked Eric, sensing Ursula's doubts. "You can stay and cover for me if you want."

She nodded, picked up the travel umbrella and walked off across the rooftop to the far edge of the apartment block. Eric picked up the large, tennis umbrella and followed. It soon began to rain and they both pulled their water proof hoods over their heads.

On the roof edge was a rusty gutter attached to a drainpipe leading down. Ursula slid over the edge and nimbly climbed down the drainpipe seven floors to the ground below. Once again Eric followed but with a large umbrella in one hand it was not as easy. He considered dropping it but did not want to risk hitting Ursula. Around halfway down he heard a crack and saw the drainpipe below him come away from the wall.

Carefully he looked down to find an alternative route but there was none. He slowly continued his descent. As he neared the broken pipe it started to shake and another section came away from the wall with a loud snap. He was still too high to jump without injuring himself but he felt sure he would be fine.

"Come on, slow coach," shouted Ursula from the ground below, oblivious to the dangerous assault course she had left behind.

Her words were followed by the sound of the drain pipe breaking clean away from the wall and throwing Eric into the air.

As if he had planned it, Eric instantly opened up his umbrella, held tightly to the handle and speedily, but relatively safely, fell towards the ground. A metre above the grass he let go, hit the ground, did a controlled roll, jumped up again and caught the umbrella.

"Show off," muttered Ursula and walked off.

Inside his hot and stuffy TV observation room, Agent Hoover was glued to the screens. He had missed Ursula's descent but caught the end of Eric's. Eric's hood and the umbrella shielded his face but Agent Hoover's interest had been piqued.

"God damn, would you look at that! That is one lucky kid," he said to himself and widened his focus again to take in all the screens.

The journey to the Stade de France was uneventful. Both Eric and Ursula kept their hoods and umbrellas up as the rain poured down. In the days leading up to their excursion they had pinpointed as many CCTV cameras as they could, in order to avoid them. This meant taking a longer route, including crossing a bridge further away, but it was safer.

When they finally arrived at the stadium Ursula stopped to take it all in. She had always lived near the Stade de France but she had never been this close to it. There had been times when she would have loved to have attended a sports game or a big concert but she never had. Residents of les banlieues just didn't go there, except to sell hotdogs or clear the rubbish away after an event. Until Eric put the idea in her head, she had never ever contemplated visiting.

From the rooftop above her grandparent's flat, the stadium was an impressive construction – an almost perfect oval, criss-crossed with huge steel cables and, when lit, glowed like an enormous halo. Now, however, as she stood looking at the large lumps of concrete blocks and metal girders she wondered what she was doing here.

Eric joined her with the tickets and she followed him into the stadium. As she questioned whether they should turn back and go home Eric spun around.

"Don't think like that," he ordered. "Wait until you get inside and then you won't want to go home." He paused and pointed towards a gate leading to their seats, "Listen to that."

It was only then that Ursula noticed the low roar of thousands of voices. Eric didn't wait for her response and sped off towards the gate with Ursula running after him. The moment they walked through the gates and towards their seats Ursula knew she had to stay. She had never been anywhere so large. All around her she could see and hear thousands of people and feel the expectant atmosphere. All eyes were watching the pitch as the two teams entered, walking into the pouring rain under the bright floodlights.

A steward impatiently motioned the children towards their seats. They sat down and placed the drenched umbrellas on the floor in front of them.

National anthems were played, the teams took their places and just before the quarter past eight kick-off the television cameras panned over the full capacity crowd.

An alarm bleeped annoyingly on the computer in front of Agent Hoover. In the thirteen weeks since the machine had been installed on his desk it had made no sound except the gentle whir of its fans.

Agent Hoover looked down at the screen. In big red letters the words, 'Suspected match,' flashed across the screen. Behind it TV5 Monde was broad casting a live soccer game from the Stade de France. For a moment Agent Hoover wondered whether the computer was having a joke with him. These thoughts soon disappeared when the footage rewound and paused on a wide shot of the crowd. Slowly the people in the crowd got larger as the computer zoomed in, scanning left and right as it did so. When it came to a halt two faces filled the screen – one black and female, the other white and male – the most wanted children on the planet. Without thinking any further Agent Hoover hit the alarm button and sat back in his swivel chair taking the two faces in.

They look happy, he thought, free as two birds! "Enjoy it while you can, kids," he said to the screen and then, under his breath he quietly sang to himself, "nowhere to run baby, nowhere to hide…"

By the time he had finished the song every screen in front of him was showing footage from every CCTV camera in a five kilometre radius of the stadium.

Before the referee had blown the final whistle Agent Angel was also standing in front of the screens. A friendly, yet intimidating, hand rested on Hoover's shoulder and he watched the two children intently.

"It is likely that we will lose them when they leave the soccer game, Sir," warned Agent Hoover. "There are eighty thousand people in that stadium."

"Do your best Hoover, but don't worry too much. We know where they are now. They've made their first mistake, it won't be their last. All we need to do is smoke'em out. Team Omicron is on their way to Paris as we speak. They're locked, stocked and ready to rock. It is time for some extreme renditioning."

"You mean kidnapping, Sir?" asked Agent Hoover nervously.

Agent Angel chuckled to himself and answered, "Kidnapping is so old-fashioned. Now we call it rendition."

Exactly as Agent Hoover had predicted, Eric and Ursula disappeared into the post-match crowd. The loss didn't dampen Agent Angel's spirits and he left the room happily smoking a big, fat, Cuban cigar.

NOTE FROM THE AUTHOR

This book is a work of fiction but contains aspects which, some would argue, are non-fiction.

In July of 1947 a piece of debris was found near the Roswell Army Airfield 509th in New Mexico, USA. The local paper reported that an alien ship had crashed, however the next day the army announced that it was a weather balloon. I will not go into details here but please refer to Guy Malone's informative website www.roswellufocrash.com.

The Austrian scientist, Victor Schauberger, was real and, depending on what you believe, invented a flying saucer which flew outside Prague in 1947. Operation Paperclip allegedly happened just after World War II but there is no documented proof that I am aware of. Again please refer to the above website which is an excellent portal if you are interested in these events.

Heinz Kohut and Hazal Siromani's separate works on the idea of self can be found on a number of websites on the internet.

All the other characters and events are entirely fictitious and any resemblance to real-life people is entirely co-incidental.

Ursula does lots of parcour (the proper expression) over buildings. This is extremely dangerous and is only attempted by extremely fit and talented people. Please do not attempt it. There are a number of organizations around the world who teach people how to do these things. Please search the internet for the one nearest to you if you are desperate to have a go.

2985814R00161

Printed in Great Britain
by Amazon.co.uk, Ltd.,
Marston Gate.